IT BEGA

GHOST STORY

IT BEGAN WITH A
GHOST STORY

JEAN HARROD

© Jean Harrod, 2023

Published by York Authors Coffee Shop Ltd

This is a work of fiction. The events in the novel did not happen. Names, characters, businesses, places, events and incidents are either the products of the author's imagination or used in a fictitious manner. Any resemblance to actual persons, living or dead, or actual events, is purely coincidental.

A CIP catalogue record for this book is available from the British Library.

ISBN 978-1-7396712-0-4 (Paperback)

Book layout and design by Clare Brayshaw

Cover by Chandler Book Design

Prepared and printed by:

York Publishing Services Ltd
64 Hallfield Road
Layerthorpe
York YO31 7ZQ

Tel: 01904 431213

Website: www.yps-publishing.co.uk

Acknowledgements

I became fascinated with the ghostly legend of Kitty Garthwaite when an employee of the Ryedale Folk Museum in Hutton-le-Hole first told me about it. In 2014, I wrote a modern-day play based on the legend and entered it into a competition. I was lucky enough to be a winner and the play was staged at the York Theatre Royal.

Now, almost ten years later and still interested in the legend, I have written this novel 'It Began with a Ghost Story'. It is the first in a new series of thrillers set in North Yorkshire.

I'm grateful to my sisters Jane and Janet for their help and advice; to my editor Alicia Makin; to my writer friends Fiona and Margaret; and to Clare Brayshaw, John Chandler, and Paula Charles for all their work in producing this novel.

I'm especially grateful to all my kind readers who buy my books and continue to urge me to write more. Thank you all.

Footnote:
The story of Kitty Garthwaite is a true legend on the North York Moors. There are several versions of what happened to Kitty, and I have chosen one for my novel. I have also taken some licence with the geography of Lowna Ford to fit my plot.

One

Present Day

Joe didn't believe in ghosts. Nor did his friends or family. But nobody liked to come to this spot after dark. Too many men had died here, and no-one had been held responsible. That is, no-one of this world. The locals knew it was absurd, but old folklore still held true. They blamed Kitty's ghost for luring those men to their deaths.

Joe had smiled to himself when his girlfriend's text popped up on his phone asking him to meet her here at midnight. She always said there was something spine-tingling about being out in the countryside at night. What we couldn't see frightened us and made us more alert to danger. We *felt* more.

And she was right. Excitement tingled through him as he thought of her luscious boobs and soft lips. She was game for anything and had shown him a thing or two. The trouble was he found himself constantly on tenterhooks waiting for her to get in touch. He knew that she did it deliberately, to keep him on his toes. Sometimes, he wouldn't hear for ages then, out of the blue, a text would arrive. *cu46* it would say, with instructions on when and where to meet up. Before her, he'd never had a clue about sexting, but he soon learnt it meant 'see you for sex'. She never gave him much notice either and that was difficult with all the work he had to do on the farm. Still, keeping him dangling and jumping to her tune is what she liked. It gave her the hots and he wasn't complaining about that.

He did feel uneasy for going along with everything on her terms though. He didn't want to be thought of as a doormat. But he considered himself lucky to have such an amazing girlfriend. She was a real character and into drama big time. She loved to dress up and had all kinds of wigs and costumes from various school productions. That was her dream, her big ambition, to be an actress.

After the first time they'd made love, she'd given herself the nickname Lady M after Shakespeare's Lady Macbeth, a character she dreamed of playing on stage in London's Globe Theatre. She insisted he call her only by that name and refused to answer to anything else. He smiled at her ambition. Until recently, she'd only appeared in amateur dramatics, but now she'd landed the lead in a play at the York Theatre Royal and was rehearsing like mad. He didn't know much about the play, except that it was called 'A Dark Vengeance'. She'd been over the moon to get the part and kept saying she was finally on her way to the top. Single-minded and determined, that was his girl. Still, that dream helped her survive the boredom of working in a local department store, a job her mother had forced her to take part-time to earn her keep since leaving school.

A soft breeze rustled through the leaves of the alder tree he was sitting under, and he looked up at the sky. There was no moon, or stars, to be seen on this damp, chilly October night, just cloud cover. He shuffled uncomfortably on the groundsheet he'd laid out for them. She hadn't picked a sensible place to meet up this time, but at least no-one would see them together in this lonely place. They could make as much noise as they liked too. And she did like to make a noise. His ears pricked up, thinking he'd heard her motorbike approaching in the distance. She loved roaring around the country lanes on it. But it was only an owl hooting from the trees. She was running late and that was unusual for her.

He propped his back up against the tree trunk and closed his eyes to enjoy the peace of the riverbank. The rushing water always soothed his soul as it flowed by, seemingly endless. Ever since he was a child, he'd fished in this river. He loved the way it meandered through the countryside and knew every spot along that stretch of its journey before it joined the River Rye in the Vale of Pickering. Sometimes the water was so clear he could see stones on the bottom, and he would cup his hand to take a drink. Tonight, it was too dark to see anything. He also liked the sense of solitude he got from being here. He wasn't antisocial. Not really. He was just used to being on his own and preferred it that way. Until he met his Lady M.

He almost broke out in a sweat thinking about their last date in that hotel in York. She'd sent him the usual text telling him to be in the hotel bar at 10pm and that she would meet him there. On the dot, in she came wearing a long blonde wig, a skirt resembling a pelmet and a blouse cut so low her breasts were spilling out. She had only to bend slightly to show everyone the tops of her black stockings and suspenders. People in the bar started to stare. Men's eyes were out on stalks. So were Joe's. She looked gorgeous and sexy. He felt ten feet tall when she came over and pretended to chat him up as if he were a stranger. Everything was going so well – until the police arrived.

Even now the memory made him cringe. Hotel security had called the police thinking his girl was a prostitute on the game. When they learnt the full story, the police let them both off with a warning. Joe could still remember the smirks and sly looks they gave her. He was embarrassed about it, but not his Lady M. She'd burst out laughing once they were out of the hotel, convinced it was her best acting performance yet. Joe dreaded his parents finding out and was even more worried about her mother. He'd never met the woman because she refused point blank to tell her about their relationship or take him home. She wouldn't let him tell his parents or friends about her either. "No-one must know about us," she insisted whenever they met. "It *must* be our secret, Joe. Mum would go mad if she knew. I'd never be allowed out of the house again."

It didn't bother Joe that she wanted to keep him a secret, although he was surprised that she allowed her mum to control her like that. After all, she was 19 and old enough to do what she liked. Still, from what he'd heard, her mother sounded a real nut job. Perhaps it *was* better to avoid her. Anyway, since that disastrous date in York, they really did have to meet away from prying eyes.

He looked at the time on his phone. Just past midnight. Where the hell was she? He scrolled to her text, to check he'd got the right place and time.

Hiya Lover. Next tryst is tonite. Bridge at Lowna Ford. Cu there at midnite. Lady M xxx

He'd been thrown by the word tryst at first and was worried about what she was going to do or would expect him to do. He'd looked it up in the dictionary and was relieved to see it was just an old-fashioned word meaning a private romantic rendezvous between lovers. Perhaps they were just going to make love this time without the shenanigans? He hoped so. It wasn't that he didn't *enjoy* her games. Far from it. It was just that she was becoming more obsessed with playing them.

He put his phone back in his pocket and told himself to be patient and play along as her moods could be unpredictable.

In temper, her eyes would flash, and her face turn white with rage. So, it was odd how completely thrown he'd been last Tuesday by her reaction when he finally plucked up the courage to tell her he'd been accepted at Belfast University to study agriculture and would be leaving for Ireland at the end of the month. Bracing himself for the blast, he'd expected her to be furious for not telling her what he had planned from the start of their relationship. He'd honestly had every intention of doing so but, as time went on, he'd never been able to find the right moment. Or rather he was too much of a coward. To his surprise, she hadn't exploded in temper. Instead, her face had crumpled, and she'd doubled over as if punched in the stomach. Then, and this is what had shocked him the most, she'd said she loved him and begged him not to go. She even started talking about wanting to settle down and have a family. He'd laughed at first, thinking she was joking or acting some part as she so often did when faced with her own emotions. Besides, they'd never even mentioned the word love or talked about being a couple, let alone about marriage or kids.

He cringed now remembering the scene. Never good with words like her, he'd mumbled something about only having fun and enjoying each other's company. Of course, he should have been kinder. But he'd been thrown by her reaction and said the wrong thing. She'd glared at him, accused him of deserting her, and stomped off home.

He was left reeling, convinced he'd never hear from her again. That upset him because he didn't want to lose her. To his surprise though, she was soon texting him again as if nothing had happened which confused him even more. In the end, he reckoned all her talk of love and marriage was another big acting performance, another one of her games to throw him off balance. He shook his head. Honestly, he never knew what to expect from one day to the next.

An image of her dressed up in stockings and suspenders in the hotel bar sprang into his mind again. He felt a rush of longing. "Hurry up, gorgeous," he said out loud.

Something fluttered in the trees in reply. He jumped and opened his eyes, hoping it wasn't a bat. He hated them and shivered when the flapping started again. Then he heard a strange noise, almost like howling. It sounded some way off. If he hadn't known for sure there were no wolves in North Yorkshire, he'd have thought there was one out there now. Ridiculous, he told himself, although he cast a careful look around anyway. This was his girl mucking about again, he was sure of it. He half-expected her to jump out of the bushes with a white sheet over her head pretending to be Kitty Garthwaite's ghost. She might even be dressed in servants' clothes like Kitty, from all those years ago.

A muffled sound, like a twig snapping underfoot, came from the bushes behind him. He turned and shouted: "Who's there?"

There was no reply, which made him nervous. His mum had always forbidden him and his sister to play around this spot when they were kids. She said it was a place of evil spirits. That warning had scared his sister to death, and she would scream her head off if he even suggested it.

That howling sound rang out again and he felt the hairs stand up on the back of his neck. Springing to his feet, he heard a voice calling...

"Joe... Joe..."

"Stop playing games," he shouted, unable to hide his anger. Or was it fear?

Silence.

"For God's sake!"

Suddenly, a white light appeared. He was rooted to the spot. Squinting, he put his hand up to shield his eyes to see who or what it was. The light got brighter and seemed to be consuming him.

"*Joe.*" He heard the woman's voice echoing all around him again. "*Joe… Joe…*"

He swung around in confusion. The light and the voice were everywhere.

His heart started thumping as he remembered the ghostly tale. *Too many men had died here.*

Shaking with the frightening thoughts in his head, he put his hands over his ears and started yelling for help as if his life depended on it. But there was no-one to hear him.

He spun around in circles, too disorientated to run, and found himself stumbling into the water at the edge of the bank. His legs buckled and he fell backwards into the river. A cracking pain seared through his head and icy cold water engulfed him. Dizzy with shock and fear, he heard that voice again.

A face appeared in his blurred vision. A strange face. Someone or something grabbed him. He tried to kick out. His hands scrabbled and punched in terror. But his limbs felt heavy and unresponsive from the blow. A hand clamped onto his face. He struggled frantically and tried to scream for help. His head was pushed under. Water rushed into his mouth and lungs. He held his breath, trying to fight, trying to stay alive, until his lungs felt they would burst. His arms and legs seemed to be floating away from him. There was nothing then but a gurgling sound before he slowly drifted off.

Too many men had died here…

Two

Grace

I was six years old the first time I saw the huge key in the red box on top of the cupboard in my mother's study. I remember it well, not just for the key, but for the scolding I got.

"Don't touch that hatbox," my mother warned one morning when she caught me eyeing it from the doorway. "I mean it, Grace." She gave me one of her 'don't mess with me' looks. "*Never* open that box." The sharpness of her tone made me nod dutifully. I had meant to obey her but forbidding me to touch it only added to its fascination and terror. I say fascination because the hatbox was a brilliant pillar-box red colour, with a gleaming gold clasp. It was the sort of box I thought a beautiful princess would keep her diamond tiara in. And I say terror because of the dreaded jack-in-the-box my aunt gave me as a present one Christmas. That box was red too. How I hated the painted man inside springing out at me, with his bulging eyes and blood red lips. I became too terrified to sleep in case he jumped out in the night and bashed me over the head as I'd seen in the Punch and Judy shows. In the end, one Guy Fawkes night, Dad threw it on the bonfire. "There," he said to me as the flames danced high in the sky and the jack-in-the-box burned to a crisp. "There's no need to be afraid anymore. He's gone for good."

I wasn't convinced though. I *wanted* to believe Dad, but that man in the box haunted my dreams. And now that there was another box in the house I couldn't rest until I was sure he wasn't in there too. But how was I going to find out? I wasn't allowed in Mum's study. At first, I tried to forget about it, but whenever I walked past and the door was open, my eyes would swivel up to the top of the cupboard. It was as if that box was calling to me, daring me to look inside.

One sunny day, I did just that. Mum was having a cup of tea in the garden with a neighbour. I was off school with chickenpox and was supposed to be having an afternoon nap. I lay in bed with my eyes closed pretending to be asleep when Mum looked in. When she'd gone, I jumped up and watched out the window until she appeared in the garden with the tea tray. That was my chance. I went into her study and looked up at the box. It would be difficult to reach, but I already had a plan. I pushed a chair up against the cupboard and stood on it. I was able to put one knee on the windowsill and grab onto the curtains to haul myself up. Then, standing on the sill, I leant over and reached the box.

My young heart was pounding as I lifted the lid and I held my breath, ready to duck in case the man pinged out in my face. Nothing happened. Emboldened, I peeked inside just to be sure. All I could see were papers and photographs. I stood on tiptoe, reached inside and swished things around to check nothing else was in there. My hand touched something cool and hard.

And there it was. The strange key. I remember thinking it must open a special door because it was bigger than my hand for sure, and very heavy. I'd never seen one like it before which added to its allure. Then I did something I've always regretted, I put the key in my trouser pocket and climbed back down. I hadn't meant to steal it, I just wanted to look at it a bit more and find out what it opened. The trouble was, once back in my room, I knew I'd done something wrong and got scared. I slipped the key into my bedside cabinet drawer out of sight. I was going to put it back in Mum's box without her ever knowing, except I forgot it was in there. Then Dad found it.

I'm shuddering even now at the memory. I couldn't understand why he was so angry, he rarely said a cross word to me. I said I was sorry and tried to appeal to his kind nature, which usually worked. But this time it was different. Mum came along to see what all the fuss was about. Her face crumpled when she saw the key and she looked at me with such pain in her eyes. Dad glared at her. Then he threw the key onto the bed and stormed out of the house.

Later that night, when he came home, they had a furious row in the kitchen. I say row but it was really Dad doing all the shouting and slamming around. Mum never even raised her voice. I was already in bed, but I wasn't asleep. I crept out to sit on the top stair and listen.

"What on earth do you think you're *doing*?" he shouted at Mum. "You said you'd get rid of that place."

I had to strain my ears to hear her voice because she was speaking so softly. "I couldn't do it," she said. "I just couldn't do it."

"For God's sake, Violet." He must have slammed his fist down on the table in temper because the whole house seemed to shake. "I thought we had an understanding."

"We *do* have an understanding." Her voice was calm. "And I've kept to it."

"Liar!" he shouted, which shocked me because I wasn't allowed to call anyone a liar. I had to use the word fibber. "You have *not* kept your promise, Violet," he bellowed. "No way!"

It was then I heard my mother crying. Long, deep sobs that made tears spill from my eyes too. I'd never heard her weep like that before and I knew it was all my fault.

There was a long pause before Dad spoke again and his voice was quieter this time, more in control. "You will *never* understand how disappointed I am Violet." He gave a weary sigh, and I heard a chair scape back on the tiled floor. "I realise now that I can't stop you. So, go there if you must, but I forbid you to involve Grace. Do you hear? You will never *ever* take Grace."

I hadn't understood what they were arguing about back then, although I knew the key that I'd found had set it off. Sadly, it was only the start of their many fights from that day until Dad passed away. He was more than 20 years older than Mum, so she found herself a widow at a fairly young age. It devastated me to know that I'd been the cause of that rift in their marriage all those years ago and I never went anywhere near that hatbox again.

Until now 30 years later. That same hatbox stood on the end of my bed, its red cover black with mildew and its clasp rusted over. I wasn't afraid of looking inside anymore because the box was mine, inherited with the rest of my mother's estate after she collapsed in the street with a heart attack. That was five months ago. It had come as an awful shock to me. I was a GP for heaven's sake. I should have known she had heart disease. I should have spotted the signs. I should have made sure she had regular check-ups. But then she never complained of chest pains or breathlessness or anything like that. To be truthful, she never complained much about anything. But that was Mum. Stubborn, proud, and independent-minded.

I picked out my favourite old photo of her from the box and propped it up against the bedside lamp. I particularly liked this one because she looked happy in it, although I didn't recognise where it had been taken. She was standing in front of an old stone building or barn wearing denim dungarees, green wellies, and a duffle coat. Her brown hair fell to her shoulders, with a wispy fringe that made her look like a student. She'd had the exact same hairstyle when she died, although grey hairs had started peppering through. I felt tears prick my eyes. She was too young to die. Far too young.

As the months ticked over, my grief at her passing became mixed with unease about the contents of the box. I didn't recognise any of the photos or the places they were taken, or the newspaper cuttings and profiles of her, or what they said about her. They triggered questions about her life that I couldn't answer. Questions that would swirl around my head and wake me up at night. Unsettling questions that made me worry incessantly about the past.

You see my mother, Violet Winter, was a successful children's author, a prolific writer in her earlier years, publishing one, sometimes two, novels a year. She conjured up some magical characters that fired children's imaginations. Her books were widely read, even in schools. Yet she never spoke about them or about her writing career at home. Nor did Dad. I didn't think much about it growing up. But I do remember her writing every morning until lunchtime at her desk in the spare bedroom she called her study. No-one was allowed in that room. Not even Dad. It only occurred to me recently how strange it was that he never went to any of her book launches or signings with her. Nor did I. And we never had any celebrations at home when she published a new novel. I just accepted what I was told. These events were for grown-ups and Dad was staying at home to look after me.

And there was something else I just accepted. Twice a year as regular as clockwork, my mother would go for weeks at a time to the seaside to write. I can still hear her parting words that would upset me to the core: "I'm off to work for a little while, Grace. Be good for your dad." I missed her terribly and would imagine her sitting on the beach writing in the notepad she took with her everywhere. I loved the sea and so dearly wanted to go with her.

Then there was this old key. It had caused a hell of a stink years ago. Now though I understood its significance. Mum's will, and her solicitor's letter, explained that it was the key to a country cottage she owned in a village on the North York Moors. As her only child, I inherited the cottage, along with the family home in Hampstead.

I fell back on the pillow and glanced out the window. The sun glowed on the watery blue horizon and lit up the red and brown leaves on the old oak tree outside my bedroom window. I loved that tree and watching its leaves change through the seasons. Solid and dependable, that's how it was, and I wondered how it survived sucking up so much carbon dioxide from the London traffic year after year. I could tell everything about the weather and the seasons by just looking at the tree every morning. In the summer, I imagined it breathing oxygen into my flat through the open windows. This year though, summer had passed me by in a whirl. It was already October, and I was about to enjoy my first proper holiday of the year. I had a whole month off work, and I was going to make the most of it.

I had just pushed back the covers to get up and finish packing when I heard a dull thud come from the kitchen. I froze. It was just the softest noise, but it told me that I was no longer alone in the flat. I knew I had to be careful, and I had to be quick. I would only have one chance to strike. But I was not quick enough...

A shape emerged from the darkness and sprang onto the bed. An excruciating pain radiated through my left foot, and I screamed in agony. Rufus had clamped his teeth around my big toe. "Bloody cat!" I shouted, before grabbing him by the scruff of his neck to make him release my toe and dumping him on the floor.

And there he sat. A large ginger tom, unrepentant and staring at me with his unfathomable green eyes. His fur was orange, except for his neck and breast which were pure white. Comically, he looked like he was wearing a dress shirt.

The cat was a less welcome inheritance from my mother. I was sure he hated me and blamed me for her death and for incarcerating him in this ground floor flat when he'd had a lovely house in Hampstead and the heath to roam around. Or perhaps he just sensed that I didn't want him and was determined to make my life hell. But my mother had loved him to bits, and I knew she'd want me to take care of him. What else could I do but take him in? It was neither practical nor easy though. I had a cat flap installed in the kitchen door which led out to a narrow terrace, so he could come and go whenever he liked. It hadn't escaped my attention that he went out for the night as I came in from work, and he came back in the following morning after I'd left. I didn't mind though. The feeling was mutual. The less we saw of each other, the better.

This morning was different though. I had plans for Rufus. I jumped out of bed, ran into the kitchen, and wedged a chair against the cat flap to stop him getting out again. He stared at me with disdain from the doorway, then marched off to the sitting room to curl up on the sofa and sleep all day. That was his usual routine.

I was about to go after him when the piercing ring of the phone stopped me. Was that the surgery ringing with an emergency? I wouldn't put it past them, as we were short staffed. I'd offered to defer my holiday, but the other doctors in the practice insisted I take it. Apart from a few days off when Mum died, I'd worked through since the New Year and I really needed a break. I looked at the phone and for a moment considered not answering. Then I picked up the receiver. "Grace Winter."

"You took your time," a weary voice complained.

I was relieved to hear it was my friend and not the practice. "Hi Sam. Are you packed?"

"Almost finished," came the reply. "I was just wondering if I might need my bikini on this trip."

I heard the longing in her voice and felt guilty. Samantha Jones was one of my oldest friends and, at this time of year, we always went on a break with our mutual friend Evie to somewhere hot. Sam loved strutting around on a beach with her size 10 figure. How she managed to stay so slim was a mystery, especially working as the Marketing Director of an advertising agency in London, amongst a hard-drinking, partying crowd. She looked as glossy as some of the professional models in her ads too, with her sleek blonde bob and fringe that took years off her age. Her make-up was always perfect, her red-painted lips the same colour as her manicured nails. Like me, Sam was in her thirties and unmarried. Unlike me, she was never without a man. She'd had so many boyfriends; it was hard to keep up.

However, this year instead of the beach, they'd both agreed to come up to Mum's cottage in Hutton-Le-Hole with me for the week. "It's the wettest autumn on record," I joked, "so you may need it."

"Very funny."

"We'll see if we can find a spa to spend time in," I said, soothingly.

"Good because I'm not sure it's the weather for traipsing over soggy moors in hiking boots. I don't think Evie will be up for that either, not in her frame of mind."

"What d'you mean?"

"She's so moody these days. I can't say anything without her jumping down my throat. I'm not sure a week away in a country cottage on the Moors with her is a good idea." She paused. "She's not herself."

That was news to me, and I felt even more concerned about not having seen Evie or Sam since Mum's funeral. I was so low after her death it had taken all my energy just to get up and go to work. I remember Evie hadn't looked great then, but who does at funerals? It was hard to tell anyway, with her pale skin. Sometimes, after swimming classes, Evie looked like a blue baby shivering in the changing rooms, her veins showing through her almost luminous white skin. She'd always been a sensitive soul too. The perfect target for school bullies until Sam had duffed them up and drawn Evie into our little gang. After that, the three of us did everything together. Even now, every year, we'd go away for a week somewhere. As soon as we were together, the intervening year would just melt away as if we'd never been apart.

Sam's words were worrying though. "What do you mean she's not herself?"

"Oh, you know what she's like, always upset about something. Teaching those kids every day must drag her down. I don't know why she became a teacher, she's not tough enough."

"Oh, come on, she's a great teacher. The kids love her."

"Well, there's something's wrong." Sam sounded cagey now. "Maybe it's trouble at home. Something to do with Trevor?"

That made me feel even worse for not being in touch with Evie. "A week away will do her the world of good," I said. "We can take her out of herself, cheer her up."

There was a pause. "I'm not sure that's going to work, Grace."

I heard the hesitation in Sam's voice and was starting to think she was trying to pull out of the trip. That upset me because I was looking forward to a week away with my two friends. And I didn't want to go up to the cottage on my own. For some reason, I was afraid of what I might find there, although I didn't say that to Sam.

"Don't you want to come?" I asked. "Is that what you're trying to say?"

"No, it's not that," she said. "I know how important this visit is for you. Anyway, I'm looking forward to seeing Violet's country cottage and where she wrote her books. I still can't believe you've never been there before."

My voice was cracking with emotion when I spoke again. "I told you I really didn't know about the cottage. I-I only found out when her solicitor read out her will and gave me the key. The truth is I don't want to go on my own."

"Of course not. I quite understand." Sam's voice was sounding emotional now, which wasn't surprising since she'd been fond of my mother too.

"Did she ever mention the cottage to you, Sam?"

"Nope. That's what's so weird." She hesitated. "Look, why don't we just go? The two of us, I mean. I think that would be for the best."

"What about Evie? She's expecting to come, and probably packing now." I paused. "I'll phone her and see if she's still up for it. If she says she'd rather not, then that's fine."

Sam sighed. "Okay, but don't force her, Grace, if she's not keen, I mean. You and I can still go and have a good break."

I felt relief wash over me. I might not have any family anymore, but I could always count on my friends. "Thanks Sam. I'll ring Evie now and see what she says. How about I pick you up around nine o'clock? Then we can go on to Evie's if she is still coming."

I heard Sam sigh again before we said our goodbyes and hung up. I wondered then if she knew more about what was going on with Evie than she'd let on. It wasn't like Sam to hold back though. She usually came straight out with whatever was on her mind, especially between the three of us.

I went back into my bedroom to phone Evie and caught sight of the old key on my bedside cabinet. The memories came flooding back of that row between my parents. It was a shock to find out all these years later that the key I'd found in her old hatbox was for the front door of a cottage on the North York Moors. Why on earth would Mum buy a place in the wilds of Yorkshire and keep it a secret? The only thing I knew about the cottage was that it had caused a deep rift between my parents. Dad had urged her to get rid of it and she'd refused. Why?

I slipped the key into my handbag, knowing I'd never be able to rest until I'd seen the place for myself. I did have an uneasy feeling in the pit of my stomach though. Or was it more a sense of foreboding? I remember thinking how difficult it must have been for Mum to keep that cottage and her visits there a secret from me. I was upset about that, for sure. But the old adage of 'you think you know someone' was rattling around in my head. Had I known my mother as well as I thought I had?

Three

The chilly night air made me shiver as we left the pub in Thirsk where we'd had dinner. I'd hoped to get to the cottage before dark, but we'd been late leaving London because Evie had overslept and wasn't ready when we arrived. And she'd looked so terrible that we had to make her a couple of strong cups of coffee to get her going. Then we sat stationery behind an awful traffic accident that closed the M1 north for several hours. Tempers started fraying in the car, so we decided to stop for dinner in the small market town before heading up onto the Moors. After all, I had no idea what we were going to find at the cottage.

The cosy atmosphere in the pub, with its lovely log fire and moreish food, encouraged us to linger longer than we'd planned. Sam wanted to stay the night in their guest rooms upstairs, but pets weren't allowed, and I didn't want to leave Rufus alone in a cold car all night. We were further delayed by Sam ordering a bottle of red wine that she insisted on finishing before she left. She'd had to drink it on her own because Evie and I were on soft drinks. So, when we finally prized her from the pub, Sam was not only tired but unsteady on her feet and trailed behind as we walked back to my car.

"I've never seen her drink like that before," I said, quietly, to Evie.

"It's that new man of hers," she whispered back. "He's a drinker."

I looked at her in surprise. "What new man?"

"Another toy boy. Years younger than her and probably bonking her into the mattress every night."

The image that conjured up made me start laughing.

"*Oi*," Sam shouted. "I *can* hear you two."

We'd reached the car now and I looked at Sam over the roof. "Why have you kept this man a secret?"

She tossed her head in reply.

"Come on," I said. "Spill the beans. Who is he? Where'd you meet him? What does he do?"

She pulled a face, opened the door, and slipped into the front passenger seat.

Rufus, upset at being left on his own in the car, made something like a growling sound as soon as he saw us, which irritated me. That morning, I'd spent ages chasing him around the flat before getting him into his pet carrier. He'd made such a racket on the journey up that Evie had to let him out and sit him on her lap to soothe him.

I went round to the boot, got his bowl out and poured in some milk from the carton in the freeze-bag. "Here," I said, handing it carefully to Evie as she slipped into the back seat beside him. "That'll keep him happy for a bit. I'll feed him when we get to the cottage. It's not far now."

Evie held the bowl and Rufus started drinking thirstily from it. I closed the boot and got into the driver seat.

"Good boy, Rufus." Sam put her hand over the seat back and went to stroke him.

He stopped drinking and hissed at her.

"Careful. Don't put your fingers anywhere near his teeth or you might regret it," I said.

Sam frowned. "Since when did Rufus bite?"

"Since this morning." I looked down at my foot. "He's the reason I'm wearing my open-toed sandals. He bit my toe. And before you ask yes, it is painful. And yes, my feet *are* freezing."

She laughed.

I pulled a face at her. "He's been a nightmare since Mum died. I think he blames me for her death."

"Don't be ridiculous," she said. "Cats are solitary creatures. They don't get close to their owners. In fact, they'd eat them if they weren't so big." She wrinkled her nose. "He whiffs a bit, Grace. Why'd you bring him?"

"I couldn't leave him for a whole week. I don't know anyone in my block well enough to trust them with a key to my flat to feed him."

"He's grieving for Violet." Evie stroked him. "He needs some love and attention, that's all."

Sam rolled her eyes. "Don't we all."

I smiled at Evie in the driver mirror. I was glad she'd decided to come. Mind you, she had been reluctant. I'd had to employ all my powers of persuasion to get her to agree. In the end, it was my appeal to her friendship and loyalty that swung it. I told her I missed her, which was true, and I needed her moral support to go to Mum's cottage and sort her things. Now though, seeing Evie even paler than usual and with dark circles under her eyes, I was wondering if I'd done the right thing. But then Evie had always been fragile and sensitive. Small and slim, with unruly auburn curls that she relentlessly tried to straighten, she had one stunning feature – beautiful green eyes.

Like me, Evie was an only child. Although we'd been friends since our early school days, our families weren't close. The only time I ever saw her mother was when she drove round to pick Evie up from our house or drop her off. My mum wouldn't allow me to go to hers because

Evie's dad was in poor health and couldn't have visitors in the house. Or that's what I'd been told. I did wonder about that because I'd overheard her telling Dad that Evie and her mum must have a terrible life with her dad. It hadn't occurred to me back then that the red marks and bruises on Evie might be caused by her own father. Mum must have known because she always welcomed Evie with open arms whenever she came to our house and made a fuss of her.

Evie had gone straight from school to university, along with Sam and me. After that, she'd trained to be a teacher, which was no surprise as she'd always loved children and wanted a family. Now, she was the only one of us who was married. She'd been with her husband Trevor for ten years, but there was a sadness in Evie's life. No matter how hard she and Trevor tried, or how many rounds of IVF they had, Evie could not get pregnant. As the years went by, it was a burden that weighed heavily on her.

"There, old boy." Evie stroked Rufus, gently. "That's better, isn't it?" She looked up at me. "He's finished drinking. Let's go."

"Good job he likes you, Evie," Sam said. "You'll have to look after him this week. He can't stand Grace or me."

Sam was right but her words niggled me. He was Mum's cat and he'd adored her. He was always curled up by her side on the sofa, or at her feet. So, why didn't he like me? Why wouldn't he let me stroke him? I'd given him a home and fed him. And what did I get for all my effort – a throbbing toe. Seeing Rufus cuddling up to Evie gave me an irrational sense of rejection.

Sam checked her watch again. "God knows what time we'll get there. It's already 10pm." She flashed a dark look over her shoulder at Evie. "If you'd been ready on time, we'd have missed all that traffic on the M1."

Evie sighed. "I've said I'm sorry for oversleeping."

"Why didn't Trevor wake you up?" I asked.

Evie looked away. "It's been a frenetic week at school in the run up to half-term. I just couldn't get going."

I studied Evie's wan face again in the mirror. "Never mind. We'll have a long lie-in tomorrow and spend our first day relaxing." I glanced at Sam. "How does that sound?"

"Good to me." Sam stretched. "I could do with some rest."

"Huh", said Evie. *Your* trouble, Sam, is that you can't rest. You always want more of everything. You should try being happy with what you've got."

It was an uncharacteristically sharp comment from Evie, and one I didn't quite understand.

But Sam didn't respond, so I started up the car and glanced over. "When are you going to tell us about this new man of yours?"

"Will you give over?" she said, huffily.

"Not until you tell us."

Sam sighed. "Well, if you must know, his name's Ashley. I met him at the gym. He runs a male-grooming salon in Kensington High Street. In fact, he owns a chain of them."

I didn't know what I was expecting Sam to say about her new boyfriend, but it wasn't that. I caught Evie's eye in the mirror.

Her face broke out into a wide grin. "Sounds a perfect match for you, Sam. You can pluck each other's eyebrows while quaffing champagne."

Evie and I started giggling and ended up with tears rolling down our cheeks. We could always set each other off and were often dismissed from class to stand outside the headmaster's study to control ourselves.

A hurt look spread over Sam's face, although I could tell by the twitch in the side of her mouth that she wasn't serious. There were three things that I loved about Sam. One, her sense of humour. Two, she couldn't stay mad for long. Three, she didn't hold a grudge. So, it wasn't long before she was laughing along with us. She was a good sport, and I felt mean for making fun of her love life.

"Sorry," I said. "I don't know where that all came from. I guess I just needed a good laugh."

"Glad to oblige." She grinned at me, and in that moment, I thought how much yet how little she'd changed since we were kids. She was a career woman through and through, but she hadn't always been like that. The youngest of three children and the only girl, she'd had to learn to stand up for herself quickly. She was brave too and had no trouble seeing off some older girls who were hellbent on bullying Evie. That earnt her the respect of everyone in the class, including the boys. They also knew that if they picked on Sam, they'd have one of her older brothers to answer to. Now, sitting next to me with her wind-blown hair, and in her cargo trousers and trainers, she reminded me more of the tomboy I'd always known.

There was something indefinable about her too. A restless soul who craved action and got high on the joy of life. She loved having a good time, and her parties were legendary. People from every walk of life would turn up at her London flat to drink and dance the night away. The sheer force of her personality pulled people into her orbit. Yet there was a vulnerability about her too. She found it hard to sustain relationships, hence the succession of boyfriends, which had become a pattern of behaviour. It was as if from the outset she expected every relationship to fail. Much of that, I guessed, was down to her independent nature, and not wanting to let herself rely on a man. But underneath that polished exterior, was a loneliness.

I wiped my eyes and pulled myself together. "Right," I said, pushing the gear into reverse, "let's get on our way."

Sam glanced over at me. "I can't wait to see Violet's cottage. I used to love her books as a kid. Such wonderful illustrations too."

"My favourite series was Rosie's Adventures," Evie said. "I suppose it makes sense now, the cottage I mean. Those books were set on the Moors when Rosie goes to stay with her aunt for the summer holidays."

"Now we know where Violet got her inspiration from," Sam said. "But why the North York Moors?" she persisted. "There must be some connection, Grace."

"If there is, I don't know about it," I said, bluntly. I'd been speculating enough in my head over recent months, and I didn't want to go there again.

Evie sensed my upset. "I'm certain Violet will have had a good reason for not saying anything."

When I glanced at Evie in the mirror again, I saw tears glisten in her eyes. I thought for a moment she was going to say something else, but she just turned to stare out the window.

I picked up the old key from the cup holder next to the gear stick and showed it to them. "At least this makes sense now."

"Looks ancient," said Sam.

"All I remember is finding this key in a hatbox in Mum's study when I was six. She was furious because she'd forbidden me to touch the box. My father was too. It caused a big row. I had no idea what the argument was about back then. I still don't really, except it was to do with this key and Mum's cottage."

"Very mysterious. The plot could have come straight out of one of your mum's books," Sam said, darkly. "Violet's supernatural series was my favourite, particularly The Fox

Spirit. He was so cute, that fox, with his magical powers. Did you read that book, Evie?"

"No. Mum said I had enough nightmares without that." Evie sighed. "What happened to the manuscript of Violet's latest novel, Grace? Did she finish her ghost story before she died?"

The question stunned me. I frowned at her in the mirror. "I didn't know she was writing a ghost story."

Evie looked momentarily flustered. "It wasn't a children's book. It was for adults."

Mum had turned her hand to one or two adult novels over the years, but they were never as successful as her children's books. But I certainly knew nothing about a ghost story. "I haven't seen any manuscript amongst her papers. How do you know about it?"

Evie shrugged. "She told me."

"What's it about?" Sam asked.

Evie hesitated. "It was based on a true legend, set up on the Moors. Violet's working title was It Began with a Ghost Story. It's a dark tale about a serving girl called Kitty Garthwaite. A local lad got her pregnant out of wedlock, then abandoned her to face the music alone." She paused. "It was all a long time ago. Late 1700s, or something like that."

"What's so dark about that story?" Sam asked.

Evie went silent for a while. I didn't think she was going to answer, then she said: "Kitty drowned herself at a place called Lowna Ford. After that, several men were killed at the same spot. The locals reported seeing Kitty's ghost sitting naked on the riverbank luring those men to their deaths. They all died with the same head injuries."

"Is this ghost supposed to have killed those men?" Sam asked.

Evie nodded.

Sam laughed. "Way to go Kitty's ghost."

I was annoyed that Evie knew all about my mother's latest book and I didn't. "When did Mum tell you about this?"

"Oh, a while ago." Evie was vague. "Last summer, I think. She asked me to research the legend. I spoke to a couple of people and looked online, but there's nothing much in any archives."

Sam reverted to our original conversation. "You know, there was one of Violet's children's books that did scare me."

I raised my eyebrows because Sam wasn't usually scared of anything. "Which one?"

"Devil Bird," she whispered in a dramatic way.

Evie stiffened. "I don't like that one. That bird is a bad omen."

"I see you've got your crystals on to protect you." Sam teased.

I'd also noticed Evie's dangly earrings glinting in the sun that streamed through the side window earlier. She believed in the power of crystals and always carried one somewhere on her. She was into complementary therapies and holistic healing too, which grated on me. Alternative medicine had its place in a patient's wellbeing but, in my view, it was no replacement for traditional medicine.

Sam went on. "Well, I liked the way that bird gives a blood-curdling shriek in the night. It's like an omen predicting death." Suddenly, she let out a loud shriek of her own. Evie and I jumped out of our skins. Unfortunately, it had the same effect on Rufus. He let out a piercing screech, shot through the gap between the front seats, and pounced on Sam.

"Aargh! Get him off me!"

Evie reached through and grabbed Rufus before he could do any damage. "Serves you right," she said, harshly to Sam. "You've terrified him."

In the mirror, I saw Rufus trembling on Evie's lap. I felt sorry for the old cat whose whole world had been turned upside down. I went to pull over, but Evie told me to drive on.

"It's all right, Rufus," she stroked him gently. "Shush…" She looked up at Sam. "You enjoy upsetting everyone, don't you? That's your trouble."

"And your trouble is you take everything too seriously," Sam shot back.

Evie bit her lip and I thought I saw tears in her eyes again.

"Look," I said. "I know we're tired, but let's not have a go at each other." I tried to sound cheerful. "It's not that far now." I was secretly worried though about what we would find at the cottage or even if the electricity would be on.

As if reading my thoughts, Sam said: "Have you got a torch in this car?"

"In the glovebox. I keep one in case I'm called out to a patient in the night."

Sam checked and nodded. "When's the last time anyone stayed in the cottage?"

"I've no idea. Mum's solicitor said her things are still there. I'm sure she'll have everything we need, and more." I glanced at Sam. "Have a look at the map, will you? Make sure I'm on the right road."

Sam reached for the map in the passenger door pocket and unfolded it. "Here we are." She traced her finger over it. "You need to take the road to Sutton Bank, which should take us all the way to Hutton-Le-Hole. Looks straight forward enough."

It wasn't long before we'd left the lights of Thirsk behind as we drove into the darkness of night towards Sutton Bank. Tiredness was creeping up on me and I opened my window a little to let in some air to keep me awake. It was a tranquil autumn night. Cool and crisp, with a clear sky. My eyes soon adjusted to the blackness of the countryside, helped by a huge moon hanging low in the sky like a luminous porcelain plate.

Now, thankfully, it was quiet inside the car. I glanced across at Sam. Her head was resting back, with her eyes closed. Evie too, I saw in the mirror, was fast asleep with Rufus stretched across her lap. Replete with food, and in Sam's case wine too, they looked peaceful. I was less comfortable. I'd had a couple of glasses of lime and soda in the pub which was a mistake on top of fish and chips. My stomach was bubbling like a cauldron.

Still, I was glad to have some quiet time to gather my thoughts. I was feeling ever more anxious as we neared the cottage. Part of me was dying to see Mum's house, a place where she came to work on her books. The other part of me was dreading it. There had to be a reason why she didn't want me to know about the cottage or ever take me there. And something told me I wasn't going to like that reason. Dad's words rang in my ears again. *I told you to get rid of the place, Violet…You must never involve Grace.* I understood now that they were arguing about the cottage, but why had he wanted her to get rid of it? And why couldn't she ever take me there?

Another thing that didn't make sense was the thought of Mum driving along this quiet road on her own. It was so out of character. She didn't like driving alone in London, never mind deep in the countryside. And she was always worried about me going out on an emergency call to a patient in the dead of night. *Make sure you have a torch in the car…make sure you change the batteries.* Those were familiar words from her, especially as the autumn nights closed in. Had she ever broken down on this lonely road?

Trying to distract myself from these negative thoughts, I peered at the stone houses lining the road as we drove through a village. There were lights on inside, but not a soul about. It was only just after 10pm, yet it seemed everyone was already battened down for the night. The smell of smoke from wood fires permeated the air and I hoped Mum's cottage had an open fire like the one in the pub.

Ahead now, the black outline of a hill stood silhouetted in the moonlight. It looked stunning on this clear night, like a dark, brooding obstacle in our path. It had to be Sutton Bank. I knew from the map that it rose 160 metres up from the Vale of York onto the North York Moors.

I could feel us climbing gently on the approach when, suddenly, a dark shape swooped across the road in front of us. I stepped on the brake and tensed, waiting for the impact. None came. I relaxed and looked all around, thinking it must have been an owl or a large bat. There was no sign of it now. In the mirror I saw Rufus, back arched and eyes gleaming, standing on all fours and staring through the windscreen. He'd seen whatever it was too. I couldn't tell whether he was excited or afraid.

Sam and Evie must have been exhausted not to be shaken awake by that jolt and I was glad of the continued silence in the car. Driving on and up the hill, I had to almost stop to negotiate a hairpin bend before chugging up another steep section of road. Eventually we reached the top where it levelled out and I saw another vast expanse of blackness spreading out in front of us.

"Talk about a journey to nowhere," said Sam.

I glanced across. "Thought you were asleep."

"I don't sleep much these days."

"Since when?" Sam was someone who could put her head on the pillow and go out like a light. "Guilty conscience?"

"I fall asleep but I'm awake after a few hours. I just can't *stay* asleep." She yawned. "Bit lonely, isn't it? I wouldn't want to live up here."

"Too far away from the party scene in London?"

"Too right. But Violet must have had *some* connection with the place to buy a house up here. Think, Grace." Her voice rose. "Maybe it was a long time ago, but there must be something you remember."

"Shush,*"* I whispered. "Keep your voice down. Let Evie sleep. She's exhausted."

I felt Sam's eyes on me. "Have *you* taken a good look at yourself in the mirror lately?"

I didn't need to because I knew what I was going to see. A pallid complexion, dark circles ringing my brown eyes, and lifeless hair framing my sunken cheeks. "It's been a difficult year."

"That's an understatement. First your partner leaves, then your mother dies. That's tough for anyone to deal with. And what do *you* do? Do you give yourself some time off? Do you take things easy? No, you throw yourself into working 24/7."

I didn't want to have this conversation, so I said nothing.

"Don't think I don't understand," Sam went on. "You've been trying to wear yourself out until you were too numb to think or feel."

"Something like that."

"Well, not only do you look completely shattered, but you've let yourself go."

Sam could be as blunt as a doorstop. "Say it as it is, why don't you?"

"Look, I'm one of your oldest friends. If I can't tell you the truth, who can?"

I hoped that was the end of her rant, but it wasn't.

"What upsets me," she said, folding her arms across her chest like some matron, "is that you wouldn't let anyone help you. Every time one of us rang to invite you out, you wouldn't come. We called round but you were always at the surgery. You've been working yourself into the ground, and there was nothing we could do about it."

Sam was right. That was exactly what I had been doing. Now though, with my two close friends, my grief bubbled up. "W-work was th-the only thing that kept me going. It helped me cope."

Sam nodded, then asked: "Where is that rat Peter, anyway? Have you heard from him?"

She asked the question casually, but I got the feeling she really wanted to know. I hadn't told her or Evie much about Peter leaving, and they were probably dying to know the details. But it wasn't a conversation I was yet comfortable with. I shrugged. "The last I heard he was in San Francisco."

"San Francisco?" She couldn't hide the surprise in her voice.

I nodded. "He sent me a postcard."

"A postcard?" She sounded even more shocked. "What did it say?"

I didn't have to think hard to remember. Peter's words were etched on my brain. "The postcard was of the Golden Gate Bridge. He wrote on the back: I'm crossing this bridge to a new life. Be happy, Grace. Always. Love P x

"When did you get it?" Sam asked.

"A few weeks after Mum died."

"Does he *know* she's dead?"

I shook my head. "His old email address just comes back as 'invalid'. He hasn't given me his new address or telephone number." My words caught in my throat. "He would have if he'd wanted me to get in touch."

Sam flopped back in her seat.

Her silence made me feel I needed to explain a bit more. "I don't blame him. I knew he'd had enough of the grind in London. He's always wanted to travel; it was a longing in him. He wanted me to go too, but I couldn't just take off. I had Mum to think about, and a busy job. So, I said to him if you want to go, then go."

"And the selfish git did."

My chest tightened. "I-I didn't realise how lost I'd be without him. Watching him go was like no other pain I've ever known. But how could I stand in his way?"

I felt a hand on my shoulder and looked in the mirror.

Evie's eyes were full of tears. "Do you think he'll come back?"

That was a question I'd been asking myself over and over. Peter had been my only love. We'd met at university and lived together since then. I'd always felt so close to him, so tuned in that I could almost predict what he was going to say or do. Had that been the problem? Had we just become too comfortable, like some old married couple? Whatever it was, I had to face up to the fact that I couldn't feel him around anymore. I couldn't sense his presence.

I patted Evie's hand. "Peter's gone from my life. I know that now. Maybe he's got a new girlfriend. He's certainly carving out a new life for himself."

She sighed. "You didn't deserve that, Grace. If it's any consolation, I don't think Peter was running away from you. He loved you, I'm sure of it."

"Just not enough to stay."

"Perhaps he just couldn't face things," Evie said.

There was a note of bitterness in her words, which I put down to her being cross with Peter for what he'd done. I was more sad than angry now.

Evie was about to say something else when Sam turned to face her. "Enough about Peter. Grace has other things to deal with right now. The important thing is to find out about Violet and her cottage, not rake over all the old muck with him."

I thought that was a bit rich since Sam had brought him up in the first place. Evie muttered something under her breath, but I was thankful the questions about Peter and Mum stopped. I was wrung out enough. Except, I couldn't get Peter's soft brown eyes and sandy hair out of my mind. And his lean, strong body lying next to me every night. I missed his warmth, the comfortable rhythm of his breathing in sleep, his arms around me. I missed his cheeriness in the mornings, the tea he would bring me in bed, the breakfast he would make. He was the proverbial lark, and I was the owl, but we got along well. We understood each other and rarely argued, which is why the pain of his leaving hit me so hard, or rather the manner of it. I had no-one to blame but myself. I'd told him to go travelling, but I hadn't expected him to leave and cut me out of his life. I thought he'd be away for a while, and we'd pick up our lives when he came back. It was only when I didn't hear from him and couldn't reach his mobile that I became frantic with worry. Had he been in an accident? Was he sick? I rang his work colleagues and was stunned to find out he'd put in his notice before going overseas. Had something gone wrong at work to make him leave in such a hurry? He was a financial consultant and often worried about investments he made for clients. His colleagues said there was nothing like that. Peter said he wanted a change of direction and wouldn't be back. Then I got that postcard.

I kept mulling it over as I drove along. He'd always been kind and considerate and I thought we'd be together for life. More fool me. There was no way I could ever have treated him like that, whatever the reason.

"Stop!" Sam suddenly shouted.

I stamped on the brake and the car screeched to a halt.

"You should have turned left back there, at the sign for Hutton-le-Hole." She shone the torch beam on the map. "The village is only a couple of miles up that road." She smiled at me. "Sorry! Nearly there."

I did a three-point turn and took the road Sam had indicated. It was deathly quiet as we drove along. The road was lined with hedgerows, and I realised we were climbing again. Trees bordered the road on both sides. Moonlight shone through the branches, giving a dappled, almost mystical effect on the tarmac. Suddenly, the car rumbled over a cattle grid at speed. Rufus went mad, springing around in the back seat and meowing.

"That damn cat," Sam huffed.

I'd had my suspicions throughout the journey that Rufus knew exactly where he was going. Now, with his excited behaviour, I was sure he did.

"Don't worry, I've got him," Evie said.

By now, my nerves were shred to pieces. I just wanted to get to the cottage. The first thing I noticed as we approached the village was the white-painted picket fence by the side of the road which stood out in the moonlight. There was a sign indicating a residents-only road to the left, but I decided to keep on the main road since it seemed to run right through the village. I drove on past a row of cottages, with dry stone walls marking their boundaries.

"Pretty, aren't they?" Evie sounded brighter now. "Look, there's the village hall on the left…and a lovely little church over there on the right."

"Why no streetlights?" Sam said. "How the hell are we going to find Violet's cottage in the dark? It's impossible to see any house names or numbers." She turned to me. "What's the cottage called?"

"Violet House," I replied.

She gave me a wry smile.

I pulled up as the road opened out onto the village green. It had a narrow beck flowing through the middle, with a wooden footbridge to cross over to the houses on the other side.

"Look." Sam sounded more cheerful. "There's a pub. They'll know all the houses in the village. I'll go in there and ask."

"Hang on, Sam. I've got a feeling we'll know Mum's cottage when we see it."

"How?" she asked.

I couldn't give her a rational explanation. "Humour me."

She flopped back in the seat.

I drove up and down the main road looking at the houses. None of them caught my eye. Then I drove back and took the residents-only road that led to the houses on the other side of the green.

"Come on, Grace," Sam said. "It's late. Let's go back to the pub and ask."

"Wait a minute." I continued along the road, but none of those houses spoke to me either. I stopped at the junction where the residents' road met up with the main road at the northern end of the village and was about to go back to the pub when Evie tapped me on the shoulder and pointed through the windscreen.

"Look, there's another house along there," she said. "I can see a light on."

I could see it too, standing some 50 yards to the north of the village and all on its own. "That can't be Mum's, there wouldn't be a light on."

"Let's go and see," she said.

I drove along and stopped at the open gate to the front of the property.

Sam clapped her hands in delight. "Look, there's Fox Spirit."

A large stone statue of Mum's popular character sat on the porch as if guarding the front door. My heart started racing as I drove through the gate and across the gravel to the front door. I parked and stared ahead. This was no cottage. This was an old stone house, with a traditional pantile roof and sash windows.

"What a fantastic old place!" Sam said.

The house had the usual two floors, plus what looked like an attic on top. There was a dormer window jutting out from the roof, where the light was on.

"Look, there's smoke coming out of the chimney," Sam opened the car door and got out.

Rufus spotted his chance. Jumping onto the passenger seat, he shot out after her and disappeared into the darkness.

"Now look what you've done," I shouted, getting out too. "I haven't even fed him yet."

"Stop worrying," Sam said. "He'll come back when he's hungry."

I knew she was right, but I was worried about poor Rufus. He seemed as emotionally strung out as I was.

"Come on." Sam nudged me in the ribs. "Get the key. Let's go in."

I ducked into the car and grabbed the old key. It was only as I shut the driver door and looked through the back window that I noticed Evie staring up at the house with a strange expression on her face.

"Hurry up!" Sam shouted from the front door. "It's freezing."

I went over and put the key in the lock. "Do you think we should knock? It looks like there's someone here."

"This is your house. You don't need to knock."

I turned the key, lifted the old black latch, and pushed

the door open. It creaked and I hesitated on the threshold. "Hello," I shouted.

Impatient as ever, Sam walked past me and went inside. Feeling around the wall, she found the light switches and flicked them all on. "Wow! Just look at this place," she said, twirling in amazement.

I followed her in. The entry hall seemed to double as a dining room and had a baronial-type dining table and chairs arranged in the middle, with a long oak sideboard to match down the length of one wall. Traditional old quarry flagstones covered the floor, and wooden beams ran the length of the ceiling.

At the far end of the room, a glass panelled door led out onto a terrace. Before that, there was another door to the right. I walked through it and found myself in a narrow hallway with a staircase leading upstairs. To the right of that was another door. I put my head around it and saw a large sitting room with a roaring log fire ablaze in a stone fireplace. At the end of the hall, another room stood in darkness. I walked along and found a gleaming kitchen. Going back to the stairs, I shouted up loudly. "Is there anyone here?"

Silence.

Meanwhile, Sam had gone into the sitting room. "Grace," she called. "Come in here."

I followed her and jolted when I saw the chintz sofa and chairs, the carpet, and tall bookcase jammed full of books. We stared at each other.

"It's an exact replica of Violet's sitting room in London," she said.

I started trembling. It had been an exhausting journey and I could hardly believe what I was seeing. "The fire's lit and there's a light on in the attic, but there's no-one here," I whispered.

There was a muffled sob from the doorway where Evie stood like a statue, her face wax-like in the firelight.

"What's wrong?" Sam asked her.

"On the stairs… I thought I saw…" Evie shook her head. "Oh, nothing…ignore me. I'm stressed out, that's all." She went over to sit in one of the fireside chairs. "Welcome home, Grace," she said, closing her eyes.

I glanced over at Sam who rolled her eyes again.

"I'm going to have a look upstairs," I said.

Sam nodded. "I'll come with you."

I was feeling strangely emotional in Mum's house. It caught me unawares and I was shaken. "I'd like to go on my own, if you don't mind," I added so as not to hurt her feelings. "This all feels weird. I want to try and make sense of things."

She smiled as if she understood and nodded towards Evie. "Look at her. Dead to the world." She sighed. "I'll go and get everything out of the car while you do that, Grace."

"Thanks. Can you have a look for Rufus while you're out there?"

"Please stop worrying about that cat!"

Four

I stood nervously at the bottom of the stairs looking up into the darkness. The house was silent now. Evie was asleep by the fire and Sam was outside at the car. Despite what she'd said, I knew she was worried about Rufus because I could hear her softly calling his name. As I climbed the stairs, I thought again how ridiculous it was that I hadn't known anything about this house. It was my mother's, for God's sake. I was close to her. She was the rock in my life, the most important person. How on earth could I not have known? But she'd taken the answers to these questions to the grave with her, and I had no idea why. Not for the first time, I wondered what else I didn't know about her.

I reached the top of the stairs and found myself looking at what seemed to be a snug or rather a small sitting room. I wondered again who had lit the fire and left the attic light on.

"Hello," I called out. "Is there anyone here?"

Silence.

I found the light switch and flicked it on. The room was lovely, with beams criss-crossing the ceiling, and a floral-patterned sofa and chairs. A TV was perched on a low unit in one corner and a small fireplace filled one wall.

I turned left, lifted the latch of an old wooden door, and peered gingerly inside to see a bedroom. The room stretched across the width of the house, with one window overlooking the back, the other over the front. I didn't know why I was so apprehensive about going in, but I was. As soon as I'd switched on the light, I knew it was Mum's bedroom because of the robe lying on the end of the bed. Mum had the same one in London. I looked around at the king-sized bed and the fitted pine wardrobes. My heart lurched when I saw her cosmetics and jewellery spread across the dressing table. Somewhere in my mind, I'd been holding on to the hope that this had all been a mistake, a bureaucratic muddle by the solicitor, and that the house belonged to someone else. But these were Mum's possessions. There was no doubt in my mind now. This was her bedroom. Her house.

With a heavy heart, I explored her ensuite bathroom, then the other two well decorated guest bedrooms, and bathroom, on that floor. They were all clean and tidy, with the beds made up. Just the way I would have expected her to leave the house. Whenever we went on holiday, she would always be vacuuming up to the front door before we left, so the house would be clean to return to.

I stopped at what I guessed was the door to the attic where the light was on. Although I didn't know why, I was afraid to go up. I told myself not to be so daft, lifted the latch, and peered inside to see a steep staircase. The light was still on in the attic, casting shadows over the stairs. As I started to climb, I felt a presence all around me. A feeling of something like hot breath on the back of my neck made me shiver. Suddenly, the attic door banged shut behind me and I jumped. Heart thumping, I turned but there was no-one there. When I'd calmed down a little, I guessed Sam had come back in through the front door and caused a draught through the house. I couldn't stop shivering though.

At the top, the staircase opened straight out onto a large room, with just a rail to stop people falling down the stairs. It was Mum's study. Her desk was positioned under the small dormer window to catch the light. A square table, strewn with index cards, was pushed into one corner, with a stack of boxes filling the other. Now, with the light on, it was as if she'd just popped out and would be back any minute.

I walked through a connecting door into a second attic room. This had a single bed in it, with a tall wardrobe and chest of drawers. The rest of the room was fitted floor to ceiling with shelves crammed with books. There was an unusual smell of perfume in this room, and one I couldn't quite fathom.

For some reason, I didn't want to linger up there and went straight back down to Mum's bedroom. I was most comfortable in this room because it felt personal to her. I opened the wardrobe and touched her clothes. There was no doubt they were hers because she'd had an almost duplicate set in London. Feeling a weariness come over me, I sat back down at her dressing table. I picked up the Paloma Picasso perfume that she always wore and sprayed a little on my wrist. The familiar scent filled the room, and a strange feeling came over me as I inhaled. It was as if I could feel her all around me. "Mum," I said, and turned. But there was no-one there. The loss I felt in that moment finally hit me and tears streamed down my face. I would never see her again. Never hear her voice. Never feel her love. I was crying both for her and for myself. For the mother she'd always been, and for the life that we'd shared, but also in bewilderment at the secret she'd kept.

★ ★ ★

Later, once we'd unpacked and settled ourselves into the house, we sat around the fire. Evie and I sipped tea while Sam drank more wine. Her face was flushed, and her words slurred. She was unpredictable when drunk and I hoped she wouldn't become argumentative. I was still on tenterhooks and in no mood for any upset. Surprisingly, Evie was doing all the talking. She'd been visibly upset when we'd arrived but had become quite animated now. Or perhaps strung out was a better way of describing her mood. She kept looking at the door as if worried someone would come walking in. She was also giving us a history lesson on Georgian-style houses, which she assured us this was.

"I'd say it was built in the 1700s, because of the pine box-shutters at the windows, she said. "Aren't they wonderful?" She went over to sit on the window seat beneath them. "And look at the ceiling beams, they're old pine too."

I had to admit the house was beautiful and full of character. But the fact that it was so big and majestic, made me even more nervous. How had Mum been able to afford it? We had a big house in Hampstead, which wasn't cheap. Now this one too. Dad was a solicitor and I'd always assumed his work paid for our family home, but perhaps it hadn't. Maybe the money had come from Mum's books. But I was more anxious about who'd lit the fire and left the attic light on. I'd walked around the house and there was no sign of anyone living there. It was clean though and there were no tell-tale signs of it being untended, such as dead woodlice or mail on the doormat. Sam reckoned someone in the village was looking after the place, which seemed the most rational explanation. But I didn't know of anyone. I wasn't paying anyone. And I hadn't told a soul we were coming. So, how did they know?

"Eeeuw!" Sam's cry jolted me out of my thoughts. She was holding the sole of her shoe out to me with one hand and pinching her nose with the other. "Sheep shit!"

I couldn't help but laugh. I'd seen sheep roaming freely on the village green as we drove in so I wasn't surprised. "You're in the country now," I said. "You can't wear your Jimmy Choos here."

She pulled a face at me. "The only thing I got on my shoes last year in Ibiza was sand." She sighed. "We had a fabulous time out there, didn't we?"

Nightclubbing in Ibiza wasn't my scene at all, and I did not enjoy it. But we had an unwritten rule that we didn't criticise each other's choice of holiday destinations.

"*You* had a fabulous time, out clubbing every night," Evie said. "Grace and I hardly saw you."

Sam laughed. "I did enjoy myself."

"You'll enjoy yourself here too, but in a different way," I said. "Now, let's get up and go for a long walk on the moors in the morning. We'll have a cooked breakfast when we come back. I brought some eggs and bacon too."

Sam held up a three-fingered salute. "Dib-dib-bloody-dib. It's the girl guides all over again."

I smiled over at Evie, who sat with her feet tucked up on the sofa staring into the fire. I got up and knelt in front of it. "There's nothing like a real fire." I picked up another log from the basket and put it on. "It throws out proper heat."

But Sam was still thinking about the girl guides and looked over at Evie. "Grace won't be happy until she has us holding hands and singing 'Kumbaya'." She laughed. "Remember those horrible girl guide uniforms and itchy knickers. And those camping weekends trying to light fires and cook in muddy fields?"

How could I forget? We were about 12 or 13 before our parents would allow us to go, and that was on the strict understanding that the three of us looked after each other. We were always so excited, and I thought it sad that we could never capture that child-like excitement again.

Sam had a mischievous glint in her eye. "What about our only university camping weekend, Evie? You *must* remember that."

Evie just stared at the fire.

"Is that what sparked the green warrior in you, Evie?" Sam persisted. "Or is that your Trev's influence?" She laughed again. "Remember when you refused to pee behind the bushes in case someone saw your fanny? You wandered off and got lost. The rescue team were hot though." She shook Evie's knee to get her attention.

Evie jumped as if she hadn't been listening.

"You okay, Evie?" I asked, thinking again there was something troubling her.

"Are *you* okay?" she asked me back. "This must be very weird for you?"

I nodded. "It's not what I expected, but Mum's been full of surprises since she died."

Evie plucked some non-existent fluff from the sleeve of her jumper. "I'm sorry about your mum, Grace. She was always so good to me, especially when I was young. I still loved visiting her in Hampstead."

"Me too," said Sam. "Violet was always welcoming. She never said so, but I'm sure she was lonely on her own in that big house. And she did love a good chat over a gin and tonic."

I don't know why, but Sam's words struck a nerve. Was she criticising me? Or did I just feel guilty? My job kept me busy 24/7 and I didn't see Mum as often as I'd have liked.

Evie shivered. "There's something about this house," she said. "C-can you two feel it?" She rubbed her arms as if she were cold. "I was watching a TV programme the other night about old houses. This expert reckoned they hold memories in their bricks and stones. It's like, well, it's like they can *talk* to you."

Sam rolled her eyes. "Perhaps it's haunted," she said.

"Oh, shut up," said Evie.

"Listen…" Sam sat forward. "Did you hear that?"

"Hear what?" Evie whispered.

"This house," Sam said. "Can't you hear it?"

Evie shook her head.

"It's crying out for a good clean and a lick of paint." Sam winked at Evie, then collapsed into laughter.

I thought it was funny too, but Evie was indignant. "You two can laugh, but just think of all the people who have lived here. All their secrets. The happiness. The grief. The heartache. All that emotion and energy trapped inside these walls."

"And it can stay there as far as I'm concerned." Sam yawned. "I think it's time I was off to bed." She grabbed Evie's knee again. "It's past the witching hour."

Evie pushed her hand away.

I saw by my watch that it was nearly one o'clock. I was exhausted too, but my head was buzzing with questions. "That's one thing this house *isn't* crying out for," I said, "a lick of paint. Or a good clean, come to that. The whole place is spotless."

Sam looked thoughtful. "When's the last time Violet came here, do you think?"

I shrugged. "She was poorly in the months before she died and didn't go anywhere. A cold had turned into flu before she had her heart attack." I paused to think. "Last October she said she went to stay with a friend in Rye. Perhaps she came up here instead?"

Sam nodded. "Well, someone's definitely been cleaning since then." She glanced at me. "Don't look so worried. Violet will have had someone looking after the place, that's all."

That did make sense. "Who though?"

Sam gave me something of a reproachful look. "You should know. She was your mother." Her voice had an accusatory edge which hit home. Of course, Sam was right. I should have known Mum owned this house. I should have spent more time with her. I should have taken her away on holiday. Perhaps then, she would have confided in me and brought me here? Yes, I *absolutely* should have known.

Five

Later, it felt strange lying in Mum's bed. The room was pitch black, with no artificial light inside or out. Apart from the occasional bleating of sheep and soft rain on the windows, there was no sound either. No traffic noise, no loud voices from the street, no TV or music from other apartments. All I could hear was the thud of my own heart and that was unnerving.

Competing emotions were rippling through me and I couldn't stop my mind sifting through memories of family holidays, day trips and get-togethers. But there was nothing in my memory bank about this house. It was comforting to feel Mum around though. I could sense her everywhere, from the lavender water she sprayed onto the pillowcases, to the pretty rose-patterned duvet cover, to the precious first edition of Agatha Christie's 'A Pocket Full of Rye' on her bedside table.

My mind was so restless, I found it hard to go to sleep. Snatches of peculiar, disconnected scenes of the past filled my head as I tried to make sense of things, until I finally drifted off…

Sometime later I was jarred awake by a familiar sound carried over from my waking life. Crying. I could hear someone crying.

I opened my eyes and stared into womb-like darkness. I panicked at first and sat up quickly, then I remembered where I was. The air in the room was cold, but I felt almost feverish. Strands of hair stuck to my damp forehead, and little beads of sweat trickled between my breasts.

It was the sound of crying that had woken me, and I was sure it wasn't a dream. I immediately thought of Evie because she'd seemed so upset earlier. I listened hard but all I could hear now was the wind blasting rain onto the windowpanes. Every so often a particularly strong gust would shake the old house and rattle the beams. I was just wondering if I should go and check on Evie when I heard another noise, a banging sound, coming from somewhere below in the house. I didn't want to leave the safety and warmth of my bed to go and investigate, but I knew I wouldn't be able to go back to sleep if I didn't.

I got up and slipped Mum's robe over my pyjamas. I lifted the latch of the bedroom door and peered out. The house was so dark that I went over to the dressing table and picked up the torch I'd seen earlier. I'd noticed several strategically placed around the house which made me think there could be a problem with the electricity supply. I switched the torch on and went out onto the landing.

Sam's bedroom was closest to mine. Rhythmic snoring reverberated through the door. She was spark out after all that alcohol. So much for her talk in the car about not being able to sleep.

I stopped at Evie's room. There was no sound from inside, no crying now. I wondered whether to go in and check she was all right. "Evie?" I whispered from outside. "Evie?"

But that banging noise downstairs distracted me. I felt a cold draught wafting up the staircase and was worried that someone was in the house. I switched the torch off and started creeping down the stairs. I tensed every time a stair creaked under my weight. At the bottom, the air was even colder, and I followed the breeze along the passage.

I stopped dead in the kitchen. The back door was wide open and banging against the wall in the wind. My heart quickened. I flicked the torch on and shone it around. No-one there. I rushed over to the door and looked out. Through the rain, I saw a flickering light at the top of the garden, next to the dark shape of what looked like an old barn. Was someone up there? Was that a torch? I watched until the light faded and disappeared.

For a second, I stood shocked then realised my bare feet were wet. I bent down and touched a puddle of water. Oh my God! Had someone come into the house and gone out again? I slammed the door shut and locked it. I found the main light switch and turned it on. My eyes watered in the dazzling light. But, when I could finally focus, I saw that nothing looked out of place. There were no cupboards or drawers open or ransacked. I went into the dining room and switched on that light. Same there. Everything was as we'd left it before going to bed. I wouldn't have known if anything had been stolen though because I didn't know what Mum had had in there in the first place.

I went back to the kitchen, trying to think what to do. The back door hadn't been jemmied open because the lock was intact. That meant someone must have had a key. Who would come in in the middle of the night and leave without closing the door? It didn't make any sense. I thought of Rufus out there in all that rain. Maybe he'd tried to get in through the cat flap and pushed the door open? Perhaps I hadn't locked the door before going to bed? I really couldn't remember. But there was water on the kitchen quarry tiles yet no muddy footprints or paw marks. That was strange. And what about that flickering light?

I went into the hall to go up and wake Sam and Evie but heard footsteps on the stairs. It was Evie coming down in a long nightdress. She stared straight through me as if I wasn't there.

"Evie," I said, following her into the sitting room.

She didn't seem to hear or see me. She was muttering under her breath and walking around the room bumping into walls and furniture.

I was stunned at first, then I realised what was happening. I'd learnt about the phenomenon of sleepwalking during my medical training. It tended to occur during a deep sleep cycle in the early hours, but I'd never seen anyone do it before. Sleep deprivation, or a sedative, could cause it and I wondered if Evie had taken a sleeping pill before going to bed. I also knew it could be dangerous to wake someone up in that state. Somehow, I would have to guide her back up the stairs and into bed.

"Evie," I said, keeping my voice soft. "Go back to bed."

She stopped.

I didn't dare touch her in case she lashed out at me. "Evie," I said again. "Go back to bed."

She didn't acknowledge me, but she must have heard because she walked out of the sitting room and climbed the stairs.

I followed to make sure she went back to her own room as the layout of the house would be unfamiliar to her. Uncannily, she went straight into her room and lay down on the bed.

I looked down at her chalk-white face. Her brow was furrowed as if in pain and beads of sweat trickled down her cheeks. The room felt ice cold, so I pulled the duvet over her and tucked her in to keep warm. "Sleep well," I whispered.

Suddenly her eyes flashed open, and she stared at me. Almost immediately, she closed them again and went back to sleep.

Startled, I stood watching her, wondering what on earth was troubling her so much to make her sleepwalk. I wanted to stay to make sure she didn't get up again, but I was shivering with cold. I thought about waking Sam to tell her about the intruder and Evie sleepwalking, but I could still hear her snoring in the next room. I decided to let her sleep and went back to bed.

My nerves were so shot through that I found it hard to relax enough to go back to sleep. I kept thinking I heard strange noises in the house and was on tenterhooks for hours. Eventually though, I fell back into another fitful sleep, full of strange dreams that made no sense at all.

Six

Kitty

Hutton-Le-Hole, North Yorkshire
June 1787 – Summer Solstice

Shaking with excitement and breathing deeply from scurrying across the Moors, Kitty Garthwaite stood in the back lane, outside the five-bar gate of Willie's house in Hutton-Le-Hole. She loved being out at night under the stars with no-one around and knew every inch of the terrain. Even as a young girl she enjoyed walking for miles, preferably alone. It was her time to think and make plans for her future. Not that a girl in her lowly position could change much, if anything, about her life. But, like most girls, she dreamed of marrying a handsome man who would love and cherish her. If he was rich and could make her and her family's life easier, then all the better. But wealth was not important to Kitty. She had told her dear, departed mother all this once, expecting her to smile and nod in approval. Instead, she had given Kitty such a pained look that Kitty resolved never to confide in her again. For Kitty was convinced that if she wished it enough, and prayed hard, it would happen.

It was after that encounter that her mother constantly scolded her for having her head in the clouds. "A handsome, rich man, indeed," she would say. "That life is not for a girl such as you, Kitty. Life is hard. It has been hard for me. It will always be hard for you too. The sooner you accept your lot, the more content you will be." But that was not enough for her mother. She kept an even closer eye on Kitty than before, wanting to know where she was every minute of the day and warning her to work hard and control her emotions. "I worry about you, Kitty," she would say, anxiously. "One minute you are singing happily around the house, the next you are in a terrifying rage, and I do not know what you are going to do next." She would shake her head, sadly. "I do believe you are capable of anything, girl."

Her mother tried to stop her trekking across the Moors too, warning her of the dangers of robbers and bad men in the wilds. But Kitty paid no heed and escaped for hours whenever she could. She loved breathing in the fresh northern air that blew the soot from the kitchen fire out of her lungs. She adored the freedom of wandering wherever she pleased, where no-one could shout at her and tell her what to do. And she especially enjoyed watching the birds. How she wished she could swoop high over the area like them and fly all the way to the sea. She picked up the hem of her long dress, her only good dress, that she kept for church on Sundays and twirled around in dreamy excitement...

Until she remembered that Willie had told her not to be seen by anyone. She swung her long cloak over her shoulders and pulled up the hood so as not to be recognised. She stared over the gate at the back of his new house, admiringly. It was built with solid blocks of local stone and had three floors. Three floors! And the latest pantile roof. She would be happy living here with Willie and his family who were not strict Quakers, like most of the people living in Hutton-le-Hole. No, Kitty would not like living with any of them. Fortunately, Willie's family were long established in the region and members of the Anglican parish of Lastingham, a village some two miles away. It would be good to live in a settlement with other people around, and see weavers and traders call by, rather than be shut away on an isolated farm.

Then she became aware of the silence all around her. Even the nightjar, one of the last birds to sleep, had stopped its unending churring love call. It was time. Her heart started fluttering like that terrified bird she had released from a poacher's trap on the way over.

Carnal desire was wrong. The vicar had preached those very words at last Sunday's service, then his eyes had fallen on her. She had felt her cheeks flame. It was as if he had delved into her mind and read her thoughts. After that, she had kept her eyes firmly on the floor for the rest of the service so that he could not penetrate her inner turmoil. Still, what did the vicar matter. God knew what she was about to do. She had prayed to him enough about Willie and told him her most private thoughts. God knew she loved Willie with all her heart and that Willie loved her. It could not be wrong to give yourself to someone you loved so much if they loved you back, could it?

She stared up at the sky, willing darkness to fall more quickly. Willie said they had to wait until it was completely black, or as dark as it could be on this warm Midsummer night. She twirled around a bit more enjoying the feel of her dress swishing around her ankles and admiring her narrow ankle boots.

She had been in a fever of anticipation all day waiting for this moment. It had not been easy getting away. The day had been hot and long, sapping every ounce of her energy as she carried out her daily chores on Mr Pickering's farm. Being a kitchen servant, it was her job to light the range, which consisted of a grate set into the brickwork of a chimney with an iron oven built to one side, and to feed it all day with coal and wood to keep it at the right temperature for cooking and heating water. She also had to scour pots and pans, clean vegetables, scrub scales off fish, pluck poultry and clean away rubbish and debris off the floors. It wasn't bad working in the kitchen in winter when it was bitterly cold outside, but in summer it was truly suffocating.

At first Kitty had considered herself lucky to get the job with the Pickerings. Their farm was the largest and most successful in the area. But she knew that Mr Pickering had only taken her on because of pressure from his wife, who considered herself a pillar of the community. Since Kitty's mother had died, her father in his grief had fallen into steady decline. Kitty had done her best to look after him, look after them both. She had tried to save him from himself, but then the beatings had started. It was the drink, of course, but it broke her heart that her own father could treat her like that. Eventually, the alcohol killed him, and she was left alone with no prospects of her own. So, yes, she had been lucky to get a job with the Pickerings.

But even luckier to have caught Willie's eye.

Her face softened as she pictured his handsome face, his dark hair tousled by the wind, and his back straight and proud as he rode his horse. Her stomach flipped over and over as she thought of his muscled arms around her, his strong body on top of her. Tonight, they would be one. And soon after, they would be married. She almost laughed out loud imagining the surprise on the faces of the Pickerings when they found out about her betrothal to Willie Dixon. They treated her as a worthless farm girl who could be pushed around and humiliated at will. But they would never behave like that once she was Willie's wife. No way. She couldn't wait to get married and out of Mr Pickering's employ and house. And particularly away from the odious Mabel, the other live-in domestic, who was older than Kitty and did most of the cooking. Mabel had made Kitty's life unbearable with her cruel taunts and comments. Kitty hated working with her and even more sharing a bedchamber in the attic. It was a living hell, so much so that Kitty had begged Mr Pickering to allow her to sleep in the kitchen. She had told him that she could carry out her first task of lighting the range more quickly if she slept in there. But he would not hear of it. She was lucky to have a good bed and a room in the attic to share with Mabel, he said. Two servants together. If she didn't like it, she could go and sleep in the barn with the labourers.

Kitty sighed again and pushed it from her mind. She would allow nothing to dampen her spirits tonight. Her and Willie's special night. Even the job of blackening the grate in the kitchen this evening, a task she loathed, had not deterred her. She had done it cheerfully and to the best of her ability. If she had not, Mrs Pickering would have made her do it again and that would have only delayed her preparations for meeting Willie.

Hot and exhausted from working twelve hours non-stop, Kitty had crept up to her bedchamber while Mabel was busy checking the food stores. There, she retrieved her treasured piece of soap wrapped in a linen cloth that she had hidden under her mattress so that Mabel could not find it. She washed her whole body carefully from the bowl on the nightstand with the cloth, breathing in the lovely perfume from the rose oil in the soap, then changed into her nightdress, and laid down on the bed as if retiring for the night. It was all a pretence. She had to wait for the whole house to go to sleep before she could sneak out.

She could not be seen. Willie insisted they keep their trysts secret until he had the chance to set all the formalities in train with his family. If they did not do everything right, he insisted, their union would be shattered before it had begun.

Their union. Kitty played those words again in her head as she stood in the back lane staring up at Willie's house waiting for his signal. Their union. Those were the exact words he had used. Kitty was sure that meant marriage. It could mean nothing else since he talked of settling formalities with his family. She was so happy she had been walking around in a dream ever since.

She smiled as the dark night clouds slipped across the moon, plunging her into darkness. A candle flame appeared at the attic window, which she knew was Willie's bedchamber. She waved furiously, not that he could see her. He knew she would be there though. She was always there. Always at the right place, at the right time for their trysts, often early. She didn't mind waiting for Willie. She would wait for him forever.

Soon, she heard his footsteps crunching along the garden path as he came near. "Willie... my love... Willie," she called, softly.

"Shush," he murmured as he opened the gate. "We must not be seen or heard. There are eyes and ears everywhere." He pulled her inside the gate. "Come in here," he whispered and ushered her into the barn, closing the door firmly behind him. Fortunately, in the height of summer, the cows and sheep were in the fields and the barn had been swept clean, with fresh hay piled in the corner. Willie had laid a cotton counterpane over it for their comfort and placed two goblets of wine on a wooden stool next to it. He went over and lit the candle he had placed next to their drinks and turned towards her.

Kitty looked around, then deep into his eyes. She had hoped he would take her to his bedchamber on this special night as he said he would.

He sighed as if reading her mind. "Mother and Father did not go to Malton to visit relatives today as planned, so we cannot go into the house." He ran his fingers through his dark hair. "I did not want to disappoint you, so I have made us a comfortable place here." He gave her an earnest look. "Is that all right, Kitty? Please tell me it is."

She hesitated.

"Look," he said, taking her hand and pulling her back over to the door. He lifted the candle high and pointed to something on the wall. "I did this carving for you today," he said. "A token of my eternal love."

"Oh Willie," she said, happily, brushing her fingers over it. "It is a heart. You have carved a heart into the stone with our initials inside. WD and KG." She turned to him, eyes shining. "It is wonderful, my love."

She saw him tremble in anticipation as he stood before her, no longer able to contain his desire for her, his love for her. Her heart softened and she nodded up at him, feeling suddenly nervous and shy.

Relief flooded his face. "Do not be afraid," he said, and took her gently in his arms.

Kitty felt his hot breath on her neck and a shiver of pleasure shuddered down her spine. "Do you love me, Willie?" she asked, anxiously. "I mean really love me?"

"Of course," he gurgled through his heavy breathing.

"Will we always be together?" she whispered. "Say that we will. Until death us do part."

"Yes, dear heart." He ran his hands over her face and through her hair. "I will never take another."

Kitty sighed with pleasure. There was no way she could stop what was about to happen even if she had wanted to.

She was completely in love with Willie and wanted him as much as she could feel he wanted her. And his promise of marriage meant she could give herself to him. She relaxed completely into his arms and felt his fiery lips on hers.

"Come," he said, as he pulled her over to the candlelight. "Let me see you." He pulled down the shoulders of her dress and helped her out of it. His hands shook as he pulled her petticoat down to her waist and cupped her breasts.

A shiver ran through Kitty as his lips moved from hers, down to her neck and then her breasts. His tongue played with her nipples making her arch her back and groan with pleasure.

"Yes, my beautiful sweetling." He picked her up and laid her down on the counterpane on the hay. Swiftly, he took off his clothes and stood before her.

Kitty marvelled at his fine looks and taut manhood. A delirious happiness rippled through her. Willie was everything she thought he would be and more. She loved him so much she could not wait to be his wife and mother to his children.

Seven

Grace

The last thing I expected the next morning was to be jolted from sleep by the sound of screeching sirens. It was a familiar noise day and night in my London world. But I wasn't in London, I was in Mum's country house. I wondered what was going on outside, but I didn't get up to look out the window. The hullabaloo was only fleeting as the emergency vehicles whizzed through the village and faded into the distance. After that, it was back to the soothing call of wood pigeons and bleating sheep.

Over at the front window, light was filtering around the edges of the curtains. Everything seemed so normal in the light of day. But memories of the comings and goings of the night before came flooding back, bringing on a familiar weary feeling. I looked at my watch on the bedside cabinet, it was 7.30. I could have happily stayed in bed, but I had to get up for Sam and Evie. And the smell of frying bacon wafting through the house was irresistible. I got up and went over to the front window to pull back the curtains. Outside, the sun shone through the red and orange leaves of a majestic beech tree, casting dappled light on the well-tended front garden. The shrubs were clipped and the earth around the faded pansies and violas in the border cleared of weeds. I saw a cattle grid across the drive at the gate which I couldn't remember driving over last night. But then I'd been so taken aback by the size of the house, I guess I hadn't noticed. The grid must be there to stop sheep wandering in and eating the plants.

I was amazed at the scene at the back when I opened those curtains. The rear garden was huge and extended all the way to what looked like a narrow lane. An old, stone barn stood next to the back gate. That was the building I'd seen in the night, where the light was flickering. Beyond that, a grassy paddock reached as far as the eye could see to the woods on the skyline. Wow! Did all that belong to Mum's house?

I slipped on her robe again and went out onto the landing. It was entirely peaceful and not the shadowy experience from the night before. Sam's door was open, but the room empty. Evie's door was still closed and there was no noise from inside. I guessed she was still asleep. I was tempted to look in, but I didn't want to wake her. She needed to rest.

Sam performed a deep curtsy when I walked into the kitchen. "Morning, Mistress. The kitchen maid has cooked your breakfast."

"Very funny."

She laughed. "Isn't this house fantastic? It belongs in some TV period drama. Maybe we'll find our Heathcliff up on the moors." She gave me a suggestive look. "Wouldn't that be fun?"

I had to admit the house and the goings-on in the middle of the night were better suited to the pages of an Emily Bronte novel, but I wasn't in the mood to encourage Sam's 'Wuthering Heights' delusions. I was pleased she was in a better frame of mind about our holiday in the English countryside though. But I find people who sleep like the dead and wake up early full of the joys very annoying. I pulled out a chair from the kitchen table and sat down, heavily.

"What's wrong?" she asked, giving me a penetrating stare. "You look like you've seen a ghost."

I pulled a face, and she put her hands up in surrender. "Okay. I'll stop with the jokes. It's obviously too early." She poured me a cup of coffee from the cafetiere and handed it to me.

"We had an intruder last night," I said, flatly.

She turned and stared at me.

"Did you hear any noise?"

"No." She shook her head.

"Well, I did, and I got up to investigate." I pointed to the back door. "I found that wide open when I got down here and puddles of water on the floor. It was bucketing down in the night. I think someone came in and went out again."

"Christ!" Sam hurried over to the back door, opened it, and inspected the frame and lock. "How'd they get in? There's no sign of the door being forced." She looked back at me. "Why didn't you wake me up?"

"You were snoring like a trooper after your skinful."

Sam bristled as she always did when I mentioned her drinking. "I'm allowed a couple of drinks on holiday, aren't I?"

It was more like a couple of bottles, but I let it go.

"Did they take anything?" she asked. "Have you had a look around?"

I shrugged. "I-I don't know what was here in the first place. There's no sign that anyone's been rummaging in drawers and the place hasn't been ransacked."

"Should we call the police?"

"I wondered about phoning them in the night. But I thought that perhaps you were right, and someone has been looking after the place for Mum. Maybe they let themselves in with a key last night."

She frowned. "In the middle of the night?"

I nodded. "I know it's weird, but I saw a light flickering at the end of the garden. There's a lane running along the back of the garden, you know."

She nodded. "I was up there this morning having a look around and..."

"If they came in from the lane and through the back garden," I interrupted, "they wouldn't have seen my car parked at the front. Maybe they got a shock when they found out we were here and made a quick exit?"

"They would have shut the door, surely? You did check it was locked before we went to bed, didn't you?"

"I can't remember."

"Me neither," she said. "What about Rufus? Could he have come in through the cat flap and somehow pushed it open?"

"I wondered that too." I looked at the untouched cat food in the dish on the floor and shook my head. "He hasn't been in here since we arrived."

"Well, he is a rather large cat," Sam said, gently.

"Are you saying Rufus is fat?"

"I'm saying that missing a meal or two won't hurt him."

I sighed. "Have you seen Evie this morning?"

"No. She's still asleep."

I took a swig of coffee and felt the hot liquid flow comfortingly down into my stomach. "You were right. I think there's something serious troubling her. She was sleepwalking last night."

"Sleepwalking?" Sam looked horrified.

I nodded. "She came down in her nightdress. I thought

she'd been woken by the intruder, but she started acting strangely. She looked right through me as if I wasn't there, then went into the sitting room and started bumping into the furniture as if she couldn't see it. That's when I realised what was going on."

For once Sam was speechless.

"No wonder she's still asleep," I said. "I don't suppose she'll remember anything about last night. Sleepwalkers don't usually." I sighed. "We'll have to try to get her to open-up while she's here. She clearly needs help."

Sam came over and gave me a warm hug. "You spend too much time worrying about everyone, Grace. You need to think about yourself for once. You don't look so great either."

"There you go again with the compliments," I said, but I knew I'd let myself go. I hadn't had my hair cut, or my roots coloured, for months. But then looking at Sam without her make-up, she didn't look so hot either with her puffy, red eyes and sagging chin. The booze wasn't helping her, and we weren't getting any younger.

She must have read my mind because she said, "Why don't we find a beauty salon or a spa. There's bound to be one around here somewhere. A massage and a facial would do us all good."

"Or you could call your boyfriend," I said. "He could drive up and do it for us."

She pulled a face at me and ran her finger along my exposed roots. "And we need a hairdresser for you. Definitely." She smiled. "Come on. Let's have some breakfast before it gets cold." She picked up two plates and spooned a large helping of scrambled eggs and bacon onto each one. "I'll leave some in the oven for Evie." She pulled out a rack of toast that she'd been keeping warm under the grill and laid everything on the kitchen table.

We sat opposite each other and ate in silence. I had a better appetite than I'd expected and managed to clean my plate. "Do you think I should call the police, Sam?"

She shrugged. "Do you think it was a burglary?"

I took another swig of coffee. "I don't know. My head's all over the place."

She gave me a sympathetic look. "It must be hard for you, being in this house. What with Violet and everything else?"

That was an understatement. My life had been turned upside down and inside out.

"Tell you what," she said. "Why don't you go out for a walk on the Moors when you've finished that. It'll give you a chance to think and let things settle in your head. We can always phone the police when you get back if you want to."

That seemed a good idea. "Some fresh air and exercise will do me good."

"While you're doing that, I'll have a mooch around the village and see if I can get some food shopping. We'll have a relaxing day around the house, and I'll cook dinner tonight, if that's okay with you?"

"Absolutely." I was glad I wouldn't have to think about that too. "I didn't see any shops as we drove around the village last night."

"Nor did I. But I saw a sign for a village called Kirkbymoorside last night just before we turned off for Hutton-le-Hole. I'll drive down there if I can't find anything here. Is it okay to use your car?"

I nodded. "The keys are on the hall table."

"My own insurance will cover me." Sam smiled. "We'll leave sleepyhead in her bunk to get up whenever she wants."

I gave her a grateful smile back. "Mum always said you were the most resourceful friend I'd ever have." I paused to remember her exact words, then said. "If you were ever in prison, you'd want to share a cell with Sam. You'd survive it with her around."

I expected Sam to laugh but she didn't. She reached across the table and squeezed my hand. "Promise me we'll always be friends, Grace, whatever happens."

I was thrown by her uncharacteristic show of affection and wondered why she looked so anxious. "Of course, we will," I said, cheerfully, trying to break the tension. "You and Evie are all I have left now."

She forced another smile. "Apart from that bad-tempered moggie."

I nodded. "Apart from Rufus, of course."

Eight

A soft breeze blew in my face as I walked along the drive, and I breathed in deeply. I felt better now I was out of the house and in the open air. I stopped at the gate and opened the map I'd found in Mum's study. I decided to go up on the moors rather than walk around the village. I turned left and followed the main road out of the northern side in the direction of Blakey Ridge. Sam had read in some booklet there was an isolated pub up there that got snowed-in most winters and was keen for us to visit it.

After walking 100 yards or so to the top of the hill, I came to a fork in the road. There was a sign indicating a left turn to Gillamoor and Farndale or, according to the map, the main road would take me to Blakey and Castleton, then over to the north-east coast. I stopped because I didn't want to go anywhere in particular, I just wanted to wander and clear my head. To my right, I saw the beck that flowed off the moors and on through the village. I thought if I followed the stream, it would take me up onto the moor. I crossed over the water by hopping carefully onto strategically placed stepping-stones and congratulated myself for reaching the other side with both feet dry. Then I took the track that ran alongside the stream up onto the moor.

I looked back as another piercing siren cut through the silence. A police car raced along the road and took the turning towards Gillamoor. I was glad I hadn't gone that way. It was the perfect morning for a walk, cool enough to make the wind nip at my cheeks and bright and clear enough for me to be able to see in all directions. I was keen to get away from everyone and have time to think.

My legs felt heavy at first as I trudged along the earthen track. The landscape was stark, with no trees. I had hoped to see a carpet of purple heather, but it was dying out for the season and had become engulfed by a rampant brown fern. Every so often a bird that looked like grouse, with grey-brown feathers and ruffs on the side of its neck, would scurry out of the undergrowth, squawk in alarm at seeing me, and run in the other direction. The bird's comical reaction made me smile and I wondered why it ran from danger rather than flew away.

A spectacular sight greeted me at the top of the hill. There was nothing but moorland stretching for miles, all the way to the sea. Small flocks of sheep roamed freely in the distance. Rays of sunlight poked through the clouds, covering the moors in a patchwork of light and shade. I felt like I was walking on the roof of England. Now, with fresh air filling my lungs and unspoiled natural beauty all around, energy started coursing through me. I was finally on my own. I could hear nothing but silence. A mysterious kind of silence, whose haunting majesty aroused a response deep within me. It was wonderful to be away from London, away from traffic and pollution, and away from a relentless queue of sick patients. I imagined Mum walking along this track, just like I was now, devising the plots and characters for her novels.

A movement above caught my eye. I looked up and saw a sparrowhawk wheeling above me, its raptor-like wings spread wide. I knew what it was because of its bluish-grey back and wings, orange belly, and spindly yellow legs. I stood and watched it swoop down on its prey, which

I guessed would be a young bird, or a mouse or shrew, perhaps even a baby rabbit. For a split second, I seemed to catch the predator's eye, and I wondered if I was its intended victim. The thought was absurd because a sparrowhawk would have trouble killing a chicken let alone a human being. I was relieved nonetheless when it flew away. In that moment, I realised that everything I was seeing – the moors, the heather, the wild birds – was familiar to me even though I'd never been here before. Mum had taught me all about it in her books. I wondered if her heroine in 'The Girl on the Moors' was based on me. Certainly, as a young girl, I fitted the description. I felt close to her again and understood why she'd loved this hauntingly beautiful place. I just couldn't understand why she'd kept it a secret from me.

As I walked on, unconscious of time, I found all sorts of thoughts and feelings washing through me. I kept coming back to Dad's angry words at my mother all those years ago. *For God's sake, Violet … go there if you must, but I forbid you to involve Grace. You will never ever take Grace.* I wanted to blame him for Mum not bringing me here. But he'd died years ago. She'd had plenty of time since then to tell me about the house. Yet she chose not to.

Then I focused on my memories of Mum and Dad when I was small. I kept trying to link scenes together like pieces of a puzzle to give me some picture or clue about their relationship. It surprised me how often Sam and Evie appeared in those memories. One or both would often come on holiday and trips with us because I was an only child and my parents thought I needed the company. To my child-like eye, Mum and Dad were happy together, but what did I know? Children can be so easily deceived. Still, I was happy as a child. But try as I might, I could not remember them ever bringing me to this place before.

I walked on, deep in thought and oblivious to everything, until a strong blast of cold wind jolted me back to the present. I looked up and was surprised to see the sunshine had disappeared. Dark clouds were advancing from the direction of the coast like a menacing army. I looked around and saw no-one and nothing but moorland. My watch told me I'd been walking for well over an hour, which meant quite a trek back. Fortunately, I hadn't strayed from the path. All I had to do was go back the way I'd come and hope to get to the house before the approaching rain hit. There was certainly no shelter anywhere up here.

I turned and started walking back. But it wasn't long before spots of rain hit my cheek. I zipped up my jacket and reached over my shoulder to pull up the hood. Then I remembered unclipping it one sunny day last week and leaving it in my flat in London. I picked up my pace. Every so often, I'd look back at the sky to monitor the progress of the dark clouds. The closer they got, the faster the light faded. The moors were starting to look bleak and hostile.

I didn't know if it was the changing atmosphere or my heightened imagination, but I started to feel a kind of presence all around me. I kept hearing a rustle of fern or the snap of a branch of heather. I told myself it was my mind playing tricks in this unfamiliar place. Never had I felt so small and insignificant as I did in that vast landscape.

Minutes later, when I looked back, I saw a thick sea-mist rolling in behind me. Had those clouds been mist rather than rain? It turned out to be freezing fog. I felt like I was walking into a cobweb as it engulfed me and clung to me, fine and yet impenetrable. Soon, my hair and face were damp with a veil of moisture. It was the suddenness of its arrival that so unnerved me because I couldn't see a thing in front of me now. I kept on walking with my head down, eyes glued to the track. I knew if I strayed one foot from the path, I might wander around lost for the rest of the day and night until I was exhausted.

I was freezing in the wind and fog. I told myself over and over to keep calm. So long as I stayed on the track, I'd come down into the village. Except I really wouldn't have known if I was still on the right track. I couldn't suppress a rising sense of panic, especially when the presence I'd begun to feel earlier seemed to press in more heavily than the fog. Eventually, when I couldn't stand it any longer, I stopped and turned. "Hello," I shouted, my voice trembling. "Who's there?" My own words echoed back in reply. Was the fog playing tricks with sound as well as sight?

That's when I thought I heard the crunch of a footstep on the track. My heart quickened. "Who's there?" I shouted again.

No reply.

I was scared now. I turned and started running, but the terrain was difficult. I kept stumbling and tripping over the roots of dead heather by the side of the path. Suddenly my foot got caught in the undergrowth and I tumbled over. A sharp pain radiated through my right ankle. I cried out as I slipped down a bank and rolled over and over until I came to a stop against a thick clump of bracken. I lay silent on the sodden ground, shaken and staring into a fog that was constantly shifting like clouds without ever parting.

I was just wondering what damage I'd done to my ankle and how I was going to make it back to the house when a dark silhouette loomed out of the fog. I stared at what I thought was the shape of a woman in a long dress. I couldn't see her head or face from where I was lying on the ground. It was her feet that I focused on. Small and dainty in old-fashioned, black lace up boots, with the hem of a long dress resting on them.

Vulnerable and petrified, I lay motionless. Suddenly, there was a rustle from the undergrowth. Rufus sprang out, with his back arched and teeth bared. He was almost growling at the figure.

I held my breath not knowing what would happen next but, almost immediately, the dark silhouette dissolved into the fog as quickly as it had appeared, leaving me shocked and silent, with only the sound of my own heart pounding in my ears.

It was Rufus who reacted first. He came closer and lay down beside me. I stroked his wet fur while almost sobbing with relief. But I felt him trembling under my touch. That apparition had scared the hell out of him too.

I checked for signs of pain around my body, but only my ankle throbbed. I sat up, loosened the wet lace of my walking boot, and pulled it off. I felt around the ankle bone and wriggled my toes. They moved okay so I guessed I'd sprained my ankle rather than broken it. I forced my boot back on before my ankle became too swollen for it to fit. I'd have to try and hobble back to the house on my own because no-one would find me up here in this weather.

Rufus also must have decided I was okay because he stood up and walked on a few paces.

"Hey, wait for me," I shouted as I struggled to my feet.

He turned round as if to say 'well, come on then'.

My ankle was painful, but I knew I'd have to put up with that to get back to the house. I gritted my teeth and clambered up the slippery bank on all fours behind Rufus until we were back on the track. Then I followed him down the path. I could hardly believe that grumpy old cat was leading me home. Despite not being able to see a thing in the fog, I kept looking nervously over my shoulder. Every time I heard a noise in the undergrowth or thought I heard a footstep, I tensed, fearing I was going to be grabbed from behind. It was Rufus who kept me sane on that slow trek home. So long as he stayed calm, I knew we were okay. Never mind Sam being the best friend I could ever have, right then it was Rufus.

Every step was a struggle though. I tried to think of everything but the pain in my ankle which began to radiate down through my toes and up to my knee. Eventually my whole lower leg and foot felt numb. I could feel us descending though and that kept me going. I almost cried with joy when I heard a car engine reverberating around, but I was so disorientated in the fog I couldn't tell which direction it was coming from.

Suddenly, at the bottom of the hill, the fog disappeared as if we'd walked through a curtain, and we were back in bright sunshine. I let out a huge sigh of relief and bent down to stroke Rufus. "Thank you, boy," I said. But he wriggled from my grasp and shot off into the distance. As I looked up to see where he was going, I saw two police cars parked outside Mum's house. I could hardly breathe such was my sense of foreboding as I hobbled quickly towards them.

Nine

The front door was ajar, and I heard voices as soon as I stepped over the threshold. I hobbled to the sitting room and stood in the doorway. Sam, Evie and two strangers sat awkwardly on the sofas and chairs as if they'd found themselves in some waiting room and were forced to make conversation. They turned to look at me. From the expressions on their faces, I must have looked a hell of a sight.

Sam jumped up from the sofa. "Good God, Grace. What happened to you?"

I looked down at my mud-covered jacket and jeans and pushed my wet hair off my face. "I got caught in fog up on the moor," I said. "I was so disorientated, I slipped down a bank and sprained my ankle." I hadn't allowed myself to think about the pain while I was trying to get back, but it was hurting now. "It's taken me ages to find my way down."

A man in a grey suit rose from the sofa. "Good morning," he said, and came over to me with his hand outstretched. "I'm Detective Chief Inspector Blake."

He was tall and thin and had to stoop a little to avoid hitting his head on the low ceiling beams. His blond hair was cropped short, and his crystal-blue eyes looked straight into mine. They were neither warm nor cold, just a neutral gaze. In fact, his whole face wore a fixed deadpan expression much like a mask to hide whatever emotions he was feeling.

I rubbed my dirty palm down the leg of my trousers and shook his hand. "Grace Winter," I said.

"I understand you're a relative of Violet Winter."

"She was my mother."

He looked surprised.

"Did you know her?" I asked.

He nodded. "Everyone knew Violet. She was a bit of a celebrity around here."

It was strange to hear Mum called a celebrity. "Then you know she passed away six months ago," I said.

"Of course. I went to her funeral in the village church."

Her funeral in the village church?

"Violet was buried in London," Sam said, quickly.

He must have seen the confusion on my face because he frowned, then he turned to his colleague. "This is Detective Sergeant Gray."

A small, slim woman stood up from one of the chairs and nodded, although she didn't come over to shake hands. I guessed she was in her forties. She was smartly dressed in a black trouser suit and lilac polo neck jumper, with silver-grey hair hanging in loose curls on her shoulders. I thought she looked quite glamorous for a detective on duty. But it was her inquisitive grey eyes sizing me up that unsettled me. And, from the sour look on her face, I reckon I hadn't made much of an impression.

Sam took charge. "Come over here, Grace." She pulled me closer to the fire and helped me out of my rain jacket.

It was only then that I noticed the bedraggled state Evie was in as she sat head bowed in the other fireside chair, close to the window. A woollen blanket was draped around her shoulders and her hands were clamped around a steaming mug. She was dressed in her walking clothes. Her muddy boots were off and standing on the hearth, but they weren't hers. Nor was the padded coat slung over the back of the chair. They were my mum's coat and boots.

"Where have you been, Evie?" I asked.

She looked over at me with a vacant stare. "I g-got lost on the moors." She nodded at DS Gray. "She found me and brought me home."

Sam intervened, and I got the impression she wanted to divert attention away from Evie. "Take your boots off, Grace," she said. "Let's have a look at that ankle."

I waved my hand. "That can wait."

"No, it can't." Sam almost pushed me down on the sofa and started untying my laces.

I felt self-conscious as everyone watched me try and get my boots off. The left one was easy, but the right one was stuck fast around my swollen ankle.

Sam tried to yank it off and I yelped in pain.

"Hold on." The Chief Inspector came over and knelt in front of me. Carefully, he gripped the heel of my boot and looked up at me. "You try and pull your foot out while I hold it still."

Up close, I noticed two thin scars on his forehead, around the hairline. The doctor in me wondered what had caused them. I also registered his voice for the first time. He didn't have a Yorkshire accent and sounded what Mum would have called posh.

"Ready?" he asked.

I nodded. After some gentle pulling, my foot came out without hurting too much. I pulled my sock down to expose a swollen, purple ankle.

"Looks nasty." The Chief Inspector stood up and wiped his muddy hands on a handkerchief. "You should see a doctor."

I felt around the bone again and wriggled my toes. "It's not broken," I said. "It's just a bad sprain. I've walked a couple of miles on it which has made the swelling worse." I glanced at him. "It's all right, I am a doctor. I can strap it up myself."

He gave me another of his inscrutable looks. I couldn't tell what he was thinking, which unsettled me further. "Well." I tried to sound cheerful. "Thanks very much for bringing Evie home. It's very good of you." I looked at the two police officers expecting them to leave, but they didn't.

There was another awkward silence before DCI Blake said: "I'd like to ask you all some questions." He looked at the three of us in turn. "There was a murder earlier today on the moors," he said in a calm voice.

We all stared at him in stunned silence. It was Sam who reacted first. "Who's been murdered?" she asked.

"A young man was found with head injuries, at Lowna Ford." His voice was calm as if it was an everyday occurrence.

Lowna Ford? That name rang a bell, and I tried to think where I'd heard it before. Then I remembered what Evie had said in the car on the way up about Mum's unfinished novel. That was about some ghost called Kitty murdering men at Lowna Ford.

Sam glanced in my direction, and I guessed the name had registered with her too.

"So that's what all the sirens were about this morning," I said.

The Chief Inspector glanced sideways at his glamorous colleague and gave her an almost imperceptible nod.

DS Gray took her cue and said: "And that's where I found your friend Evie early this morning. Walking all over the crime scene."

I stared at Evie in surprise, but she wouldn't meet my eye.

"Evie?" It was DCI Blake who spoke again. "Why were you at Lowna Ford this morning?"

She shrugged. "I-I d-don't know."

"Lowna is three miles from here," he went on. "How did you get there? It's a long way."

Evie shrugged again. "I must have walked further than I'd planned to."

His voice remained steady. "Where had you planned to walk to?"

Her brow wrinkled. "I c-can't remember. N-nowhere in particular, I guess."

His right eyelid twitched as he repeated: "Nowhere in particular, you guess." Was that a nervous tic, or was he annoyed? "What time did you leave the house?" he asked her.

Evie sank further down in the chair. "I c-can't remember."

"Was it still dark when you left?" he persisted.

Evie looked at Sam and me with desperation in her eyes. "I can't remember anything about this morning. I really can't."

Glamour cop let out a soft sigh and crossed her arms. Her face took on a sceptical expression every time Evie spoke. She wouldn't take her eyes off her either, which I thought was intimidating.

I jumped in to defend her. "Evie was still asleep in her room when I went out for a walk this morning." I paused. "That must have been at around nine o'clock, after breakfast." I turned to Sam, expecting her to back me up.

But she just squeezed my knee, as if warning me to be quiet.

DCI Blake noticed. "Are you *sure* you went out at that time, Miss Winter?"

I wondered why he was addressing me more formally than Evie. "Yes," I said, firmly. "Absolutely sure."

"And are you absolutely sure that Evie was still in bed then?" he asked.

There was a look in his eye that made me think I was walking into a trap. I hesitated, realising that I hadn't seen Evie that morning. I'd *assumed* she was still in bed, but maybe she hadn't been. I looked over at her.

Her eyes glistened. "I can't remember," she said. "Why won't you believe me? I really can't remember."

I gazed at Mum's boots on the hearth and her coat over Evie's chair. I so wished Mum was here now to sort everything out. I dearly wanted the comfort of her presence in this strange place.

Evie noticed my gaze. "Violet said I could borrow her things whenever I liked," she said.

I didn't care one bit that Evie had gone out in Mum's coat and boots. But why would she say Mum had told her she could borrow them? It sounded mad. I knew I had to intervene. "I think I can explain what happened, Chief Inspector. Evie may have left the house without realising it." I gave Evie an apologetic look. "You see, I found her sleepwalking in the night."

"*Grace!*" Evie's voice quivered with indignation. "I do *not* sleepwalk."

I heard another tut from Glamour Cop. So did the Chief Inspector and he gave her a sharp glance.

"I'm sorry, Evie," I said. "But you did last night." I turned to the Chief Inspector. "You see, I heard a noise in the night and got up to investigate. When I came down, I found the kitchen door wide open." I paused. "I thought someone had broken in, but the door wasn't forced. None of the drawers or cupboards were open or ransacked like in any normal burglary."

His eyes held mine. He had a face made for interrogation and I imagined criminals squirming under those inscrutable eyes.

"Was anything taken?" he asked.

I shrugged. "I can't be sure because I've no idea what was here in the first place. I've never been here before."

His voice rose a notch. "*Never?*"

"No."

His eyes stayed on me. What was he thinking? That I was the kind of daughter who was too busy and too wrapped up in herself to visit her own mother. I looked away, reluctant to admit to him and his watchful sidekick that I hadn't even known Mum had this house until she'd passed away.

To my relief, he turned his attention back to the intruder. "What did you do when you found the back door open last night?" he asked.

"I didn't really know what to do. It didn't look like a burglary so I thought someone must have come in with a key." I shrugged. "Someone who was looking after the house for Mum."

"And who might that be?"

"I don't know," I said, flatly. "So, I just locked the door. I was on my way back to bed when Evie came down the stairs in her nightdress. She was bumping into walls and muttering under her breath, clearly unaware of what she was doing." I looked over at Evie whose cheeks were bright red. "I'm sorry," I said again, "but it's true." I turned to the Inspector. "It was a classic case of sleepwalking."

"Are you *sure*?" he asked.

That came over as patronising and I bristled.

"Look," Sam said. "I can confirm what Grace has said. This morning, she and I had breakfast together in the belief that Evie was still asleep in bed. We decided not to wake her because she was exhausted. She's a teacher and in need of a holiday," she added, as if that explained everything. "As for my movements, after Grace went for a walk, I drove into Kirkbymoorside to get some shopping for dinner tonight." She straightened her back. "Now, if that's all, we need to take care of Evie and get Grace's ankle strapped up."

DCI Blake didn't move. "We need to discuss the murder."

We all looked at him.

"Well," he went on, "we can't confirm the man's identity yet. But, as I said before, he suffered a blunt trauma to the back of the head."

"Blunt trauma?" I frowned. "What makes you so sure it's murder? Could the lad have slipped over and hit his head? Presumably, you won't know until you get the post-mortem results, unless you have other evidence, of course."

DCI Blake looked uncomfortable and glanced at DS Gray. There was something unspoken in that look. He was about to speak again when his mobile rang. He checked it and stood up. "Excuse me, but I must take this." He walked through the kitchen and out into the back garden for privacy as if he already knew his way around Mum's house.

The four of us sat in silence while we waited for him to return until DS Gray decided to ask some questions of her own. She turned to me.

"Are you sure you've never been here before, Miss Winter, even as a young girl?" she asked.

"Certain," I said.

She turned to Evie. "And you?"

It was Sam who answered. "None of us have been here before. We already told you that."

"Do any of you know the history of Lowna Ford?" she went on, "where the murder took place."

I looked at her. "We know about some ghost story, but I'm sure you're not referring to that."

DS Gray turned to Evie and said: "You know about the legend of Kitty Garthwaite, don't you, Evie? Is that why you went to Lowna this morning?"

I saw the blood drain from Evie's face, and she looked at me.

I replied for her. "My mother's latest novel was based on that legend. That's how we all know about it."

DS Gray ignored me and kept her eyes on Evie. "I just wanted to establish if Evie knew about it."

Evie nodded. "Yes. I do."

"What if she does know?" Sam said, irritably. "What are you trying to imply?"

"It's not my position to imply anything." DS Gray kept her eyes on Evie. "Do you know the rest of the legend, Evie?"

"We all know," I said, quickly.

Sam let out an impatient sigh and turned to me. "Come on, Grace, let's get that ankle of yours cleaned up."

"Stay where you are," DS Gray ordered. "Blake will be back soon." She looked at me. "Is Evie taking special medication, or having psychiatric care, for her sleepwalking?" she asked.

I was surprised at her bluntness. Was she insinuating that Evie was mentally ill?

It riled Evie too. "That's exactly how people treated Kitty back then," she said, hotly. "Full of contempt. Like she was crazy."

"Evie…" I said, attempting to warn her to keep quiet.

But Evie wouldn't stop. "People like you," she said to DS Gray, "have turned the poor, destitute girl into a murdering monster. It's pure nonsense to say Kitty's ghost lured those 16 men on horseback into the ford and killed them on the spot. Absolute nonsense." She slumped back down in the chair.

I saw a small smile on DS Gray's face. I was sure then she had deliberately provoked Evie into revealing all that she knew about the legend and the subsequent killings. Why though?

I'm not sure if Sam realised that too, but she was irritated. "You can't be serious if you believe a ridiculous ghost story could in any way be connected to this lad's murder?"

"Ah," DS Gray said, in a reasonable voice. "It's not what *I* believe that's in question here." She looked over at Evie. "It's what *others* believe that's important. Even today, some local people still report sightings of Kitty stalking the moors."

I felt chills run up my spine, remembering that presence all around me as I walked in the fog earlier. Those footsteps. That dark silhouette. Those small feet in lace up boots, perhaps belonging to another time. I was so engrossed in my thoughts I didn't notice DCI Blake come back into the room and I jumped when he spoke.

He looked at me, curiously. "Just one more question for now, Miss Winter, if I may? Did you see anyone while you were out walking on the moors today?"

Suddenly, it felt as if all the warmth was being sucked out of the room, and I shivered.

"Miss Winter?"

He would think I was truly mad if I mentioned some ghostly apparition. "No," I said. "I didn't see anyone." It was true in a way because I didn't know who or what I'd seen.

DCI Blake pursed his lips in a way that made clear he didn't believe me.

"May I suggest you ladies don't go walking around on the Moors on your own," he said, "not with a killer on the loose."

If he'd wanted to put the fear of God into us, he couldn't have done any better.

DS Gray got out of her chair. "I'll need to take that coat and boots for forensics." She pulled two large plastic evidence bags out of her backpack and stuffed Mum's boots into one and her coat into the other. "We're keeping Violet's car for forensics too."

I looked up, sharply. "What car?"

DCI Blake pointed to the back garden. "The Mercedes your mother parked on the gravel, next to the barn. We found it at Lowna Ford this morning, with the keys still in the ignition." He looked over at Evie. "Is that how you got up to Lowna, Evie? Did you drive Violet's car?"

Evie stared in bewilderment. "I d–don't remember."

My mind was racing. Evie *had* taken Mum's boots and coat. Had she taken her car too? Impossible, I thought. How would she have known about it? "Evie couldn't have taken it," I said. "It was dark when we arrived here last night. We were delayed leaving London and got stuck in heavy traffic, so we stopped for dinner in Thirsk. It was so late that we just unpacked and went to bed. We didn't go up to the barn." I gave him a firm look. "I can assure you that none of us knew there was car up there."

He looked at me for what seemed an eternity. "That's all for now. Don't go anywhere or leave the area. We'll want to take statements from all three of you at the station. We'll need a DNA sample and fingerprints from Evie too."

We stared at him.

"We'll be in touch very soon." And with that, he got up and walked out, followed by his sidekick.

It was the triumphant look on *her* face that I couldn't get out of my mind. Why had she provoked Evie in that way? Did she really think Evie was capable of murder? None of it made any sense. This was our first trip to the North York Moors, and we didn't know anyone here. So, why on earth would Evie murder some poor lad? And why had DS Gray taken such a hostile stance from the beginning. She had openly tutted and sighed whenever Evie spoke as if she really doubted her. Perhaps she was like that with all strangers in this rural community. Or perhaps I was just imagining it. Still, to be fair, it was weird thing for Evie to do, even if she was sleepwalking. And the more I thought about it, the more bizarre it seemed. Why on earth would Evie go to Lowna Ford in the middle of the night?

Ten

"Did you see his eyes?" Sam poured herself a glass of wine, took a swig, and tipped the rest into the pan of risotto on the hob. "Like lasers they were."

It was pure theatre watching Sam cook. She never measured anything out and threw in bits of this and that, along with lots of wine. Not that I was going to complain, I was grateful she was doing the cooking. "Smells good," I said. "Chicken and mushroom?"

She nodded but was more pre-occupied with DCI Blake than in what she was cooking. "Interesting man, don't you think? Not someone you'd expect to be in the police. Not up here anyway."

I remembered his intelligent eyes boring into me: "Mm. I felt I was being questioned by a sharp city trader."

She chuckled. "He couldn't take his eyes off you." She glanced over. "Don't get too excited. You came in looking like a bag lady."

I smiled at her. "You say the sweetest things." I never expected any sympathy from Sam. Empathy wasn't in her nature. She said it like it was.

She looked me up and down and shook her head. "You really should take better care of yourself, Grace. You're not getting any younger."

Before I could say anything about her slackening jaw and alcohol-ruddy complexion, she started talking about the Chief Inspector again. "Rather posh, isn't he?"

"No hint of a Yorkshire accent. Where do you think he's from?"

"Oh, he'll be from up here somewhere," she said. "Probably the son of a wealthy farmer or even landed gentry. He'll have gone to boarding school and university and been taught to speak proper." She laughed. "I've had clients like that. I can sniff them out."

I didn't doubt she was right. Sam had spent most of her life working or socialising with successful men, but I found DCI Blake more unsettling than interesting. He was no fool, and I was scared for Evie. I lowered my voice to a whisper. "I'm really worried about Evie. What the hell was she doing out there in the early hours?"

A shadow passed over Sam's face and she looked away. "I told you she wasn't well. I said it would be a mistake to bring her up here." She glanced at me. "I bet you pressurised her to come."

I wanted to say that I hadn't, but I had. Evie hadn't wanted to come and I'd guilt-tripped her into it. "I feel terrible about it."

"Well, what's done is done," Sam said. "I'll tell you what though. I think that sidekick of the Chief Inspector is a piece of work."

"Miss Glamour Cop, you mean?"

Sam grinned, gleefully. "Did you see her black patent ankle boots? They're from Russell and Bromley. And her red-painted talons surprised me. She was all dolled up for a policewoman on duty." She paused. "Perhaps she's got the hots for the DCI?"

"Did you see the look on her face as she left?" I asked. "She thinks Evie's lying about not being able to remember what she was doing."

"She didn't believe you either," Sam said. "All that nonsense about sleepwalking. What made you say that?"

"Because it's true," I said, hotly. "I saw her with my own eyes in the middle of the night. I'm not lying and I'm not imagining it. I'm certain Evie was sleepwalking."

Sam stared at me as if to gauge whether I was telling the truth or not. "Okay. I believe you, but the police didn't." She shook her head. "Evie's very disturbed, isn't she? Christ knows what's going on with her."

The decisive way Sam said that made me somehow think she *did* have some idea of what was going on with Evie. I wondered if she was being honest with me, but I let it go. "Do you think we should pack up and go home?" I asked.

"You heard the man. He told us not to leave the area."

"Yes, but what if the police get their claws into Evie. We both know she'd never hurt the proverbial fly let alone bash some young lad over the head."

"Yes. *We* know that. But if she persists in carrying on with this 'I can't remember, I was sleepwalking' routine, then she'll have no defence at all."

"That's why I want to go home," I said. "It won't get Evie off answering more questions. But it will put some distance between us and the local police."

"Oh, come on, Grace, be sensible. We're stuck here now, for a few days at least. We'll just have to deal with it as best we can, like it or lump it." She picked up the wine and poured another glass. "Here, sit down and have a drink. It'll relax you."

"We'll need to find a lawyer for Evie," I said.

"It may not come to that," Sam said. "Now come on. Sit down and relax. Your face is lined with worry."

I took the glass and sat down at the kitchen table.

"This is such a lovely kitchen," Sam said. "Bespoke, I reckon. For me, the kitchen is the most important room. I don't care how old a house is, it must have all the mod cons, like this one."

I looked around at the beautiful wooden cabinets and black granite worktops. The food mixer, kettle, and microwave were the latest models.

"Violet had such good taste," Sam said. "I love the red and black colour scheme. I can just picture her cooking in here."

My heart squeezed again. I was sad I'd never seen my mother in this kitchen. Sad she'd never cooked for me in here. Sad I'd never see her again.

Sam gave me a smile as if she'd read my thoughts. Then she nodded at my ankle. "Is that getting any better?"

I could feel it throbbing under the bandage, but I didn't want to complain. "It's okay."

"There's a bag of frozen peas in the freezer. Do you want to put that on it?"

I shook my head. "It'll be fine now I've strapped it up." I took a long swig of wine. "Where did you say you got the shopping from?"

"Kirkbymoorside. I drove back to the main road, turned right and the market town was just off the next roundabout. I found the Co-op open and managed to get all the ingredients for tonight's supper in there." She smiled. "I haven't been in a Co-op since I was a kid. It was well stocked for a small store."

They obviously had a good range of wine too because Sam had several bottles lined up on the counter and was knocking it back liberally. She gave the risotto pan another satisfied stir, then pushed it off the heat and put the lid on. "There," she said. "We'll let that rest for a while." She came over and sat beside me at the table. "What are you going to do with this place, Grace? Sell it?"

My head was too scrambled to even think about it, let alone take a decision like that quickly. "I don't know."

"You're quite the lady of the manor, aren't you? What with your mother's Hampstead house and your own flat? They'll be worth a bit now."

"Yeah, but… oh, I don't know. I'm still taking it all in."

"Well, don't think for too long or you'll have squatters in."

I didn't reply because I heard creaking noises coming from the stairs. We both looked up as Evie came through the doorway. I was glad to see her looking a little better. She'd had a nap, a long soak in the bath, and washed her hair, which was now scraped back into a ponytail. Her face looked innocent and child-like with no make-up on.

"I could do with a drink," she said, sitting down heavily at the table.

Sam got up and poured her a glass of wine. "Here you go."

Evie took a long gulp and closed her eyes as the warm liquid permeated through her. "Lovely," she said. "How's your ankle, Grace. Any better?"

"It'll be fine in the morning after some rest."

She nodded and turned to Sam. "I'm starving. Is that one of your risottos?"

"Yes," Sam said, "real wholesome food. Not like that take-away stuff you and Trev exist on." She studied Evie. "You've put on a few pounds with all that garbage you eat."

I expected Evie to flare up, but she didn't. She touched her jawline and blew out her cheeks. "Listen to you, chipmunk-chops."

That had been Evie's childhood nickname for Sam, and I couldn't help but laugh. But the jibe had hit home, and Sam looked downcast. She knew she'd put on weight, and I guessed much of that was due to the booze.

"Okay, you two," I said to change the subject. "Do you want to eat in here? Or shall we do it in style in the dining room?"

"Dining room," they said in unison.

It was Evie who set about laying the old, polished, refectory table with Mum's bone china and crystal from the oak sideboard while I sat and watched. She padded around straightening a knife here and a spoon there to make sure everything was symmetrical. That was Evie's personality at heart – clever and precise. She loved Bohemian clothes and crystals and was kind and sensitive, but she was not a chaotic person. That's why I couldn't understand her sleepwalking in the night. It seemed so out of character.

"I love this room," Evie said with a sigh and handed me a box of matches. "Light the candles, Grace."

I stood up, struck a match, and leant over to put the flame to each candle in the silver candelabra in the middle of the table. The flickering lights shone on the cutlery and glass, casting a warm glow all around. It was a beautiful room and my heart squeezed with unbearable sadness. I pictured Mum and me together at the table eating and chatting about our day. We'd always liked to go walking and I could see us setting off over the moors on a long hike to the coast. Wouldn't that have been wonderful?

I was shaken from my daydreaming by a scratching sound. I'd been aware of it for a while, but it had become louder, more insistent, and something I couldn't ignore. It seemed to be coming from outside. I got up and went over to the terrace doors to look out over the back garden.

Suddenly, someone darted across the terrace. At least that's what I *thought* I saw. My mind flashed back to the figure on the moors in the mist earlier and my heart quickened. I cupped my hands over the windowpane and pressed my nose against it, but I couldn't see anyone. Then something whipped against the glass pane making me gasp and jump back.

Evie cried out: "What is it? What have you seen?"

"I thought I saw someone on the terrace," I said.

She dashed over and peered out the window.

I could feel her shaking beside me. "It's all right," I said, trying to calm her. "Look, it was probably that branch from the old pear tree blowing about in the wind." I pointed to the tree. "It must have hit the windowpane. The wind is fierce tonight." I gave her a confident smile, more confident than I felt inside.

I didn't think Evie was convinced because she stared out into the dark again, then gave me a sceptical shake of the head.

Fortunately, Sam came in with the food just then. "Sit down you two," she ordered, cheerfully, as she put a large dish of steaming risotto and a bowl of salad on the mats in the middle of the table. "Be careful though. The risotto dish is very hot." She plonked herself down on the chair nearest the kitchen door and reached for the bottle of white wine in the cooler on the table. "You haven't even opened this," she chided, and unscrewed the cap. "Come on. Let's have a toast." She poured us all a glass of wine, then raised hers. "To Violet," she said, beaming at me, "Grace's lovely mum and a wonderful friend to Evie and me. May she rest in peace and live on in our hearts forever."

For some reason, I was annoyed with Sam for thinking she should be the one proposing a toast for Mum and not me. But Evie raised her glass, her voice choking when she said: "To Violet who was like a second mum to me. Love you, Violet."

I looked at them both, raised my glass, and simply added: "To my mum." The truth was, I didn't really know what else to say. I was too shell-shocked with all her lies.

Sam seemed to read my mind and gave me a sad smile. "Go on, Grace. You, first. Help yourself to some risotto."

We sat quietly eating and sipping wine, enjoying the food. I was at the head of the table and couldn't help but glance up at the terrace doors from time to time. I didn't know who or what I was expecting to see outside. Evie must have noticed because she stood up and pulled all the curtains closed, even the ones across the terrace doors that were obviously there to keep out the draughts. Except she couldn't shut out the sound of the wind sighing and moaning around the old house. It felt like we were marooned in the middle of nowhere, but at least we were warm and cosy. I just wished Rufus was inside with us. If Mum were here, he'd be lying flat out under the table at her feet. Perhaps Evie was right? Perhaps he was feeling grief too in some cat-like way and wanted to be alone.

"Well," I said with a sigh as I put down my knife and fork after devouring a second helping of risotto. "That was lovely, Sam. Thanks for shopping and cooking for us. You're a life saver."

Sam smiled and glanced over at Evie who just looked away. "You okay, Evie?" she asked.

"Evie?" She asked again.

Evie gave her a pointed look and I wondered what it was supposed to mean. It certainly made Sam uncomfortable because she stood up and collected our plates. "I'll go and get the cheese and biscuits and we can finish off the wine," she said.

"Let me help." I went to stand up.

Sam stopped me. "No. You stay there. I can manage these few dishes perfectly well."

"Thanks," I said, and I meant it. My ankle was throbbing.

When Sam had gone, Evie turned to me. "Who did you see on the terrace earlier?"

I shook my head. "No-one."

"You saw something," she said. "I know you did."

I shrugged. "I thought I saw someone outside." I remembered my experience on the moors earlier, but I didn't want to scare Evie by telling her about the woman. Anyway, I wasn't sure who or what I'd seen up there.

Evie looked down at her hands. "You know that ghost story Violet was writing?"

I nodded.

"It's true that people still report sightings of Kitty's ghost on the Moors." She paused. "Kitty comes here too because this is where her lover Willie lived."

I smiled at her. "It's just folklore, Evie. There's nothing like a good ghost story to get tourists visiting and spending money."

"No." She shook her head. "It's not just folklore. I've, well, I've…"

She was clasping her hands together to stop them shaking, and I wondered why she was getting so worked up about some old ghost story. "You surely don't believe all that, Evie, do you?" I asked the question in a light-hearted way, but she looked scared.

"I didn't murder that lad, Grace. It wasn't me. And I didn't drive Violet's car up to Lowna. I'm sure I didn't."

"You remember now, do you?" I said, hoping everything was coming back to her.

"Well, yes," she said. "Or rather… no, I don't remember anything. But I'm sure I didn't do it. I couldn't do anything like that and certainly not without knowing about it. Really, I couldn't. You know that Grace, don't you?"

We were still staring at each other when Sam breezed back into the room and put a plate of cheese and crackers down on the table. She'd even thought to buy some grapes too. She looked from Evie to me, then back at Evie. "What have I missed?"

Evie shook her head at me as if to say, 'don't say anything'. And I didn't because I knew Sam would pooh-pooh it and I needed time to reconcile what Evie had said with my experience of seeing that misty apparition on the moors. Not that I believed in ghosts for one minute. "We were just chatting," I said.

"Here." Sam handed us both small plates and knives and told us to tuck into the cheese. But she was not going to let things drop. "Have you remembered anything about your walk on the Moors today, Evie? Is that what you were talking about when I came in?"

Evie stared at her plate, and I noticed her hands were still trembling as she picked up her knife.

"You can tell us if there's something troubling you," Sam persisted. "You know we won't judge you. We're your friends."

Evie flashed her a dagger-like look but stayed silent.

"Come on," Sam said. "Out with it."

Evie's face turned red, the tell-tale sign that she was on the brink of an outburst. She rarely got mad but when she did, she let rip.

I intervened. "It's all right," I said to her. "You won't remember everything straightway. I'm sure things will come slowly back when you've had some sleep and a reset."

Sam pulled a face at me for letting Evie off the hook. But at least she stopped asking questions.

Then something weird happened. Music rang out making us all jump. I froze in shock as I recognised the beautiful voice of Celine Dion, Mum's favourite singer.

Evie reacted first. "It's only the iPod." She pointed to the sideboard. "I set it up when I was laying the table." She frowned. "I don't remember loading that track though."

"Switch it off," Sam said. "Can't you see it's upsetting Grace." She held out her hand to Evie. "Give me the remote."

"I haven't got a remote," Evie said.

"How did it switch itself on, then?" Sam asked.

"I d–don't know."

Sam went to stand up, but I stopped her. "It's okay. Leave it on. I don't mind." But, as the music continued, I found I did mind. A lump came into my throat when the track 'My Heart Will Go On' played. Titanic was Mum's favourite film, and that song was the soundtrack. Hot tears pricked my eyes, and I fought them back.

Evie reached over to squeeze my hand. "You must really miss her. I know I do."

I nodded. "I do, but I'm angry with her too for keeping this house a secret."

"I'm sure she had a good reason," Evie said, softly.

"And what would that be?" My voice was sharp. "How would you feel if your mother had had a secret life and you only found out about it after she'd died?"

"Honestly," Evie sighed, "I'd be very hurt."

Sam chimed in. "Don't you think it's best to let go of the past? We should live in the present and look to the future. That's my take on life anyway."

I shook my head. "That won't work for me. I need to know the truth. Otherwise, it'll eat away at me forever."

"What if you find out something awful?" Sam asked. "What then?"

"At least I'd know the truth."

Evie nodded. "We all deserve that." She glared again at Sam, who gave her a stern look back.

"Grace is a good person," Evie went on at Sam. "She doesn't deserve to be treated like this. She needs to know the truth to understand why things happened the way they did and get on with her life."

It was good to hear that from Evie. "I'm glad you understand," I said to her.

Evie's eyes suddenly welled up. Tears began flowing down her cheeks so freely that she couldn't speak.

I looked over at Sam who just shrugged.

"Tell us what's wrong, Evie," I said. "I mean I know you're upset about Mum. But there's something else, isn't there? I've sensed it from the moment I first saw you."

Evie's head drooped and she let out a loud moan that reverberated around the room. A despairing moan that filled me with dread.

I grabbed her hand. "What is it?" I whispered.

There was such a look of pain in her eyes when she lifted her head that I shivered. "We want to help you," I said.

"You can't," she said, closing her eyes. "Trev's left me." She whispered the words as if saying them out loud would make it all too real.

"Oh, Evie!" I could hardly believe it. She'd been with Trevor since university. Their marriage seemed rock solid. "I'm so sorry," I said. "When on earth did this happen?"

"A-about six weeks ago."

"*Six* weeks?" Sam said. "Why didn't you tell us?"

But I knew why Evie hadn't said anything. I'd been with Peter for years before he'd suddenly left. It was like a bereavement, the loss indescribable. I wanted to be on my own to process what had happened. "Why did he leave?" I asked, gently.

"For another woman," Evie whispered. "Someone he met at work."

"Bastard!" Sam said.

Evie's chin hung low on her chest as if the last ounce of energy had been knocked out of her.

"Do you know this woman?" Sam asked.

Evie shook her head. "All I know is that she's divorced, with two young kids."

"Bastard!" Sam said, again.

I was thinking the same. Evie and Trevor had been trying for a family for years. I knew how much they both longed for children. Had Trevor given up on Evie and left her for a woman with a ready-made family? I thought that might be the case, but I wasn't going to say so to Evie. And I wasn't going to let Sam interrogate her either. "Why don't you go up and have an early night, Evie? You'll feel better after some rest."

She smiled at me. "I think I might relax on the sofa and watch some TV first. If that's all right with you?"

"Of course."

Sam got to her feet. "You do that, Evie. I thought I'd go over to the pub for a drink." She looked at me. "Want to come?"

I shook my head. I didn't want to leave Evie alone and anyway I needed to rest my ankle. "You go, Sam, if you don't mind drinking on your own. My ankle's throbbing."

She nodded. "I'll just have one drink, so I won't be long. I want to get all the gossip from the locals on this murder."

That set off alarm bells in my head. Sam stirring things up was the last thing we needed. "Probably best to stay off that subject. Feelings will be running high."

"Nonsense. I'm just going to have a chat with the locals. And while I'm there, I'll see if I can find out who's been looking after this place. Someone is bound to know something."

I wasn't sure that was the way to go about things, but how else was I going to find out? "Take my car if you want. Best not walk around in the dark with some nutter on the loose."

Sam laughed. "The pub's only a couple of hundred yards down the road. I'll take a torch." She jumped up and started collecting the plates. "I'll clear these before I go."

I nodded. "I'll settle Evie in front of the TV, then I'll come and help you."

Evie looked worried as I helped her to the sofa in the sitting room. "Will Sam be all right out there on her own?"

I laughed as I covered Evie's legs with a woollen throw. "Are you kidding? The good folk of Hutton-le-Hole don't know what's about to hit them."

Evie sighed. "You never know with her though, do you? She's not always what she seems. It's impossible to know whether she's telling the truth or not sometimes."

I was surprised at Evie. True, there were times when I'd caught Sam out in a lie. Nothing serious. Just things like saying she was going out when she wasn't, or not being where she said she was going to be. But I wasn't her keeper. She could do what she liked.

Evie laid her head on the cushion. "If it hadn't been for you and Violet when I was a kid, I don't know what would have become of me."

That was another odd thing for her to say. "Don't forget Sam," I said. "She was the one who saw off those school bullies."

Evie nodded. "She doesn't always do the right thing though, does she?"

I got the feeling there was more behind Evie's words. "Are you trying to tell me something?"

She looked away. "The point I'm making is that Sam doesn't think about anyone but herself. Or about the impact of her actions on others."

"That's a bit harsh, isn't it?"

"Is it?" Evie sighed. "I'm just so tired, Grace. Of everything. I think I could sleep forever."

"Look, I know it's hard. But take it from me, you will get through this. I did when Peter left."

"I'm not as strong as you."

"You're stronger than you think."

She gave me a weak smile. "It's so good to see you again, Grace. I've missed you."

"I've missed you too." I smiled at her. "Now, you lie there and relax while I go and help Sam in the kitchen."

Evie nodded and closed her eyes.

I limped back to the kitchen where I found Sam loading up the dishwasher.

"How is she?" she asked.

"Physically and emotionally exhausted," I said. "She's been bottling everything up since Trevor left and probably working too hard."

"Can you give her something to relax? Sleeping pills, perhaps?"

"No." I shook my head. "They can be highly addictive. She might be on them already for all I know. It could explain her sleepwalking."

"What about tranquilisers?"

"I can't. I'm not her doctor."

"But you've known her for years."

"Yes, but she may have some medical condition that I don't know about or be on some other medication." I paused. "She does seem rather delusional. She's really preoccupied with this Kitty Garthwaite ghost story."

Sam's eyes twinkled. "This *is* Evie we're talking about. You know what she's like. She *feels* everything. She'll be telling us next that she's seen this ghost."

"Don't be unkind, Sam."

"I'm not being unkind. You know full well that I love Evie to bits. It's just that, well, she does go over the top." She paused. "I mean, what a dramatic reaction to Trevor leaving."

I stared at her. "Trevor was Evie's husband and soulmate. They've been together for years. Him leaving would be devastating enough, but to leave her for another woman with children after all they've been though. Well, that's just like stabbing her and turning the knife in the wound."

Sam just shrugged her shoulders which provoked me even more. "She's not like you," I flared. "She hasn't had a shedload of men. She won't find a man around every corner like you do. She may never find another man."

As soon as I'd finished my rant, I knew I'd gone too far. The truth was, I wasn't sure if I'd been talking about Evie or myself. "Oh God," I said, wearily. "I shouldn't have gone off at you like that. You've done all the shopping and cooking and all you get is a rocket in return."

Sam wasn't upset though. "I'm sorry too, Grace," she said. "I'm not *trying* to be flippant. I just have a different outlook. We've only got one life and I prefer to fill it with fun, not misery."

Suddenly, something Peter said once during a row flashed into my head. It wasn't the cause of the argument that stuck in my mind, it was the words he'd flung at me afterwards. *You know your trouble, Grace, you suck the fun out of everything.*

Did I? Did Peter leave because he wanted some fun? Had I become so bogged down with my work and patients' problems that I'd become a misery to live with? I turned to Sam and smiled at her. "Go on. You go and glam yourself up for the pub. I'll finish this."

Sam didn't need to be asked twice. "Thanks." She laid the tea towel over the back of a chair and rushed out of the kitchen as if she couldn't wait to get away.

After she'd gone, I pottered around putting things away and wiping down surfaces, but my thoughts returned to Peter. I thought we'd had fun along the way. But then I was obviously no good at reading relationships, or I'd have known he was planning to leave for good when he said he was going travelling for a while.

I was clearly wrong about my parents too. I thought they'd been happy together. Sure, they never showed any kind of affection publicly, never kissing or holding hands, but nor did my friends' parents. They were different times. But Mum wouldn't have bought this house if she'd been happy with us at home, would she? Had that been my fault? Had I been a noisy child? A needy child? I would never know because she never spoke about it, not even after Dad died. But I should have known. I really should have known.

Eleven

Evie was asleep in front of the TV when I popped my head in to check on her. That gave me the chance to go up to Mum's study and have another look around. On my way up, I remembered to bend over on the stairs up to the attic to avoid hitting my head on the low stone ceiling. The two rooms up there were light and airy though. The roof was high and supported by tree trunks fashioned as beams. Not only could I stand up straight but there was plenty of room to move about too. I switched on the main light, the one that was blazing when we arrived at the house. The blind at the front dormer window was up and I could see the night sky. At the back, the moon glowed through a skylight in the roof.

I'd been surprised downstairs to find the same furniture in the sitting room as in Mum's London home. Her study was different though. Her desk was mahogany, with a green leather inlay, and positioned under the dormer window to get as much light as possible. There was a matching table in one corner, covered with index cards, but no computer. Mum always said she had no use for them and wrote her manuscripts by hand. She never employed a secretary either as far as I knew. I'd always assumed her publisher formatted everything for her, but was that right?

I went over to the stack of coloured boxes that I'd seen earlier. Each one contained a bundle of manuscripts in series order. I'd been wondering about them because I hadn't found any in London, and Mum always said she'd never throw them away. They were too precious to her.

I was determined to go through everything in her study and adjoining bedroom to find something to explain why she'd kept the house a secret from me. I searched the desk drawers first. They were tidy and full of the usual stationery items, except for an unusual fountain pen that caught my eye. It was made of blue and black marble with a gold nib and trim. I noticed tiny gold words engraved in a spiral pattern around the entire top of the pen. I flicked on her desk lamp and held it to the light. I had to use her magnifying glass to make out the words and was surprised to read a quote from CS Lewis, one of Mum's favourite authors: *A children's story that can only be enjoyed by children is not a good children's story in the slightest*. I smiled at first, then frowned. My practical mother would never have bought this pen and had it engraved for herself.

I continued searching the desk but found nothing else of interest. Next, I went over to the table with the index cards. I knew Mum used them when working on a new novel to help plot scenes. I read the cards one by one, but couldn't make sense of her random scribbles, except the name Kitty kept cropping up. It was only when I picked up the central card that I saw the working title, 'It Began with a Ghost Story: Kitty's Revenge'. So, Evie *was* right. Mum was working on a ghost story. Underneath the title was another quote, which she'd attributed to Stephen King: *We need ghost stories because we, in fact, are the ghosts*. Now some of his novels were terrifying. So, Evie was right again. Mum's ghost story was for adults.

I was still taking all this in when I got that strange feeling again, the one I'd had on the stairs when I'd first arrived at the house. There was a presence in the attic. I wasn't alone.

Suddenly that same sensation of hot breath on the back of my neck sent goosebumps shivering up my spine. I froze, hardly daring to turn. A tapping sound on the glass of the dormer window made me look up.

Outside, a white figure with two enormous eyes stared through the glass. My fear melted away when I realised what I was seeing. There, perched on a tiny ledge and looking in, stood a huge barn owl. Its snowy breast and unblinking eyes were mesmerising. We gawped at each other for a moment until it spread its wings and flew away. When I'd got over the shock, I burst out laughing at my own paranoia. It was a beautiful creature, and I reminded myself that I was in its territory now. We humans, especially those of us living in cities, tended to forget that there was an amazing natural world living all around us, and generally keeping out of our way.

I turned my attention back to my search. My eyes rested on a bookcase under the skylight. It was full of Mum's books and seeing them lined up like that reminded me what a prolific author she'd been in her earlier life. On the bottom shelf, I noticed a photograph album. I picked it up and started leafing through. It was full of snaps of my parents and me through the years. Some were at the seaside on holiday, others were taken in parks and other places we'd often visit. Sam and Evie appeared in many too. It was poignant seeing the three of us growing up in photos, and Mum and Dad ageing. It was frustrating too because I couldn't find one single photo of this house or garden. I was getting nowhere fast. "Think, Grace!" I said out loud. "Where would Mum hide something she didn't want you to see?"

Of course! I went into the bedroom adjoining the study. When I was young Mum had hidden the key to this house in the red hatbox on top of her wardrobe. In this room, there was just one single bed and a large wooden wardrobe. The rest of the walls were lined with bookshelves. I stood on the bed to see if there was anything on top of this wardrobe. *Bingo!* There was another box. This time it was grey, and more like a document box you'd find in a stationery shop. I pulled it down, expecting it to be covered in dust. It wasn't, so it must have been put there recently.

Butterflies fluttered in my stomach as I took off the lid. I didn't know what I was expecting to find. Certainly not the jack-in-the-box that had terrorised me as a child. But I need not have worried. Inside, I found a large, leather binder. When I opened it, a lump came into my throat. It was full of beautiful illustrations which I recognised immediately. There was Fox Spirit, door mice, rabbits, and all kinds of birds from Mum's books. I couldn't help but smile as I flicked through the pages and at the memories they brought back.

Then I noticed each drawing had the same initials in the bottom right-hand corner. I turned the pages again and studied the initials. Each one had been written in blue ink, but with such a flourish that I couldn't quite make them out. I tried to remember who'd illustrated Mum's books, and realised I had no idea.

My delight at finding the illustrations soon faded when I reached the back of the binder. On the inside back cover, written in the same blue ink and signed with the same initials, were the words: *The greatest happiness of life, Violet, is the conviction that we are loved; loved for ourselves, or rather, loved in spite of ourselves.* I was puzzled. Who was this person with the indecipherable initials?

The sound of car tyres crunching on the gravel drive distracted me from some worrying thoughts. I looked at my watch. Nine o'clock. Who'd be calling at this time of night?

I ran down the stairs and opened the front door. There on the porch stood DCI Blake. The rain fell onto his coat and hair like glitter. The dull beam from the porch light made his face look sunken and grey.

My mind flashed to Sam. "What's happened?" I asked, anxiously, thinking the worst.

"Oh, it's nothing to worry about," he said, as if only just realising what his presence at this time of night might mean. "Sorry to disturb you so late. I wanted to have another word if I may."

I was surprised. "Can't it wait until morning?"

"It won't take long," he said. "Can I come in?"

He was the last person I wanted to see, but I couldn't really refuse. Reluctantly, I opened the door and stood back to let him in.

"Thank you." He stepped over the threshold and wiped his wet feet several times on the doormat.

"Do you mind if we talk in the kitchen?" I closed the door. "Evie's asleep on the sofa in the sitting room and I don't want to disturb her. She'll only get upset again if she sees you."

He nodded and followed me along the hallway. I heard the TV as we walked past the sitting room but there was no sound from Evie. I guessed she was still asleep.

In the kitchen, I invited him to sit at the table and I sat down opposite. The bright kitchen light made his weary face look almost yellow with fatigue now. "Are you still on duty?" I asked.

He shook his head. "I'm on my way home. I live in the next village, Lastingham. It's a couple of miles east of here." He paused. "How's your ankle?"

"It'll be a lot better in the morning after some rest."

"And Evie? How's she doing?"

"A little better now she's had some food and rest."

He nodded. "I came to tell you that we've identified the murder victim. A young lad working on a farm in Gillamoor." He shook his head, sadly. "His name was Joe Dunstan. Did you know him?" he asked.

I shook my head. "No."

"He was only 22."

So that was the reason for his bleak face. He'd been in the morgue. It was an unpleasant task, as I well knew. "I'm sorry to hear that," I said, knowing what a bereavement like that did to families and communities. "His family must be devastated."

"They are," he said, his voice low and sad.

I looked at him for a while. That's when I noticed something else in his eyes. The thing about being a doctor is that I have all of humanity sitting before me, telling me their most private thoughts and feelings. I can see if they're sad, or happy. I can tell if they're being truthful, or lying, or if they're just lonely. But there's something else I see in my patients, something that has both physical and mental symptoms. Pain. And that's what I saw in DCI Blake's eyes at that moment. My doctor's instincts took over. "You look like you could do with a drink," I said. Without waiting for a reply, I got up and went over to the dresser to get the remains of the wine from dinner. I came back and poured two glasses from the bottle. I pushed one towards him. "Take your raincoat off. It'll dry out a little if you hang it on the hook on the back of the door."

He gave me a small smile and hung his coat up. "I'm not sure I should drink that." He looked at the wine, then at me.

"Are you on duty or not?" I asked.

"I'm not on duty."

"You're worried about fraternising off-duty with suspects, then," I said.

"Something like that." He looked at me, then decided he could stay because he sat back down, took a long gulp of wine, and gave a satisfied sigh. "Thanks. I needed that."

As the tension slackened from his shoulders, I noticed his fingers touch the two scars on his forehead. I wondered again how he'd got them. "Doesn't matter how often you see bodies," I said. "They always get to you, especially one so young."

He nodded, and we sat drinking our wine in silence.

After a while, when he'd relaxed a bit more, I asked: "Are you sure yet what happened to the lad?"

"It's been confirmed that he had a blow to the back of the head. That didn't kill him though. The cause of death was drowning."

I looked at him. "So, why do you think it's murder. He could have tripped, hit his head, fallen into the water, and drowned."

"There were pressure marks on his face and shoulders. Someone held him under."

I sighed, deeply. "Do you have any more idea about who did it?"

He looked straight at me. "We're following several lines of enquiry at present." He paused. "I'm afraid Evie will need to come down to the station."

I tensed. "You can't honestly believe she killed this young man. Anyway, you've seen how slight she is. She wouldn't have the strength to hold him under."

"She was found at the crime scene by my colleague DS Gray. Evie has no explanation for what she was doing there. Forensics are examining Violet's Mercedes too." He paused. "I told you we found it parked up near Lowna this morning."

I nodded.

"They've found a scarf inside the car, and a crystal bead that probably came off a necklace or earrings. Could they belong to Evie?"

I felt myself freeze, as his blue eyes pierced mine. "They could," I said, evenly. "Or they could be Mum's. She had lots of scarves and jewellery."

He nodded. "So, you see, there are many questions for Evie to answer."

I stiffened. "But she couldn't possibly have known this young lad. Why would she kill him?"

A frown flickered across his forehead. "Are you sure none of you have been here before?"

"I told you." My voice was frosty now. "This is my first visit. There's no way my friends could have been here before either."

"You weren't close to your mother, then?" he asked.

His words cut me like a knife.

I think he noticed my reaction because he added: "Things can get difficult sometimes in families. Relationships are complicated."

I drew myself up in the chair. "On the contrary. Mum and I were very close. There was no difficulty in our relationship," I said with as much conviction as I could muster. Of course, I'd always thought that was true, but perhaps it wasn't. Perhaps there had been some difficulty that I didn't know about.

He gave me another of his penetrating looks but didn't push the point. He turned the conversation back to Evie. "We need to find out what Evie was doing up at Lowna in the early hours."

I was fed up with this man not believing a word I said, but I didn't want to antagonise him because of Evie's situation. "Look." I tried to adopt a reasonable tone. "I explained before that I found Evie sleepwalking around the house in the middle of the night. I put her back to bed, but she must have got up again and gone out." I shrugged. "People do all sorts of things while they're in that state. They walk, they drive, they run, they even cook meals. They won't remember anything about it when they wake up."

"Hm." He paused as if considering what I'd said. "Nevertheless, Miss Winter." His tone was business-like now. "I'd like you and your friend, Sam, to bring Evie to Police HQ in Scarborough in the morning. We'll want statements from all three of you as to your exact movements yesterday and today."

I looked at him. "Are you suggesting that all three of us are murder suspects?"

"Afraid so," he said in an unapologetic way. "Like everyone else at the moment."

"Why Scarborough?" I asked. "That's quite a way from here, isn't it?"

"Our main HQ is in the market town of Northallerton. That's where the regional murder squad work from. But there was a big fire a month ago that caused a lot of damage throughout the building. We've moved our location to Scarborough until our building's fixed."

"I see."

In the silence that followed, he picked up his glass and finished the wine.

I hoped that was the end of the conversation and that he'd leave, but he didn't move. I knew from my patients that if they didn't get up when I thought we'd finished, there was something else on their minds. I waited for him to say whatever it was.

He put the glass back on the table. "Now," he said, fixing those eyes on me again. "Will you tell me who *you* saw this afternoon while you were out walking on the moors?"

"What makes you think I saw someone?"

"Policeman's hunch."

Was that the ghost of a smile? This man was so buttoned up, his every gesture was hard to read. But he was certainly no fool.

I decided there was nothing for it but to be honest. "You're going to think this is crazy," I said.

"Try me."

I shrugged. "I honestly don't know who or what I saw up there." I went on to tell him everything that had happened that afternoon: the walk, the moors, the weather, how happy I'd been to be out in the fresh air and away from everyone. I told him how the clouds had rolled in from the coast, the fog, and not being able to see my hand in front of me. I explained about my sense of being followed, the footsteps behind me. And I told him about the woman I thought I'd seen, leaving out the bit about being terrified.

I expected him to dismiss the whole thing as nonsense, a fertile imagination, a city dweller spooked by the bleakness of the moors. He didn't.

"This woman, you saw. Can you describe her?" he asked.

I shook my head. "All I really saw was the hem of her long dress and her feet. Dainty feet in narrow, worn, boots. Old-fashioned."

He looked at me with another expression I found hard to read. "It is desolate up on the moors at times, even for those of us who know our way around. Walking for miles with your own thoughts, in the same landscape, can distort your sense of time and distance. It plays with your head."

"Not to mention experiencing all four seasons of weather in just one hour," I chipped in. "It's hauntingly beautiful though."

He nodded. "Unexpected things can happen up there. And, of course, there's the folklore…"

I stopped him. "If you're talking about the resident ghost, I already know the story. Mum was writing a novel about Kitty Garthwaite."

He gave a wry smile.

I went on. "Kitty's ghost is said to have murdered many men at Lowna Ford over the years. You don't think she killed Joe Dunstan too, do you?" I said, tongue-in-cheek, meaning it as a joke.

"The locals may be talking about that possibility," he said. "I just wanted you to know."

I couldn't tell from the look he gave me whether there was amusement or devilment in his eyes.

"Kitty's ghost was said to sit naked on the riverbank luring those men to their deaths. The murders only stopped when the parish priest went up and performed an exorcism," he said.

He was keeping such a straight face that I had to say. "You don't believe all that tosh, do you?"

"Doesn't matter what I believe," he said. "It's what *others* believe, that's the problem."

I remembered DS Gray coming out with the exact same thing earlier. I was about to say that when his face suddenly fell, and he looked past me towards the door.

I turned and saw Evie standing in the kitchen doorway staring at us. Her face was like alabaster, her eyes glued on DCI Blake. The ferocity of that stare prompted him to stand up.

"Make fun of Kitty if you dare," Evie hissed at him. "She's standing right behind you."

At that moment, the back door flew open, making us all jump. A gust of wind sprinkled raindrops on the floor and Sam stumbled in. She was dripping wet, but it took only one look at her rosy cheeks and crooked smile to know that she was drunk.

She pushed her coat hood back and looked at the three of us in turn. "Evening," she said, gaily. "I'm glad you're here, Chief Inspector." She slurred the words, and I felt myself cringe. "I've just been talking to villagers in the pub. They've cracked your murder. It was the ghost who did it… Kitty."

I gave her a warning shake of the head to stop.

But she was too far gone to notice. "Did he tell you Kitty's lover, Willie Dixon, who left her pregnant and suicidal, lived in this house, Grace?" She turned to DCI Blake. "Go on. Tell her. She won't believe me."

DCI Blake didn't respond.

Sam's eyes were glowing with mischief as she turned to Evie. "Fancy that, Evie. We've got our very own resident ghost. Perhaps it was the ghost who lit the fire and put the light on for us when we arrived."

"That's enough, Sam," I said, sharply.

But she was enjoying herself too much. "And did he tell you that Kitty and Willie met here sometimes for their trysts?" Sam winked, suggestively. "Kitty might have got pregnant in here."

"Will you shut up!" Evie shouted and turned on her heels.

I was exasperated. "For goodness' sake, Sam. Why do you have to aggravate her?"

"I was only joking." Sam turned and stumbled after her. "Wait, Evie." I heard her shout. "I'm sorry. I was only mucking about… Evie!"

My cheeks must have been flaming. "I'm sorry about that," I said to the Chief Inspector when we were alone again.

His eyebrows were still raised when he walked over to get his raincoat. "I'd better be off," he said. "I'll see the three of you at Scarborough Police Station at 11 o'clock tomorrow morning."

I nodded, meekly. How could I refuse after that embarrassing performance?

"I'll go out the back way." Then he hesitated as if he had something else on his mind but wasn't sure whether to say it or not. Finally, he turned back to me. "You might want to talk to Patrick Hardy. He lives in the end cottage on this side of the village." He pointed in a vaguely southerly direction. "He might be able to help you understand why Violet came here."

"Really?" I jumped up. "I'll give him a call. What's his number?"

When the Chief Inspector looked at me again, for the first time I saw kindness in his eyes. "Just call round," he said. "That'll be for the best."

Twelve

I always found it hard to sleep on the first night of staying somewhere new, but I would have expected to sleep well on the second night in my own mother's house. I didn't. I lay awake, tossing and turning, aware of the minutes and hours ticking by, punctuated by the infuriating chime of the grandfather clock in the dining room. It hadn't been working when we arrived, but Sam had managed to wind it up and get it going. She said she'd muffled the sound of the chime, and we hadn't really heard it in the rest of the house during the day. But now, in my sleepless state, there was no ignoring it. I pulled a pillow over my head to shut out the noise, but I couldn't get rid of the chatter in my mind.

I was seriously worried about Evie's connection to this murder and her mental health. I kept going over our conversations in the car on the way up and with the police. She knew all about the ghost story. Still, if she'd been researching it for Mum's novel, that made sense. But nothing else did. Why would she take Mum's car up to Lowna in the dead of night and murder some lad? That was ridiculous. Evie wasn't capable of murder. She was though on the verge of a nervous breakdown. I was sure of that. Fancy telling DCI Blake that Kitty's ghost was standing behind him in the kitchen. Honestly, she wasn't doing herself any favours.

With sleep becoming more elusive as time ticked by, I gave up trying and propped myself up on the pillows. I listened, but there was no banging downstairs like last night or any noise from Sam's or Evie's rooms either. They had to be asleep. I got up, pulled a sweater over my pyjamas, and went to the window. It was so magical seeing the back garden bathed in moonlight that it took my breath away. I pulled a chair round to sit and look out. The rain had stopped, and the clouds cleared to reveal a myriad of stars. In the far distance, the black silhouette of the trees atop the bank stood out against the clear sky. Below them, the paddock stretched down to the back lane. The grazing sheep in the field looked almost ghostly in the brightness, except I knew they were real. Inside the garden gate and the dry-stone wall bordering the garden, there was the gravelled area where Mum must have parked her car, and the old stone barn that I still hadn't had a chance to explore.

Then I saw Rufus. He was perched on top of the gatepost, sitting as still as the statues at Mum's front door. He had his back to me and seemed to be staring at the paddock. I wondered if he was hunting for field mice or baby rabbits, but he didn't move. I decided to go out and try to entice him in with some food.

I walked quietly along the landing so as not to wake Sam and Evie and crept down the stairs. I didn't put any house lights on for fear of alerting Rufus. He would only run off if he thought I was coming. My eyes soon adjusted to the dark as moonbeams spilled in through the windows. In the kitchen I put on Mum's long Barbour raincoat and pushed my feet into her rubber garden clogs as they were big enough to give my strapped ankle some room. I grabbed a torch from the sideboard, picked up Rufus's bowl and slipped out of the back door into the night.

The chilly air caught in my throat as I stared up at the clear sky and stars. I switched on the torch to light my way and kept the beam down on the ground. At the end of the terrace, I stepped gingerly onto the moss-covered flagstones that stretched up the garden. They glistened with rain and were slippery and treacherous underfoot. An earthy smell from the holly hedge wafted into my face as I made my way along, giving me a real shot of aromatherapy. The moment I stepped off the path and onto the gravel at the top of the garden, Rufus heard the crunch and spun around.

I stood still and put his food bowl down on the ground. He let out a soft, mewing sound as if in greeting, jumped down from the gatepost and came running towards me. Then he stopped dead and stared at me. Quickly, he turned, ran over to the barn, and wriggled under the rotten wood at the bottom of the door.

That irrational fear of rejection swept over me again. Rufus clearly thought I was Mum at first because I was wearing her raincoat and shoes. He soon scarpered when he realised it was me. Well, I thought, he might have given up on me, but I wasn't going to give up on him so easily. I picked up his bowl and limped to the barn. The old door creaked open as I lifted the latch. "Rufus," I called, and went inside. I wasn't expecting the fragrant smell that hit me. Roses perhaps? I switched on the torch to have a look around, but there were no flowers real or dried in there. I saw that the old flagstone floor had a pile of straw swept into one corner. Metal rings were hammered into the stone walls at intervals presumably for tethering animals. At the far end of the barn stood a workbench, its wood was grey and rotten with age. Next to it were some rickety pigeon-holes with rusty old tools pushed into every slot. There was a thick layer of dust and droppings everywhere. No bats *please*. I shivered because I hate bats.

I tilted the torch beam upwards to see a hayloft and a patchwork of massive cobwebs hanging from the ceiling and draping the stone walls like curtains. I couldn't see any bats roosting, but I wasn't going to look too hard. Rufus would probably see them pretty much as mice with wings. Perhaps that's what he was eating?

"Rufus?" I called again. I heard a soft rustling in the hayloft. I looked around but the only way up seemed to be a rickety ladder. I put his bowl down on the floor and pushed the torch into my pocket. I shouldn't have gone up with my sprained ankle, but I wanted to get Rufus. I grabbed the ladder with both hands and shook it to see if it stayed in one piece. It did. I leant it up against the hayloft and put my foot on the bottom rung to see if it would hold my weight. Satisfied that it would, I started to climb. It was perilous, but I made it to the top. I shone the beam along the loft and saw Rufus lying at the far end curled up on a pile of old straw, looking warm and comfortable.

He opened his sleepy eyes and looked at me. He didn't bother to move because he knew I was too far away to grab him.

"So, this is where you've been hiding out," I said.

He continued to look at me.

"Are you coming into the house?"

He just closed his eyes.

"I'll take that as a 'no'," I said, grumpily, and I swear that cat smiled. "Right, I'm done worrying about you, Rufus. You can damn well get on with it on your own." I shoved the torch back in my pocket and climbed down the ladder carefully. At least now I knew he had shelter, a cosy bed in the hay, and a ready larder of food in the fields if he could be bothered to catch it. But I still left his bowl of food on the barn floor just in case. Other creatures might steal it, but that was up to him.

I shone the torch around the walls and floor one last time. And that's when I noticed a kind of image on the wall near the door. I held the beam directly onto it to see better. A large heart shape had been chiselled crudely into the stone. It had an arrow through it and two sets of initials carved inside. I brushed the dirt away to try to read them. Age had disintegrated them, but they appeared to be *WD* and *KG*. I smiled to think of couples through the ages declaring their love in this timeless way.

Oh God! I realised their significance. Did they belong to Willie Dixon and Kitty Garthwaite? Did those two lovers really exist? Did they meet up in this house? In this barn?

Suddenly, I had that same feeling as in the attic earlier. A presence all around me. A sense that I was no longer alone. My heart started pounding and I was rooted to the spot, not daring to move. Then, as before, I felt something brush the back of my neck and shivers ran up my spine. Without turning round, I sped out of the barn and down the path, slipping and sliding on the stones as I went. Back in the kitchen, I locked the door, threw the bolts, and stood breathless with dread. If I'd stopped to think about it, I wouldn't have known who or what I was running from. A terrifying thought ran through my head. Could this Kitty ghost story be true? Did her ghost still visit this house to meet her lover, Willie? Was it *her* presence I'd felt in the attic and just now in the barn? Was *her* ghost still killing men at Lowna Ford?

My rational brain was screaming at me not to be ridiculous. The trouble was I couldn't think straight. My world had been turned upside down by Mum's death and the revelation of her secret life. I couldn't even be sure if memories of my childhood and family life were true or false. I'd been shaken to the core by her deception, so much so that nothing in my life seemed real anymore. And because I couldn't make sense of that, I no longer knew what to think or believe.

Thirteen

Kitty

Sunday, 1787 – **Autumn Equinox**

Kitty awoke with a start as freezing cold water splashed onto her face. She looked up to see Mabel standing next to her bed with a jug of water poised to pour over her. She struggled to sit up. "What are you *doing*?"

Mabel's piggy brown eyes glared back, and Kitty shuddered. What a sight Mabel looked in that voluminous nightdress covering her ample figure. With her frizzy red hair and fleshy cheeks, she was enough to frighten anyone.

"Get up, you lazy girl." Mabel grasped Kitty's bedcovers and flung them back. "You should have lit the kitchen range ages ago. Mrs Pickering is down there now and sent me to find you." A satisfied smile spread across her lips. "You will be in trouble."

Kitty groaned and rubbed her eyes. "Why did you not wake me?" she asked, although she already knew the answer. Mabel hated her. From the first morning Kitty had arrived at the house, Mabel's moon shaped face had formed into an ugly frown. She had not met Mabel before, so there was no previous animosity between them. But she guessed anyone coming in to work in the kitchen would receive the same treatment. Mabel was determined to assert her authority, no doubt terrified she would be pushed out by any newcomer. Their jobs were vital to the survival of their families. Although Kitty had no family to worry about now, the only thing keeping her sane was the thought of marrying Willie and moving in with his family.

She swung her legs out of bed and stood up. The room swam and she gripped the wall to stop herself falling.

"What is wrong with you?" Mabel asked. "You were dead on your feet all day yesterday."

"I am fine," said Kitty, unwilling to admit to Mabel of all people that she felt unwell. "Would you please light the range this morning for me," she asked. "Just this once. I will not sleep in again."

Mabel stared at her in annoyance and stomped out of the room.

Kitty closed her eyes. Whenever that feeling of hopelessness came over her, she conjured up a picture of Willie's smiling face and remembered that wonderful first night together in the barn. He had been so gentle in his lovemaking. From then on, they had met every Sunday afternoon in secret at Lowna Ford up on the Moors. It was a private place where they could swim in the river together and make love without prying eyes around. What a wonderful couple of months it had been.

She suddenly jolted. Today was Sunday. *Their* day. She had not seen Willie for three weeks because the weather had been so bad. Storms and relentless rain made the fields and tracks soggy and treacherous. Despite the weather, she had walked up to Lowna Ford every Sunday afternoon in the hope he would be there. He had not been, but she understood why. He always refused to ride his horse far in those conditions. And she could not remember a wetter time. Would she be able to see him today? There were no windows in the stone walls of the attic where she and

Mabel slept, so she listened hard. Her heart sank at the sound of rain pattering down on the thatch. Oh Lord, not again. Please, not again.

Kitty felt total despair at first, then she straightened up resolutely. She would see Willie today. She could not wait any longer. She must urge him to tell his family about her and get on with their marriage plans. There was no time to lose.

She went over to the bowl of water on the stool and splashed her face, gasping at the icy coldness of it. Then she dressed and went down to the kitchen. She stopped outside the door and steeled herself for the scolding she would get from Mrs Pickering. To her relief, the mistress was nowhere to be seen. Only Mabel was in there, bent over the range and stoking up the fire.

"Oh, you have lit it," Kitty cried with pleasure. "Thank you, Mabel."

Mabel scowled and went over to sit at the table where she had prepared two bowls of hot milk and slices of bread. "Sit down and eat," she said.

Kitty's stomach lurched at the sight of food. "I am not hungry."

Mabel pushed the kitchen chair opposite out with her foot. "Sit!" she barked. "You will feel better with food inside you."

Reluctantly, Kitty did as she was told and tore off a piece of bread. She dipped it in the milk and tried to eat. However much she chewed though, she just could not swallow anything.

Mabel looked at her. "You're as pale as a ghost. Do you need to see the doctor?"

Kitty's eyes widened with fear. "No," she said, quickly. "I am ailing a little this morning, that is all. It must have been something I ate last night."

Mabel's eyes narrowed. "You ate exactly the same as me, and I am not ill."

Kitty swallowed some bread in an act of defiance and felt her stomach turn again. Determined, she tore off another piece to dip into the milk. "Do not worry yourself, Mabel. I am fine."

Mabel raised her eyebrows but said nothing more as she slurped her way through her food. Watching Mabel eat always put Kitty off her own. She tried to ignore the droplets of milk running down Mabel's wobbly chin and prayed she would get up and leave when she had finished her breakfast. Mabel did not. She sat back in her chair and smacked her lips with satisfaction. Then she gave Kitty a sly glance.

"You know that Willie Dixon, over in Hutton-Le-Hole," she said.

Kitty's heart squeezed at the mention of his name, but she did not dare show any reaction.

"They say he is getting married," Mabel went on.

Kitty's spirits soared with happiness. Willie must have told his family about her. They must have agreed. Oh, thank you, Lord. Everything was going to be all right.

"Yes," Mabel went on. "He has been seen with the daughter of that wealthy farmer over in Castleton. What is her name now?" She made a show of trying to think hard. "You know the girl I am talking about, do you not? The big heifer, with the bouncy curls." Mabel let out a raucous laugh. "Never done a day's work in her life that one. Hands as smooth as silk."

The stab of shock Kitty felt was swift and true, as if someone had pushed a knife into her. Her heart started pounding and her head swam. It could not be true. Willie would never do that. Never.

Mabel's eyes bored into her. "You should see your face, girl. Why are you so shocked?"

Kitty felt tears pricking behind her eyes and she fought to hold them back. Mabel was the last person she would ever talk to about Willie. But there was a cruel gleam of amusement in Mabel's eyes that made Kitty wonder if she already knew. How could that be possible? They had kept everything so secret. She felt panic rising inside her. Had someone seen her standing outside Willie's house on Midsummer night? Or heard them making love in the barn? She felt her cheeks redden. Maybe someone had seen them swimming naked and canoodling at Lowna Ford, their secret place.

Her head was pounding as hard as her heart now and she shivered as ripples of nausea washed through her. She fought to keep the sickness inside, but she could not stop it. Jumping up from the table, she bolted out of the back door into the rain. She had just made it round to the back of the stable building when she heaved her breakfast up all over the sodden grass. Bent over double, she groaned as every wave shuddered through her.

"That must have been a right horrible breakfast," a voice behind her said.

She spun round to see John, the stable lad, grinning at her. "Oh, it is you," she said, glad it was him and not anyone else. They had known each other since childhood, having lived in neighbouring tied cottages on the Lord of the Manor's estate. A few years older than her, John was a cheeky lad, with his ruddy face and lanky dark hair, and not much taller than her. He had been initially employed by Mr Pickering to labour in the fields, but John was an accomplished rider. His father looked after the Lord of the Manor's horses on the estate and had taught John everything he knew about riding and caring for them. Because they were so close as children, John's father had kindly taught Kitty to ride too, and her mother never ceased to tell her what a lucky girl she was. One day, John hoped to take over his father's job on the estate. Meanwhile, proving himself such a hard worker, Mr Pickering had elevated John to taking care of his horses. A position John treasured.

"Come inside the stable," John said to Kitty. "You will catch your death out here in the rain." He shepherded her inside and pulled out a wooden stool. "Sit there," he said, gently pushing her down onto it. He went over to a bucket of water, dipped a beaker into it, and came back to offer it to her.

She turned up her nose.

"The water is fresh," he said. "The horses have not drunk from it yet."

She accepted the beaker and took a swig. The cold water rushed down into her stomach, cooling the inferno inside her. "Thank you," she said, softly.

"What is the matter, lass?" he asked. "You look awful."

"Just something I ate."

He made a grimace. "My mutton stew last night was nothing but fat. Enough to make anyone sick up their guts." He beamed a warm grin at her.

Just looking at John's round face, and mess of uncombed hair made Kitty smile. His clothes were always covered in a film of dust and mud, but that was because he worked all the time. His diligence had not only been rewarded with the job of looking after the horses but taking care of Mr Pickering's brand-new carriage too. John was so delighted with it; he cleaned and polished it to a shine every day. Even Kitty admired its four wheels and harness for two horses. But the best thing of all was the latest leather folding top that kept passengers dry. It was so much better than their single horse cart. Once a month, John would drive the horses to York with Mr Pickering sitting proudly in the carriage. Sometimes Mrs Pickering would go too to do some shopping. But the outing was mostly for business. York was a centre for the wool trade in the north and Mr Pickering had one of the largest flocks of sheep in the area and in turn was one of the wealthiest farmers. The only other outings were to visit relatives or neighbours in the area and to church on Sunday.

"Are you driving the carriage to church today?" she asked.

John nodded, happily. "We are going over to Lastingham, to St Mary's Church. The new vicar has arrived at last, and Mrs Pickering is keen to be one of the first to meet him."

Kitty's heart leapt. That meant Willie and his family would be there too. His mother would not want to miss out on such an occasion. She glanced up at John. "Could I come to church with you?"

He looked surprised. "In the carriage?"

"Yes."

"You will have to ask Mrs Pickering."

Kitty looked dejected. "She will not let me ride in the carriage."

John gave her a sympathetic smile. "Well, the whole family are going so-"

"Can I borrow one of the horses, then? You know I ride well."

He looked shocked. "No, lass. You cannot. I would lose my job." His brow knitted into a frown. "Why do you want to go to St Mary's so badly?" His eyes locked onto hers. "Are you wanting to see someone in particular?" he asked. "And do not tell me it is the new vicar that you are so anxious to meet?"

Kitty jolted. Did he know about her and Willie? Did everyone know? She stiffened. "Why should I not want to see the new vicar?" she asked.

His eyes lingered on hers, then travelled down to her stomach. "That sickness," he said, gently. "I hope that…"

His words trailed away as Kitty stood up abruptly and smoothed down her dress.

"Be careful, lass," he said. "You do not want to lose your job, do you?"

Kitty tossed her head and walked away with as much dignity as she could muster. Underneath, she frantically worried that everyone knew about her and Willie. But then, she reasoned, they were going to find out soon enough anyway. Perhaps it would not be so bad if word had got out. But she was in turmoil nonetheless with all sorts of emotions bubbling around. There was no way she would be able to calm down until she saw Willie again and told him their news. She had not dared to go to the doctor to confirm it, but she did not need to. She recognised the changes in her body and the morning sickness. A baby! She hugged herself and felt a warm glow ripple through her. One thing was for sure. Willie had to marry her quickly now that she was pregnant.

She looked over her shoulder at the stables as she walked back to the house. John was still staring after her, but a plan was coming together in her mind. When they had all left in the carriage for St Mary's, she would saddle up one of the other horses and ride over on her own. She could tether the horse in a nearby field where no-one would see it. The church was large, the biggest in the area, so she could creep in once the service had started and hide at the back behind the pillars. Willie never liked going to church. He always sat away from his family at the back so that he could get out quickly and before the vicar got up the aisle to talk to everyone as they left. She would be able to get Willie outside on his own, talk to him, and be back at the farm long before the Pickerings returned, especially as they were attending a meal in honour of the new vicar after the service. It was also Mabel's day off and she was going to see her family.

No-one would ever know that she had taken the horse and no-one, but Willie, would see her. Relief flooded through her. Now that she had a plan, it felt like a weight had been lifted. She did not believe Mabel's nonsense about that Castleton girl. Willie would never do that. Nonetheless, a little warning voice in the back of her head told her it was more important than ever to see him today, claim him as her betrothed, and tell him their happy news.

Fourteen

Grace

Hutton-Le-Hole
Present Day

Next morning, I was woken up by a banging on my bedroom door. "Yoo-hoo," a cheerful voice shouted from outside. "You up yet, Grace?"

I was still in a deep sleep after my disturbed night, and it took a while for me to come round. "What time is it?" I croaked back.

"Time you were up." Sam waltzed in with a tray. "Tea, milady?" She curtsied while trying not to drop anything, then laughed at herself. "Honestly, Grace, I don't know how you can sleep in so late. It's nearly nine o'clock. We must be at Scarborough police station at 11." She put the tray down on the bedside table and went over to pull open the front curtains. Watery October sunshine filtered in through the window, lighting up the room.

"Ha!" she said, peering out the window. "Come and have a look at this."

I propped myself up on the pillow, in no mood to spring out of bed. "Just tell me," I said.

"It's Evie." She smiled at me, then turned back. "She's out there on her yoga mat meditating. She's got her crystals out too. She says they protect her. God knows what from though?"

"From you," I said. "And the negative energy you radiate towards her."

"I do not," Sam said, huffily. "Anyway, you'll be pleased to know she's in a better frame of mind this morning. She got up at 7.30 and had some breakfast. Now she's out there doing yoga and meditation. It's all good, wouldn't you say?"

I wasn't so sure about that, remembering last night in the kitchen, when Evie told DCI Blake that Kitty's ghost was in the room listening to him. That was neither rational nor sane. Nor, I had to admit, was my reaction in the middle of the night after my trip to the barn. I sighed and reached over to pour myself a cup of tea. This house was getting to Evie and me. I wondered if Sam had picked up on anything too. "What do you think about this house, Sam?"

She turned to me. "It's just lovely."

"Yes, but…" I hesitated. "Have you felt any strange vibes?"

"Strange vibes?" She gave me a stern look. "Don't tell me you believe Evie's ghostly nonsense?"

"No," I said, quickly. "But, well…" So, I started telling her the story from the night before about going out to feed Rufus and finding him living in the barn.

"That cat is driving you crazy," Sam said. "And climbing up some old ladder was madness. Supposing you'd fallen? We wouldn't have heard you calling for help."

I told her about the heart and initials carved into the wall and my feeling that they belonged to Kitty and Willie.

Sam shrugged in her nonchalant way. "So what? If Willie had lived in this house, they could well be his and Kitty's."

Then I told her about the presence I'd felt both in the attic and barn last night, and the breath on the back of my neck. I expected her to laugh or call me an idiot, but she didn't. She frowned which prompted me to ask: "Have you experienced anything like that in the house, Sam? Or noticed anything strange?"

"Well…" It was her turn to hesitate. "Now that you mention it, I have felt somehow that I'm not *welcome* here." She turned to me. "But I just thought that was Evie. She's been on my case since we left London."

It was the first time I'd looked at Sam close-up since she'd come into the room. She was avoiding my eye, but I saw hers were bloodshot, with dark circles underneath. That was the alcohol. But there was something else in her expression, an underlying tension. Worry even. That wasn't like Sam.

She went on: "I thought, well, I thought maybe I was getting some negative vibes from you." She searched my eyes. "Am I, Grace? You do want me here, don't you?"

I was surprised she would ever think such a thing. "Don't be ridiculous. I love having you here. And Evie."

She looked at me as if to check I was being serious, then gave a relieved smile. "Now," she said, checking her watch. "I'd better go and start your breakfast, or we'll never get to Scarborough. Poached eggs on toast all right?"

"Wonderful." I smiled. "I'll have to hire you as housekeeper, seeing as you curtsy so well."

"Cheeky mare." She went to get up then stopped. "I'm sorry about last night, Grace, I had a bit too much to drink in the pub. I'll apologise to DCI Blake when I see him today." Then she left the room before I could say anything else.

As I sat sipping my tea, I thought about what Sam had said. I couldn't have coped here without her. Yes, she could be annoying, especially when drunk, but she was also a good friend. So, why would she feel she wasn't wanted in this house?

★ ★ ★

When we eventually got into the car, I sat in the front passenger seat, Evie in the back, with Sam driving. She was a surprisingly cautious driver, given her boundless energy.

"Can you drive out of the village that way, Sam." I pointed to the narrow road with the residents-only sign. "Last night, DCI Blake told me a man called Patrick Hardy lives in the end cottage. He thought I should have a word with him about Mum."

"Has he been looking after the house?" Sam asked.

"I don't know, but I'm going to call on him when we get back this afternoon."

We studied the quaint houses and cottages lining the road as we drove along.

"Amazing that we never seem to see anyone out and about," Sam said. "All sorts of people live here, you know. I found out in the pub last night that there's even a space engineer who used to work for NASA living in a house that used to be the old post office. Apparently, he was born here, spent most of his career working in America and came back to retire."

"Just shows you how strong the pull is to return to our roots," Evie piped up from the back. "It's who we are." She paused. "Maybe that's why ghosts hang around. They don't want to leave their roots."

Sam and I ignored that. We didn't want to encourage Evie with any more conversation about ghosts. "Stop outside the last cottage, Sam," I said. "I want to have a look."

She pulled up and we sat looking at the dwelling. It was at the opposite end of the village to Mum's house and built from the same old stone, with a pantile roof. A wooden picket fence encircled a small front garden. A gate and path led up to a white-painted door. The cottage had the same sash windows as Mum's and was probably just as old. I noticed an unsealed road running alongside it, which had to be the entrance to the lane that ran along the back of all the houses on this side of the village.

"Sweet little cottage," Evie said. "Look at those pink roses. They've done well to last into October."

Sam glanced at me. "Want me to come with you later to see this Patrick Hardy?"

I shook my head. "Thanks, but I'll be fine." I wasn't feeling so sure though. If he had been such a good friend of Mum's, why hadn't he been in touch with me before? Or come along to see us? For some inexplicable reason, I felt strange, exposed even, sitting there, I said: "Come on. Let's go or we'll be late."

"Okay." Sam pressed down on the accelerator and off we went. "If I've read the map correctly," she said, "we drive to the end of this road and turn left onto the A170 which should take us most of the way to Scarborough."

We were quiet for a while as Sam drove, each with our own thoughts. Now I was out of the house and village, the sunshine and fluffy clouds scudding across the blue sky lifted my spirits. There wasn't much traffic about, but the farmers were active in the fields. "Look at the size of those combine harvesters," I said, "they're massive."

"Tell me about it," Sam said. "I met one on the road coming back from the shops yesterday and almost ended up in a ditch. They're too wide for these lanes."

"They're late finishing the harvest," Evie said. "Michaelmas was the 29th of September. It should have all been in by then."

"Not in this wet autumn," I said. "I bet they've lost a lot of crops. Must be hard farming in our unpredictable climate?"

"Oh, look," Evie said. "There's a corn doll hanging on that gate."

I looked out the window, but we'd gone past it. "What's a corn doll?" I asked.

"Saxon farmers began the custom," Evie said. "They believed the last sheath contained the spirit of the corn, who was a descendent of the Roman goddess of grain, Ceres." She smiled. "No-one wanted to anger her for fear of the next harvest failing, so they kept the corn dolls until the following spring to ensure the continuation of a good crop."

It seemed there was nothing that teacher Evie didn't know about. We all lapsed into silence again until Evie suddenly asked: "What were you doing in the garden in the middle of the night, Grace?"

I looked over my shoulder. "You saw me?"

"Yes. Something woke me up."

"That must have been me," I said. "Sorry. I couldn't sleep, so I got up. It was a clear night. The rain had stopped, and a stunning full moon lit up the garden. I saw Rufus sitting on the gatepost, as if he was guarding the house."

"I expect he was," Evie said.

"Don't be daft," Sam said. "Cats don't protect property like dogs."

"Yes, they do," Evie said. "Not in the same way, of course, but they do define their patch and protect it. They probably consider humans as part of their territory. In their minds, I guess they own the humans. It's the other way around with dogs." She paused, then continued. "Just look back in history. Cats have always been mysterious creatures and associated with the supernatural. Look at witchcraft. In ancient times, they were said to have the ability to ward off evil spirits."

Sam gave an impatient sigh, which she did whenever Evie went on about spirits and ghosts. She didn't say anything though. Nor did I.

"How was Rufus?" Evie asked.

"He's been living in the old barn," I said. "Probably on mice and bats."

Evie chuckled. "I'm glad he's all right."

"Seems to be," I said. "God knows how I'm going to catch him when it's time to go home."

"He'll come when he knows we're leaving," Evie said. "He's just enjoying the freedom of the countryside."

Sam rolled her eyes.

"What else did you find in the barn, Grace?" Evie asked.

I hadn't told her I'd been in the barn so she must have seen me go in. "Nothing much. Just an old workbench and tools." I was going to say I'd got spooked in there but stopped myself. I didn't want to add to Evie's paranoia. "I saw a lovers' heart chiselled into the stone wall by the door of the barn," I went on, "with the initials WD and KG inside it?"

She nodded. "Willie Dixon and Kitty Garthwaite."

"They could be anybody's initials," Sam said.

Evie shook her head. "They're Kitty and Willie's." She paused. "Kitty died in 1787 so they must have been done around that time or just before."

Sam was losing patience. "You must stop thinking about this ghost story, Evie," she said. "And please stop talking about it. If you come out with this at the police station and you stick to your story that you can't remember anything about Saturday night, or rather the early hours of Sunday morning, they'll think you're crazy. I'm sorry if that sounds blunt, but…" She paused for breath. "Look, why don't you tell us why you went to Lowna Ford? And why drive Violet's car up there?"

Evie's green eyes flashed in my passenger mirror.

Sam went on. "We only want to help you, Evie. A lad has been murdered. You were at the crime scene. It's serious."

"I've *told* you the truth," Evie said, hotly. "I don't know... I can't remember." She paused. "I'm sure I didn't kill that lad. It can't have been me," she said, her voice pleading with us to believe her. "I'm telling you the truth. I don't remember *anything* about that night."

Sam glanced across at me. "They're going to arrest her if she sticks to this story. You know that; don't you?"

I knew Sam was right. The police didn't believe my explanation that Evie was sleepwalking either. Now, it suddenly occurred to me that we were all sleepwalking into disaster. "What the hell are we thinking," I said. "We need a solicitor. We should have one with us."

"Where are we going to get one from now?" Sam looked at her watch. "We're due at the police station in 30 minutes."

"We'll ask for the duty solicitor," I said. "The police can't question us without legal representation if we insist."

"I don't think we are being questioned," Sam said. "DCI Blake said he wanted a voluntary statement from each of us." She paused. "By the way, I found out all about our Detective Chief Inspector in the pub last night." She nodded when I looked at her. "The village of Hutton-le-Hole is part of the Manor of Spaunton," she went on. "It's all common land, 7,000 acres apparently, and owned by the same family – DCI Blake's family. His father lives in a huge house on the Moors when he's not in London, which is most of the time it seems. He's still got the title Lord of the Manor, would you believe? DCI Blake doesn't live with him. He lives in a house in Lastingham, which is the next village to ours. Alone by all accounts."

"You missed your vocation," I said, drily. "*You* should be the detective."

"What I did find interesting," she went on, "is that no-one wanted to tell me anything else about him. I did try, but every time I asked a direct question, they changed the subject. I got the distinct impression there's something about Chief Inspector Blake that people weren't comfortable talking about." She shrugged. "Black sheep of the family perhaps?"

"He's a *liar*, that's what he is," Evie shouted from the back. "He said Kitty's ghost was responsible for killing several men at the same spot where Kitty died."

"No, he didn't, Evie." I had to put her straight. "He said that's what some people believe."

Evie didn't want to be corrected. "I heard you both talking. *He* said Kitty's ghost sat naked on the banks of the river luring those men to their deaths. That's a *lie*," she said, darkly. "Made up by men and kept alive by men like DCI Blake."

I wanted to let the subject drop so as not to throw any more fuel onto Evie's fire. I noticed Sam's lips were pursed tight too. She was showing unusual restraint.

But Evie wouldn't shut up. "They treated Kitty shamefully," she went on. "Men get away with everything. They get women pregnant and then move on. I suppose it was some *jampot* who enticed Willie away. That's what they called loose women back then. Jampots. Bees around honey. *You* should know the meaning of that word, Sam."

I saw Sam shudder, but still she said nothing.

Evie wasn't finished. "Kitty had no-one to turn to," she said. "Not a soul in the world. Those *treacherous* men deserved to die."

That was the final straw for Sam. She braked, swung into the kerb next to a row of shops, and parked the car. I braced myself for a slanging match between them, but it never came. Sam grabbed her bag and pointed to a cafe by the side of the road. "I'm going in there for coffee." She took a deep breath and turned round to face Evie. "And when I come back, let's not say another word about Kitty and that ghost story, all right?"

It was the venom in Evie's eyes as she glared back that shook me. If the old saying was right and looks could kill, Sam would have been dead on the spot.

Fifteen

The cry of seagulls rang out when Evie and I stood on the pavement outside Scarborough's Police HQ. I looked up to see them wheeling about in their never-ending quest for food. In the distance, over the tops of buildings, water glistened in sunlight. The sea always drew a sense of excitement from me. There was something about its vastness, and the fascinating world beyond its horizon. I was dying to get down to the seafront, but we had to deal with the police first. I looked up at their two nondescript low-rise office blocks and gave Evie's arm an encouraging squeeze. I felt anything but optimistic though. This was all my fault. I'd encouraged Evie to come on this holiday. Now she'd somehow found herself mixed up in a murder and we were all implicated.

"Don't worry," she said, as if reading my thoughts. "I'm not going to say anything wrong. I will continue my line that I can't remember what happened while I was out on the Moors." She gave me a sideways look and winked. I wasn't sure how to take that. "Anyway," she went on, "if they had any real evidence that I killed that lad, they'd have arrested me by now." She gave me a small smile that lit up her green eyes as she pulled me towards the entrance. For a moment, she seemed more like her old self. "Come on, Grace. The sooner we get this over with, the sooner we can go for a paddle."

Things immediately got off on the wrong foot when it wasn't DCI Blake who greeted us in the waiting room, it was his sidekick, Stella Gray, or *Detective* Sergeant Gray as she emphasised when she came in. Today, she was all in black. Trouser suit, polo neck jumper and the same shiny Chelsea boots. Her silver-grey hair looked even more striking against her clothes and sun-tanned skin. She must spend all her spare time on the beach or out on the sea sailing or paddleboarding to get that bronzed. She looked fit too. Standing there now, despite her small stature, she somehow oozed authority and power.

She smiled as if she could read my thoughts. "Where's your friend, Sam?"

"Parking the car," I said. "She'll be here soon."

DS Gray nodded and turned to Evie. "I'd like to take your statement first."

It sounded more like an order than a request and I intervened. "We'd like a solicitor, please. We haven't had time to organise one. Can we request your duty solicitor?"

DS Gray's face fell ever so slightly. "There's no duty solicitor here," she said. "We'll have to call for one and you might have to wait a long time. Hours even."

"That's fine," I said. "We can come back later."

She shook her head. "Evie is a person of interest and DCI Blake wants her statement this morning." She paused. "We'll have to keep her here in the cells otherwise."

That really irritated me. "Where is DCI Blake?"

"Out on a call."

"We'll wait for him to come back," I said.

Evie sighed and put a hand on my arm. "It's fine, Grace. I'll give my statement now. I've got nothing to hide." She faced Glamour Cop and said: "Please put it on the record that I'm giving you a voluntary statement."

DS Gray nodded. "Follow me." She turned and walked out with Evie trailing behind.

I sat down and glanced at the clock, 11.15. I wished I'd brought a book with me because I had nothing to do but read the crime stopper notices on the wall opposite. It didn't help that the whole waiting room was dreary. Grey walls, grey desk, plastic chairs. Depressing in every way.

At 11.34 I looked at my watch, wondering where Sam was. I sent her a text. *Having trouble parking? Evie's giving her statement now. The police will need yours too. Gx*

Ten minutes went by before she replied. *Had to park in multi-storey place in town. Be there in 10. S x*

I watched the minutes tick by on the wall clock, getting ever more anxious about Evie. How long did it take to make a voluntary statement? I'd never had to do one before.

It was Sam who appeared first just before noon. She looked just as slim and stylish as DS Gray in her black trousers and leopard-print fleece.

"Is Evie still in there?" she asked, breezily, as if we were in a doctor's waiting room.

"Yes. I'm worried. I asked for the duty solicitor, but DS Gray said we'd have to wait for hours to get one and that she'd have to keep Evie here until then."

Sam frowned. "Has she gone in without one?"

"Yes."

"Is that wise?"

I sighed. "Probably not, but Evie is just giving a voluntary statement."

"I thought DCI Blake was going to be here."

"He's been called out, so we've got Glamour Cop instead." I looked at her. "Evie's going to stick to her story and say she can't remember anything about going out on the Moors."

Sam groaned. "The police aren't going to believe her."

"Well, I'll confirm that I saw Evie sleepwalking that evening. I am a doctor. As I've already said umpteen times, it's perfectly possible for people to walk, drive, cook or whatever while in that phase of deep sleep." I looked at Sam.

But she wouldn't meet my eye. "Let's just hope she doesn't start going on about seeing Kitty Garthwaite's ghost," she said.

We chatted on for a while about Evie and her partner Trevor, speculating about the woman he'd gone off with. Finally, at 12.30, Evie came back in followed by DS Gray. Evie's cheeks were flushed and her eyes feverish.

I stood up. "Everything all right?"

Evie sat down on the chair next to mine. Her hands were shaking in her lap.

DS Gray turned to us. "I'd like to take your statement next, Sam."

Sam looked her straight in the eye. "I'm Samantha," she said. "Samantha Whitlock."

DS Gray gave a curt nod.

For God's sake, don't rile her Sam, I thought. It'll only make things worse for Evie. Maybe for all three of us.

After they'd both left the room, I turned to Evie. "How'd you get on?"

Evie clenched her fists. "That woman is convinced I did it. She *accused* me of murdering Joe Dunstan."

My stomach turned. I should never have let Evie go in there without a solicitor.

Evie's voice was cracking with emotion. "She kept asking me the same questions over and over. She didn't believe a word I said and kept saying I should tell the truth and not waste police time. I thought she was going to charge me with murder. I really did."

Inside, I was furious. Furious with DS Gray, but even more so with myself for letting things get this far. "I thought you were just making a voluntary statement," I said.

"So did I, but she just kept going on and on."

"I expect she was just testing you, Evie." I was trying to make her feel better. "She probably came over a bit strong."

Evie shook her head. "I'm telling you that woman is convinced I'm guilty. I can see it in her eyes."

I didn't know what else to say to comfort Evie, so I put my arm around her and felt her trembling. She was emotionally and physically in turmoil, and I was afraid for her.

Fortunately, we didn't have to wait long for Sam. She was back in 15 minutes.

"I've done my statement," she said. "Stella said to send you in, Grace."

"Stella?" I asked, drily, surprised they were on Christian name terms after their frostiness earlier.

Sam shrugged in her usual way. "I didn't have much to say. I told her that all I did was get to the house late with you two on Saturday night, go to bed, and do some shopping in Kirkbymoorside the next day, which was after the body was found." She paused. "She was fine with me."

"Well, she really upset Evie," I said, glancing over at her hunched and silent figure.

"She should have had a solicitor with her," Sam said.

Of course, Sam was right, but I could have thumped her anyway.

"She's trying to frame me," Evie said, flatly, her eyes glued to the floor.

Sam gave me a resigned look. "You'd better go in, Grace. The sooner you get your statement over and done with, the sooner we can get out of here."

I nodded. "Where do I go?"

"Turn left out of here. It's the last door on the right."

"Wait here for me," I whispered in Sam's ear. "And don't let Evie out of your sight."

I was cross when I walked into the interview room. Very cross. I had allowed Evie to make a statement without a solicitor and that was stupid of me. Now, I needed to deal with the police in an entirely professional manner. I steeled myself for the encounter.

But DS Gray just smiled and stood politely as I entered the room. "Please," she said, indicating to a chair opposite her at the large table in the room. "Take a seat."

I sat down. The only furniture in the room was that table, the two chairs we were sitting on, and a smaller table with a machine on. Yet another drab, nondescript room, with a very musty smell that made me wonder who'd been in there overnight. I sat down on the edge of the chair, back upright. "My friend Evie is upset." I kept my voice low and even. "Last night, DCI Blake said he wanted statements from all three of us. When we arrived, that's what you said too. We thought we were giving *voluntary* statements. Evie says you grilled her, then accused her of murder."

The DS frowned and put her pen down on the table. She had the table lamp on between us which lit up her face rather than mine, making her angular features seem more pronounced.

"DCI Blake did ask me to take voluntary statements from you ladies." Her tone was firm but reasonable. "That's all I'm doing." She looked up at me. "I assure you I did not accuse Evie of murder."

I looked at the machine on the adjacent table. "Are we being recorded?"

"No."

"Why is Evie so upset then?"

"Let's be honest," she said in a calm voice. "Evie was upset before she walked in here, wasn't she?"

That was true. Evie had been truculent on the drive over and wasn't in the best of moods. "In that case," I said, "perhaps it wasn't a good idea to question her in that way?"

"This is a murder investigation, Grace." She paused. "May I call you Grace?"

I nodded, thinking it was better to keep on her good side if I could.

"Then please call me Stella. It's easier." She hesitated. "As I said, this is a murder investigation. We are a small team and under pressure to get a result. Unfortunately, we don't have a lot of time." She sighed. "All I asked Evie for was a statement about her movements after she arrived in Hutton-le-Hole with you on Saturday night and when she went out on Sunday morning."

I studied the woman's impassive face and wasn't sure what to think. Had Evie got it all wrong? She *was* in a highly strung state. I had some sympathy for the pressures of police work too. I knew all about stress and dealing with the public and DS Gray did seem reasonable. I felt uncomfortable though, but that could have been down to being in a police station and the seriousness of the crime of murder. Wanting to get this over with, I took the initiative. "Shall I just explain my movements?"

"Please do." She picked up her pen again and started writing as I spoke.

"On Saturday, Evie was with Sam and me in the car all the way to Hutton-le-Hole. We arrived late at the house, having stopped in Thirsk for dinner. I can give you the name and address of the pub if you want to check that out."

I paused to allow DS Gray to finish writing, then went on. "It was dark when we arrived at the house. I couldn't tell you the exact time, but it was around 10.30 or 11 o'clock. We unpacked the car, settled in, and went to bed." I paused again. "I woke up in the night." I hesitated at that point, I wasn't going to tell her I'd heard crying or anything strange. "When I came down to the kitchen," I continued, "as I told you when you brought Evie home yesterday, I found the back door open and wet footprints nearby. Someone had been in the house and left quickly, probably when they heard me."

This time, as the DS scribbled down my words, I noticed the large, silver ring on the middle finger of her right hand. The black stone in the centre looked like Whitby jet, which I knew was produced in the area.

"Did you see anyone in the garden?" she asked. "Can you give me a description?"

"I'm afraid not. All I saw was a flickering light up at the barn, at the end of the garden. It could have been a torch."

"Who did you think it was?" she asked.

I shrugged. "I have no idea."

She looked at me. "Did you think of calling us…the police?"

"We went through all this when you called at the house with DCI Blake yesterday."

She tapped her pen on the paper. "For the record, please."

I sighed. "Yes, I did think of calling the police because I thought it was a burglary. Then I saw the door hadn't been forced and could only think that someone had let themselves in with a key. I wondered if someone had been looking after the house and came in to investigate when they saw the lights on."

"Someone?" She looked up from her writing at that point. "You don't know if anyone was looking after the house. Your mother's house."

I stiffened. "No."

"How are you finding it?" she asked. "The house, I mean."

I looked at her. "I'm not sure what you are asking."

She explained. "All houses have an atmosphere of some kind, don't you think? Peaceful. Sad. Happy. Welcoming or unwelcoming."

The question was strange, and I wondered if Evie had been talking about seeing Kitty's ghost. I wasn't going to stray into that territory. "I find my mother's house entirely peaceful," I said, although that wasn't true.

She shuffled in her chair. "Did it occur to you that the middle of the night was an odd time for whoever was looking after your mother's house to come in?"

"As I said before, they must have seen the lights on and were worried. They probably panicked when they came in and discovered we were there."

"And left without closing the door?"

That point had stuck in my mind too, but I wasn't going to say so.

"Right, let's move on." DS Gray paused to reread her notes. "Yesterday," she went on, "you told us that Evie had been sleepwalking that evening."

"Yes. After I'd locked the kitchen door, I was about to go back to bed when Evie came down the stairs and started pacing around. She looked right through me and kept bumping into the furniture. I knew from my medical training it was a classic case of sleepwalking."

The DS's eyes were bright with interest. "Did Evie say anything at the time?"

"She was mumbling under her breath, but nothing coherent that I could make out."

The DS leant forward. "What did Evie look like while she was sleepwalking?"

Another weird question. "What do you mean?"

"What expression did she have on her face?" she asked. "Smiling? Laughing? Upset?"

I hesitated to answer because I didn't know what this woman was getting at. I remembered Evie's face was as pale as a wax mask and her eyes dark and feverish as they stared ahead. But I didn't want to say that. "No expression at all," I said. "Much like you would expect from someone sleepwalking."

The DS flicked her biro on and off, impatient with my neutral answers.

"So," I went on, briskly, "I made sure Evie went back to bed, then I returned to my own room. When I got up the next morning, Sam had cooked breakfast. Neither of us had seen Evie. We thought she was still asleep in bed. I went out for a walk on the Moors and well, you and DCI Blake were there when I got back to the house."

The DS's eyes pierced mine. "Do you think Evie was sleepwalking when she dressed and left the house?"

"She must have been because she says she can't remember anything."

"Did you hear your mother's car start up at the back of the house?"

"No. I didn't even know Mum had a car up there." I shrugged. "It's a wonder it started at all. It must have been parked up for the best part of a year."

"We found the car at Lowna Ford on the morning of the murder, with the keys in the ignition. Do you accept that Evie could have driven it up there?"

I shrugged. "I don't know."

"If she didn't drive it there, who did?"

"I have no idea DS Gray. As I said, I didn't even know Mum had a car parked at the back of her house. Perhaps someone else knew it was there and took it."

"If Evie didn't drive the car, then how did she get to Lowna? It's a few miles from Violet's house. Do you think she could sleepwalk all that way in the darkness of the early hours?"

The tone of her voice told me that she didn't believe it for one minute. I just shrugged, not wanting to give DS Gray any more ammunition to fire at Evie. "I don't know," I said. "I haven't been to Lowna."

She gave me a sceptical look. "Evie *was* there when I arrived."

"Evie says she can't remember anything about that night," I said. "I believe her. She wouldn't remember if she'd been sleepwalking."

"*If* she'd been sleepwalking."

"What are you suggesting?" I asked, sharply.

She leant towards me. "My job is to take the evidence and test it, Grace."

"Evie *was* sleepwalking earlier in the night. I saw her myself. As a practising doctor, I would be willing to swear to that on oath in a court of law."

I saw two pink spots appears on DS Gray's cheeks as if she were either hot or annoyed. Then she said: "Do you want to record in your statement that you've never been to Lowna before?"

"Yes."

"Are you sure?"

"Absolutely."

"Can you confirm that neither of your two friends have been there before either?"

Stick to the truth, I thought. Just stick to the truth. "This is Evie's first visit to the area," I said. "Mine too. And Sam's. None of us have been here before."

I noticed DS Gray raise her left eyebrow ever so slightly. There was something in that gesture that worried me. And when she looked up again, her eyes seemed to pierce right through me if as she were reaching into the corners of my mind. Then she frowned as if she didn't like what she was seeing.

Sixteen

To say I was relieved when the three of us walked out of that police station was an understatement. I glanced at Evie who kept her eyes down as she walked along between Sam and me. While I was being interviewed, another police officer had taken Evie's fingerprints and a DNA sample, which made her even more upset and withdrawn. I was very worried now. The police would surely come knocking again and I could understand why. Even I was having doubts. I was burning to ask Evie all sorts of questions, but her body language was telling me to wait for the right moment. I didn't want to send her over the edge.

I glanced at Sam who was looking every bit as glum as Evie, then up at the sky. The sun was poking out from behind a fluffy cloud, and the wind had dropped. "What shall we do now?" I asked. "Do you want to go down to the sea or return to the house?"

Sam spoke first. "I'd like to walk along the beach and blow away the cobwebs, if that's all right with you two."

"How far is it to the seafront?" I asked.

"Not far," Sam said. "I know the way because I was driving around for ages looking for a parking space." She pointed ahead. "At those traffic lights, we turn left into a pedestrian precinct which will take us down to the seafront." She paused. "Is your ankle up for a walk, Grace?"

I'd been so worried about Evie and the police that I'd almost forgotten about my sprained ankle. It felt so much easier this morning anyway, just some discomfort when I put my weight on. "I'm up for it," I said.

"There are seats along the promenade. You and Evie can have a sit down while I go and explore."

I nodded. "Let's do that, then." I turned to Evie. "If that's okay with you?"

Evie agreed and we set off. The shopping precinct was disappointing, with the same chain stores as in most town centres. I did notice we were descending sharply, which meant a steep climb back up.

"Don't worry," Sam said, as if reading my mind. "I'll get the car when we're ready to go home and pick you up from the seafront."

"Thanks," I said. "What would we do without you, Sam?"

Evie suddenly stopped outside an arts and crafts shop displaying stones and crystals in the window. "I'm going to pop in here for a quick look," she said. "Won't be long."

"Okay," Sam said. "While you're in there, I'll get us some takeaway coffees."

I sat down on a bench while they both disappeared into the shops. All the while my mind was racing through events at the police station. Had DS Gray accused Evie of murdering that boy? Or had Evie misunderstood or overreacted to her questions? Maybe the latter, given Evie's sensitive frame of mind.

Suddenly, as I sat there, goosebumps shivered up my spine despite the sunshine. It was a strange feeling that I couldn't quite put my finger on. It was almost as if I was being watched. I casually looked over my shoulder and thought I saw a figure dart into a shop. It was just a flash of black from the corner of my eye. It could have been anyone or no-one for there were a lot of shoppers around. I told myself I was becoming as paranoid as Evie and was still mulling this over when she came out of the shop and sat down beside me.

"I've got you a present," she said, smiling. Then her face fell as she spotted Sam coming back with the coffees. "I'll give it to you when we're down on the seafront," she whispered.

I knew that meant when Sam wasn't around. She tended to pooh-pooh Evie's belief in crystals. I admit I didn't believe in their healing properties, but I took the view that whatever made people happy or helped them in their daily lives was fine with me.

As I stood up, I glanced fleetingly over my shoulder. No sign of that figure now and I felt ridiculously relieved. The three of us continued walking down the steep hill, still lined with shops and cafes. When we turned the corner, Evie gave a small cry of delight.

There, before us, stretched a stunning beach and sea. It was so unexpectedly glorious that we stood staring at it for a while. The autumn sun sparkled on the water, giving it an almost Mediterranean feel. We walked down to the bottom of the hill and only stopped when we reached the promenade. To the left, I saw what I guessed from the architecture was the older part of town. Set out around a harbour and protected by a rocky headland, the dramatic ruins of a castle stood on the promontory. Behind us, limestone cliffs towered above.

"Look!" Evie pointed. "An old railway lift, to carry people up the cliff to town. We should have come down on it."

"We'll go back up that way," I said.

We stopped at an empty wooden bench, and Evie and I sat down. Sam pointed to the right. "Look, there's a sign for a pavilion and theatre. I'm going to wander along and have a look." She put the tray of coffees down on the seat next to me, pulled one out and strode off, her blonde hair bobbing in the sunshine.

"Look at her," Evie said. "She can't wait to get away."

"She probably feels confined with the pair of us. You know she likes to do her own thing."

"Don't you think she's always had a bit of a selfish streak?"

I pulled a coffee from the tray, took the lid off and saw it was black. That was Evie's and I handed it to her. "Sam has a restless soul and likes to be active."

"Mm, but she puts herself first. Doesn't care much who gets hurt in the process."

I pulled the lid off my latte and took a sip. The liquid slipped down and warmed me up. "That's only because Sam lives on her own and is used to doing whatever she wants. She works in a cut-throat business too. Can't be a wallflower in advertising." I glanced at Evie. "She's been great on this holiday, shopping, cooking and cleaning." I held up my right ankle. "Now she's having to drive us around too."

"That's because she owes you."

"Owes me?" That thought triggered something in my mind and I turned to Evie. "Yesterday you said Sam wasn't the person she seemed to be. You also said it was hard to know whether she was telling the truth or not. Now you say she owes me." I paused. "Why?"

Evie looked down. "Perhaps you should ask *her*."

"About what?"

Evie sighed. "Oh, just ignore me. Sam winds me up, that's all." She pulled a paper bag out of her pocket and handed it to me. "Here. This is for you."

"Oh, thank you." I took the bag and pulled out a small parcel wrapped in pink tissue paper. I carefully opened it to reveal a pretty, silver pendant with an amber stone in the middle. "It's gorgeous, Evie," I said, genuinely delighted. I slipped the long silver chain over my head and the pendant dangled on my jumper.

"I bought it to protect you," Evie said.

I frowned at her. "Do I need protecting?"

"Amber is known as the 'seeing' stone. It's so powerful, it'll help you see things and people clearly."

"Are we back to Sam again?"

"You have a lot to work out for the future, Grace. It's vital you see and understand the past clearly. Only then will you be able to move on and follow your heart."

I chuckled. "You sound like a fortune teller," I said, kindly, knowing she meant well. "Thank you for the pendant, Evie. I really love it."

She looked happy and we fell silent again until she said: "Did you see what that awful policewoman was wearing?"

We were back to DS Gray again. "Her Chelsea boots, you mean?"

"No, the ring."

I remembered it well. "It was silver with a black stone, Whitby jet I thought."

Evie shook her head. "It was black obsidian." She looked at me. "Black obsidian is generally worn for healing and dispelling negative energies. But some people believe it creates a veil of protection, like a cloak that others can't see through or penetrate." She glanced at me. "I know you think I'm going crazy, but I'm not, Grace. That woman is clever. She wants me to be guilty of Joe's murder."

I was silent for a while, turning over what Evie had said in my mind. I agreed that DS Gray was clever but, if I put myself in her shoes, I had to admit that I would be suspicious of Evie too given the facts and circumstances of her being at the crime scene. Of course, I'd known Evie since she was a small child and knew she didn't have a bad bone in her body and couldn't kill anyone. "DS Gray's just doing her job, Evie. Think of all the lowlife she deals with every day. She's probably adopted that brusque approach over the years for self-preservation. It's not easy dealing with the public, is it?" I smiled at her. "Look, let's forget about the police for the time being and enjoy the day. Anyway, once they start following up other leads of enquiry, I'm sure their attention will move away from us. We'll just try and keep our heads down until then."

Evie said nothing more and we drank our coffees in companionable silence until she suddenly asked, "Do you still miss Peter?"

Do I still miss Peter? I knew why she was asking. She was wondering if she'd ever get over Trevor leaving her for another woman.

I sighed. "I missed him like crazy at first. We'd lived together for years, so there were reminders of him everywhere in the flat. I'd get a stab of pain seeing little things of his around the place, like his favourite mug in the cupboard." I turned to Evie. "You know he had this leather tray on the hall table. He'd empty his pockets into it whenever he came in, keys, loose change, that kind of thing. Then he'd load his pockets back up before leaving the next morning. I got so upset at seeing that empty tray all the time I threw the damn thing away."

Evie nodded.

"I kept expecting Peter to walk back in at any moment with all his dirty washing. I kept replaying our last conversation over and over in my head, blaming myself for not going travelling with him as he'd asked so many times." I shook my head at my own turmoil. "As time dragged on and he never got in touch, not even to see how I was or to let me know he was okay, it slowly dawned on me that he wasn't coming back."

"Oh, Grace..."

The sympathy in Evie's voice brought tears to my eyes. "He chose to make a complete break from me, and everything we'd had together," I said. "He could be dead for all I know."

"Do you think he knows Violet's gone?"

I shrugged. "He's cut off all communication, so I haven't told him. No, he's started a new life and he doesn't want me in it. That's just the way it is."

Evie linked her arm through mine. "I guess he thought he was doing the right thing. He loved you and didn't want to hurt you."

Didn't want to hurt me? I stared at her. "He couldn't have hurt me more if he'd tried." Suddenly anger bubbled up. "To say you're going off travelling, then cut all ties is a terrible thing to do. Unkind. Cowardly. You talk about Sam being selfish. Well, Peter has shown his true colours too."

Evie asked, softly: "Would you take him back?"

I had of course asked myself that question over and over until I realised that I was never going to have to answer it. "He's not coming back." My voice was flat. "I know that now."

"Aw, Grace. You didn't deserve that."

I looked at her. "Would you take Trevor back?"

She looked away. "I–I'm not as strong as you. But he's made his choice. He's with this other woman now. She has children from her first marriage and now she's pregnant with Trevor's child." Evie sucked in her breath as if summoning the strength to go on. "It's what he's always wanted... a child. He thought I could never give him one, so he's gone off with someone who can." She paused. "Th–that's how much he loved me."

I squeezed her hand. "I'm sorry, Evie." The words sounded lame, but I didn't know what else to say. "Neither of us picked our men wisely, did we?"

She rested her head on my shoulder. "It's j–just that, well, I don't know w–what to do." Her voice trailed away. "I'm not sure I can face things alone."

"You're not alone. You've got me… and Sam."

"I miss talking to your mother. Violet was always so wise. She loved you, Grace, you know that don't you?"

I tensed. "She's hurt me too, with her secret life up here. I don't know what to think anymore, Evie. I feel like I've been let down by the two people I loved the most, and both at the same time."

"Violet will have had her reasons," Evie said. "I'm sure they were for the best, at least in her mind."

"But she'll never be able to tell me those reasons, will she? Never be able to explain."

Evie shook her head. "I could never think badly of Violet." She paused. "Do you remember the time I played the piano in my first school music exam?"

How could I forget? Evie was a nervous wreck for weeks in the run–up to it.

"Only parents were allowed to watch their children perform," Evie said. "Mum told me she couldn't come because she had an appointment that she couldn't change. Even then I knew she was lying. The truth was my dad wouldn't let her, controlling bastard that he was." Evie's face hardened. "He didn't approve of my piano lessons. Thought they were a waste of time and money." She turned to me. "It was *your* mum who came on the day to support me. Violet told the examiners she was my mother.

They were from outside the school and didn't know the parents anyway, so it wasn't a problem."

I stared at her. I'd had no idea that my mum had supported her in that way. I'd never heard Evie talk about her father like that before either.

She nodded at the surprise on my face. "It was wonderful having Violet there. When I'd finished, she shouted 'bravo' and gave me the loudest clap ever." Evie smiled. "No, I could never think badly of Violet."

We said no more as we watched people walking along the damp sand near the water's edge. They were mostly older folk. I guessed that the flat beach would be crowded in the height of summer, with children eating ice creams and riding donkeys up and down. No-one wanted to brave the water and go for a swim today. The North Sea was too cold at this time of year. It was peaceful though sitting out in the fresh air.

Evie sat up. "Let's go for a paddle."

I lifted my foot. "I'll get my bandage wet."

"Well, I'm going." She pulled off her trainers and socks, trod carefully down the steps to the beach and ran across the sand to the water's edge. There she stopped, waiting for a wave to roll in and cover her feet in cold foamy water. "It's *freezing,*" she squealed, then laughed.

It was good to get a glimpse of the old Evie again and I sat watching her. I was aware of the sound of a car pulling up behind me, but it was only when I heard the door slam and a shadow fell over me that I twisted round to see DCI Blake standing there, blocking out the sun. "Are you following us?" I asked, more sharply than I'd meant to.

He looked surprised. "I saw your friend Sam walking along the promenade and guessed you and Evie wouldn't be too far away."

I pointed to the water's edge. "Evie's down there, but I hope you're not here to ask her any more questions," I said, stiffly.

He sat down next to me on the bench, and we both watched Evie paddling for a moment. He was his usual silent self, which made me start talking. Why did I always fall into that trap? This time, though, I had something I wanted to say. "We had quite a time at the station this morning. Evie was very upset when she came out from her grilling." I turned to him. "We weren't there just to give routine voluntary statements, were we?"

"You were."

"That's not what it felt like with your DS. Evie says she accused her of murdering Joe Dunstan."

DCI Blake wasn't a man to show any reaction, so I continued.

"Apparently, she said she would arrest Evie for wasting police time if she didn't tell her the truth." I turned to him. "Evie's not a liar. She says she can't remember what happened, and I believe her. I keep saying that it's not unusual behaviour in sleepwalkers."

He nodded. "DS Gray is rather direct. She has a heavy workload and doesn't mince her words. She's a good detective though." He sighed. "She's also a single mother, with a couple of grown-up teenagers. They're a right handful that pair, especially the eldest girl. Stella's a devoted mother though. There's nothing she wouldn't do for her kids."

I had of course expected him to defend his colleague, but I wanted to stand up for my friend too. I tried to keep the frostiness out of my voice when I said: "If you want to question us again, we'll need legal representation."

"Of course. But please remember we have a job to do, Grace. This is a murder investigation and Evie's a person of interest. She was found at the crime scene by my Sergeant and says she has no memory of how she got there. Highly suspicious behaviour, don't you think?"

"Well, DCI Blake…"

"Just call me Blake," he said. "Everyone else does."

I wondered about this informality, but then he was calling me Grace. "Well, Blake," I said, "here's another fact. Evie wouldn't hurt the proverbial fly. She doesn't have a vicious bone in her body."

He sighed. "You'd be surprised what people can do when provoked."

I shook my head. "Not Evie."

He rubbed his hand across his brow, and I noticed his fingers stop on the old scars on his forehead. They'd healed up ages ago but the fact that he kept touching them interested me. Perhaps the psychology of what caused them had not healed so well.

"Have you found out anything else about that intruder on Saturday night?" he asked.

"Not yet. I'm going to call on Patrick Hardy when I get back, as you suggested. I hope he can shed some light on things."

He nodded. "Patrick is my father's oldest friend. He's lived in Hutton-le-Hole for a long time. Retired now, of course." He glanced sideways at me. "Patrick's wife was American, but she died young, of cancer." He paused. "If it *was* him who came into your house on Saturday night, we can relax."

We can relax. Blake seemed more concerned about the break-in than I was. "Should we be worried?" I asked. "Is there a burglar active in the area?"

"No. Nothing like that." He paused and this time I waited for him to continue. "The local lads are fired up about this Kitty business. A group of them went up to Lowna

Ford after the pub closed last night. They're all farmers and friends of the lad who was killed. I don't know what they thought they were going to do, but they trampled all over the crime scene and caused a ruckus."

"How brave of them," I said, tongue-in-cheek, "since this ghost has a habit of killing men."

Blake did not smile. "The lads can get hot-headed after a night on the beer." He flicked a sideways glance at me. "They know you and your friends are staying in Violet's house. They've started asking questions about the three of you."

I raised my eyebrows at him.

He shrugged. "It's human nature. People prefer to think of a stranger killing their loved ones rather than someone living in the community."

"That's madness!"

He nodded. "I just wanted to warn you. Make sure you lock all the doors and windows tonight. Call us immediately if there's any trouble."

"And how long would it take for the police to get from Scarborough?" I asked. "It took us an hour to drive here."

"We have roving patrol cars. But there's no need to be overly worried. I just wanted you to know that feelings are running high." He gave me a small smile as if to reassure me after delivering that bombshell. "Anyway," he asked, "how are you settling into the house?"

"It's a lovely old place. I can see why my mother chose to write her novels there."

He nodded. "I was brought up on Violet's books, you know. Most kids read her books back then."

I was genuinely surprised. "Did you know my mother well?"

He nodded. "Everyone knew Violet. She came to her house at least once, sometimes twice, a year and always joined in village life." He paused. "I was surprised when you said you'd never visited before. Why was that if you don't mind me asking? You said you were close to your mother."

I did mind him asking. Very much. I wondered then just how much I should tell the police about myself and my friends. He was after all investigating a murder and I didn't want to give him any more reason to focus on Evie. So, I did what I always do with awkward questions, I changed the subject. "That reminds me," I said, "I meant to ask if you knew who'd owned the house before Mother."

His brow wrinkled. "I can only remember Violet living there. She must have owned it for years, for as long as I can remember anyway." He looked at me, knowing I'd avoided his original question. He didn't repeat it though. "Do you find the house peaceful?" he asked.

I stared at him in surprise. There was that question again and I never expected it to come from him. "How could I find my own mother's house anything but peaceful?"

He nodded. "Back in the day, there was a lot of superstition about houses. You know, like where they were situated, where the windows and doors were." He turned to me. "There's a rowan tree planted beside the back gate, isn't there? You know, the one with red berries. Did you know a rowan tree had to be planted in the garden to protect the house from witches?"

It was only when I saw the corner of his mouth twitch that I realised he was teasing me. Then he smiled. It was good to see his face relax for once.

"So, no more nocturnal activity to report?" he asked.

I thought about my visit to the barn in the night to look for Rufus, and the heart chiselled into the stone wall. "Everyone talks about this domestic servant, Kitty, and her ghost, being a legend," I said. "But did she really exist?"

Blake shrugged. "As far as I know, she did. So did Willie Dixon."

I hesitated. "Last night I went out to the garden to look for Rufus, my cat. I was worried about him because he hasn't been into the house since we've been here or touched his food and–"

"Oh, I know Rufus," he said. "Violet always brought him up here with her. He knows the area and is used to hunting for his own food. I often see him on the Moors when I go out for my early morning run. No need to worry about him."

That was good to hear. "Well," I said, "last night I saw him in the garden and went out to try and entice him in. I discovered he's been living in the barn. When I followed him into the old building…" I paused, thinking about the feeling of soft breath or someone brushing the back of my neck. "Well, I had the feeling I wasn't alone in there." I looked at Blake. "And I don't just mean Rufus."

He frowned. "Go on."

I shrugged. "I felt a presence, that's all. Anyway, on my way out I noticed someone had chiselled a heart shape into the old stone wall by the door. Inside that heart were the initials WD and KG."

I saw the realisation slowly dawn on his face. "You think they stand for Willie Dixon and Kitty Garthwaite?"

"Perhaps."

"I'd like to get a look at that if I can. Check whether it was done recently or not." He paused to think. "Would it be all right if I call in this evening on my way home from work and take a look?"

"Of course."

"Right." He glanced at his watch and stood up. "If you want to, you can find out more about Kitty in the museum in Hutton-le-Hole." He must have seen my blank stare because he added: "The Ryedale Folk Museum, it's on the other side of the village to you."

I nodded. "I haven't had a chance to look around yet."

He checked his watch. "And I must go."

"See you later, then," I said. "Roughly what time?"

"Probably around nine if that's not too late?"

"That's fine."

He stopped and took out his mobile. "What's your number? I'll text before I arrive."

I gave it to him, and he punched it into his phone. "I'll send you a text now," he said, "so you've got mine too. Call if you have any problems."

It felt a bit odd exchanging phone numbers with a police chief inspector, but I was glad too. It was reassuring to know we'd have help if we needed it. When I glanced up again, I noticed him staring along the beach. I followed his gaze and saw Evie and Sam by the water's edge some way off. Sam stood rigid with her hands on her hips. Evie leant towards her, hands waving in the air. A knot formed in my stomach.

"Looks like a proper barney going on over there," he said, with a smile. "I'll let you sort that one out." And with that, he jumped in his car and drove away.

I sat watching Sam and Evie, wondering why they were so upset with each other. But I didn't move to intervene because I was fed up with their bickering. Anyway, something far more worrying was taking shape in my mind. It was DS Gray's raised eyebrow when I'd told her at the station that none of us had ever visited the area before. It was clear from the smug expression on her face that she hadn't believed me. Did she know something that I didn't? I started thinking about other things that had come up during this trip. For a start, I hadn't known Mum had masqueraded as Evie's mother to support her in that school piano exam. Nor that Mum was writing a ghostly thriller. I hadn't known about the Kitty Garthwaite legend that was the basis of Mum's novel either. But Evie had known all of that. She'd also visited Mum regularly in London, again something that I hadn't been aware of.

Evie... Everything kept coming back to Evie...

I shivered as a chilly breeze whipped around me and shook me out of my daydream. On the horizon, dark clouds were gathering, turning the colour of the sea grey and the waves rolling harder onto the beach. Was that a storm approaching? Sitting there watching Sam and Evie arguing, I felt this was somehow only the beginning of the turbulence.

Seventeen

The mood in the car on the way back to Hutton-le-Hole was subdued. I realised I'd made a mistake bringing Sam and Evie on holiday with me. What I'd really needed was time and space on my own to come to terms with Mum's other life, without having to worry about my friends' simmering tensions. And now, because of my insistence that Evie should come, despite Sam trying to persuade me otherwise, we'd all got mixed up in a murder. Of course, we'd had nothing to do with it. But I wondered just how bad things were going to get for Evie. For all of us, come to that.

On the way out of Scarborough, we stopped at a supermarket to stock up on ingredients for a beef curry that I wanted to cook that evening. Other than a brief discussion about food, we were silent for the rest of the journey, all immersed in our own thoughts.

When we got back to the house, I went straight up to my bedroom to change into some comfortable jeans. Then I went down to the kitchen to cook supper. I planned to shut myself in and have some peace on my own. I needed to distance myself from my friends to sort my head out. But I had only just begun chopping the onions when Evie came in, followed by Sam.

"I'll cook tonight," Evie said.

"Don't worry," I said. "I'll do it."

"No," Evie insisted. "I haven't done anything since I got here. Let me cook, please."

I opened my mouth to protest, then closed it again. "Fine. You cook the curry. I'll go and see Patrick Hardy."

"Want me to come?" Sam asked.

"No, thanks," I said, flatly. I slipped on my mother's raincoat and garden clogs and walked out of the back door. I was glad to be outside and away from the two of them, although I was nervous of seeing Patrick. I looked at my watch, 4.45pm. The light was already beginning to fade in the gloomy weather. In one week, the clocks would go back and plunge us into darkness. I wasn't looking forward to that, or another chaotic, covid and flu-filled winter.

I kept a nervous eye on the barn as I passed by. I would wait for Blake to come this evening before going in there again…*Damn!* I'd forgotten to bring a torch. It would be dark by the time I returned from Patrick's and there were no streetlights anywhere in the village. I looked back and saw Sam and Evie watching me through the kitchen window. I couldn't face going back in there, so I carried on through the gate and into the lane. My clogs scrunched over the fallen berries from the rowan tree and my mind wandered back to my conversation with Blake earlier. At least the house was protected from witches, I thought, ruefully.

It was very muddy underfoot. Rainwater had collected in the two deep ruts worn into the unsealed road by car tyres. I sloshed along in Mum's clogs like a ten-year-old, glancing over hedges into back gardens that lined one side of the lane as I went. The houses were all built from a light-coloured stone, York stone I presumed. I guessed it was mandatory in villages in the national park. There was nothing uniform about the houses though, they were all shapes and sizes. Most had garages that led out into the back lane.

On the right, stretched a patchwork of paddocks marked out by wire fencing and hedges. I guessed they belonged to the owners of the houses, almost like extensions to their gardens. A light mist clung to the trees and hovered above the grass, creating an eerie backdrop in the twilight. A creeping, yet familiar, sense of unease shivered through me. There it was again, that feeling of being watched. I stopped and looked around. No-one there. Part of me wanted to go back to the house, but I was almost halfway along the lane now and I refused to be spooked.

I carried on walking, pushing all anxious thoughts from my head, and trying to focus on an action plan to uncover as much as I could about Mum's life here. First, I decided, I'd find out what I could from Patrick. Then I'd visit the church over the road. If she'd taken part in village life as Blake had said, the vicar would have known her. The parish records might also tell me how long she'd lived in the house. After that, I'd visit the Ryedale Folk Museum and see what else I could find out about Kitty Garthwaite and her ghost story. My mother might have some research notes in the attic too. I resolved to continue my search for her manuscript after dinner.

Ahead of me, apples had fallen onto the ground from an overhanging branch from one of the gardens. I stopped and stuffed a few into my pockets. Next, I saw a hedgerow of what looked like blackthorn. I recognised its bluey-black berries because Dad loved to make sloe gin for Christmas every year. Did Mum ever bring him back sloes from her so-called writing trips? I couldn't remember her ever doing so and I felt sad for Dad.

Then I started wondering if Kitty Garthwaite had ever walked along this lane. I told myself to stop thinking about that ghost story or I'd get as obsessed as Evie. Still, if Kitty had visited Willie Dixon in Mum's house, she'd have walked along this lane, just as I was now. The weight of history was all around, in every wall and hedgerow.

"Grace…" Someone called my name. I stopped and turned, but there was no-one there. I looked in the paddocks and all around. No-one. My heart quickened and I strode on, anxious to get to Patrick's, and not daring to look back for fear of what or whom I might see. Ridiculous, I know, but I felt a presence I couldn't shake off.

When I reached the last house, Patrick's cottage, I burst through the gate and hobbled up the path. "Hello!" I banged my fist on the back door. "Hello." But there was no reply. I saw a cat flap in the door, just like the one in Mum's house, but there were no lights on inside the cottage.

I ran along to the terrace doors and rapped on the window. "Hello, anyone in?" I cupped my hands over my eyes and pressed my nose to the window to see inside. The sitting room was dark too, but I could just make out a sofa and chairs, a coffee table, a TV. All the normal things, except a piano stood near the terrace doors. It was arranged in such a way as to allow as much light as possible to fall on the keys. On top of the piano, there was a photo in a large frame. I looked closer. My stomach turned. Mother!

Suddenly, in my upset and confusion, I thought I felt that familiar breath on the back of my neck. I put my hands over my head like some crazy woman, thinking someone was going to attack me from behind. "Go away," I shouted. "I don't want to see you." Refusing to look back, I scurried around the path to the front of the cottage and out of the gate. I headed straight for the bridge and crossed over the beck and village green. Only when I was standing shaking and breathless next to the main road right on the other side of the village, did I dare turn around.

And there she stood. Outside Patrick's front gate. A young woman, staring directly at me. Her dark hair was parted in the middle, with two long plaits falling either side of her pale face. From that distance and in the twilight, I couldn't make out her features, but she was wearing a long dress, probably grey, with a dark cloak and hood draped over her shoulders.

I was rooted to the spot. My heart was pounding so much that I could hardly breathe. Terrified that she was going to follow me over the bridge, I kept shuffling back until I tripped up a kerb and fell flat on my back. I scrambled up into a sitting position and looked across the green again. The woman had gone. Frantically, I checked all around in case she was creeping up on me. But there was no sign of her anywhere. She'd simply vanished.

By the time I reached the house I was in an awful state from the exertion and fear. I didn't know who or what I'd seen, but I was scared witless. All the time I was heading for home, I was praying the front door would be unlocked. Fortunately, it was. I ducked inside and slammed the door behind me, the sound of it reverberating around the room. I turned the key in the lock and just about managed to sit down on one of the dining room chairs before my knees buckled. I put my head in my hands and heard blood roaring in my ears. I didn't believe in ghosts but out there in the village just now, in that misty light, I'd seen a young woman whose presence and clothes were out of keeping with the reality of present day. I *had* seen her. She wasn't a figment of my imagination. She'd looked solid too, not like some transparent or disappearing ghost in a book or a film. Yet there was something about her stillness, her silent presence, as she stood on the other side of the green that had momentarily paralysed me.

As I sank back on the chair to think about what to do, I became conscious of voices and the smell of curry wafting from the kitchen at the other end of the house. Evie and

Sam must have called a truce and started cooking together. It was good to hear them talking and banging about, a return to normality, although they clearly hadn't heard me come in. I was glad I wasn't alone, yet I didn't want to see them. I didn't want to tell them what had happened, not yet anyway. Not until I'd got my thoughts together.

I took off Mum's raincoat, hung it on the coat-stand and left her cogs on the doormat to dry. I crept out of the dining room and up the stairs to the attic. Once in her study, I felt calmer, but I was struggling more and more to discern what was real and what was not. Mum would never have lived in a haunted house. Whenever I'd been afraid as a child of a film or story about ghosts, she'd smile and say: "You have more to fear from real people than ghosts, Grace." I could hear her words now, and that gave me purpose. I needed to find out more about Kitty Garthwaite and this ghost story.

I went over to the table where Mum had laid out index cards for her new novel and picked up the central one with the title on, 'It Began with a Ghost Story: Kitty's Revenge'. I needed to find the draft manuscript. It had to be here somewhere.

My eyes swivelled to the stack of coloured boxes in which I'd seen some of her manuscripts earlier. I went over and pulled them out one by one. A wave of emotion came over me, like an overwhelming sadness, when I saw the bold, forward strokes of her distinctive handwriting. It was as if she were still alive and speaking to me from the page. I slumped to my knees on the carpet when I reached the last manuscript in the last box. Her ghost story wasn't there.

I stayed like that on the floor for some time until pins and needles crept into my right foot. I rolled back onto my bottom and stretched my legs out in front of me, jiggling them up and down to get the feeling back. That didn't work, so I lay flat on my back to try some yoga moves. Turning my head to the left in a sideways stretch, I could see through the door into the adjoining bedroom. Something under the bed in there caught my eye. Curious, I crawled on my hands and knees through the interconnecting door up to the bed and lay flat on my stomach.

That's when I saw the metal rings of what looked like a large notebook under the bed. I reached under and pulled out an A4 project book with the words on the front cover I'd been looking for, 'It Began with a Ghost Story: Kitty's Revenge'.

Yes! I propped my back up against the side of the bed and opened the cover to begin reading Mum's unfinished novel.

Eighteen

Kitty

Sunday 1787 – Autumn Equinox

Kitty was in a high state of anxiety as she paced around the kitchen like a caged animal thinking about what Mabel had said. Willie and that Castleton girl. It could not be possible. Mabel was lying and trying to make trouble, as usual. Nonetheless, as hard as she tried, Kitty could not get the vision of that buxom girl out of her head. She was not pretty in the usual sense of the word, but she was young, well dressed, and from a good farming family.

Feeling herself on the brink of slipping into one of her rages, Kitty got to work peeling the apples she had collected from the orchard the day before. She made a pie crust and fitted it into the tart mould for supper. She would bake it over the fire when she got back from church. She liked to cook but was only allowed to do so when Mabel was out of the house. However, not even the distraction of cooking could calm her that morning. And the chatter and laughter filling the house as the Pickering family took ages to get ready for church made her even more jittery. "Go!" she muttered under her breath, impatiently. "Just go."

Finally, the family were off. With John wearing his greatcoat to keep out the rain in the driving seat, Mr and Mrs Pickering and their daughter squeezed into the carriage at the back under the leather hood, looking the picture of elegance in their Sunday best. Kitty watched from the front door as the carriage travelled down the front track and through the farm's front gate. As soon as they were out of sight, she slammed the door shut, locked it, and hurried up to her room. Quickly retrieving her soap from under her mattress, she breathed in its scent as she washed her face and hands and changed into her best Sunday dress. She slipped her small feet into her boots and tied the laces tight. Grabbing her cloak, she flung it around her shoulders and ran down the stairs. Mrs Pickering would throw a terrible fit if she discovered that Kitty had left the house unattended, but she would never know. Kitty planned to be back well before the family got home.

Before she dashed out the back door, Kitty picked out a couple of Mrs Pickering's prized orange carrots from the pantry and stuffed them into her dress pocket. The carrots had come all the way by ship from Holland and Mrs Pickering adored them. Kitty wondered if she would ever be able to travel to another country. She would ask Willie once they were married.

As she entered the stables, Kitty smiled at the big chestnut horse, glad to see he had not been hitched up to the carriage. He was big and strong, and her favourite on the farm. If she ever had a horse of her own, it would be one just like him. Patting his neck, she gave him one of the carrots and he crunched it down noisily before nuzzling her neck appreciatively. Once he was saddled and ready to ride, she took the long way out of the farm, over the back field so that no-one saw her, and up onto the Moor. She knew every track up there. Not only would it be quicker that way than taking the lower tracks that others used, but she could come straight down into the village of Lastingham.

The wind whipped her hair around her face once she was on top of the Moor and misty air engulfed her. She wasn't cold though because the warmth of the horse radiated through her. However, she could not contain her anxiety and that made the horse nervous. He kept shaking his head as if something was wrong, perhaps knowing that he should not be out with her. He did not like the mist blinding his eyes either. She leant forward and spoke reassuringly in his ear. "It's all right, boy," she said, softly. "It's all right."

Fortunately, it was not pouring with rain, but the going was tough with the ground so wet. While the horse might not have known the way, *she* certainly did. She could have done the journey blindfolded and had often walked the route. But she was too tired to walk that far today, and Lastingham was a good two miles further on from Hutton-Le-Hole where Willie lived. She patted the horse's neck and spoke kindly to him at regular intervals. "Soon be there," she whispered to him. "Not far now."

He nodded and snorted in reply as if he understood every word.

Indeed, it was not long before the magnificent church spire of St Mary's came into view. Kitty's spirits always lifted when she saw it. She was especially happy today because she was convinced her beloved Willie would be there. She heard the ancient bells pealing out their call to service. That reassuring sound gave her courage, convincing her that God was with her and all around her.

Dismounting in a field at the back of the church adjoining the graveyard, Kitty tethered the horse under a tree next to some bushes where he would have some shelter if it started raining again. "I will not be long," she whispered to him, stroking his ear. "Then we will go home and dry off." She fed him the second carrot and left him munching happily. An image of Mrs Pickering's outraged face on seeing her precious carrots being fed to a horse sprang into Kitty's mind and she smiled.

Glancing furtively all around, she climbed over the dry-stone wall that bordered the graveyard and hid behind one of the larger gravestones. It was covered in green mould, which made her shiver. She was superstitious enough not to step on the grave's earth for fear of upsetting its occupant and have their ghost come looking for her. Now, from her vantage point, she could see parishioners walking up the path. Some went straight into the church while others stopped outside to chat. Her eyes were glued for a sight of Willie, but she did not see him. He must be inside already. She was so focused on the parishioners that she jumped out of her skin when the bells pealed out a second time and fell backwards across the grave. Startled, she scrambled to her feet and apologised profusely to its occupant.

Now though it was all quiet outside the church and the great wooden door had closed. She picked her way carefully around the rest of the graves and stood outside to listen. The vicar's melodious voice boomed out and bounced around the church's stone walls and floors. She waited nervously for him to announce the first hymn. There was a collective shuffle and bustle as the crowd stood up, followed by the sound of singing that became louder as the congregation got into their stride.

Heart pounding with nerves, Kitty lifted the latch and pushed the great door open gingerly. She poked her head inside and peered around. Fortunately, the door was on the east side of the church at the back so the vicar preaching from the altar could not see her, nor she him. Most of the congregation were in the centre pews either side of the main aisle, rather than sitting on the side near her. She slipped inside, closed the door quietly, and ducked behind a huge stone pillar.

After a minute to restore her breathing, she crouched down and peered around the pillar. Her eyes ranged over the back pews, but she could not see Willie. Her heart sank in despair. Please be here, she whispered. Please. She crawled along the floor on her hands and knees to the next pillar and stood up behind it to be able to see the front rows. She had to be careful now in case the vicar saw her. She waited for the hymn to finish and everyone to sit again. Then, once the vicar had turned his back to the congregation and knelt before the altar, and everyone had sunk to their knees in prayer, Kitty took her chance. She came out from behind the pillar and frantically looked at the people in the front pews. Her heart skipped a beat. There was Willie right in the front, she would recognise the back of his head and shoulders anywhere. His mother and father sat on one side of him but… oh my Lord, next to him on the other side sat that Castleton girl. Kitty did not have to see her face; she knew from the shiny curls and fine clothes who it was. Kitty clutched the pillar for support to stop herself fainting. Unable to move or speak, her eyes bored into the back of Willie's head.

Willie shuffled uncomfortably on his knees, as if he knew someone was watching him. He lifted his head and looked over his shoulder, visibly jolting when he saw her. Murmuring something to his mother, he stood up and quietly moved down the aisle towards her. When he reached her, he grabbed her arm and pulled her outside.

"What are you doing here?" he whispered, his face a picture of shock. "You should not have come."

Kitty tried to swallow down the bile that had risen in her throat. "I have not seen you for three Sundays," she choked.

His face turned softer when he saw her distress. "Your face is so white. You are shivering with the cold. How did you get here?"

"By horse." She pointed over to the back field.

He gasped. "Did Mr Pickering give you permission?"

She shook her head.

"Oh, Kitty. He will sack you."

"Does that matter?" She stared into his eyes. "When we are soon to be married."

He flinched. "Look, we cannot talk here. Let us meet at Lowna Ford this afternoon as usual."

She gave him a sceptical look. "You have not come for three Sundays. Every week I have walked there in the wind and rain and waited for you. But you have not come."

"I could not come," he said. "I cannot ride my horse in such bad weather."

"Yet I have ridden over the Moor perfectly well to see you today."

"Oh, Kitty. Kitty." He sighed and pulled her into his arms. "I am sorry," he said. "I am so very sorry."

Kitty felt the warmth of his body and heart beating against her chest. She was where she always wanted to be, in his arms. At first, tears pricked at her eyes as she pictured that girl next to him in the front pew, then anger rose in her. "They say you are to marry that… that fat jampot from Castleton." She swivelled her wounded eyes up to him. "Why are people saying that?"

The blood drained from Willie's face.

"Is it true?" she demanded.

Willie looked all around. "Come," he said, pulling her around to the back of the church where no-one would see them. "Kitty, my sweetling," he crooned as he wrapped his arms around her again. "You know how much I love you, but…" He hesitated. "My parents want me to marry that girl."

"You cannot." Kitty's eyes locked onto his. "You are betrothed to me."

"Alas, it is not that simple. My father knows her father. They want a union of our two families… for farming and business. You must understand."

"No," she breathed. "I do not understand. You promised marriage to me. I gave myself to you."

"Marriage?" He looked genuinely anguished. "I did not–"

"You did," she urged. "You spoke of our union."

"Yes," he said, cupping one hand around her breast. "Our union of love."

Her knees buckled and he held her up. "I am sorry, Kitty. This pains me as much as it does you. Look, you know I would choose you… not that girl. But my parents–"

"No," Kitty cried. "You cannot marry her."

"What about my father? I cannot disobey him."

Kitty's head swam with shock and despair. "What about our baby?" she said, shaking herself free of his arms and clasping her stomach. "*Your* baby," she whispered. "I am with child."

A shudder rippled through Willie as that news hit him like a thunderbolt. He stared at her, open-mouthed.

"It is true," she said, softly, putting her arms around his neck and pulling him close to her again. "You must keep your promise to me. And we must marry soon because of the child."

When the immediate shock had passed and Willie had got his thoughts together, he pulled Kitty's arms from around his neck and clasped both of her hands in his. Face ashen, he said: "I will discuss this with my parents and sort things out, Kitty."

"Promise me," she begged.

"Of course, my sweetling." He kissed her gently and released her hands. "Now you must go home," he said.

She clutched at him again. "When will I see you again, Willie? Please… when?"

"Next Sunday afternoon," he said. "Give me a week to arrange things with my family. I will meet you at Lowna Ford next Sunday."

"Even if it is pouring with rain?"

He nodded. "Whatever the weather, I will be there."

She smiled up at him again. "Promise?"

"I promise, dear heart."

Nineteen

Grace

Present day — Hutton-Le-Hole

The strained atmosphere between Evie and Sam continued over dinner. It felt like a piece of elastic was being stretched further and further, and I prayed it wouldn't snap. To compound things, Sam was already tipsy. Despite that, she'd done a great job in setting the table in the dining room, adorning it with Mum's best crockery and glass again. Evie had cooked the curry and looked quite radiant in the candlelight as the three of us sat down to eat. I dared to hope that she might be starting to feel like her old self again. But I was on tenterhooks throughout the meal because Sam kept topping up everyone's glasses, especially her own. Even my head was woozy. At every opportunity, I moved the wine bottle out of her reach, but she outmanoeuvred me as if playing a game of chess. I was more convinced than ever that she was totally dependent on alcohol, but she was also stubborn. It was going to be hard to convince her to get the help she needed to stop drinking.

We were still at the table drinking coffee when there was a knock on the front door. I looked at my watch. Just past nine. "Oh, that'll be Blake," I said.

"Blake?" Sam's eyes gleamed.

I shrugged. "The Chief Inspector told me to call him that. Everyone does, apparently. Anyway, he said he'd call in on his way home to look at that chiselled heart on the wall in the barn."

Evie's face fell.

"He won't be here long," I said to her. "I'll take him up to the barn straightaway."

"Nonsense," said Sam. "Bring the poor man in for a glass of something. He's been working all day."

I went to answer the door and brought Blake through to the dining room.

"Evening, Blake," Sam called out, taking her cue from me, and dropping his Chief Inspector title. "Come and have a drink." She pulled out the chair at the table next to her and patted the seat.

He looked awkwardly at me.

"You're welcome to have a drink before we go up to the barn, or a cup of coffee if you prefer," I said.

He nodded and took off the long, luminous yellow raincoat he was wearing. "I'll have a quick coffee please. It's bucketing down out there. Hopefully it'll ease off in a minute."

Sam decided to ignore his request for coffee and poured him out a large glass of red wine. She put it down on the table in front of the seat next to her. "Here. No need to be polite. Get that down you."

"She'll get you drunk if you let her," I said, with a laugh, although I was deadly serious. I knew Sam was going to say or do something that evening to embarrass or rile him. She was well gone, and I could see mischief in her eyes.

He went over, picked up the glass and took a swig of wine, but he didn't sit next to Sam. He walked around to the other side of the table and sat down next to Evie. She in turn shuffled to the furthest edge of her chair to get away from him.

He didn't react. "How are you, Evie?" he asked. "I saw you paddling in the sea this afternoon when I was speaking to Grace."

"I'm fine." Evie's voice was frosty.

I was embarrassed by my two friends' behaviour which in turn made me start babbling again. I talked non-stop about our day trip, about the beach, the sea, the town and how lovely it all was. I even showed him the amber pendant around my neck that Evie had bought me."

He nodded. "I know the shop. My Sergeant is always buying something in there. She's into crystals and all that too."

Evie visibly stiffened at the mention of DS Gray. I hoped she wasn't going to kick off about what happened at the police station again, even though she had a right to.

"Your DS wore a black obsidian ring today, Chief Inspector," Evie said, using his formal title. "Did you know that people who wear black obsidian are secretive? It's like they're wearing a veil."

I expected Blake to smile, but again he didn't react. I guessed he didn't want to aggravate Evie, and he was of course a master of the inscrutable face.

"How long has she worked for the police?" Evie asked.

"A long time," he said, vaguely.

"Is she married?"

Blake shuffled on his chair no doubt uncomfortable at being asked personal questions about his colleague but not wanting to be rude either. "She's a single mother. I say mother but her two children are all grown up now." His eyes bore into Evie. "You're very interested in my DS."

Evie met his stare. "On the contrary, *she's* very interested in *me*. She thinks I killed Joe Dunstan."

"No-one thinks you killed Joe Dunstan," I said.

"*She* does," Evie insisted.

Blake was gentle yet firm when he spoke. It struck me then that he was not a man to be swayed in his judgement or blown off course. "She needs to ask searching questions, Evie. To corroborate statements and people's movements. It's just police procedure."

Evie gave him a pointed look. "Is it usual procedure to harass people in the way she did me? Is it usual to accuse people of murder when they are there voluntarily?"

Again, Blake didn't react. "This is a lovely dining room, isn't it?" he said, so obviously changing the subject. "Violet was a great cook. I came to some of her dinner parties here." He sniffed the air. "Don't think I ever had curry though."

I was stunned and didn't know what to say. We rarely had dinner parties at home. A weariness came over me and I sank back in the chair. It seemed that everyone knew my mother well, except me.

Sam took up the reins. "Now Blake," she said, putting her elbow on the table and cupping her chin in her hand, seductively. "Should you be drinking wine with murder suspects?"

"I did wait for you to drink yours first," he said, with a gleam in his eye. "You seem all right."

Sam burst out laughing, causing her elbow to slip off the table and almost take her plate with it. "Oops!" She reached behind her and lifted another bottle of Pinot off the sideboard. "Since you're here," she said to him, "you can tell us how the investigation is going?"

He looked at her. "That wouldn't be very professional, would it?"

"Oh, come off it," Sam said, as she twisted the cap off the bottle. "You're amongst friends now."

He gave a wry smile. "All I *can* say is that we're following several leads of enquiry."

"You can at least tell us how you're conducting the investigation," she said. "I mean, are you doing house to house enquiries in this village?"

He nodded. "And in the surrounding villages."

"And what about this boy's family and friends?" Sam went on. "They say people are more often than not murdered by someone they know."

"As I said, we're following several leads of enquiry."

"Have you found his mobile phone?" she asked. "Police work must be so much easier since they were invented. The youngsters have their whole life on their phones."

Blake didn't answer, but I saw a shadow pass over his face.

Much to Sam's frustration, the rest of her questions were met with his repeated mantra about 'following several leads of enquiry'. I could sense her mounting frustration at being stonewalled. "So," she said, sweetly, "I hear your father is the Lord of the Manor?"

Blake blushed to the roots of his hair.

Sam gave a satisfied smile at his discomfort. "So, why did you become a policeman?" she asked. "I'd expect a man like you to be working in the city, or in some global corporation."

"Sam!" I was annoyed at her rudeness.

Blake touched my arm, as if to say, 'it's all right'. Then he turned to Sam. "I went to university as I guess you did. I went to all the parties, drank anything and everything on offer, even smoked pot. Fortunately, I got past that phase while I was there. It may sound trite, but I found more to life, a deeper meaning." He fixed his gaze on Sam. "Unfortunately, some people never get past that phase."

It was a blatant shot at Sam, and Evie gave a hoot of laughter.

"It was well after I'd left university that…" Blake stopped and looked down as if the memory was difficult… "I made up my mind to become a policeman. I was born up here. I love the moors, the space, the freedom, and outdoor pursuits. I'm living *my* dream. Are you living *yours*, Sam?"

A shadow fell over her face, and she went quiet.

That gave Evie an opportunity to have a go at Blake. "I suppose you're into shooting and chasing foxes around the countryside," she said, stiffly.

He turned to her. "No, Evie. But I do understand how people in the countryside live," he said. "The natural world must be managed alongside an ever-growing human population. Who do you think builds the dry-stone walls? Who keeps the grass and hedgerows under control? Who manages the forests and national parks?" He paused to give effect to his words. "Farmers and country folk, that's who. And what chaos there would be if they didn't." He took another gulp of wine. "Unfortunately, some culling of species is inevitable to allow them and others to survive sustainably. It's all about ecological balance."

I smiled inwardly. I need not have worried about my rude friends. Blake could look after himself.

"When I said I liked outdoor pursuits," he went on, "I meant hill running, horse riding and such like."

"I like running." Sam had already forgotten his barb. "I've done the London marathon a few times. Where do you run?" she asked.

"Across the moors, and sometimes over to the coast. Hill running's just like cross-country running, but longer and over gradients."

"How far do you run?" Sam asked.

"Ten to 20 kilometres usually. You need to carry survival equipment and have navigation skills to do it."

"I'd like to try that," Sam said. "Mind you, I'm not as fit as I used to be. I'd need to do some training first." She sighed. "And now, as it happens, I need the ladies." She stood up, held onto the edge of the table to steady herself, then launched herself towards the stairs.

"You'll have to forgive Sam," I said, once she'd gone. "She overdoes it on the drink sometimes."

Evie rolled her eyes and stood up. "I'd better go and help her." But she had no intention of helping Sam. It was just an excuse to get away from Blake. She kept her eyes on him all the time until she'd reached the stairs, as if she thought he might jump up and grab her.

I apologised when they'd gone. "Sam really is a good runner," I said. "She's fit and was always winning prizes at school. She *has* run the London marathon too, several times, for charity." I paused. "Don't think too badly of her, will you?"

He shrugged. "I see all human frailty in my line of work. I try not to judge people."

"Good, because Sam and Evie are like family to me. We've been close friends since school. They're all I have left now."

Blake's eyes fixed on me. "No family? Not even on your father's side?"

"Nope." I shook my head. "Both sets of grandparents have gone. My mother was an only child, my father too. Must be in the genes and I'm the end of the line."

He gave me a serious look and opened his mouth to say something. He must have thought better of it because he closed it again. I guessed it was going to be some platitude like I should think myself lucky because families can be a pain in the proverbial. That's what most people said whenever I told them. Keen to bring this conversation to a halt, I said: "I think the rain has eased off."

He paused to listen, then nodded. "Shall we go up to the barn?"

"Good idea."

The night was freezing and pitch black under heavy cloud cover when Blake and I started up the garden path. The smell of woodsmoke from chimneys filled the air, along with the scent of rain-soaked earth and leaves. I was back in Mum's clogs and raincoat. He was in his police issue raincoat and holding the heavy-duty flashlight he'd brought with him.

"Careful, Grace. It's slippery." He put a hand on my shoulder. "Can't you get your feet into your wellies?"

"No, my bandaged ankle won't let me."

"Let me go first, then. This flashlight has a wide beam."

I let him pass. It was a good couple of hundred yards to the end of the garden and I had to lengthen my stride to keep up with him.

He stopped outside the barn door and scanned the beam of light over the building façade and the roof. "This needs some work," he said.

"I know." I didn't want him to think I was a complete fool. "The wood on the door's rotten and I reckon from the damp patches on the inside walls that the roof needs doing too."

"Hm. Well, you'll have a problem with that." He turned to look at me. "It looks like there are bats roosting up there. They're protected, you know."

I shuddered. My bat phobia started as a child, probably from watching vampire movies, and had never left me.

"And see these holes in between the stones," he went on in his no-nonsense way. "Wasps have been nesting in there." He glanced at me in the dark. "They've gone now. Fortunately, they don't usually return to the same place to breed every year." He shook his head. "Jackdaws do though. The blighters will kill themselves getting back into the same chimney to nest. I've seen their dead bodies hanging from wire on chimney pots where they've been trapped." He turned to me. "The pots on your house need to be covered with galvanised steel. It's the only thing those birds can't peck through."

He lifted the latch and the old barn door creaked open. He stood on the threshold and shone the beam around inside. "Just look at these cobwebs. No-one's used this barn for years. Looks like it should be condemned if you ask me."

No-one is asking you, I thought, but I didn't want to engage in some conversation about the state of the place. I glanced up at the hayloft, wondering if Rufus was up there. I grabbed the ladder to go up and check.

"What *are* you doing?" Blake asked.

"I'm going to see if Rufus is up there." I was whispering because there was something about the atmosphere in the barn that made me nervous. "He's made a bed in the straw."

"The wood on that ladder's rotten."

"I've been up it before," I said. "Look, you stand underneath and hold it still for me."

He shook his head. "I'll go up." He handed me his flashlight and started climbing one step at a time, making sure each rung held firm before stepping onto the next. When he was at the top, I handed him up the flashlight and he directed the beam along the hayloft. "Rufus isn't here." He paused. "But there is something." I heard the rustle of hay, then he held something up. "It's a silver chain and pendant." He pulled a plastic evidence bag out of his pocket and slipped it inside. Then he climbed down.

On the ground again, he held up the transparent bag and shone some light on it.

"Is that a pentagon charm on the chain?" I asked. "I can't remember if it's a sign for witches or Satan."

Blake was unimpressed and shoved the bag into his pocket. "I'll get it checked for prints and DNA." He turned to me. "Now where's this heart?"

I pointed to the wall by the door, and he went over.

"Ah, I see what you mean." He held the flashlight to it. "I think you're right about the initials. They look like WD and KG."

"So, what do you think? Are they old or not?"

He rubbed his fingertips over the carving as if to brush away any dirt. "Hm. I'd say they were chiselled into the stone a long time ago." He paused. "But I'll get forensics out in the morning to do a proper check. We'll do the whole barn while we're at it."

Suddenly, a strong gust of wind blew the door shut. That in turn disturbed the bats in the roof. Several started flying crazily around, screeching their high-pitched squeak. One landed on Blake's head, but he just brushed it off.

I wasn't so sanguine. I covered my head with my arms and fled out of the barn like some mad woman. Only when I was outside and over by the path did I pluck up the courage to stop and look back. And in that moment, I saw a figure flash past the gate. I started shouting in terror.

Blake came running out of the barn.

"Quick," I said. "There's someone in the lane."

He had no idea what I was talking about, but the fear and urgency in my voice must have prompted him to rush through the gate into the lane and shout: "Stop! Police!"

I watched from my safe distance behind the gate as he walked up and down the lane, flashing his light into gardens and paddocks. "Come out," he kept shouting, with real authority in his voice. "Show yourself."

I already knew it was a fruitless task. There was no-one there.

He came back through the gate. "Who did you see?"

"I-I don't know," I said. "It was just a dark figure flashing by."

He looked at me with a puzzled expression. "What made you start shouting, then?"

"Well…" I hesitated. "For a moment I thought it was the same woman I saw this afternoon when I went to Patrick's." I stopped, wondering how to continue without sounding crazy. "You see, I got this feeling while I was walking down the lane earlier that I was being followed. I even thought I heard someone call my name. But when I turned back, there was no-one there."

"Go on." His voice was brusque.

"I was spooked. I ran into Patrick's back garden, and banged on the door, but he wasn't in. So, I bolted around to the front of the house, and over the bridge to the other side of the village. When I got to the main road, I looked back and saw a woman standing outside his front gate, staring at me." I paused. "She looked a bit strange. She was dressed in clothes that didn't really belong in this time."

His brow furrowed. "What are you saying?"

"Well, I don't believe in ghosts but…"

"What did she look like?" he interrupted.

It wasn't hard to remember; her image was imprinted on my brain. "She was a young woman. Early twenties maybe, and wearing a long dress, with a dark cloak over her shoulders." I paused. "She had dark hair parted in the middle, with two plaits falling to her shoulders."

He gave me a strange look that I couldn't read. "Have you seen her in the village before?"

"No."

"Right." He sighed. "Well, there's no-one there now." He shut the gate, making sure the metal latch was securely fastened. "Would you recognise this young woman if you saw her again?"

I shook my head. "I was too far away this afternoon to see her features."

We walked in silence back to the house. This time, he held onto my arm as we negotiated the path. I wasn't sure if that was to reassure me or hold me up in case I slipped.

"There's something weird going on, Blake," I said. "I don't know what exactly, but something feels very wrong."

"Mm."

There was something emphatic in that murmur that made me think he agreed. "Please tell me if there's something important that I should know about," I said. "It feels like we're caught in the middle of a nightmare, and we don't have a clue what's going on."

"I'm afraid I can't talk about the investigation right now," he said. "But I promise you, Grace, as soon as I can, you'll be the first to know." We'd reached the terrace now and he stopped to face me. "There's something *I* need to know from you too." He paused. "Are you *sure* you've never been to this house before?"

There it was again. The question I hadn't wanted to answer because of my own sense of hurt and guilt. Now, I had no choice. "*Yes*, I'm sure," I said. "The truth is I didn't even know this house existed until after my mother died and I inherited it." I wanted to make him understand that I was telling the truth. "How could I have been here before when I knew nothing about it? Or about my mother's life here?"

Suddenly there was a loud crash from inside the kitchen. We stared over at the open window as angry voices carried through it.

"Now look what you've done," Evie shouted. "You've smashed Violet's crockery."

"I didn't do it on purpose," Sam shouted back.

"You're a hideous drunk!"

"And you're a hideous liar!" Sam flashed back at her. "Why won't you tell Grace you've been here before? Don't shake your head at me, Evie. I *know* Violet brought you up to this house last summer.

"How *dare* you?"

"Don't bother to deny it. Violet told me all about it. She knew you and Trevor were having problems even back then. *And* she knew you were losing it."

"Bitch!"

"You can call me all the names you like, but Trevor knew how close you were to Violet. He went to see her and told her about his affair. He wanted to leave you last year but thought you might have a nervous breakdown. He was afraid you might try to top yourself. So, he asked Violet to take care of you. *That's* why she brought you up here for a break."

I shuddered and walked over to the kitchen window. Through the glass, I saw my two so-called friends facing each other across the kitchen.

Tears streaked down Evie's cheeks. "You're horrible when you're drunk, Sam. If you could only see yourself."

"And you're horrible when you're so self-righteous."

"*Self-righteous?*" Evie shouted. "Tormented more like. You see, I *know* what it's like to live with an alcoholic. I lived with one as a child, my so-called father. I *know* what drink does to someone and I especially know what it does to those around them. I was terrified of him," she went on. "He b-beat me and criticised me, until I never knew what I should say or do. He gave away my t-toys and books and told me I was too worthless to have them." The despair in Evie's voice was heart breaking and she sank to her knees. "H-how could you possibly understand what that's like?" Her head jerked up towards Sam, her eyes fierce. "B-because *you're* the drunk wreaking havoc on other people's lives? On Grace's life. How could you *do* that to her?"

I was shaking at the ferocity of their argument. I felt Blake's hands on my shoulders. "It's all right," he whispered.

All right? My two friends screaming at each other. Lying to me. Smashing up my mother's treasured crockery. No, it was *not* all right. I struggled from his grip and stormed into the kitchen.

"Stop it!" I shouted. "Stop it the pair of you!"

Twenty

"I'm sorry, Grace… I promised Violet I wouldn't tell you." Evie was rambling incoherently, her body shuddering as if the effort of speaking was draining the last ounce of energy from her. "I'd have done anything for Violet… anything."

I looked down at my friend as she lay in bed. Blake had helped me carry her upstairs before disappearing back to the kitchen. Now, with the yellow light from the bedside lamp reflecting on her face, she looked sickly, and her eyes feverish. I desperately wanted to know why she'd lied to me about visiting this house before, but I was too worried about her state of mind to force her to tell me. I didn't want to send her any further over the edge. "Let's talk about it in the morning," I said, with a calm I didn't feel. "After we've all had a good night's sleep."

"*Please* understand, Grace. *Please…*"

"Shush…" She felt frail under my touch, like an old woman with the life ebbing away from her.

"I'm so sorry," Evie repeated over and over. "I did it for her… for Violet, you see."

"Shush," I whispered again, as I pulled the covers up and tucked her into bed. Evie was in no fit state to discuss anything, and I was in no mood to listen. I felt in an almost dream-like state, detached from my friends and from everything going on around me.

Evie was still muttering as I went to leave. "It was up to Violet to tell you." She clutched my arm. "It was *her* place to tell you…"

"Tell me what, Evie?" I asked, gently. "What?"

"Your mum and dad didn't want you to know." She shook her head and closed her eyes. "I can't… don't you see? I promised."

I looked at my friend lying in a confused and emotional state. I was furious with her for lying, but I could see just how fragile she was. She'd never been a confident person, but I never realised how rejected and worthless she'd always felt. And no wonder. Why hadn't I known about her abusive, alcoholic father? And now Trevor had left, she'd slid into a very dark place. "Get some sleep, Evie," I whispered. "You'll feel better in the morning. We can talk then."

She nodded and pulled the duvet up around her head and ears like a tortoise withdrawing into its shell.

I switched off the light and stood in the doorway watching her. I wished I had some medication to calm her down and help her sleep. I was worried she'd get up again and start wandering around. I decided to lock all the doors and hide the keys so that she couldn't get out of the house. But, as soon as the light went off, she stopped moving and lay still. I closed the door, praying she would get some much-needed sleep.

When I went into Sam's room to check on her, she was still fully dressed and lying flat on her back on top of the covers, snoring in a drunken sleep. I was so angry, I thought about throwing cold water over her face to give her a shock. But when I looked down at her flushed cheeks and tousled blonde hair, I wondered why I hadn't noticed her decline into alcoholism before. I must have been so wrapped up in my own life that I hadn't really *seen* what was happening to my friends. I pulled off her high heels and stood them next to the bed. Then I yanked the duvet out from under her legs and threw it over her. She could sleep off her alcohol binge like that until morning.

Back in the kitchen, Blake had cleared up the smashed crockery, and laid some of the bigger pieces of a vegetable tureen out on the kitchen table. "I don't think they'll glue back together again," he said. "May be worth a try though."

"Broken crockery isn't the only thing that won't glue back together again," I said with a sigh. "Both of my so-called friends have been lying to me."

He gave me a sympathetic look. "How are they?"

"Sam will sleep off her alcoholic stupor and probably be fine in the morning. But I'm worried about Evie. It's like she's snapped in two. I really need to get her some medication and treatment."

"There's a surgery in Kirkbymoorside." He pulled out his mobile. "Here's their number. I'm sure one of the doctors will talk to you tomorrow."

"Thanks." I picked up my mobile from the table and punched in the number that Blake read out to me. "I'll ring them first thing."

He stood before me running his fingers through his hair in a rather agitated way. "I'm worried about this intruder hanging around the house." He glanced at me. "Do you want me to stay the night? I'll sleep on the sofa. I'm used to that."

I looked at his weary face. It would have been good to have his protection in the house, but I couldn't impose. "You've got a lot on your plate with this murder investigation. You need to get some proper rest." I gave him a small smile. "Don't worry, we'll be fine."

He looked at me. "You understand that we'll have to interview Evie again, don't you?"

I nodded. Of course, he would. She'd been lying to all of us.

"Have you got any idea *when* Evie came up to this house with your mother?" he asked.

I shook my head. "I'm the only one who *doesn't* know anything about any of this." I could hear the despair in my own voice. "It seems my mother wanted to keep it a secret from me." I shrugged. "God knows why!"

He gave me a searching look. "You really don't know?"

"No, I don't."

He sighed. "Right, we're going to have to sort this out. I'll find Patrick and get him to talk to you."

I stared at him. "Is he the key to all this?"

"To some of it."

"To what exactly?"

"Just talk to him," Blake said.

I sighed when I saw from Blake's closed expression that I wasn't going to get any more out of him. "What about poor Joe Dunstan?" I asked. "You don't think Evie could be involved in his murder, do you?" I paused. "*Could* she have met him when she was here before?"

He looked thoughtful. "It's possible."

I waited for him to say more, but he didn't. "It doesn't make sense though," I said. "Even if she had met him before, why would she want to kill a young man like that? She'd have to be crazy." I stopped, realising just what I'd said. "I know you don't believe in ghosts, Blake. But you once said it's not what *you* believe; it's what *others* believe."

He nodded. "The question is, has Evie become so obsessed with this legend that she really *believes* Kitty, or rather Kitty's ghost, exists?"

I frowned. "I don't understand *why* people think Kitty's ghost lured those men to their deaths. To put it in your police language, what would be her motive?"

"Revenge, I suppose, if she believed Willie Dixon had deserted her and their unborn child." He shrugged. "Revenge on men in general and the society of that time."

I nodded. "You said it was only when the vicar performed an exorcism at Lowna Ford that the deaths ceased." I paused. "Is it possible that Evie *believes* she's doing Kitty's bidding by killing Joe Dunstan?" I stopped, unable to believe what just came out of my mouth. "My God, what am I saying? Honestly, Blake, I really don't think my friend is capable of anything like that. I'm sure she's not."

"Hm." He looked thoughtful again. "The other pressing question is w*ho* did you see in the back lane this afternoon and a few minutes ago?" He turned to me.

"I can't be sure I saw anybody just now." I was sounding exasperated. "This is all making me jumpy. Perhaps there was no-one there." I hesitated. "But I did see that young woman this afternoon. I've no doubt about that."

He nodded. "Well, I don't think I can leave you all alone in this house tonight."

I frowned at him. While I was pleased that he was looking out for us, I didn't want to impose. "Yes, you can." I pulled his raincoat off the back of the kitchen chair. "We'll be fine."

I was taken aback by the fearful look on his face. "What is it, Blake? What is it you're not telling me?"

He touched the scars on his forehead and stood silently for a while. Then he spoke: "I made a mistake one night, Grace. A mistake I've never recovered from." He swallowed almost as if the words were getting stuck in his throat. "I left someone on their own one night and she was, well, she was murdered."

I stared at him in shock.

"She was my fiancée," he said. "Gina was being stalked by her ex. He was always following her, ringing her up in the middle of the night, sending her abusive letters and texts." He shook his head as if he still couldn't believe it. "She didn't think he was dangerous or that he'd hurt her." Blake's shoulders stooped. "Nor did I."

The pain was raw on his face and present in every word he spoke. I didn't know what to do or say. I was surprised he'd told me something so personal. I wanted to comfort him, but I hardly knew this man and couldn't find the words. So, I just listened.

"It was the night of our engagement party at her house," he went on. "Everyone was there, friends, family. We'd had a lovely evening. I should have thought about what that bastard might do. I should have stayed over. I didn't because I had to get up early for work. Nobody thought... *I* never thought..."

"Oh, Blake." I could hardly bear to listen.

"He broke into her house. There must have been a frenzied struggle because she was beaten black and blue. And that battering..." His voice faltered. "Killed her."

I gasped at the horror of his words.

"I knew something was wrong that night because I couldn't go to sleep. I phoned Gina, but there was no reply, so I drove back to her house. As soon as I saw the front door ajar, I knew. I ran inside and found her on the kitchen floor."

"Oh my God! That's horrifying."

"There was nothing I could do. She was dead, but that maniac was still in the house. He crept up behind me while I was trying to revive her and smashed a bottle over my head. We had a vicious fight. I ended up punching him so hard that he fell and cracked his head open on the aga.

Staring at Blake's desolate face, I didn't have to ask if the man had died.

He nodded, dejectedly. "It was self-defence, and I was never charged with manslaughter or murder." He touched the scars on his forehead. "These are the only physical reminder of that night."

To say I was shocked was an understatement.

"That's why I'm a detective," he said. "I know it sounds trite, but I joined up to stop dangerous lunatics like him." He looked at me again. "Perhaps now you can understand why I'm nervous of leaving you all alone tonight, Grace."

"You think we're in *that* kind of danger?"

He shook his head. "No, but as you said earlier, something feels very wrong here." His mobile rang before I could say anything else, and he answered immediately.

While he was talking, I pottered around the kitchen opening drawers and putting things away. I was so rattled; I hardly knew what I was doing. Why had he told me all that? What kind of danger did he think we were in? *Christ!*

I was still shell-shocked when he came off the phone, although I'd had some time to marshal my thoughts. "I don't know what to say, Blake. I'm so sorry about your fiancée. It's beyond horrific. What a terrible thing for you to have to go through." I knew I was babbling, but I couldn't seem to stop.

He looked into my eyes. "I've frightened you."

"N-no," I stammered. But the truth was he had. "It's just that I, well, I…"

He held his hand up to stop me talking. "I'm sorry I heaped all that on you, Grace. To be honest, I don't know why I did."

"It's all right," I blustered. "It's fine. Really. I'm glad you told me." And, in some way, I *was*.

He looked embarrassed and couldn't meet my eye. "That was my boss on the phone. He wants me back at the station. I'll tell him I'm staying here if–"

"No." I shook my head. "You have to get on with your job and catch Joe's killer." I paused. "Don't worry. We'll be okay on our own."

He looked at me, then sighed. "All right. But I won't leave you completely in the lurch." He draped the raincoat over his arm. "I'll arrange for a patrol car to park outside all night. If there's *any* problem, or *any* hint of one, go out to them or ring me immediately." He stared at me. "Promise me you'll do that."

"Of course."

He nodded and went over to the back door. "Make sure you lock this behind me. And don't leave the key in the lock in case Evie tries to go out sleepwalking again."

Ah. So, he *does* believe me about Evie sleepwalking.

He turned. "Sorry again for dumping all that on you, Grace. I just wanted to make you understand the possible danger… and I went too far." He sighed. "Thanks for listening though."

I managed a small smile. "Goodnight, Blake."

"Goodnight, Grace."

I locked the door after him and waved through the window as he disappeared into the night. I heard his car start up and drive away. As I stood all alone in the kitchen in the silence, with Evie and Sam out for the count upstairs, I felt desperately alone. I plopped down on a kitchen chair and started sorting distractedly through the pieces of broken crockery on the table. As I tried to fit them together like a jigsaw puzzle, my head was trying to fit together the events of the evening. All the conversations, all the details. The trouble was some of the pieces were missing.

But I was scared now. Very scared. The intruder on Saturday night; the ghostly woman in the back lane; and now the image of Blake's fiancée lying dead on the kitchen floor – all these happenings were crowding my mind.

There was no way I'd get any sleep, that's for sure. I walked into the sitting room and banked up the fire with more logs and moved from room to room switching on all the lights. Then I went upstairs and pulled the duvet and a pillow off Mum's bed. I was going to sleep downstairs on the sofa, in front of the fire, and be ready for anyone who tried to break in. The last thing I did was to go into the kitchen and pull one of Mum's carving knives out of the block. It seemed an irrational thing to do, but it was down to me to make sure the three of us came through the night unscathed.

Twenty-one

A deep ache radiating through my neck and shoulders woke me the next morning. I groaned as I stretched out my stiff limbs after my night on the sofa. The embers were still smouldering in the fireplace, casting the room in a cheerful glow. There was something comforting and relaxing about an open fire and I managed to get some sleep after all. I lifted my head to look at the clock on the mantelpiece and was surprised to see it was 8.15. I sank back down on the pillow and looked up at the beams as the madness of the night before came flooding back. A heavy gloom settled over me and I listened for any noise to tell me if Evie or Sam were up. It was all quiet. That was a relief because I didn't want to see them. I didn't want the confrontation, all the talking, the explanations, the tears, and tantrums. I was hurt and angry with Evie. She'd lied to me about visiting the house. She'd come up with Mum last summer and hadn't told me because Mum didn't want her to. Sam knew, but she didn't tell me either. For God's sake!

As I trudged up the stairs to go for a shower, Blake's words about tracking down Patrick to 'sort all this out' popped into my head. It wasn't the first time he'd told me to talk to Patrick and it seemed more urgent than ever. I decided then that I wouldn't put up with this secrecy for a moment longer. I wouldn't wait for Blake to find Patrick either. I'd find him myself.

There was no sound from Sam's room as I passed by, and I didn't bother to go in. She could look after herself. But I hesitated outside Evie's door, feeling the need to check she was all right. I opened it and peered in. She was still as I'd left her, wrapped up in her duvet. I tiptoed over to the bed so as not to wake her. Her face and lips were still pale, but thankfully she was breathing rhythmically in deep sleep. That was the best medicine she could have, so I went out and closed the door again.

I showered quickly and dressed. And, when I got back in the kitchen, I happened to glance out the window. To my surprise, Rufus was sitting on the terrace. He was perfectly still, his eyes scanning the horizon. He looked bedraggled though, his wet fur hanging in sodden clumps. I immediately went out to him. "Morning, boy," I said, bending down. I knew better than to try and stroke him. He disliked any display of affection from me. His big green eyes studied me. To my surprise, he got up and rubbed himself against my ankles. I took that as a sign of greeting. I bent down and stroked behind his ears which he allowed. After a few moments, he strolled off up the garden path. He was ready to be friends, but not to eat tinned cat food or come into the house. I glanced nervously up at the barn. The memory of that ghostly woman made me go back inside the house and lock the door.

Still, seeing Rufus had cheered me up. I made a pot of coffee and some porridge, enough for all three of us. I brushed the pieces of broken crockery that still lay on the table into a dustpan and threw them in the bin before sitting down to eat breakfast. It didn't matter to me that some of Mum's crockery was broken. I was more upset about all her lies. I made up my mind there and then to take all her stuff to an auction or charity shop. None of it meant anything to me.

A text popped into my mobile inbox, from Blake. *How are you, Grace? Everything all right?*

I replied immediately. *We're fine. A quiet night, with no disturbances. How about you?*

At work. Will send forensics officer out this am to check the barn. I can't accompany, too much to do here but will ring again later. Take care.

Okay. Speak later.

I should have told Blake that I was going down to Patrick's cottage to see if he was in, but I didn't. It was like a mist had been lifted that morning and everything was coming into sharp focus in my mind. I didn't know why I hadn't worked it out before. Maybe I had and hadn't wanted to admit it to myself. Patrick Hardy was the reason Mum came to this village and why she'd bought this house. I remembered the burning fire in the grate when we arrived, the spotlessly clean rooms, the well-tended garden. Patrick was keeping this house as a shrine to her, and there was only one reason he'd do that. He'd been her lover. I just couldn't understand why it was such a damn secret. And why he hadn't been in touch with me after her death? What sort of man does that? Well, I was going to confront him and find out.

Misty rain engulfed me the moment I stepped outside the front door for there was no way I was walking down the back lane again. It was as if a sea fret had blown in across the moors and settled over the land. The air was refreshing though. I took a furtive glance all around. Everything was quiet as usual apart from the sound of the rushing torrent that was the beck. After the night's heavy deluge, water sloshed over the top of its grassy banks as it bubbled and swirled down to the farms and pastures below. Thank goodness the village was on a hill, and the incline too steep for the beck to flood. Those people living downstream might not be so lucky though.

I pulled up the hood of Mum's raincoat and turned right out of the front gate onto the main road. A couple of cars flashed by on their way over the moors to the coast. I raised my hand in a sign of greeting to a farmer sitting high on a tractor piled with hay bales, and he waved back. In the distance, I spotted a group of children in their uniforms climbing into a school bus. Everything seemed so normal that morning.

At the junction, I turned right into the residents' road leading to Patrick's cottage. As I got closer, my anger turned to anxiety about seeing this man. Standing outside his front gate, Dad's words rang in my head. *You go there if you must, Violet, but I forbid you to ever take Grace. You will never ever take Grace.* I knew Dad would hate me being here. He'd known about Mum's relationship with this man and forbidden her to bring me here. Their affair must have been going on for years because Blake said he'd never known anyone but Violet owning her house. How could she *do* that to Dad and me? And why on earth would Dad put up with it?

I went up to Patrick's front door and raised my hand to knock. It swung open before I made contact, and I jumped back.

"Sorry to startle you, my dear."

A small, bird-like woman stood in the doorway. She wore a blue skirt down to her calves, with her grey-white hair tied back into a ponytail. Her face was freckled from the sun and a life outside in the country. She wasn't in the first flush of youth, that's for sure. Sixties, maybe? But her inquisitive blue eyes sparkled with energy as she gave me a penetrating look. "You must be Grace." She didn't wait for me to reply before continuing: "Yes, yes. Of course, you are. I can see Violet in you."

I was so taken aback, I didn't speak.

"Come in, my dear," she said. "Don't stand out there in the rain."

I went to cross the threshold, then looked down at my muddy shoes.

"Just leave them under the porch," she said.

I slipped them off my feet and stood nervously in the hallway in my socks.

"It's never going to stop raining this autumn," the woman said. "Look at that beck. I've never seen it like that in all my years." She shook her head and closed the door. "Come into the kitchen, my dear, and dry off. The Aga's on and I'm just making a pot of tea."

"I–I'm sorry to disturb you," I said as I followed her into the kitchen. "I was looking for Mr Hardy. Mr Patrick Hardy."

"Of course, you are." She smiled at me. "But I'm afraid he's not here."

My heart sank. "Do you know when he'll be back?"

She shrugged. "He left yesterday. Told me he'd be away for a day or two, visiting a friend." She suddenly laughed. "I'm the cleaner, by the way, if you're wondering. Annie Jennings." She pulled out a chair and gestured for me to sit down. "Take your coat off. I'll get that tea and we can have a chat."

I smiled at her. She was the first friendly soul I'd met since we'd been here. I hung my raincoat on the hook behind the door and sat down.

Annie busied herself pulling cups and saucers out of a cupboard. It was clear we weren't going to have our tea in some old mugs. The best tea set was being laid out on the table, along with milk jug, sugar bowl and biscuits. It was Royal Worcester, just like Mum's. Looking around, I realised the whole kitchen was almost identical to hers – the same lovely wooden cabinets, black granite worktops, kettle, and food mixer. It confirmed my suspicion about Mother and Patrick. "Do you live in the village?" I asked Annie.

"I wish." She shook her head. "I live in Kirkbymoorside."

"Have you worked for Mr Hardy long?"

"Oh, about eight years now."

Music to my ears. This woman should know quite a bit about him. "You knew my mother, then?"

"Yes." Annie filled the teapot with boiling water and carried it over to the table. "She was a lovely lady, your mum," she said, sitting down opposite. "I was so upset when I got the news from Patrick that she'd passed." She gave me a sympathetic look that brought a lump to my throat until she said: "What a shame you couldn't get to the funeral, Grace. Still, it's a long way to come from Australia. Violet was always so proud of you being a doctor and said you were dedicated to your patients."

Australia? This woman thought I lived in Australia. Had Mum told everyone the same lie? Was that her excuse for a daughter who never visited?

"It was a lovely service," Annie went on. "Patrick did your mother proud. There were so many people there. Everyone knew Violet and Patrick, of course."

I sat dumbstruck. I wanted to shout out the truth. To tell this woman and everyone else that I didn't live in Australia; that my mother had had a funeral in London and was cremated there. Something stopped me. I didn't know if it was out of embarrassment at the lies Mum had told, or my loyalty to her, or the fact that I still didn't know the full truth. I swallowed the bile in my throat and looked away.

I didn't fool Annie though. She picked up on my distress and patted my hand as she poured me a cup of tea. "I'll put a bit of sugar in it." She dug the spoon deep into the bowl. "It's the shock... the emotion of it all... coming back to your mother's house." She pushed the tea towards me. "There, have a sip. It'll warm you up and you'll feel better." She got up and went over to get the box of tissues from the dresser and handed it to me. "Dry your eyes, my dear. I know it's hard laying a loved one to rest when you haven't been able to go to the funeral. But you're here now. You can go and say a proper goodbye."

I looked at her.

"Violet's grave," she said, seeing my confusion. "Over at St Mary's Church in Lastingham." She patted my hand again. "There's a plaque for her on the wall in our village church too, St Chad's, just over the road. Why don't you go and have a look?" She sighed. "Oh, I do wish Patrick were here. He'd loved to have taken you to Violet's grave. You were the two closest people in her life."

The *two* closest people? Her words were still reverberating around my head when the telephone in the hall rang.

Annie jumped up. "I'll have to get that. You sit quietly with your thoughts and finish your tea." Although she closed the door behind her, I could still hear her voice in the hall. From the noisy chatter, it sounded like she knew the caller well.

As I sat sipping my tea, I got cross again. How dare that bloody man put on a funeral service for my mother here and take a burial plot in the local church? *I* was her next of kin. He should have consulted *me*. Anyway, Mum didn't want to be buried. She wanted to be *cremated*, which she was, in London. Who did he think he was?

That's when I remembered the framed photo of Mum that I'd seen on top of his piano through the window the evening before. I wanted to have another look. Satisfied Annie was chatting happily on the phone, I slipped through a connecting door from the kitchen into the sitting room and went over to the piano to pick up the photo. It was a beautiful full-face shot of Mum smiling, but it must have been taken at least 15 or 20 years ago. I couldn't help but smile back at her. She looked so happy.

I put it back on the piano and looked around. There were more photos on the mantelpiece, so I went over. They were all of the same man and a woman who was not my mother, at different stages of their lives. I smiled at the one in which the man was young. His hair was longer and just brushing his shoulders as was the fashion in the 1960s. He was wearing a white T-shirt tucked into the wide belt on his trousers, with a check shirt loose over the top like a young Mick Jagger. He was tall and handsome in a rugged kind of way. In the same photo, the woman wore bright green bell-bottom trousers. Her hair was blonde and straight, with a fringe and a hairband of flowers. The photo was signed: *To Lizzie, with all my love. Patrick.* The woman had to be his wife or partner as they were holding hands or linking arms in all the photos. I remembered Blake telling me Patrick's wife had died young of cancer which was probably the reason why there were no photos of the woman past 40-ish.

I glanced around the room to see if there was anything else to tell me about Mum's relationship with this man. My eyes rested on a row of pictures hanging on the far wall. I went closer and was surprised to see Bugbear, Spirit Fox, Barn Owl, and other illustrations from Mum's books.

Then I froze. The signature on all the pictures was identical. I went back to the photo on the mantelpiece that Patrick had signed with his name to the woman called Lizzie. It was the way he'd drawn the 'P' of Patrick, with such a flourish, that made it unmistakable. It was *his* signature on all the book illustrations in the album in Mum's attic. He must have illustrated all her books.

"Ah, there you are, Grace." Annie came up behind me. "Wonderful illustrations, aren't they?" She sighed. "They were such a lovely couple, Patrick and Violet."

By now, I was feeling quite nauseous. "I m-must go," I said. "My friends will be wondering where I am. Thank you, Annie. You've been so kind."

"Oh, don't mention it." She beamed at me, then gave me a sideways glance as if there was something else on her mind. "Can I ask you a question, Grace? About Violet's house, I mean?"

I felt sick to the stomach and desperately wanted to get out of this cottage, but I also didn't want to offend this woman who'd been kind to me. "Of course, I don't mind," I said.

She looked straight into my eyes and her expression turned grave. "I was wondering how you were getting on in the house?"

"Oh fine," I said. "It's lovely."

"Mm." She looked uneasy, which made me realise exactly what she was asking. "Did you ever clean for my mother, Annie?" I asked.

She nodded. "Yes, I was happy to help her. But I was glad to stop when she died." Then she realised how that had come out. "Oh, I'm sorry, my dear. I shouldn't have said anything, especially to you. But I feel I should warn you that Violet's house has a history. A rather dark history."

"You mean the Kitty and Willie ghost story," I said.

"You know about it?" She sounded surprised.

"I do." I studied her. "Do you think it's true?"

She shrugged in a non-committal way. "It was all a long time ago."

I pressed her. "Tell me, Annie, did you ever see or hear anything unusual when you were working in the house?"

She looked uncomfortable, as if she wished she'd never started this conversation. "Patrick always tells me off if I mention it. He says it's all nonsense and that I've listened to too many stories over the years."

"And my mother?" I asked. "Did she think it was nonsense too?"

"Violet *said* it was." Annie ran her hand over her already smooth hair. "But I did wonder sometimes."

I nodded. "Will you tell me what you've seen or heard in the house, Annie?"

She shook her head. "I don't think it's my place to say."

"Please. I *should* know, don't you think?"

She looked thoughtful. "Maybe you should. After all, it is your house now."

I waited, hoping she would tell me whatever it was. And she did.

"Sometimes I thought I heard crying." She shivered. "And once, on the attic stairs, I saw a figure." She paused. "It was young woman in a long dress, with a cloak over her shoulders. I only saw her from the back so I couldn't describe her face. It was her feet that I remember. They were small and dainty… even in her old lace-up boots."

I felt my stomach flip.

"It was just a fleeting glimpse, like a shadow passing over." Annie clutched her chest as if she was in pain. "Her clothes were the same as in the portrait of Kitty in the museum over the road." Annie's eyes pierced mine and she lowered her voice to a whisper. "You said you knew about the Kitty and Willie ghost story."

"Yes," I was whispering too, although I didn't know why.

"Have you heard about the murder on Saturday night?" She shook her head as if in despair. "Poor Joe, he was *such* a good lad." She made the sign of a cross over her face and chest. "He was killed in the same place as the other young men, all those years ago." Her blue eyes were no longer sparkling. "They say history repeats itself, don't they?"

I looked at Annie, wondering whether I should ask my next question. Then I did. "Do you think Kitty's ghost killed those men all those years ago?" I asked, softly, for it struck me that Annie was just the kind of woman who might believe such a thing.

She studied me, then said: "Sounds ridiculous when you say it like that, doesn't it?" She sighed. "But I know what I heard and saw in your mother's house."

I nodded. "And Joe?"

She folded her arms across her chest. "The police are all over the village knocking on doors, talking to everyone." She started whispering again. "You mind out for Stella Gray. That Detective Sergeant is a piece of work, so are her kids." Annie pursed her lips. "Her son's a druggie and her daughter's a trollop."

"Oh, I–I see." I was too surprised at her frankness to say anything else.

"Poor Joe," Annie said again. "He had everything to live for. He was going off to college in Ireland, you know."

"It's all very sad," I said. "Anyway, thank you, Annie, but I must get back to my friends now."

"Of course." She led me to the front door and opened it. "Patrick will be sorry to have missed you. I'm sure he'll be in touch as soon as he gets back. You'll be around for a while longer, won't you?"

"Yes," I said, although it wasn't true. I wanted to go back to my life in London as soon as I could. "Will you please tell him I called."

"Of course." Annie suddenly looked stern. "And don't be tempted to go visiting Lowna Ford while you're here, my dear, will you? It's an unholy place."

Twenty-two

I felt Annie watching me as I walked away so I didn't look back. I was still reeling from what I'd discovered in Patrick's cottage. At least now I knew the truth. Mum had been working with Patrick on her novels for decades and I was sure they'd been lovers. Annie had confirmed it anyway by calling them a lovely couple.

I pulled my raincoat hood up again and sloshed along in puddles of water, deep in thought. I didn't walk back in the direction of Mum's house though. I didn't want to see Sam and Evie and deal with their problems. I needed to be on my own to process what I'd learnt at Patrick's. I found myself crossing over the bridge to the other side of the village and heading for the church where Annie said there was a plaque for Mum. I ought to see it before I left.

I stood outside the church at first studying the simple, stone building. St Chad's Church. It had the same pantile roof as most of the houses, with an old bell tower on top. I glanced around. There was no-one about. The wet weather was clearly keeping people away. The trees in the churchyard looked beautiful in their autumn colours. Large drops of rainwater trembled on their branches in the stillness. Red berries hung from the tree closest to the church, framing its old façade as if in a painting.

I went through the gate and picked my way carefully through the dead leaves that floated in the puddles on the flagstone path towards the door. "Hello?" I called out, as I stood on the threshold and peered in.

Rows of plain wooden pews filled the small space inside, with only enough room for two people to walk down the central aisle to the altar. The stone walls were stark, but the windows were made of a lovely lead glass. It was a plain, country church and charming for its simplicity, but there was no-one in there.

I walked down the aisle and sat in the front pew. As I looked up at the image of Christ on the cross and the stained-glass window beyond, I imagined Mum sitting there for the weekly Sunday service. Had Patrick sat next to her?

I felt sad for Dad. He'd always been there for me, dropping me off and picking me up from school, helping me with my homework and encouraging me to go to university. He'd looked after me when Mum was 'away writing'. Now I knew why he'd never gone to any of her book launches or signings. Because *Patrick* would have been there. Every step of the way it had been *Patrick* helping Mum with her books and career. *Patrick* taking her from us. *Patrick* interfering in our lives.

"What a deception, Mum," I said out loud. "You had us all fooled. Even my friends, who thought you were *so* lonely after Dad died. I used to feel guilty about being caught up in my work and not seeing you as much as I'd have liked to. You never complained, and I loved you for your strength and independence. Except all the time you were with *him*."

Then I wondered if I'd ever met Patrick in London without knowing who he was. Perhaps Mum had introduced him to me as one of her friends? I tried to remember his features in the photos in his cottage, but I didn't recognise him at all. No, I was sure I'd never met him before.

"What a web of lies, Mum. Telling everyone I lived and worked in Australia to explain why I never visited you here. The stark truth was you never wanted me here. You never wanted me to be part of your life here. Perhaps you never wanted me at all?"

That's when I could no longer hold back the floodgates. Tears streaked down my cheeks, and I wept in a way that I hadn't when Mum died or at the funeral. Back then, I'd had to keep myself buttoned up to deal with everything. Now, in the quiet peace of this country church, everything came bubbling to the surface. I wondered how many other people over the years had sat there weeping for their loved ones. I was glad there was no-one around to see or hear me.

My feet were sopping wet in Mum's clogs, so was the bandage on my ankle. Slowly, I unwound it and slipped it into my pocket. My ankle felt much better now it was free and exposed to the air.

I must have sat there for ages in my misery because when I went to get up, I discovered I was frozen stiff. I shook my hands and stamped my feet to get the blood flowing again. I turned and made my way down the aisle. Then I noticed a narrow staircase at the back leading up to a balcony and the church organ. Patrick played the piano in his house, and I wondered if he played this organ for church services. Curiosity got the better of me and I climbed the narrow wooden staircase to the balcony. Above the organ hung a brass plaque with Mum's name and date of birth at the top. The second line read: *The greatest happiness of life is the conviction that we are loved.*

It was the same quote as in the binder of book illustrations in Mum's attic. Patrick had given her that binder, of course, and written that quote inside. He'd hung this plaque where he could see it while he played the organ, in the same way he'd put her framed photo on top of his piano. Like she was his muse, or inspiration.

That familiar sick feeling hit me again. I ran down the stairs and out into the fresh air. I leant against the stone wall to steady myself and waited to see if I would throw up this time. Fat droplets of rain dripped down my face and neck, but I was too upset to care.

Twenty-three

As I trudged along the road, feeling more miserable than ever, I came across a single-storey stone building with a sign above the glass entrance doors: Ryedale Folk Museum. I remembered what Annie had said about the young woman she'd once seen in Mum's house, particularly about her clothes and hair being the same as in the portrait of Kitty in the museum over the road.

I was feeling completely drained and I knew I should have gone back to the house to see the forensics officer who was coming to check out the barn. But I didn't. For a start, I still couldn't face Sam and Evie; and I really wanted to see the portrait of Kitty. I pushed through the glass doors and went inside the museum.

Immediately, a young woman looked up from the desk.

"Morning," I said, and pulled back my hood to shake off the rain. I was dripping wet and must have looked a sight. She was something to behold too, but for a different reason. Her face was deathly pale against her glossy black hair. Her eyes were smudged black with kohl and her lips painted bright red. Dressed all in black, and with two gold rings pierced into each eyebrow, I guessed this girl was a 'Goth'. I'd read in some tourist blurb that the nearby seaside town of Whitby was the Goth capital of the UK.

She studied me. The brightness of her grey eyes had a magnetic quality and I found it hard to look away.

"Are you Grace Winter?" she asked.

I must have looked surprised because she added: "I heard Violet's daughter was in the village. You look like her." She flicked her black hair off her shoulders. "Residents can enter the museum free of charge," she said, "if you'd like to go in."

She spoke in a rather aloof way, and I thought she was an odd choice as a receptionist for such a museum. I wondered if she was like this with all visitors, or if it was just me. "Thank you," I said, and went to walk inside.

"The Kitty Garthwaite portrait is hanging on the wall in the Iron Age roundhouse right at the back of the property," she said.

That stopped me in my tracks. How did she know I wanted to see it?

There was something familiar about the watchful eyes she trained on me. "With Joe's murder, and the goings-on in your mother's house," she said. "I was expecting you."

I stared at this young woman. She could only have been in her late teens or early twenties, but there was something strange about her. Her piercing eyes, maybe. Or her voice perhaps, which was low and melodious. Or was it the extraordinary confidence she exuded? And what did she mean about the 'goings-on' in Mum's house? I looked back at her, then decided not to engage in any more conversation. The villagers would be talking about us enough as it was. I didn't want to give her and them anything more to gossip about. "Thank you," I said, curtly, and went through another glass door into the museum.

I found myself back out in the rain again and I pulled up my hood. It was not the day for a visit to an open-air museum which would explain why there was no-one else about. The first noticeboard I came across explained that the museum stood on a five-acre plot and had 20 historic buildings for visitors to view. It all looked fascinating, but I didn't have time to mooch about today. I just wanted to see Kitty's portrait. So, I walked on, past an old-fashioned village shop and post office; a blacksmith's workshop; several thatched cruck cottages; an Elizabethan manor; the museum cafe which was closed; several tractors and other agricultural machinery exhibits; and across a stretch of muddy grass until I eventually stood outside the Iron Age roundhouse. Butterflies started up in my stomach. I was reluctant to step over the threshold. I was scared about seeing Kitty's portrait, scared I might see the same woman I'd seen standing outside Patrick's cottage yesterday.

Then that strange feeling kicked in again. That sense of being watched. I looked around. There were no other visitors, but I was reassured to see a man clearing fallen leaves into a wheelbarrow over by the boundary fence. He had to be a member of the museum staff. I shrugged at my own paranoia, took a deep breath, and stepped inside the roundhouse.

The interior was set up like a small theatre in the round. There was a clearing in the middle for the stage, and chairs for the audience encircling it. The walls were made of wooden posts and wattle-and-daub panels. The building had a high, conical thatched roof, with a small hole in the top. I guessed the central 'stage' was where the fire was originally set up for heating and cooking in these ancient houses, and the hole in the roof for smoke to escape.

There were several posters hanging on the walls advertising all kinds of plays and I walked along studying them. Quite a mix of productions had been on: 'A Midsummer Night's Dream', Alan Ayckbourn's 'A Chorus of Disapproval'…Oh, I stopped dead. There was a poster for a play called 'Sarkless Kitty'. Next to it hung the portrait of Kitty Garthwaite. Goosebumps shivered along my back and arms. The woman in this painting *was* just like the figure I'd seen yesterday afternoon in the back lane. Or at least her clothes were. The same grey dress. Same cloak. Same hair with two plaits falling to her shoulders. The woman's eyes in the painting seemed to bore right through me. She seemed as real to me as any person I'd ever seen in the flesh.

Suddenly I felt a draught of cold air blow over me, and my heart quickened. I didn't like the atmosphere in the roundhouse, and I turned to leave.

There, behind me, stood the young woman from the reception. She was taller standing up than I expected, and her red lips formed into a tight smile. She moved silently to the stage and stood in the centre. Bowing her head theatrically, she opened her arms wide and started to perform.

I stood like a rabbit caught in headlights. I wanted to leave. I was desperate to leave, but I didn't want to appear rude. I thought perhaps she regularly put on a show or recital for all visitors, so I stood politely to listen.

"I was just a servant girl when I met Willie," she said, her face softening at the mention of his name. "How handsome he was. He rode so proud and upright in the saddle, like a real gentleman. I loved the way his dark eyes lit up when he saw me sitting on the trunk of the alder tree at Lowna just waiting for him. It was *our* tree. Our trysting tree." The girl's face lit up as she spoke as if she were reliving every moment. "The tricks he did on horseback were wonderful." She shook her head. "He always made me laugh. He loved to make me laugh."

She was mesmerising and I couldn't take my eyes off her. "Very good," I said, clapping. "What's your name?"

She seemed to look right through me. "Kitty," she said. "Kitty Garthwaite."

I stood paralysed, not knowing what to do. In the end, I think I said something like: "Thank you, but I'm afraid I have to go now."

She ignored me and continued with her performance. "Willie did not turn up for our tryst on the Sunday afternoon I died. He *promised* me he would be there. I waited at the tree all afternoon, but he did not come." She started pacing around the stage in an agitated way, making me increasingly nervous. "How could he leave me waiting for hours by the raging river in the wind and rain?" she said. "He knew I was with child." She stopped and looked over at me. "Yes," she whispered, holding her stomach. "I was with child."

She took a few paces towards me and shouted: "He did not come because he was with *her,* that creature from Castleton. But he was betrothed to *me*. He promised *me*. But he would not marry me because of *her*. That is why he kept insisting I tell no-one about us and our baby. Because of *her*."

Her words started hitting me like hammer blows. My God! This woman was reciting the opening chapter of Mum's novel word for word. How did she know it? The manuscript was under the bed in the attic. My head was throbbing hard now, and I inched backwards towards the door.

The girl jumped from the stage towards me. "You are living in Willie's house." Her voice cut the air like a saw. "Sometimes I think I see him on the stairs or hear his footsteps. That small, quick step of his. Do you think he is here now?" she asked, her voice malevolent. "Do you think the dead come back and watch the living?"

Jesus! I turned and headed for the exit.

"Go on, run away!" she shouted after me. "Leave me to face the world alone. I will not let you get away with it, do you hear? Just like I would not let Willie and all those rotten men get away with it. I will kill you all, just like I killed them."

At the exit, I glanced quickly over my shoulder to see if she was following me. But she was back performing on stage again, arms lifted to the heavens. Suddenly her eyes swivelled to mine. "Get out of my house!" she screamed.

I needed no further invitation. Heart thudding, I ducked outside and dashed across the grass. To my dismay, there was still no-one around. Even the man picking up leaves had disappeared. But there was a gate on the boundary fence near to where I'd last seen him. Running over, I barged through it and found myself in a field of cows. They looked up curiously from their pasture as I stood panting like a woman possessed. I bolted across the field to another gate directly opposite, praying that it would lead back to the village. It was hard going squelching along in mud and cow pats, but I got there in the end.

It was only when I was back in the safety of the centre of the village and standing by the side of the main road that I stopped and bent over to catch my breath. When I looked up again, I saw a police car and CSI van on the drive of Mum's house.

Twenty-four

I'd hardly had time to process the madness at the museum before standing in a breathless daze on the back terrace of Mum's house. In the distance, up at the barn, I could see forensics officers in white suits going in and out of the building. I was about to go up and talk to them when I noticed the kitchen door was ajar. That worried me because I'd asked Sam to keep all the doors locked while I was out. I walked along the terrace towards the kitchen and stopped halfway to look through the glass doors into the sitting room. I saw DS Gray standing over Evie who was sitting in the fireside chair on the far side of the room and still in her pyjamas. She was so focused on Evie that she didn't see me outside and she didn't hear me come through the open kitchen door either.

"Why did you lie, Evie?" I heard her say as I stopped to listen. "Why did you say you'd never been here before when you had?"

Evie didn't reply.

"We know you were here last summer with Violet," DS Gray continued.

I crept closer to the open door between the kitchen and sitting room. I should have made my presence known but I wanted to hear what they both had to say.

"If you don't co-operate," DS Gray raised her voice a notch, "we can do this down at the police station." She paused. "I ask you again, Evie. Why did you lie?"

"To protect Grace." Evie's voice was just a whisper and I had to wedge myself between the door and the cooker to be able to hear her.

"Protect her from what?"

"Violet didn't want her to know about this house."

I held my breath.

"Is that so?" DS Gray sounded like she didn't believe her. "Why was that?"

"Family business," Evie said. "Nothing to do with me. Or you."

There was a pause, then DS Gray said: "Why would Violet bring *you* here and not her own daughter?"

"Grace and I have been friends since school. Violet always helped me. Kept an eye on me." Evie was choosing her words carefully. "I was helping her with the research for her latest novel."

My stomach churned. Why did Mum want Evie to help her and not me?

DS Gray's voice became more strident. "You met Joe Dunstan when you were here last summer, didn't you?" She paused. "Don't deny it. I know you did."

"Why ask me questions if you're going to answer them?" Evie said.

"Did you or did you not meet Joe Dunstan when you were last here?"

"I don't know." Evie sounded genuinely unsure. "I–I'm not sure I remember him."

"You met him at the village museum." DS Gray sounded like she was enjoying herself. "I know you did. I attended the same performance of the play as you and Violet. 'Sarkless Kitty', it was called."

Oh my God! So, Evie *had* met Joe Dunstan before. What's more, DS Gray had known that from the start of the investigation.

"You and Violet were in the front row that night," she went on. "Joe was a stagehand and helped change the scenery at the interval. He sat next to you."

"I don't remember."

"Oh, come on, Evie. Joe was a volunteer in the museum. He looked after the agricultural machinery on display." The DS chuckled. "I remember you plain as day with your orange hair and crystals."

"My hair is auburn," Evie protested. "And, oh…"

"A-ha. I see from your face that you do remember Joe. You learnt all about the story of Kitty Garthwaite and Willie Dixon at that play. Research, was it? For Violet's book?"

"Yes," Evie said.

"So, why did you kill Joe?"

"I didn't."

"It *was* you."

"No. It wasn't."

"How can you be so sure when you say you were sleepwalking and can't remember?"

Silence.

"So, Evie, if you didn't kill Joe, then tell me who did."

There was another silence that seemed to go on for ages and I felt I really should reveal myself before this went any further. But I didn't.

"Come on," DS Gray goaded. "Tell me."

Then Evie said in a low voice. "Perhaps it was Kitty? You do know she's standing beside you, don't you?"

I heard a gasp which I was sure came from DS Gray.

Evie's voice rose to a higher pitch. "Perhaps Kitty killed Joe in the same way she killed all those other men. They deserved to die. Scumbags. They had their pleasure and dumped us like we were nothing. Like we were discarded dolls. Don't you see? Kitty's been trying to protect women from men like that for over two centuries."

Shut up, Evie, I thought. For goodness sakes, shut up. For your own sake.

"It wasn't Kitty who killed Joe." DS Gray continued. "You killed him, Evie, because you thought that's what Kitty wanted you to do."

Silence.

"I found you at the crime scene, Evie. You were there." She paused. "I know it was you who killed him."

I couldn't take any more. "That's enough," I said, stepping into the room.

DS Gray's head jerked round in surprise. For a brief moment, I saw dismay on her face before she resumed her neutral look.

I didn't know if it was the shock of seeing me, or DS Gray's badgering behaviour, but Evie started dry retching. I'd seen this happen before when she was deeply upset. It came in waves from the depths of her stomach. I rushed back into the kitchen to grab the plastic bowl from the sink and returned just in time to see her lean forward and project vomit all over the hearth and Glamour Cop's shiny Chelsea boots. Divine intervention, I thought.

Evie's eyes rolled upwards as if she were about to pass out.

I ran over to pin her back in the chair and stop her tumbling into the fireplace. I looked up at DS Gray. "You had no right to badger her like that," I said, crossly. "She's sick. Will you get her a glass of water." It was more an order than a request.

DS Gray looked at me from under her lashes, but she went out into the kitchen anyway.

"Don't say another word," I whispered in Evie's ear once DS Gray had left the room. "Not another word."

"Sorry," Evie whispered back. "Sorry."

I looked over at the hearth. There was nothing but stomach acid splattered around. "Have you eaten anything this morning?"

She shook her head.

"Where's Sam?"

Evie shrugged. "She went to look for you."

I held Evie's wrist, pressed my fingers on her pulse point and looked at my watch. The beat was a little rapid and she felt burning hot. I went over to the table to get my medical bag. I pulled out my thermometer and pushed it under her tongue. Then I grabbed my stethoscope. "Can I listen to your heart?"

I saw panic in Evie's eyes as I quickly pulled up her pyjama top and put my stethoscope against her chest. "Oh." I hesitated when I saw her full breasts and dark nipples. My eyes took in her swollen stomach.

Tears glistened in Evie's eyes, and she pulled the thermometer out of her mouth. "I can't do this, Grace," she whispered, grabbing my hand so tightly I thought the blood would stop flowing to my fingers. "I can't have this baby on my own. I can't."

"You're not on your own," I whispered back. "Now, listen to me. Don't say another word to DS Gray, do you hear?"

Evie nodded.

I quickly pulled down Evie's top to hide her pregnancy before DS Gray returned with the water. I held the glass to Evie's lips and urged her to drink. "Now, let's make you comfortable on the sofa." I helped her over and told her to lie down. "You'll feel better with more rest."

She relaxed back and closed her eyes.

DS Gray was hovering. "I need to take Evie to the station for more questioning," she said.

"Questioning?" I spun round. "Is that what you call it?" I saw the unease in her eyes. "I heard every word."

"Then you'll have heard Evie admit to killing Joe Dunstan."

I looked at her, steadily. "She did not. She kept saying she didn't do it."

DS Gray sighed. "You heard her say that *Kitty* killed Joe. Your friend is clearly disturbed. She's become so obsessed with this legend; she thinks she's doing Kitty's bidding."

"Are you saying you believe Evie killed Joe because some ghost told her to?" I narrowed my eyes in a dramatic way. "Or are you saying this ghost has possessed Evie?" I hesitated. "Do you realise how ridiculous that sounds?"

She chose her words more carefully before she spoke again. "Evie needs help. Psychiatric help. She's having a mental breakdown, as I'm sure you know."

Yes, I did know that, but I wouldn't give the woman the satisfaction of agreeing. I was cross with Evie for lying to me about visiting the house with Mum, but I had to defend her. I would not believe she could murder anyone. "Evie *is* sick," I said, "but it's just temporary. She's been working too hard." I wanted to say Evie's husband had just left her for another woman, and that Evie was pregnant, which would be enough to send anyone over the edge. I didn't though. I didn't want to give this woman any more information about Evie before we'd spoken to a solicitor.

DS Gray tried to take charge. "We'll arrange for a psychiatrist to see her at the station. They'll be able to judge her mental state."

I shook my head. "Evie is not in any fit state to go anywhere, except perhaps to hospital." I paused. "Why are you so keen to pin this murder on her?"

DS Gray bristled. "I am not trying to *pin* anything on Evie. The facts are that your friend has been lying the whole time, even to you it seems. She came here with your mother last summer. She met Joe Dunstan at the museum when she went to see the play 'Sarkless Kitty'. And she was found at the crime scene early on Sunday morning in a distressed state supposedly sleepwalking." She drew herself up in an authoritative way. "I need to take her to the station for official questioning."

I stood up to face her. "Well, I'm a doctor and I say that Evie is too sick to go anywhere or answer any more questions right now."

There was a long silence. I thought she was going to read Evie her rights and march her out to the car. Then I saw hesitation in her eyes.

"You do know your friend is dangerous, don't you?" she said.

We stared at each other, and I didn't dare look away for fear of losing the battle of wills.

Finally, she gave me a curt nod. "Very well." Her voice was icy. "I'll go now…but I'll be back."

I nodded but said nothing more for fear of giving her a reason to change her mind. I knew she would be back. Before then, I'd make sure Evie got some medical treatment and the best lawyer I could find.

Twenty-five

Only when I looked out the front window and saw DS Gray's car driving off did I start to relax. I turned back to Evie, who was watching me from the sofa, her green eyes calm now we were alone.

"Has she gone?" Evie asked.

"Yes… for now."

"Thank you, Grace, for standing up for me."

"You know I'll always do that." I shook my head at her. "Why didn't you tell me you were pregnant?"

She sighed. "I couldn't believe it at first," she said, softly. "Or rather wouldn't believe it. After all those years of trying." A single tear streaked out of the corner of her eye and onto the cushion. "Anyway, I wasn't sure what I was going to do about the baby," she whispered.

I felt so sorry for her. She and Trevor had been desperately trying for a baby for years. Now that she was pregnant, he'd left her. "Does Trevor know?" I asked.

"No." She raised her head up and gave me a fierce look. "He got that woman pregnant and left me. He's not having my baby too."

"But he's the father. He needs to step up and help you, financially at least."

"I said no!" Evie was getting agitated again. "Absolutely not." She glared at me. "I forbid you to tell him."

I held up my hands in defeat. "I wouldn't dream of telling him. It's your business, not mine."

Evie looked a little mollified. She flopped back on the cushion and after a while asked: "Did you see Patrick?"

I shook my head. "No. He's away, at least that's what his cleaner said. I think he's avoiding me." I gave her a cool look. "I suppose you met him when you were here with Mum."

She nodded. "I liked him."

"Did you now? Well, I have a very low opinion of him." I gave her a sour look. "You can drop the pretence, Evie. I know he was having an affair with Mum."

Evie blushed and looked distraught. "I'm sorry, Grace. Really sorry."

"You should have told me," I said. "You're supposed to be my friend."

Her eyes glistened. "I wanted to, but Violet made me promise not to."

"Why? Because she didn't want me to know about her affair?"

"I guess…"

"You could have told me after she died?"

"I didn't know what to do." Her voice was soft, pleading. "You'd been through so much with Peter leaving and then Violet dying. I didn't want to load any more hurt on you." She must have seen the pain on my face because she said: "I kept Violet's secret because she'd always been good to me. Anyway, she said she was going to explain everything to you about the house *and* Patrick before she died."

It was only then I realised the implication of her words. "Are you saying Mum *knew* she was going to die?"

Evie shook her head, defensively. "I don't know that for sure, Grace. She never told me there was anything wrong with her. I didn't know about her heart problems,

I promise. But she kept saying she had to put her affairs in order before she died. That she had to tell you everything." Evie had a wistful look now. "I guess we all know when our time is up." She sighed. "Trevor called me a barren bitch before he left, you know."

"He said *that?*"

She nodded. "He could be a hurtful bully when he couldn't have his own way."

"Oh, Evie."

"None of us knows what goes on inside other people's marriages," she said, stiffly.

That was true. I had no idea why Peter left in the way that he did. Sure, we'd had our arguments like everyone else, but they were short-lived and neither of us held grudges.

"You have every right to hate me for not telling you the truth about your mum and Patrick, Grace."

"I don't hate you," I said, and I meant it. "It's just hard for me to believe anything you say at the moment."

Evie nodded, her face a picture of sadness.

"Is there anything else you need to tell me?" I asked. "You'd better say so now if there is. I don't want any more secrets between us."

Evie looked away.

That's when I knew. "You're holding something back, Evie. Tell me now. I won't forgive you again."

She bit her lip, and I could see her thinking hard.

"I mean it," I said.

She gave a resigned sigh. "All right, but this is going to hurt you too, Grace. Very much."

"Go on," I said, bracing myself.

"I know why Peter left."

That surprised me. "You do?"

"Yes. You've noticed the tension between Sam and me, haven't you?"

I nodded.

"Well, I didn't want to come on this trip with *her* in the first place." Evie looked into my eyes. "What Sam won't tell you is that Peter didn't just leave because he wanted to travel." She shook her head. "He left because of Sam. They slept together."

At first, I couldn't quite take in what she was saying. Then I staggered back as if she'd punched me.

"Sam wanted Peter to tell you," Evie went on. "But he refused. She threatened to tell you herself if he didn't. The poor man was quite desperate in the end. And that's why he left. He couldn't bear to tell you, Grace. He loved you and didn't want to hurt you." Evie suddenly froze and gazed at a point over my shoulder.

I knew Sam was there. I turned to see her in the doorway. Rain dripped off her raincoat, and her blonde hair hung in wet clumps.

"Is that true?" I asked, sharply. "Did you sleep with Peter?"

"Grace, I..."

My voice rose. "Did you sleep with Peter? Yes, or no?"

"Look, I-"

"Yes, or no?"

Sam sighed, then nodded. "Neither of us meant for it to happen. I was just in this bar one night with friends and Peter walked in. I was on the rebound and he..." She looked at me, "Well, you were working, and he needed company. Th-that's all."

I stared at her. The misery I felt inside could not have been more intense. These women were supposed to be my friends. Both had deceived me. Sam with my partner. Evie with my mother. I turned to Sam. "Is that why Peter left?" I asked Sam, softly. "Because of you?"

"It was just the once, Grace. We didn't have some long-standing affair. I wanted him to tell you. Get it all out into the open and put it behind us. I didn't want you to find out like this. But he refused."

My head was throbbing. I felt wretched. I had to get away from these women, and away from the misery they poured on me. I strode over to the kitchen door and pushed Sam aside.

"Grace," she said. "Please!"

I didn't want to hear another word. I wanted to get out of this house. I easily slipped my feet into Mum's wellies now that I had no bandage on, grabbed her raincoat, my bag and car keys and headed for the door.

"Grace..." Sam was pleading. "Don't go like this. We need to talk."

Talk? I couldn't bear to even look at her. I strode out through the back door, and around to the front of the house where I clambered into my car and started up the engine. In my mirror I saw her rush out of the front door.

"Stop." She banged on the rear window. "*Please,* Grace.*"

But I was stopping for no-one, least of all for her. She was still shouting for me to come back as I pushed down on the accelerator and drove through the gate.

Twenty-six

I drove along in a daze, with no idea of where I was going. The windscreen wipers swished back and forth in their mesmerising way and the car shuddered as I drove through deep pools of rainwater running across the road. But I was oblivious to the weather and conditions. All I could think about was Sam and Peter. I sifted through memories of get-togethers over the last year or so, but I couldn't remember one single occasion to suggest an attraction between them.

You were working and he needed company that night. Sam's words made me feel sick to the stomach. She'd chosen them to deflect the blame onto me. She knew I had to be on duty and go out to very sick patients some nights. Peter understood that too. What if he did have to cook himself meals and be alone sometimes? He was a grown-up, for God's sake. It didn't give him… them… the right to sleep together behind my back.

The car suddenly jolted as I drove through a deep puddle and the steering wheel spun dangerously in my hands. That brought me to my senses. I was in no fit state to concentrate on driving. I braked when I saw a sign saying Chimney Bank. The steep, twisty drop down to Rosedale village looked treacherous so I braked and parked up on a grassy moorland verge. God, what a nightmare this holiday had turned into. It was supposed to have been my chance to get over Peter and Mum and recharge my batteries. Instead, I felt shattered in every sense of the word. Everything I'd ever known had been turned on its head. My childhood, my family, my friends, my partner were all a sham. I sank lower into my seat as a kind of despair washed over me. It was comforting to be locked in the car away from everyone, with just the rain pattering on the roof. Tears streaked down my face again as all sorts of images and memories from the past flashed through my head until I was totally exhausted. Eventually, I found myself drifting off.

Sometime later, I became aware of a rocking sensation that woke me. I sat up quickly. A flock of sheep had surrounded the car and were rubbing their flanks along the bumper as if to satisfy an itch. I started up the engine to scare them off. They just looked at me, unperturbed, and trundled off into the mist.

It seemed to be a weather pattern in these parts for a blanket of fog to descend after rain. I shivered and looked at my watch. Almost 4pm. I couldn't believe I'd been asleep for a couple of hours, although it wasn't really that surprising. I hadn't had a good night's sleep since arriving at the house. I was still upset though. Very upset. But in some way, the rest had helped me think more clearly. For my own sanity, there was no option now but to let go of the past. If I sold Mum's house in Hutton-le-Hole, and everything in it, that would put an end to her secret life. I could sell my London flat too and rid myself of any memories of Peter. And why stop there? I could sell Mum's home in Hampstead as well and buy myself a lovely property with all the proceeds. I could even use some of the money to go travelling, or work in another country like Australia or New Zealand where my GP skills would be welcome. I didn't have to continue my life as before. I could make some drastic changes now that I had resources and options. The more I thought about it, the better I began to feel. And focusing on a plan for the future cheered me up a little.

The hard part now was having to go back to the house. I wanted nothing to do with Sam, but it would be dark soon and too late in the day to send her packing. In my usual practical way, I concluded that we'd all have to spend another night in the house. There was no way I could spend hours in the car with Sam driving her back to London though. I would arrange for a taxi to collect her in the morning and drive her to York, where she could get a train home.

Evie was more of a problem. I couldn't just leave her at the train station. I didn't trust Sam to look after her either, not with the friction between them. No, I'd have to drive Evie back with me. She also needed medical treatment, which meant I couldn't just drop her off at her flat given her state of mind. I would have to take her home with me until she'd recovered something of her old self. At the time, somewhere deep inside, a voice was telling me I was behaving like an ostrich with its head in the sand. I was refusing to think about Evie's situation and the murder. But even then, I never thought her capable of hurting anyone. And there was another thing I was refusing to consider: that Evie might be more desperate than I'd ever imagined.

Mind made up about the way forward, I turned round and drove back along the road until I came to a T-junction where there was a sign indicating a right turn to Hutton-le-Hole and a left turn to the village of Lastingham. I remembered Annie saying that Patrick had a burial plot for Mum in the church graveyard there. I glanced up at the darkening clouds and reckoned I had another hour or so of daylight left to visit Mum's 'grave'. This would be my only chance because I could never see myself coming back to this place again.

That settled it. I turned left towards Lastingham and drove along the narrow road for a mile until I came into the village. On the right, I saw an imposing old stone church with a sign outside saying St Mary's. It stood atop a mound of grass, which itself was dotted with old gravestones. The whole site was encircled with a dry-stone wall. I parked the car in a lay-by and stared up at the ancient building. I was struck by its majesty for such a small village on the edge of the moors. It must have an interesting history, I thought, as I got out. The wind was beginning to blow harder, and I buttoned up my raincoat.

Putting my head down, I went through a wooden gate and up the wet path to the church door. I turned the metal ring to lift the latch and pushed, but the door was locked tight. Disappointed, I wandered around the gravestones looking for Mum's. It was so wet my wellies squelched on the sodden grass and the wind blew in my face in squally gusts. I couldn't read the inscriptions on the stones because of all the lichen and moss clinging to them. It was clear the occupants of these graves were long dead. I walked around to the other side of the church and found another entrance. This one was covered by a long porch and had a carved stone bench near the door. When I turned its metal ring, the door creaked open. I hesitated on the threshold wondering if I should go in, but it felt like something was driving me on. I stepped inside and wiped my boots on the mat. Nothing could have prepared me for the magnificence of the cathedral-like interior. Beautiful stone arches reached to the ceiling and colourful stained-glass framed the windows.

I stood at the welcome sign for visitors and was stunned to read I was in one of the oldest churches in England. St Cedd of Lindisfarne had founded a Celtic monastery on the site in AD654, which had been destroyed. The building of the existing church had begun as early as 1078, just 12 years after Norman the Conqueror invaded Britain.

Captivated by its history, I wandered around looking at the window designs, the hangings on the walls, and stone carvings. I was surprised at how peaceful it felt in there, and I wasn't at all worried about seeing ghouls and ghosts. My only moment of hesitation came when I stood at the top of a narrow stone staircase in front of a sign saying that it led down to the Norman crypt and a shrine built for St Cedd. Was it sensible to go down? I looked over my shoulder and all around, but there was no-one else in the church. Again, it was as if something was carrying me along and I had to see the crypt. I went down the rough stone steps which were steep but well lit. At the bottom, a low archway led up to a plain stone altar and I had to bend my head to walk along and reach it. The atmosphere was so tranquil that I sat on a stone bench near the altar to absorb the silence and pervading aura of history. This was a special place and I wondered if Mum had sat on this bench. Of course, she had. She'd have explored every nook and cranny of this church.

Suddenly, in the silence, I heard a voice, or more like whispering and my heart quickened. I was trapped down here in the crypt, with the staircase the only way in and out. I listened. The sound seemed to be echoing down the stairs from the nave above. I tiptoed back to the steps, climbed them quietly, and stood behind a pillar at the back of the church. Peering out from behind it, I saw an old man in the front pew, head bowed, and hands clasped deep in prayer. There was something moving about the hunched figure, as if a deep sadness radiated from him. I came out from behind the pillar and sat down in a pew at the back so as not to disturb him.

I was conscious that I was intruding into this man's private prayer, although he seemed to have no sense of my presence. I was somehow drawn to him. I couldn't help but watch while he made the sign of the cross and struggled to his feet. He had to haul himself up with the aid of a stick. And when he turned, I looked down, not wanting him to think I'd been watching him. His stick tapped on the flagstones as he walked slowly down the aisle. When he stopped close to me, I raised my eyes.

He physically jolted when he saw me. "Grace," he whispered. That one word conveyed so much emotion that we just stared at each other.

I'd never met this old man before, but I recognised him immediately. That once young and tall physique in the photo on the mantelpiece of his cottage was now bent over with age, and that handsome, rugged face deeply lined. It was Patrick.

I should have stormed out of that church without acknowledging him. I should have given him a piece of my mind for what he'd done to our family. I didn't do any of that. It was as if all the anger and hurt had been sucked out of me in the car on the Moors that afternoon. All I saw was a dignified, sad old man who'd loved my mother. Tears sprang into my eyes and down my cheeks.

His face crumpled. "I'm sorry we had to meet like this, Grace." His eyes glistened. "So very sorry."

His voice was kind, without rancour.

"Why didn't Mum tell me about you?" I asked.

There was a pause. "May I sit down?" he asked.

To be honest, I wasn't sure if I wanted him to. I was afraid of discovering more upsetting secrets. But my desire to know the truth was stronger and I nodded.

He sat down, heavily, next to me.

"Violet was afraid of losing you," he said. "That's why she didn't tell you. She was afraid Max would prevent her from seeing you."

That surprised me and I had to think. "I can understand that," I said, after a while, "but why not tell me *after* Dad died? Or before *she* died? Why leave me to unravel all this in the most hurtful way?"

His brow wrinkled into a frown. "She left a letter with her solicitor explaining everything, with instructions to give it to you on her death, with the contents of her will."

"I didn't get any letter." I didn't know whether to be mollified by that or even more hurt. "Why didn't she just *tell* me?"

He sucked in his teeth. "You know your mother, Grace. She was a writer, good with words on paper. It's how she best expressed herself."

"More like she was too much of a coward to tell me."

He shook his head. "Your mother was no coward. She was more afraid you'd despise her."

I turned to him. "I wouldn't have minded about your friendship in later life. She was lonely after Dad died."

He shuffled on his seat.

I saw his discomfort. "Tell me the truth," I said. "I don't want to hear any lies, or half-truths. I don't want some sanitised version you think would make me feel better either. I want the whole truth. I'm tired of all the deceit."

"So am I," he said with feeling.

"Then, *please*."

I felt his eyes on me, but I refused to meet them.

He gave a long sigh. "I should start at the beginning," he said, softly. "You see, Violet and I met years ago, in a publishing house in London when we were both trying to sell our first children's novel."

I could hear the warmth in his voice at the memory.

"She was an attractive woman, your mother, inside and out." He gave a little shrug. "Her book was published, but not mine. However, the publisher loved the illustrations I'd done for my own book and engaged me on a freelance basis to do Violet's illustrations." He paused. "Do you believe in love at first sight, Grace?"

"No," I said.

He gave me a sympathetic smile. "Well, that's how it was when I met your mother."

I waited for him to continue, but he seemed lost in his memories. "And then?" I prompted.

"Ah, it was an exciting time in London. Pop music, rock bands, long hair." His voice became more animated as the memories flowed. "It was a heady time for young people, a time for hippies… flowers in their hair, free love, and all that. The economy was finally recovering and there was a sense that anything was possible. It was an optimistic time."

I nodded, impatient for him to continue.

"Violet and I started dating. We spent a lot of time at concerts, the pictures and theatre and started talking about a future together. Then, out of the blue, I was offered a job in New York, a well-paid job, doing illustrations for a publishing house over there. It was too good an opportunity to miss, or so Violet said. I didn't want to leave without her, but she insisted I go and see what the job and New York were like. She said she'd come over later when I was settled." He stopped and shook his head as if the memory was painful. "So, off I went, to travel and see the world. Or rather America." He smiled again. "It was exciting being in New York. The job was great and the people warm and welcoming. I loved it."

"And my mother?" I asked, thinking of the parallels in the way Peter had left me.

He nodded. "We wrote to one another for a few months," he said. "Letter was the only means of communication back then, apart from the telephone. But transatlantic calls cost a fortune, so we didn't talk on the phone. But then…" He paused for ages until a kind of desolation came into his voice. "Violet stopped writing. I kept writing to her, several letters, but got no reply. Frantic with worry, I phoned but I was told she'd moved and left no forwarding address." He was speaking as if feeling the pain all over again. "I couldn't believe it. I *wouldn't* believe it until I finally got a letter from her saying she'd met someone else and was getting married." He fumbled in his pocket and pulled out a handkerchief to dab his eyes.

I was touched by his distress, and cross with Mum too. It seems she'd hurt just about everyone who'd ever loved her.

We fell silent for a while. I was conscious of rain pattering on the windows. The altar candles started flickering in the breeze that rattled through the old church, casting shadows on the stone floor. I was reluctant to break that spell, but I was desperate to know the full truth. "So, when did you meet up with Mum again?" I asked.

He stared ahead. "Ten years later, at the same London publisher. Your mother's career was going from strength to strength by then. She was very well known." He gave a rueful smile. "You see, I'd continued doing her illustrations, even though I was living in New York. I watched her meteoric rise from a distance."

"You stayed in America?"

He nodded. "I'd married my American wife Lizzie by then. I wasn't just interested in illustrating though, I had another passion."

"Ah," I said, remembering Mum's framed photo in his sitting room. "The piano?"

He looked surprised. "Yes. I wanted to realise my dream of becoming a concert pianist. So, I came back to London with Lizzie to try and further that career. And that's when I saw Violet again. All through the years, I'd still been doing her book illustrations for her publisher, and we met up again in their offices."

"Is that when you started your affair?" I hadn't meant to be tactless. It just came out that way.

He shook his head. "That came later."

"While my father was still alive?" I knew in my heart that was the truth, but I wanted to hear it from him.

"Yes," he said. "You see I'd never stopped loving Violet and, well…"

"She'd never stopped loving you." I was quite sanguine when I said that because it all made sense now. My parents' cool relationship and the fact that Dad and I never went to any of her book launches or signings. Dad must have been so hurt yet they kept up the pretence of a marriage for years, probably because of me. I remembered the key I'd found in the hatbox all those years ago and shuddered to think I'd stumbled on her secret.

"Mum lied to me when she said she was going to the seaside to write," I said. "She came up here to see you, didn't she?"

Patrick nodded. "By then Lizzie and I had moved into our cottage in Hutton-le-Hole. Lizzie was suffering from cancer, and we thought the country air and peaceful life would be good for her in those final years. And it was." His voice shook. "She fought the disease for three years before she finally succumbed."

I could hear the grief in his voice. "I'm sorry," I said.

He nodded. "At first your mother and I were just friends, collaborating on her books. It was only after Lizzie passed away that we resumed… our relationship." His voice trailed away.

"And Dad found out about the pair of you because of me," I said, softly. "When I found the key to Mum's house in her old hatbox."

He shook his head. "You're not to blame for any of this, Grace. Max found out about the house before that and was furious. He'd already confronted Violet and demanded that she sell it and never come up here again." He swallowed as if the memory was difficult. "He threatened to divorce her and fight for sole custody of you. He said he would drag her through the courts and ruin her name and career with all the publicity." He turned to me. "And it *would* have ruined her, Grace. They were different times. And she *was* guilty of…"

"Adultery."

"Yes," he said. "She thought she'd lose custody of you, and she couldn't risk that." He shook his head. "I couldn't have lived with myself if that had happened either. So," he continued with a deep sigh, "Violet agreed to sell the house in Hutton-le-Hole and never to see me again."

"But she didn't keep to that agreement, did she?"

He shook his head. "She did put the house on the market and found a buyer. But, when it came to the crunch, she couldn't go through with it."

"Then I found that key in the hatbox, and Dad went ballistic."

Patrick nodded. "They had a blazing row. Violet was racked with guilt. She didn't want to hurt Max or bring shame on the family, but she told him she couldn't lose you. She said she would fight him for custody whatever damage it did to her career. Max just as passionately vowed that she would never take you."

You will never ever take Grace. Those were the words etched on my brain from that night too. I'd never understood their implication until now. "So," I sighed, with the sadness of it all. "I assume my parents came to an arrangement of some kind?"

"Yes. Violet agreed with Max that she would come here twice a year to write. One of his stipulations was that she never bring you with her or involve you in her life here in any way." He glanced at me. "Max was determined you should never meet me."

I couldn't hide the bitterness in my voice. "You do know that you wrecked my parents' marriage *and* our family life together, don't you?"

"Grace …" His eyes glistened again. "I should never have gone to New York, never have left your mother."

"But you did," I said, hotly. "You did."

"Please, Grace," he pleaded. "I need to explain how much we loved each other. We had no choice, you see, your mother and I…"

"You had every choice," I interrupted. "You should have walked away. Done the right thing for my parents and me."

"Grace, please listen…"

Suddenly the church door creaked opened, and we both turned.

Blake hurried towards us, his footsteps echoing on the stone floor. "There you are, Grace." He sounded so relieved. "Your friends are worried senseless back at the house. Sam rang and told me what happened."

"*Did* she now?"

Blake faltered and looked from me to Patrick. Something in that hesitation and the way he searched our faces told me that he already knew about Mum and Patrick.

"You can relax," I said to him. "Patrick has already owned up to an affair with Mum."

"I see."

"You already knew that though, didn't you?" I went on before Blake could answer. "I suppose they told you that my so-called friend Sam slept with my partner, Peter, too. He left because he couldn't face telling me the truth either." Then I spun back to Patrick. "I suppose my mother knew about Sam and Peter? Evie would have told her."

He had the good grace to look embarrassed. "Yes, and Violet told me."

I felt chilled to the bone with both the cold and deception. Unable to bear the look of pity on their faces, I stood up, pushed past Blake and hurried to the door, anxious to get away.

"Grace," Blake called.

I kept going. The moment I stepped outside into the dark, a strong blast of wind almost bowled me over and Blake pulled me back under the porch light.

"The weather's turned. It's dangerous to go wandering around out there." He hesitated. "Look, we need to talk about Evie, and Joe's murder. Can we just go back inside for a few minutes?"

I stared at him.

"Please, Grace."

The wind tugged at my coat and hair, and I shivered.

"Come on." Blake led me back inside.

Patrick was at the altar relighting the candles that the wind had blown out when Blake opened the door. He smiled at me. "I've never seen them all blow out in one go before. The weather's atrocious."

Blake nodded. "There's a yellow weather warning out for storms and heavy rain tonight." He cleared pamphlets off a table, pulled up some chairs for us to sit down and called to Patrick to join us.

I watched Patrick walk slowly back down the aisle. I could see he was in pain, and I guessed his legs were stiff with arthritis. Somehow, that stooped figure tugged at my heart strings and I looked away as he pulled out a chair and sat down with a whoosh of air.

"Right," said Blake. "Now, I know it's hard for you to be here with us, Grace, but we must put that aside while we talk about Joe Dunstan's murder and Evie. Now, tell me about Evie. What happened earlier?"

"You must have heard it all from your DS," I said, although the look in his eyes did make me wonder. "She came to our house this morning, at the same time as your forensics officer."

"Tell me what happened," he said.

"I was over at the village museum when they all arrived."

He nodded. "What happened with my Sergeant?" he asked.

The thought of DS Gray got me all fired up again. "When I got back to the house, I found her questioning Evie again. She was pushing her to confess to killing Joe... all in the name of Kitty Garthwaite."

Patrick frowned. "I don't understand. What do you mean in Kitty's name?"

"DS Gray says Evie is mentally ill," I said. "She believes that Evie went out in the early hours of Sunday morning to Lowna Ford and killed Joe for Kitty Garthwaite. That Kitty told her to do it. That somehow Kitty has possessed Evie."

"Goodness." Patrick turned to Blake. "How awful for Evie."

That made me warm to Patrick. "I've known Evie all my life," I said. "She would never hurt anyone." I paused. "The thing is..." I was unsure whether I was about to make things better or worse for her. "Evie's become rather obsessed with this Kitty ghost story. And now I understand why." I stopped to choose my words carefully. "You see, Evie's situation is mirroring that of Kitty's all those years ago. Evie is identifying with Kitty because she too is pregnant, and her husband has left her for another woman."

"Poor girl," Patrick said.

"I only found out yesterday when I examined her," I continued. "Evie and her husband Trevor have been trying for a baby for years. Despite IVF, it never happened for them, until this cruel twist of fate." I sighed. "You see, it turns out that Trevor was having an affair and left Evie a couple of months ago when he got his lover pregnant. Evie only discovered she was carrying his child too after he'd left."

"Does he know Evie's pregnant?" Patrick asked.

I shook my head. "She won't tell him."

"But she must," he said. "She *must*."

I studied him. "Evie told me she met you when she came up with Mum last summer."

He nodded. "And I quite agree with you, Grace, Evie has the sweetest nature. Not a violent bone in her body."

I turned back to Blake. "You see. That's what I've been saying all along."

Blake's face betrayed no emotion, but I was used to his cool demeanour.

"Your DS seems determined to put Evie in the frame for this murder," I said.

He looked at me. "That woman you saw in the back lane when you went to call on Patrick. A woman not of this world I think were your words. Can you remind me what she looked like?"

I shrugged. "She was a young woman, wearing a long grey dress. She had a cloak over her shoulders with a hood at the back. She had dark hair, parted in the middle with plaits falling onto her shoulders. I was too far away then to see her face clearly."

"How old?" he asked.

"Late teens or early twenties. Something like that."

"Have either Sam or Evie seen her?" he asked.

"Sam's never mentioned it and I'm sure she would have if she'd seen her." I paused because I didn't want to make things worse for Evie, but I needed to tell the truth. "Evie said she'd seen Kitty in the house. She even rattled your DS by saying Kitty was standing behind her. Proper scared her."

He nodded. "Evie tried that on me in the kitchen last night too."

I gave him a grim smile. "I believe she is having a nervous breakdown, what with her pregnancy and husband leaving."

Patrick raised his eyebrows.

"Did my mother ever say anything about seeing Kitty's ghost in the house?" I asked Patrick. "I know she was writing about her. I've seen the manuscript of her unfinished novel – 'It Began with a Ghost Story'."

"It's all nonsense," Patrick said. "I told Violet that."

"Are you saying she *had* seen the ghost?"

"Violet said she felt a presence in the house, but it didn't bother her because it wasn't upsetting or threatening. I've never seen this ghost, and I've been in and out of that house for years, plus taking care of it when your mother wasn't there."

"Did you light the fire on the night we arrived?" I asked.

He nodded. "I've been lighting it for a few hours every night since Violet died. I wanted the house to feel lived in, as if she were still there. And I knew you'd come eventually, Grace."

The sadness in his voice brought a lump to my throat. "Did you come into the house in the early hours of Sunday morning, the first night we were there?" I asked him.

His brow wrinkled again. "No. Why?"

"I heard a noise in the middle of the night and went downstairs to find the back door wide open. The lock hadn't been forced. Someone must have had a key."

"A key?" Patrick gasped. "Oh, no."

We both looked at him.

"I always leave a spare key to Violet's house on a hook in the barn. It's in a dark corner where no-one can see it." He hesitated. "You don't think someone *found* it, do you?"

Blake sighed.

"I'm sorry." Patrick was getting distraught. "I kept forgetting to bring the key with me and it's a long walk back to my cottage at the other end of the village."

Blake looked tense as he glanced at his watch again.

I said to Patrick: "Your cleaner, Annie, told me she saw Kitty in Mum's house once when she did some work for her."

"Oh." He gave a dismissive wave. "Don't take what Annie says to heart. She's been affected by all the gossip over the years and loves a good ghost story."

"And you?" I turned to Blake. "Do you think we're imagining it too?"

For a moment, he touched the scars on his forehead. "I've said before that I think ghosts probably exist in the hearts and minds of those who want to believe in them."

"Well," I said to him, "if you want a good description of the young woman I saw outside the front gate of Patrick's house, just stop by the museum. She looked identical to the woman in the painting of Kitty on the wall in the roundhouse. Same clothes and hairstyle. Apparently, they had some play on in there about Kitty."

Blake stared at me.

"It's a strange place, that museum." I shivered. "I don't think I'll be going back."

"Why?"

"The young woman on the front desk was weird. She knew my name and said she'd been expecting me."

He frowned.

"And when I was in the roundhouse, she came in, jumped on stage, and started performing. Playing the role of Kitty or something like that." I shook my head. "I wasn't sure if it was something she did for all visitors. It was bizarre."

"Right," he said, suddenly, as if a thought had just come to him. "I must get back to the station. Come on, let's get you home."

"I've got my car out front," I said.

He nodded. "I saw it. That's how I found you. Look, I'll follow you back to Hutton-le-Hole. Make sure you get inside okay."

I shook my head. "I don't need a chaperone. I'm sure you've wasted enough time already looking for me."

He stood his ground. "Grace, there's a killer out there. Who knows what they're going to do next?"

"Steady on, Blake," Patrick said. "That's a bit strong."

"It isn't," Blake insisted. "Grace should be made aware of the potential danger she and her friends are in. And Violet's house figures in all this somehow." He turned to me. "Look, I know you're upset with your friends, and you have every reason to be. But you must all stay together in the house tonight, whatever the provocation. Is that understood?"

I nodded. "I'd already come to that conclusion," I said. "But I'm telling you now, we're going back to London tomorrow morning. Sam will get a taxi to York station, and I'll drive Evie home with me."

Blake shook his head. "You need to stay here. Evie is still a suspect."

"She's in no fit state to answer your questions. Any lawyer will tell you that," I insisted. "And I assure you she is not being questioned again either in my house or in your police station without one." I paused. "Anyway, you've just said we're targets. We need to get out of the house." I drew myself up. "It's not like we're leaving the country, we're only returning home to London. You've got all our contact details."

"I can stay in the house with you tonight, Grace," Patrick said. "It would be no trouble."

I shook my head. "Thank you, but we'll be fine."

"Well, I'm just along the road, if you need me," he said.

"Come on, Grace." Blake was impatient to leave. "I want to make sure you get home safely before I go back to work. You too, Patrick."

I didn't protest anymore. Blake looked shattered and needed to get on with his job without any more argument from me. But I was more determined than ever to leave this place first thing in the morning.

Blake hurried us to the door and braced for the wind as he opened it. "Remember," he said to Patrick and me as we filed past. "Stay indoors tonight."

Twenty-seven

My heart was heavy with dread as I opened the front door. The last thing I could handle was more upset and confrontation with Sam and Evie. I listened, but there was no sound of voices. That was a relief. I slipped off my raincoat and wellies and padded into the sitting room in my socks. The fire was lit, with the guard around to prevent spitting embers burning the rug. I warmed myself for a bit, then went into the kitchen. No-one in there either. The signs of Sam's messy cooking were all around, and I had to push away the memories of her smashing up Mum's crockery in her drunken state the night before. I spotted a heavy casserole dish on the hob and went over to lift the lid. Inside were the remnants of what looked like a lamb stew, with dollops of white fat solidifying on top. Dirty plates covered the draining board, which suggested Sam and Evie had already eaten. I checked my watch and was amazed to see it was just past 8pm. In my agitated state, I'd been unaware of time passing and the day had gone by in a flash. Just as well, I thought. The sooner this night was over, the better. We'd be out of here in the morning.

I decided I couldn't stomach the stew and put the lid back on the pan. Instead, I found some eggs in the fridge and was busy poaching them when I heard the stairs creak and footsteps approach. I hoped it wasn't Sam, but it was.

"I'm glad you're okay, Grace," she said in a soft voice as she came into the kitchen.

I kept my eyes on the pan of eggs, hoping she would just give up and go away if I didn't answer.

She sighed. "I didn't mean to hurt you, Grace. You must believe me."

I was in a strangely detached mood now, almost as if I wasn't in the room. I just wanted to be left alone.

But she kept on talking. "I know it sounds trite, but it just happened between Peter and me. Really it did. I was in that bar with friends when he came in one night and…"

"Stop!" I turned to face her. "You slept with my partner behind my back. There's nothing you can say or do to make up for that." I was surprised how controlled I sounded. "I don't want to hear any more about it."

"It didn't mean anything," she said. "Peter just told me I was fun to be around."

Her words felt like a knife slicing through my heart because I understood their meaning. *You suck the fun out of everything.* Peter had flung those words at me and now I knew why.

Footsteps came tripping down the stairs and Evie appeared. "Thank God!" She flung her arms around me. "I was so worried." Tears sprung into her eyes. "I'm sorry, Grace. So very sorry." She turned on Sam. "Leave Grace alone. You've done enough damage."

I felt my body tense. This was just what I'd wanted to avoid.

But Evie was in full flow. "Women like you should be put in the stocks and stoned," she shouted at Sam. "You're nothing but a floozy. A fat heifer. A jampot." Pure rage flashed across her face. She picked up Mum's rolling pin from the counter and raised it to strike Sam.

I grabbed her arm, and the rolling pin clattered to the floor.

The three of us stared at each other as if frozen on film. None of us, including Evie, could quite believe the violence she had been about to unleash.

I reacted first. "Right," I said in a voice that brooked no argument. "This is what's going to happen next." I looked at them both in turn. "Evie and I are driving back to London in the morning. You, Sam, are going by train."

"Grace," Sam pleaded, arms outstretched. "It doesn't have to be like this."

"I'm afraid it does." My voice was still calm. "Everything we do has some consequence."

"Aw, Grace, *please*…"

I shook my head. "I'll order a taxi to pick you up first thing in the morning and take you to York station. You can get the train to King's Cross from there." I looked directly into her eyes. "Now, will you please leave me alone?"

She stared at me for a while, then her face and shoulders drooped, and she slunk off. I remembered our conversation in the kitchen the day before when she'd grasped my hand and asked if we'd always be friends. Now I understood what lay behind that gesture. But I was both hurt and furious. It wasn't just that she'd slept with Peter, it was the way she'd let me worry myself sick when he went off and didn't get in touch. I'd been imagining him lying dead in a ditch somewhere, or on his deathbed in hospital, with no-one to help him. Not knowing what had happened to him was sheer torment. That's what I couldn't forgive her for. Or him.

When Sam had gone, I turned to Evie. "Go and pack up your stuff. We'll get an early night and be away first thing." I hesitated. "I think you should stay with me in the flat for a while, at least until you've had the baby and sorted yourself out."

Her eyes widened. "You'd do that for me... after everything."

"Yes," I said. It was Mum I blamed for putting Evie in the position of having to lie to me. "Now go on. Get some sleep."

She stood for a moment, smiling at me, although I noticed her hands were shaking. Her eyes glistened as she planted a kiss on my cheek and hugged me tight. "You've been such a good friend to me," she said, her voice breaking with emotion. "I don't deserve your kindness. I've let you down, just like I let everyone down. But thank you, Grace. Thank you so much."

The sadness in her voice brought a lump to my throat. "You haven't let me down." I pulled a tissue out of the box on the dresser and handed it to her. "Let's focus all our energy now on leaving here in the morning. We'll have plenty of time to talk when we get back to London."

She took the tissue and gave me another sad smile. "Goodnight, Grace," she whispered.

"Night, Evie." I watched her leave the kitchen and trudge dejectedly along to the stairs. I sighed and turned to my now hard poached eggs. I spooned them out of the pan and onto a plate of cold toast. I didn't care though; food was the last thing on my mind. I was just glad to be alone again. It was the only time I could think properly. At least things were making sense now. Mum's long-standing affair with Patrick explained why she'd bought this house and visited a couple of times a year without Dad and me to 'write'. And Sam and Peter's treachery had prompted him to do a runner, although I knew he'd been hankering after travelling overseas for some time. The truth made me feel calmer, but it hurt more than ever.

When I'd finished eating, I started washing up all the dirty pots and pans and happened to glance out the window. There was another pressing problem that I still had to work out. How was I going to find Rufus and get him into the car in the morning? I pondered this for some time, although I knew in my heart that I was going to have to leave him behind. That made me sad because he was the only living link to Mum I had left. Still, he seemed happy here. The truth was the grumpy old cat had abandoned me rather than the other way around. And I was sure Patrick would look after him. Rufus no doubt preferred his company anyway.

Knowing that Mum always did like a tidy kitchen, I busied myself putting all the dishes back exactly where I'd found them. I considered it my last daughterly duty before leaving the house for good. Then I boiled the kettle, made myself a hot mug of tea and went back into the sitting room to drink it in front of the fire.

After a while of just staring at the glowing embers, I began to relax a little. I looked up at the ornamental figurines and crystal animals that Mum displayed on the mantelpiece alongside an old slate clock and wondered whether to take them, or anything else, back to my London flat. But I couldn't summon up the enthusiasm. I'd never seen any of her possessions in this house before, and they had no sentimental value for me whatsoever. I did seriously consider taking the first editions of her novels, but even they left me cold. The woman I'd called 'Mum', who'd lived in this house, was like a stranger to me now. She'd bought the place to be close to her lover. She'd collaborated with him on all her books and spent as much time here with him as she could. It wasn't hard for me to decide that Patrick was the rightful heir to this house and everything in it.

Once I'd made that decision, it felt like a weight had been lifted from my shoulders. I was coming to terms with her double life. It had been a real shock to find out that she'd hidden such a terrible secret from me. As an only child, my parents had always been the centre of my world. But perhaps I'd never been as important to her as she'd been to me. That thought stung, but I was a grown-up. I had to live with it and get on with my own life.

In the silence, I became aware of the rain still pattering on the windows. The duvet I'd pulled off Mum's bed the night before was folded up at the end of the sofa. I'd had my best night's sleep down here in front of the fire, so I thought I'd do it again. I'd stay fully dressed too, just in case. Laying down, I pulled the duvet over me. I wasn't scared of the unfamiliar creaking noises in this old house anymore or of the wind howling through the trees outside. I was getting used to rural life.

I listened for any movement above from Sam and Evie. It was all quiet and I guessed they were already in bed asleep. Lucky them. I desperately wanted to drift away into oblivion and refresh my tired body, but my mind wouldn't let go. Yes, I had the answers to Mum buying this house and Peter leaving me, but I didn't have a logical answer for the presence of the ghostly woman I'd seen in the back lane and on the Moor. It was ridiculous, but the idea that she might be Kitty Garthwaite's ghost wouldn't go away. And what about that crazy young woman in the museum? Where did she fit into all this?

I remembered reading somewhere that in Kitty's time, it was considered such a sin to take your own life that those pour souls who did were denied a proper funeral and burial. Had that happened to Kitty? With no resting place, perhaps it was her eternal quest to wander the lanes and houses where she'd found happiness with her lover Willie Dixon. I shivered. I didn't like anything about Kitty's dark story and the haunting of Lowna Ford. Why on earth would Mum want to write about something like that? And

I certainly didn't like, and refused to believe, that Evie had anything to do with Joe Dunstan's murder.

However, as I lay there thinking about the legend, that familiar creeping sense of foreboding swept through me again. Somehow, I knew the nightmare we'd been caught up in wasn't yet over. But if I'd had the slightest inkling of what was going to happen that night, I'd have bundled us all into the car and away from that place there and then. But I didn't, and I was too shattered to go anywhere. So, eventually, in the warmth of the fire, my eyes started to feel heavy, and I drifted off to sleep.

Only to be woken later by the sound of screaming.

Twenty-eight

Kitty

1787 – one week after the Autumn Equinox
Lowna Ford

Kitty shuffled uncomfortably as she sat on a thick branch that grew sideways out of the trunk of the old alder tree. She had been in a fever of anticipation all week waiting for today and had arrived early at Lowna. Willie had promised to speak to his father about marrying her and meet her here today, Sunday. This was the exact day of their tryst. She had believed with all her heart that he would come. But she had been waiting a long time and a voice in her head was now starting to doubt that he would. She tried to ignore it, but every time she distracted herself with blissful thoughts of their first night of lovemaking in the barn, and the many wonderful Sundays swimming and canoodling with Willie at this very spot, that nagging distrust returned to shatter her dreams. "Come on, Willie", she shouted to the wind. "Hurry. *Please.*" The only reply was the plop of a frightened water vole as it poked a head out of its riverbank home and plunged into the water to get away from her.

She waited and waited, but Willie did not heed her call. Frozen in her sitting position on the branch, she was now thoroughly wet, cold, and miserable. She shook her hands and swung her legs in the air to get the blood moving around her body and release her stiff joints. She did not want to get down from the tree though. It was the perfect spot to stare across the swollen river for a sight of Willie arriving on his horse. She loved that first vision of him coming to meet her. He always looked so handsome on horseback, but time was getting on. She looked down at the water nervously. The level had risen since she arrived, but she was sure Willie could still ride across it to reach her, if he came soon.

She stared up through the branches of the old tree that were protecting her from the worst of the rain and marvelled at the shivering leaves that were still in full bloom. She could not believe it was already Autumn. Now, the days were the same length as the nights, and the household had changed its daily routines. Because of the rains, the harvest had been difficult for the labourers to collect. Much of the crop had been destroyed which meant a harder year for provisions. Mrs Pickering would be ruling the kitchen with a rod of iron from now on. Only the sheep grazing in the fields and on the Moors seemed to be oblivious to the wet weather, though shearing their coats for wool had been more difficult than usual.

The problem with Autumn, especially a wet one, was that daylight faded much earlier. Now that the twilight gloom had descended, the river looked as black and as uninviting as her mood. She would need to start walking back to the farm soon. Mrs Pickering would send men out to look for her if she did not return before dark.

Oh, Lord, Mrs Pickering! Kitty dared not face her. She could not tell her, or Mabel, that she was with child. She could not bear to witness the looks on their faces. She was certain to be sacked and cast out in shame. But where would she go? She had no family and no-one else would take her in in her condition. "Oh, Willie…Willie," she cried. "What have you done to me?"

Eventually, when total darkness had fallen and she was sure Willie would not come, her mood turned from despair to anger. "You coward, Willie," she screamed out. She had given herself to him because they were betrothed. He *had* promised marriage, there was no doubt in her mind about that. She could not, and would not, give him up now she was with child. She would go and see that Castleton girl and tell her. She would tell Willie's father. She would tell the Pickerings and everyone else who would listen that Willie had promised marriage when he made love to her. She *would* marry Willie. She would make him marry her. Fury powered her along as she trudged wearily back to the farm, with all sorts of thoughts bubbling irrationally in her head. So much so that she feared she was losing her mind.

Back in the farmyard, that rage had turned to abject fear, and she stood at the kitchen door unable to go inside. She shivered uncontrollably. What would become of her? And her baby? She went to lift the door latch but could not do it. Clutching her stomach, she turned and walked across to the stables. She stumbled inside, took off her cloak, and shook out the water. Hanging it on a hook, she went over to where the chestnut horse was tethered. She stroked his nose with her frozen fingers, and leaned against him, feeling the only warmth and comfort she had known in weeks. He nuzzled her gently. She was weeping silent tears into its soft back when a voice barked out: "What is going on in here?"

"It's only me, John," she called out, softly.

"Kitty?" He came over and held the oil lamp up to look at her. "Goodness, lass. You are soaked to the skin. Where have you been? Why are you crying?"

Kitty did not reply.

"Answer me, lass," he said.

"I was walking on the Moors and got caught in the rain."

He made a tutting sound and went over to Mr Pickering's carriage to retrieve a blanket. "Here," he said, pulling out a stool. "Sit down there and put this around you before you catch your death." He stared into her eyes and put his hand on her forehead. "That is if you have not already. You feel feverish."

Kitty collapsed onto the stool while John put the blanket around her.

"Now," John said. "Are you going to tell me what has happened? Why would you do a crazy thing and walk the Moors for hours in this weather?"

Kitty stared up at him, unable to hold back any longer. "Did you drive the family to St Mary's Church again today?"

"Aye."

She bit her lip, then said. "Did you see Willie Dixon?"

John stared at her for what seemed like ages. "So, it is him, then?"

She nodded.

"Oh Kitty. Kitty," he said, softly. "Are you out of your mind?"

"Willie promised marriage," she said, weakly. "He said he loved me."

A pitying look came over John's face, but he seemed at a loss to find the words to comfort her.

"He promised to meet me this afternoon at Lowna Ford. I waited for hours in the rain, but he did not come. He promised," she said, bitterly. "He promised."

John gave a deep sigh. "Look lass, maybe that is just as well. You will need to forget him.

Kitty stared at him. "Why do you say that?"

"Well," John continued, gently. "I was talking to one of Willie's father's labourers outside church today while I was waiting for the family. He told me there has been great upset in the Dixon household. Willie's father has been in a bad temper all week. My friend did not know all the details but knew enough to say it concerned Willie's betrothal to a girl from Castleton." John bit his lip as if wondering whether to continue, then decided he should. "Anyway, Willie was in church with his family and this girl this morning." He frowned in concentration as he recalled the scene. "Willie left the church before everyone else and rode off on his horse alone." He shook his head. "Mrs Pickering chattered about nothing but the wedding in the carriage on the way home. She is so excited about it."

Kitty was not listening anymore. Her head drooped, and tears flowed down her cheeks.

"Now, now, lass," John soothed. "Do not upset yourself so. The man is not worth it. Forget him and find someone who deserves you."

"You do not understand," she choked. "I am with child. *Willie's* child."

John visibly jolted with shock. "Was that the sickness the other morning?"

She nodded.

His face hardened. He went over to the stable wall and took his driving hammer off a nail. "I will ride over to Hutton-Le-Hole and see young Willie Dixon."

Kitty stood up and grabbed his arm. "You will not," she said, firmly. "I do not want you getting into trouble and sacked on my account."

"Willie cannot treat you like that," he growled. "I will not let him get away with it."

Kitty pulled the hammer out of John's hand and hung it back on the wall. "You will not do anything," she insisted.

"This is my life and my baby. I will not let Willie get away with it. I will not let his father stop our marriage. These treacherous men must be stopped."

"Kitty," John breathed. "You must know that you cannot make Willie marry you."

"I am carrying *his* child. His mother and father's grandchild."

Willie pointed at her stomach. "What if Willie denies the child is his?"

"It *is* his," she said, hotly.

"You know that, and I know that. But it would be Willie's word against yours." He shook his head. "Anyway, let us face the truth. Willie will not be able to defy his father. He would be cast out."

Kitty stood up abruptly, grabbed her cloak, and stomped out of the stables. "We will see about that," she hissed over her shoulder.

"Kitty," John called. "Come back. Let us talk about this. Come back, lass."

But Kitty did not.

Later, as she lay in bed, the hammering rain on thatch made sleep impossible. That, and the north wind whistling through the old farmhouse. It did not often blow directly from the north but, when it did, it was able to squeeze in through the attic beams and window frames and freeze the air. Every so often it would tug at the metal latch on the door as if demanding to be let into the rest of the house.

Shivering with cold, or perhaps fear at her predicament, Kitty pulled the blanket up over her head for comfort, but that only served to suffocate her even more. She tossed and turned on her straw mattress. She was ice cold, yet her sark was covered in sweat. The rough cotton of the night robe was itchy, but usually kept her warm. Tonight though, she was freezing. Had she caught a fever out in the wind and rain all afternoon? Were the dark thoughts swirling around in her head due to the fever too? Sad thoughts. Angry thoughts. Her head was spinning so much she could not think straight. She was sure of one thing though – she hated working in this house. She hated Mabel and she hated the Pickerings. She wanted to run away and never come back. Trouble was, she had nowhere else to go.

Murderous thoughts took hold now. She pushed back the blanket and glanced over at Mabel who lay on her back in her bed softly snoring. That night, as they had washed the pans in the scullery sink, the old witch had started gossiping again about Willie and that Castleton girl, having heard the news about their supposed marriage from John on his return. Pain seared through Kitty's chest at the thought of Willie with that woman, followed by other darker feelings. One minute she was sure she loved Willie with all her heart. The next, she hated him with a dark vengeance.

Had he abandoned her? Certainly, he had not shown up for their tryst that afternoon. Had he deceived her all along? Taken her for a fool? Strung her along to trick her into giving herself to him, then cast her aside like an old shoe? So much for his promise of love. So much for his promise of arranging matters with his family. Kitty could feel a rage like nothing she had ever known building up inside her. He had left her waiting for hours all afternoon by the swollen river at Lowna in the wind and rain knowing she was with child. *His* child. He had said he loved her and promised to marry her. That was a lie.

Or was it a lie? Perhaps John and Mabel were telling lies. Spiteful lies, to hurt her. But why had Willie not shown up that afternoon? John said he'd left church early and ridden off on his horse. Had he had an accident or been thrown from his horse in the bad weather? There she was feeling sorry for herself, and he could be lying injured somewhere. Or maybe Willie had not been able to get away that afternoon. Could he be at their tree now? In the summer, they had often stayed up there until first light, before anyone was about, and before she started her morning duties.

Suddenly, a fierce gust of wind rattled the latch. The attic door swung open and banged against the wall. Kitty sat up with a start, while Mabel just rolled over and carried on snoring.

Kitty's head was throbbing so hard, she could not think straight. Was that the fever? Or the incessant rain pounding on the thatch? Or the overwhelming loneliness that settled on her the moment the rain had started; that familiar dread of the elements she had had since childhood. It arrived unannounced from time to time like an unwelcome visitor. She knew that fear was absurd, but she had never been able to stop it. The death of her mother had only made it worse since there was no-one to comfort her now, except Willie.

Or were Mabel's lies and wretched snoring making her crazy? Kitty pulled her woollen shawl off the metal hook in the beam above her head and wrapped it around her shoulders. She had to get away from Mabel and the Pickerings. Away from this house. She needed to see Willie, to know that everything would be all right.

The cold, pine floorboards creaked as she stepped onto them. Mabel had purloined the old rug from the master's bedroom that was meant for the labourers and laid it beside her own bed so that her feet would not be cold when she got up of a morning. Kitty picked up the chamber pot to fling the slops into the ratbag's face as she slept, but then managed to stop herself. She would never get out of the house if she made a scene and woke the master and mistress. They would set her to work clearing up the mess, and she would have no chance of seeing Willie.

She placed the chamber pot on Mabel's rug hoping she would step into it as she got out of bed. Closing the door behind her as she left, she clicked the metal latch into position, then crept down the stairs, all the while listening for any noise. The house was deadly quiet. At the bottom of the staircase, she had to be especially careful because the master and his family slept in rooms leading off this landing.

Again, no-one stirred. Kitty headed down the main staircase to the kitchen. There, she slipped on her boots, flinching as her bare feet touched the cold leather that was still wet from her earlier soaking. Hands shaking, she put on her bonnet and cloak. She turned the key in the scullery door and slipped out of the house.

Outside, the first gust of wind caught in her throat, and she put her hand on the cold stone to steady herself. In the east, she saw a faint purple glow on the horizon. Almost dawn. She blinked to dispel the blurriness in her eyes. She had to get to their tree. Willie would be waiting for her, she was sure. Resolute, she pulled the cloak tight around her and ran across the yard. The rain was light and misty now, which was a relief. She would take the shortcut to Lowna. If she stayed off the cart track, no-one would see her.

Climbing over the gate, she ran across the field towards the river. Grazing sheep scattered in surprise, bleating out alarm calls, as she ran through them. All she could think about was getting to the tree and to Willie. Her heart soared at the thought of seeing him. She tried to focus on his image, standing there, waiting for her. But all she could see was that Castleton mare, with her lily-white hands and fine clothes. *She* didn't have to scrub the scullery floors and blacken the stove.

What hope do you have against her? Kitty shuddered at the voice in her head.

Desperate now, she trudged on through water-logged fields, her boots slowing her down as they sunk in the mud. Her head throbbed. Her chest felt it would burst with the effort. Then she heard a noise behind her. A noise like squelching footsteps in the mud. Had someone seen her leave the farmhouse? Were they following her?

She stood still, suddenly fearful, and peered back into the darkness. "Who's there?"

No reply.

On she ran towards the tree on the riverbank. As she got closer, she could hear nothing over the noise of water rushing down from the Moors above. The usually calm stream had crept over its banks and was now a torrent.

"Willie?" she called. "Willie?"

She waded through the ankle-high water to their tree and climbed up onto the sideways branch to sit and wait for him. Faint and feverish, she clung to the tree trunk to stop herself falling off. All the while, she could not take her eyes off the opposite riverbank. Willie would come. He *would* come.

As she waited, head swimming, she hardly noticed the water rising. Dark thoughts bubbled up again, and she tried to push them away. But all she could see was *that* Castleton girl, with her rosy cheeks and sleek curls.

Kitty let out a sob as her mind replayed those thoughts over and over. It was almost as if someone was whispering in her ear. *Why would Willie choose a penniless servant girl when he could have a rich farmer's daughter? Why would he want you?*

As she clung to the tree trunk a primeval howl bubbled up from the depths of her soul and came out through her lips. It reverberated on the wind and all around her, filling the valley with the haunting sound of despair.

She had listened to Willie's promises of love, of marriage, of a life together and believed him. Why? Because she loved him more than anything in the world and wanted nothing more than to be his wife and live as a family with their child.

Tears flowed down her cheeks, mingling with the rain. Sobs racked her body. *Now you're with child, Willie doesn't want you anymore.* That voice in her head again.

But it was the truth. She knew it. And she had nobody to help her out of her terrible predicament. Not a soul in the world. She put a hand on her stomach. "I'm sorry," she whispered to her child. "I'm so sorry."

Her body slumped as if every breath had been knocked out of her. She looked down at the water, swirling beneath her feet. It seemed like a blessed relief. A final way out. Succumbing to her misery and fever, her arms slackened, and she let herself slip off the branch into the water.

"Willie," she cried out, as rage replaced the love in her heart. "You will pay for this. As God is my witness, *Willie,* you will pay!"

Twenty-nine

Grace

Present Day
Hutton-le-Hole

I winced as another loud scream echoed through the night and sat up on the sofa, my heart pounding through the fog of sleep. It sounded like it was coming from the back garden. I looked over to the terrace doors and saw the curtains edged in an orange glow, as if it were already light. But it wasn't the normal soft glow of morning.

I jumped up, pulled back the curtains and gasped in shock. Flames flickered in the old barn at the end of the garden and smoke billowed up into the night sky.

Another terrifying shriek shuddered through the night. It didn't sound human. Then I realised it wasn't. I could see Rufus struggling and howling to free himself from that ghostly woman's grip as she held him aloft in her arms. Her cloak hood was down, but I couldn't make out her features in the dark even though she was looking in my direction. Then, as if to taunt me, she turned towards the barn.

Oh my God! Was she going to throw Rufus into the fire?

"Stop!" I shouted, banging on the windows with both fists. "Stop!"

Rufus must have heard me and started screeching even louder.

I stumbled into the kitchen, unlocked the back door, and rushed outside. The wind drove a wall of rain into my face as if I'd had a bucket of water thrown over me. I hardly noticed the feel of my bare feet on icy flagstones. All I could hear was Rufus's cries and the crackle of flames.

I bolted along the terrace and ran across sodden grass towards the barn, mud and water oozing through my toes. Fire lit up the sky. Smoke filled my nostrils.

I looked around frantically, but the woman had disappeared. I ran up to the barn, but the heat was so fierce it held me back. "Rufus," I half screamed, half sobbed. "Rufus!"

Suddenly he appeared from nowhere and flung himself into my arms, knocking me flat onto my back on the wet grass. As I lay winded, clutching him to my chest, I felt his heart pounding right through me. "It's all right," I whispered. "It's all right."

I didn't know how long I lay there. Seconds probably. But Sam was soon beside me. She'd had the presence of mind to slip her raincoat over her nightdress and was holding onto the hood to keep it up in the wind. "What the hell-?"

"Go back to the house!" I shouted as I struggled to my knees.

She stared wide-eyed at the fire as if mesmerised, the red glow reflecting eerily on her face.

"Quick!" I scrambled to my feet, tucked Rufus under my arm with one hand, and grabbed Sam with the other. "Get inside the house."

She tried to shrug me off, but I held her in a vice-like grip. "Do as I say!"

The fear in my voice jolted her and she ran back to the house beside me. Once in the kitchen, I slammed the door, locked it, and threw the bolts.

When I turned round, Sam was staring at me, face stony as a mask.

I was shivering with cold and shock. My teeth chattered so hard that I could barely speak. "S-someone set fire to the b-barn."

She nodded. "I've called the fire brigade. They're on their way."

Rufus started whining in my arms and I realised I was squeezing the life out of him. I grabbed a towel from the rail and wrapped him up in it. "Good boy," I murmured as I laid him in his bed and stroked his head. Normally, he would have protested at any sign of affection from me, but he lay still and quiet.

Sam picked up a kitchen chair and wedged it sideways against the cat flap. "There, that'll stop him getting out again." She went over to the dresser and pulled out a large towel. "Here." She handed it to me and watched me rub my face and hair, before saying: "I want to know what's going on, Grace."

I was still shivering too hard to speak. My clothes felt like an ice-cold compress on my skin. I stripped them off and wrapped the towel around me. Then stared out the window at the blaze.

"There's nothing we can do but wait for the fire brigade," Sam said. "There's no water source up at the barn to put it out."

"I'm worried it'll spread to the trees and paddocks. Maybe to neighbouring gardens."

Sam looked out the window and shook her head. "It's too wet. The ground's saturated." Her eyes swivelled back to me. "I smelt petrol up there. That's the only way anyone could get a blaze like that going in these conditions."

I nodded. There was no electricity or gas supply up there to start it.

"Why would anyone set fire to your barn?" Sam's voice was tight.

I was still furious with her, but she deserved to know what was going on. So, standing there shivering under the glare of the kitchen lights, I quickly told her everything that had happened with that ghostly woman on the Moors and in the back lane; about Rufus's shrieks waking me up and that woman holding him aloft like some sacrifice she was going to throw into the fire. "I know it sounds mad," I continued after a slight pause, "but–"

"I've seen her too," Sam said.

"You have?" I was stunned because she'd never mentioned it before.

She nodded. "On our first morning here. I was up early and went for a quick look around while I was waiting for you and Evie to appear." She frowned. "She didn't look like any ghost to me."

"Tell me exactly what you saw," I urged.

Sam shrugged. "I went outside to have a look around the garden. The old barn seemed interesting, so I went inside. That's when I heard footsteps crunching along in the back lane. There's no window in the barn to look through, so I went back outside and saw a young woman in a long dress walk past."

"Did you see her face?"

Sam shook her head. "She'd already gone past the barn by the time I came out. I only saw her from behind as she carried on down the lane.

"Did you notice anything strange about her?"

"I did a double take because of the old-fashioned clothes she was wearing. I was intrigued enough to follow her."

"You *followed* her?"

"Yes. I thought I'd have a walk down the lane anyway and see where it led to." She paused. "It continues past all the houses on this side and eventually opens up into the village."

"Did the woman see you?" I was impatient now. "Do you think she knew you were behind her?"

Sam shrugged again. "She didn't stop or look back at me."

"What happened then?" I asked. "Where did she go?"

"Into the museum. When she got to the end of the lane, she walked across the village green and straight into the museum."

I frowned. "Didn't it strike you as odd that she was dressed like that?"

"Not really. I assumed she was part of some historical re-enactment or demonstration in the museum."

Of course! The young woman I'd seen over in the museum, the one who'd chilled me to the bone with her menacing performance of Kitty.

Sam's eyes narrowed. "Who is she?"

"I don't know."

"You've got some idea though. I can see it in your eyes."

"Well…it's just that when I was over at the museum this morning, there was a young woman in there acting strangely."

"Acting strangely how?" Sam asked, then added: "You think *she* set fire to the barn?"

"Maybe." I was flustered now. "I-I don't know."

"I think you do," Sam insisted. "Come on, tell me."

I sighed, knowing what I was about to say would sound mad. "I think she might be Kitty's ghost."

Sam's jaw dropped, her face a picture of incredulity. "You can't be serious, Grace. You of all people. A respected doctor."

"What other explanation is there?" I asked, hotly.

She pursed her lips. "This is Evie's fault, filling your head with all this nonsense." She ran her fingers through her hair. "Look, Grace, I know things have been difficult for you over the last year. And I'm sorry about Peter, truly sorry. But you need to get a grip. You really do. You don't want to end up like Evie."

I glared back, indignantly. But was she right? Had I been too influenced by Evie? Too ready to believe all this ghostly nonsense. Something jarred inside me, and I looked around. "Where is Evie? She can't possibly have slept through all this."

Sam looked startled, then shrugged.

There it was again, that feeling of dread. I brushed past Sam, ran upstairs, and darted into Evie's room. "Oh, God!"

There was no sign of Evie. Her bedroom was completely empty, with the bed neatly made and her small suitcase standing next it.

Sam rushed over to the wardrobe and flung open the door. It was empty. "Evie's gone." She ran over to the window, her shoulders slumping as she pulled back the curtains. "So's your car!"

I stood like a rabbit in headlights, wondering what to do. Then, my eyes focused on the only thing on the dressing table. A notepad. My hand shook as I picked it up and flicked open the cover. "It's a note," I said, "from Evie."

Sam turned back from the window, her eyes desperately searching my face. "What does she say?"

I began reading out loud.

"Dearest Grace. I'm so sorry, but I feel like such a failure that I don't have the strength to go on. I just can't face this world alone and I want to end the hurt and sadness for good. We have been through so much of our lives together and the certainty of your love and kindness seems to be all I have

left. But I don't want to be a burden to you and spoil your life like I have everyone else's.

I'm sorry I can't be stronger. Please forgive me. Evie." x

I stumbled back onto the bed.

Sam snatched the pad out of my hand. Her face crumpled in pain as she read it again. "She's going to kill herself."

She whispered the words, but they shuddered through me. "We've got to stop her," I said.

"But where the hell's she gone?" Sam started pacing anxiously around the room. "Think Grace. Where would she go?"

"I don't know, unless..." My mind cleared, and I jumped up off the bed. "She's going to drown herself."

The colour drained from Sam's face.

"Don't you see?" I went on. "She's obsessed with this Kitty ghost story because *her* circumstances mirror Kitty's exactly... Evie's pregnant."

"*Pregnant?*"

"Yes, and her lover, or rather husband Trev, has been unfaithful too. I reckon she's going to drown herself like Kitty."

"*Christ!* Don't tell me she's gone to Lowna Ford."

"I bet she has."

"We've got to stop her." Sam turned to run out. "But she's taken the car."

"I'll call Blake."

"It'll take him too long to get here."

"What else can I do?" We stood staring helplessly at each other. "I know," I said, "I'll run down to Patrick's."

Sam stared at me.

"I finally met him when I was out today," I explained. "He'll take me to Lowna. He's bound to know the way." I rushed into my bedroom and threw on some dry jeans and two thick jumpers on top of each other.

Sam followed me in. "I'll come with you."

I shook my head. "You stay here for the fire brigade."

"No," she argued. "I want to help you find Evie. The fire brigade will deal with the blaze whether I'm here or not."

"*Please,* Sam," I said. "Stay here and sort out the fire. Make sure they come and put it out. *Please* don't let it spread to the house and to neighbouring properties. I couldn't bear that." I bolted down the stairs before she could say anything else.

She came running down behind me. "You'll need to take a torch." She picked one up from the kitchen table and thrust it into my hands. "Shall I make a flask of something hot for Evie, just in case."

"There's no time." I slipped into Mum's wellies and raincoat.

Sam picked up her woolly hat and rammed it on my head. "Here." She grabbed her small silver hip flask and stuffed it into my pocket. "There's whiskey in there."

At the door, she hugged me tight. "Find her Grace," her voice was hoarse with fear. "And tell her I'm sorry."

I nodded. "Stay in here and keep the door locked. If someone did set fire to the barn, they're still out there."

Sam shuddered. "Are you sure you should go alone, Grace? I mean, it's not safe."

"I won't be alone. Patrick will help me."

Sam gave a resigned sigh. "Be careful, Grace."

"You too," I said, and set out for Patrick's cottage.

It was still pitch black and raining hard. The wind was strong. It took my breath away as I struggled to run into it. Blake had been right about the forecast. It was a filthy night. I would have loved to stay snuggled under the duvet in front of the fire, but I had to find Evie and stop her.

What if I was wrong though? What if she *hadn't* gone to Lowna Ford? What then? I pushed those thoughts away and pulled the raincoat hood up over my hat. I *was* going to find Evie in time.

The houses were all in darkness as I ran along the residents' road. Only porch or outside security lights gave any indication that there was anyone living in them at all. I didn't know what the time was but, as everyone seemed to be in deep slumber, I reckoned it must have been around 3am.

Patrick's cottage at the end of the row finally came into sight. My heart soared when I saw a light on in the sitting room. I ran through the front gate, up the path, and knocked hard on the door. "Patrick!" I pushed the letterbox open and shouted. "Patrick. It's me, Grace. Please open-up. I need your help."

After a moment, the hall light came on and I heard Patrick shuffling to the door. Impatiently I waited as the key turned in the lock and the door opened. I almost fell inside. "Please help me," I said. "Evie's taken my car. She's gone to Lowna Ford, to kill herself."

Patrick stared at me open-mouthed, his eyes rheumy. I must have woken him from sleep because he looked disorientated as if he couldn't understand what was going on.

"I'm sorry to wake you like this," I said. "I didn't know who else to ask for help."

"I was snoozing in the armchair," he said, rubbing his eyes. "I don't find it easy to sleep much in bed these days." His bushy grey eyebrows suddenly knitted together in a frown. "What did you say?" His voice was incredulous. "You think Evie's gone to Lowna Ford to kill herself?"

"Yes. We found a suicide note in her bedroom. She didn't say she was going to Lowna Ford, but she's taken my car. I feel sure that's what she's going to do." The last sentence caught in my throat like a sob. "She's going to drown herself, like Kitty."

He stood for a second, then nodded. "You did right to come to me, lass." He took my hand and squeezed it. "I'll get the car keys." He paused. "Where's Sam?"

"Back at the house. The barn's on fire. Sam's called the fire brigade. We think someone's set it on fire."

He stopped dead again. "*What*?"

"We could smell petrol."

"Good Lord!"

Now in the dim light of the hallway, I saw how grey his weathered skin was and how old and fragile he looked. That made me hesitate. "Put your warm coat and hat on," I said. "It's a terrible night out there."

I helped him into his long, padded raincoat and he pulled a thick, woolly hat onto his head. I grabbed a scarf off the rack and wound it around his neck.

"My stick," he said. "By the chair in the sitting room."

I ran into the room and grabbed his stick. I was worried now about dragging him out in the middle of the night in such foul weather. "Are you okay to do this?" I asked. "I could take your car, but I don't know the way."

"Come on, lass." He smiled at me. "There's not a moment to lose."

"Thank you." I was truly grateful for his help when I'd been unkind to him earlier. I grabbed the key, locked the door, and followed him to the car. He tried to hurry but I saw how hard it was for him to walk with his arthritic legs. He got inside, threw his stick over the back, and the old Range Rover sprang to life.

I jumped in and threw his house key in the well by the gear stick.

While Patrick might have been slow at walking, he was the reverse behind the wheel. Headlights blazing, he sped through the village as if his own life depended on it. His foot only slackened on the accelerator when we got to Mum's house, and he saw the orange glow lighting the sky round the back. Even inside the car, we could smell acrid smoke. Tears pricked my eyes. I wasn't sure if that was due to the smoke, or the emotion of seeing the fire, or knowing the fire brigade hadn't turned up yet.

"Dear God!" Patrick glanced over at me, anxiously. "I always keep a can of petrol in Violet's barn for her old mower. Do you think someone used that to start the fire?"

I sighed. "I don't know. But if they did, it's not your fault, Patrick."

"Let's hope the fire brigade get here soon," he said.

"I'm worried about Sam. I don't know if whoever did this has gone. Sam's feisty at the best of times. She'll challenge them if she sees them. Anything could happen." I looked across at him and saw the sadness on his face as he stared at the fire.

He turned to me. "Do you want to see if Sam's all right first, or go straight to Lowna Ford?"

It was a dilemma, but I thought Evie was in the most danger at that moment. "Lowna," I said. "I've no idea what time Evie left the house." My voice was almost a whisper. "She may already be dead for all I know."

"Don't think like that, lass." Patrick reached over and patted my hand. "We'll find her."

Yes, but would she still be alive? Despite the coldness of the night, his hand felt warm and comforting.

He drove like the wind out of the village and up onto the Moors. His old Range Rover rode easily through puddles and brushed aside any dead bracken and heather blown in its path. He obviously knew the road like the proverbial back of his hand. I was glad I'd gone to him for help.

I was silent now with my thoughts. Why on earth had I brought Evie and Sam up here with me? If I'd come alone, none of this would have happened. And why didn't I just drive us all home when I knew how sick in mind and heart Evie was? I'd never forgive myself if anything happened to her. Never.

Again, it was as if Patrick was reading my mind. "You can't blame yourself, Grace," he said. "Evie's a grown woman, with a life and mind of her own. She wouldn't have just started thinking about killing herself. She'll have been struggling with those dark thoughts for a long time. She's a sensitive soul and deeply scarred by her father's abuse. Life's been a struggle for her ever since. Now she's been rejected by that husband of hers, she feels worthless all over again."

I was surprised by the depth of his understanding. "That's what she said in her note. She felt such a failure she didn't have the strength to carry on."

"There you are, then."

"She said she didn't want to face the world alone." I turned to him in desperation. "I told her that she wouldn't be alone. I said she could stay with me, and I'd look after her and the baby." A tear spilled down my cheek. "She wrote that she didn't want to spoil my life like she had everyone else's." I put my head in my hands. "I should have known. I should have stopped her."

"No, Grace," he insisted. "You couldn't have stopped her. Believe me if someone decides to commit suicide, it's their own decision. You must never think it's your fault because it's not."

"It's that bloody ghost story," I said, bitterly. "I wish Violet hadn't brought her up here last year and filled her head with all that nonsense. She was too vulnerable. If I'd known..." My voice trailed off when it struck me that I was calling Mum Violet, as if she wasn't even my mother. Perhaps somewhere deep in my subconscious I'd always felt distanced from her, as if she were never totally committed to our family.

It didn't go unnoticed by Patrick. He glanced over but said nothing.

We lapsed into silence as he pushed the accelerator to the floor. We raced through another moorland village where all the houses were in darkness, and back out into the countryside again. "Not far now," he said, "just a bit further along this road."

I strained to see out the windscreen but there was only darkness beyond the headlights. Rain still lashed the windows, and the wind rocked the car as we turned off the road onto an unsealed track. We bumped along the uneven ground for a while until, suddenly, Patrick stamped hard on the brakes and the car slithered to an abrupt halt.

Lying across the track was a fallen tree, its branches and leaves glistening and trembling in the headlights. It wasn't a huge tree, but the trunk was big enough to stop us passing. I turned to Patrick. "Can we drive around it?"

He shook his head and pointed out his side window. "We're next to a steep bank. It's so muddy, the car might slip down and roll over."

It was so dark that I couldn't see anything ahead. "How far is the Ford?"

"A few hundred yards further along."

"Right." I pulled on Sam's woolly hat and pulled my raincoat hood over it. "I'll go on foot."

Patrick grabbed my arm. "No, lass. You don't know the way."

"I'll find it," I said, and switched on my torch.

"Wait! I'll come with you."

"No." I shook my head. It would take him forever to walk that far, especially in this weather. "Thank you," I said, "but we both know I'll be quicker on my own." I looked over at his anxious face. "Don't worry. I'll find her."

"I'm worried about you too."

"I'll be all right." I forced myself to sound upbeat. "Just tell me the way."

He threw up his hands in a sign of defeat and pointed ahead. "Follow the track. You'll come to a place where visitors park their cars. It's not a proper carpark, just a patch of rough ground. Keep following the track, alongside the water, until you get to a footbridge. That's Lowna Ford."

I took a deep breath. "Right."

He gave me a desperate smile as I struggled to open the door against the wind and got out. I gave him a small wave as I slammed the door shut. Then I clambered over the fallen tree trunk, put my head down against the elements, and set off down the track.

Thirty

I made my way blindly along in the pitch black and relentless rain. At first, Patrick's car headlights shone a corridor of light to help me see the way ahead. That soon faded, and I stopped when I realised my boots were squelching through mud. I flashed the torch around to get my bearings. To my left were bushes and bracken and I could see the river on my right now. I was surprised how narrow it was given the rushing noise coming from it. In normal times it was probably nothing more than a narrow tributary or stream. Today, it was swollen and flowing fast after weeks of rainwater cascading down from the Moors. I could see water lapping over the top of the bank in places and knew I had to be careful not to stumble in.

I ploughed on in the dark, my eyes glued to the small arc of light from my torch picking the way along the ground. Every so often I had to stop and turn my back to get some respite from the non-stop blasts of wind and rain in my face. I desperately wanted to dry my eyes to see better but every inch of me was soaked.

"Evie!" I shouted as I stood catching my breath. "Evie!" All I heard in reply was the gurgling and bubbling water alongside me.

I shone the beam onto the water-logged track ahead and froze as two yellow eyes looked up at me. A hare stood hypnotised in the light. For a moment, we stared at each other in surprise before it made the first move and darted into the bushes.

Head back down against the weather, I struggled on for another hundred yards or so before stopping again. Patrick said I'd come to a carpark, but I couldn't see anything that looked like one. Had I missed it? It was difficult to say in this blackness and with flood water starting to conceal the track. I was beginning to lose all sense of direction and a kind of hopelessness settled on me. Perhaps I was wrong in thinking Evie had come up here? I was having serious doubts when suddenly a streak of lightning lit up the sky. In that moment, I caught the glimpse of what looked like a car ahead. I walked on quickly. It was a car. My car. A mixture of terror and elation took hold. Elation because I was sure now Evie *was* here. And terror because I was convinced of her suicide mission.

I shone the torch through the car window, scared I'd find Evie slumped in the driver seat. I tried the door and it opened. The interior car light came on and I saw the key in the ignition. There was no sign of Evie though. Every fibre of my being wanted to jump in my car and drive it back along the track to Patrick and safety. I was scared witless of being out in this hostile terrain on such a stormy night. Would I be walking to my own death if I carried on? Would there be a flash flood? Would I drown too? But then I thought about Evie in her lonely and vulnerable state. I was sure she was heading for the Ford. I shut the car door and turned. I had to go on. I had to try and find her before she drowned herself.

I steeled myself to continue but I was confused about which way to go. Patrick said that from the carpark I should continue to follow the track alongside the river and that it would lead me to the bridge. But the flood water was beginning to cover the track. I felt a rising panic.

"Evie!" I shouted again in desperation. "Evie!"

It was then that a woman's voice rang out clearly over the noise of the wind and water. "Grace," she called.

"Evie?" My heart leapt. "Is that you?"

There was no reply. I shouted Evie's name again. Suddenly, the torch beam picked out a terrifying sight.

A dark figure loomed ahead, the dress and cloak unforgettable.

I stopped dead as if rooted to the spot and stared at this apparition through the pulses of rain. For a moment, neither of us moved. The woman was much smaller than I'd first imagined. She had her cloak hood up so I couldn't see her face, but she wasn't too far away from me. I wanted to turn and run, but I couldn't move. I was paralysed with fear like that hare in the torch beam.

My heart pounded in my ears, and I tensed ready to run. But the woman made no attempt to come closer. I cupped my free hand over my eyes to shield them from the wind and rain. I could hardly believe what I was seeing. Was this Kitty Garthwaite's ghost? Could the folklore be true? Could people come back from the dead? The figure stood so still that I calmed down a little and found a shaky voice. "W-where's my friend?" I shouted. "W-where's Evie?"

The woman didn't speak or move.

"*Please*," I pleaded. "Help me find her. She's pregnant. She's going to drown herself. I…"

The woman beckoned me to follow her.

I didn't move at first, both suspicious and terrified of her intentions. Was she going to show me the way to Evie or lead me into a trap?

She beckoned again and turned to walk on.

My legs were like jelly, but I took a few steps in her direction. She kept on walking, and I followed, not daring to take my eyes off her for a moment. It was the most surreal experience I've ever had as I kept the torch beam focused on those dainty feet in the old-fashioned lace-up boots. The same feet and boots I'd seen when walking on the Moors, and the same hem of a long dress swishing along the track before me. The strange thing was that however fast I walked, I was never able to catch up with her. I tried, but she always seemed to keep the same distance from me as if she had some forcefield around her.

We went on like that for some time until she suddenly disappeared, just as she had up on the Moors. One minute she was there, and the next she'd gone. I spun around flashing the beam wildly, half expecting her to creep up on me from behind. But no terrifying figure ran at me. No blow smashed into my head or body. No hands gripped my throat. I was simply alone. Overcome with emotion, my knees buckled, and I collapsed to the ground.

It was the sudden, high-pitched scream that made me pull myself together. "Evie?" I put my hand out to pull myself up and realised the ground felt muddy, but not water-logged, which probably meant the bank was higher at that point and holding the water back.

I shone my torch around. The beam picked out something sparkling on the ground. I reached out to pick it up and felt a prickle of excitement. Evie's crystal necklace. The one she'd been wearing in the kitchen earlier. If only I'd realised when she'd hugged me then that she was really saying goodbye.

I shoved the necklace into my pocket and hauled myself to my feet. That's when I saw footprints in the muddy earth ahead. Real footprints. Heavy boots too, by the look of it, and not the dainty feet that had shown me the way to this spot. As I swung the beam around again, it picked out the silhouette of a low footbridge.

Lowna Ford – I'd made it.

"Evie," I shouted, running up to the bridge, and flashing the torch both ways along the bank. "It's me... Grace." I listened but heard nothing over the whoosh of wind and rushing water. I ran onto the bridge shouting her name over and over, but there was no sign of her.

I ran across to the other side and flashed the light along the bank over there. Still no sign. Desperate, I ran back to the centre of the bridge and swept the torch beam across the water. That's when I saw what looked like a bundle of clothes wedged around the bridge's central struts.

Oh God! Evie's shiny, yellow raincoat. She was in the water.

I ran back to the bank, threw the torch onto the ground, pulled off my boots and raincoat, and waded into the icy water. The cold made me gasp with shock. The force of the fast-flowing water pulled at my legs, and I clung onto the footbridge with both hands, taking side steps like a crab towards the middle. The water bubbled like a jacuzzi, splashing into my face and mouth, before being forced under the low bridge.

I was up to my chest when I finally reached Evie. She'd somehow got trapped around the bridge's central structure which had stopped her floating off downstream. "Help!" I screamed as I struggled to turn her lifeless body onto her back and get her face out of the water. "Help!"

But there was no-one to answer my call. I had to find the strength to get Evie back to the bank alone. I manoeuvred myself behind her and circled my arms under hers so that I could drag her on her back. I kept my legs wide, and my feet firmly planted on the riverbed to stop the water knocking me over. I shuffled backwards to the bank, dragging us step by step and holding onto Evie as tightly as I could. If I let her go, I knew the water would sweep her away.

I don't know where I got the strength from that night, but I made it to the edge of the bank. I dug my heels into the riverbed to anchor myself for one last effort and heaved Evie's limp body out of the water and onto the bank. Exhausted, I dropped down beside her coughing and choking for breath. But I knew there was no time to lose, and my medical training kicked in. I scrambled to my knees beside Evie and checked to see if she was breathing. She wasn't. There was no pulse either.

I opened her mouth and turned her head sideways to let the water drain out. I turned her head back, took some huge gulps of air, put my mouth over hers and blew five rescue breaths into her lungs. Then I clasped my hands over her chest and started compressions to restart her heart. My arms and shoulders were already aching from dragging her out of the river, but I pumped away as best I could for what seemed like ages, before sitting back on my heels.

I checked again for signs of life from Evie. None.

I took more gulps of air and blew another five breaths into her lungs before starting chest compressions again. This time I spoke to her as I tried to keep count. I wanted her to hear my voice. I wanted her to know I was there. "Come on, Evie. Come on," I kept saying, as I pressed down on her chest over and over. "Stay with me, Evie. *Please.* You won't be alone with the baby. I promise." I could hardly feel my arms and hands, but I kept working away, urging her over and over to choose life.

There was no response. A sense of despair took over me, but I still wasn't ready to give up on her. I tried again, blowing more breaths into her lungs. "Think of your baby, Evie," I said, as I pumped as hard as I could. "Your baby deserves to live. Your baby deserves to live."

Suddenly, I felt a faint rise and fall in her chest. "That's it, Evie," I urged. "Breathe… breathe."

She gave a kind of splutter and coughed weakly. I turned her head sideways again to let the water drain away. I put my ear to her mouth. I've never felt anything so wonderful as her breath on my cheek at that moment. I put my fingers on her throat and felt a faint pulse. "That's it, Evie," I shouted. "You're going to be fine. Just fine."

I could feel her shivering though. Hypothermia was setting in. I grabbed the raincoat I'd thrown on the ground and wrapped it tightly around her, even though it was wet. Everything else was sopping too, but I pulled my woolly hat off and tucked it on her head. I knew I couldn't carry her back to the car and that I'd have to run and raise the alarm. "Hold on while I get some help, Evie," I urged. "I promise I won't be long."

I was still kneeling beside her when a sudden bright light made me look up. Help was already here. I jumped up and started shouting and waving like a lunatic. "Over here. Over here."

Footsteps squelched in our direction and then it happened so quickly, it took me by surprise. The light was blinding. I shielded my eyes with my hands to try to see who it was. A young woman stood in front of me, holding a bright halogen lamp. She was dressed in black, bikers' leathers and boots and had black hair down to her shoulders. She also had a face I recognised. The girl from the museum!

At first, I didn't see what she had in her other hand but, before I realised what was happening, an object came hurtling in my direction. Instinctively, I ducked sideways. It missed my head and thumped me hard on the shoulder. The blow was forceful enough to knock me off my feet and onto my back. I stared up in time to see what looked like a metal poker come down again and feel it crunch against the side of my body. Pain seared through me, and I looked up into the young woman's crazy eyes.

"Why did you have to interfere?" she shouted. "Evie *wanted* to die." She raised the poker again with both hands.

I stared up in shock and horror as I realised what she was about to do. "No," I babbled. "Evie didn't want to die... she's alive... she chose to live... to save her baby."

I saw a look of surprise flit across the girl's face.

"You didn't know Evie was pregnant, did you?" I said, quickly.

The girl looked confused.

"She's four months pregnant."

A look of indecision flashed across the girl's face. I knew then I had to try and connect with her somehow, distract her from her deadly mission. "It's always women who suffer," I said. "Men take their pleasure, then leave us to face the consequences." I knew I sounded trite, but I couldn't think of anything else to say. "Evie's husband left her," I said, slipping my hand over Evie's to reassure her in case she could hear me. She was ice cold. "It was a shock," I went on. "Evie always wanted children. So did her husband. Then he had an affair, made that woman pregnant and walked out on Evie just as she fell pregnant too."

"Bastard!" the girl said.

"Let me get Evie some help," I pleaded. "Please don't let her and the baby die."

The girl stared at me. "But Evie *has* to die."

For a moment, I was confused. "Why?"

"To take the blame for Joe's murder."

"Why would Evie need to take the blame..." I hesitated as it all fell into place in my head. "Were you Joe's girlfriend?" I asked.

She nodded.

"You killed him, didn't you?"

"No," she said, her voice breaking. "No, I didn't kill him. I loved Joe. I was just trying to scare him. I didn't mean it.

Really… It was just a shove, that's all. He fell backwards, hit his head on a rock and then… and then…" She stopped, as if incapable of continuing.

"But he didn't die from a head injury," I said. "He drowned. That was the cause of death. And the police say it was murder?"

"I didn't kill him," she said, half-sobbing. "I wouldn't." She looked agonisingly into my eyes for me to believe her. "I was angry with him, for sure. He was going to piss off to college in Ireland without a second thought for me. The bastard hadn't even told me he wanted to go to college let alone that he'd applied."

I saw the girl's hand slacken on the poker as she continued speaking. "That's when I knew he didn't give a toss about me. He'd just used me for sex." Her face crumpled, then she put on a man's voice. "But Jenny," he said to me. "This was just a bit of fun. You know that. You said as much yourself. All those sex games…" The voice dwindled away.

Jenny. Her name was Jenny, I thought, pleased that I'd managed to get her talking. "So, why didn't you just tell the police what happened?" I went on. "Why not explain that he fell?"

"No," she wailed like a distraught child. "I can't do that. You don't understand."

"If you tell me, I might understand. I might be able to help you."

Her face took on a hopeful expression as she considered this. Then she shook her head, sadly. "I can't. It would hurt my… family, don't you see? Mum is the only person who has ever loved me." She let out a sob. "My selfish Dad abandoned us when we were kids. He said he hated living with Mum and me and my brother. That we were spoilt brats." She brushed the tears roughly from her cheeks. "Things were hard for Mum bringing us up on her own, but she always said she would do anything for us. And she did." She took a deep breath and said, darkly. "Then Joe told me he was leaving me too."

"Is that why you killed him, Jenny, because he was leaving you just like your dad?"

"I didn't kill him," she shouted. "I didn't kill him."

Why was she so adamant that she hadn't killed Joe? She admitted that she'd been here at the time. She said that she'd shoved him, and he'd fallen back and hit his head. But the post-mortem report said the cause of death was drowning. The police were convinced it was murder. Perhaps she was just in denial at what she'd done. Or… perhaps someone else had been here that night. I looked down at Evie. Could she have been here that night? "If you didn't kill Joe, then who did?" I asked, dreading the answer.

Jenny looked confused, conflicted even.

"You said earlier that Evie had to die to take the blame for Joe's murder," I said, calmly. "You yourself said that he'd been murdered. So, what I don't understand is why the police would think Evie killed Joe. She had no link to him. And the police have no evidence that she did it."

The girl gave a brittle laugh. "That's where you're wrong. The police *do* believe Evie killed Joe. Don't forget they found her here at the crime scene on the night of the murder. They found Violet's car here too. Only she could have driven it up." She smiled at me and there was a craziness in that gesture. "Everyone knows your friend Evie is obsessed with the Kitty ghost story. She came to our play 'Sarkless Kitty' in the museum last summer when she visited with Violet. She was researching the ghost story for Violet's latest novel even then. I played Kitty, the lead role," she said, proudly. "Evie came over to the museum several times after the play to talk to me about the ghost story and research the archives."

My head was whirling with all this and the revelation that Evie knew this girl. Oh my God! Was it possible that Evie had killed Joe? I stared at Jenny. "Did Evie kill Joe?"

She shook her head and gave another of her strange laughs. "That's what's so funny. Everyone knows your friend Evie is a nut job. She even told the police she'd seen Kitty's ghost in your house and garden. In your friend's own mixed-up head, she believes Kitty's ghost told her to start killing young men at Lowna Ford again. Joe was the next victim."

How the hell did this girl know what the police were thinking? Or what Evie did or didn't say to them?

She gave me a smug look. "DS Gray will swear an oath to say that she found Evie here that night."

DS Gray? Of course! That's when I saw the likeness. The piercing eyes. The angular face. This girl was Stella Gray's daughter; the troubled daughter Blake had talked about. "I know who you are now, Jenny. Well, DS Gray, or rather your mum, might be prepared to lie on oath, but Blake will work everything out. He'll find out that Joe was your boyfriend and-"

"Wrong again," she snapped. "No-one knew about Joe and me. It was a secret. Mum wouldn't allow me to go out with boys. Why do you think we were meeting in secret up here?"

"Blake will check your phone for emails and text messages."

"He won't find any." The girl was gleeful. "We used pay-as-you-go mobiles to send texts about when and where to meet. You know, like they do in films. It added to the fun and excitement. We never emailed."

I stared at her. "If it wasn't you who killed Joe. And it wasn't Evie. Then who was it?"

"I told you I can't say. I must protect my mum… my family."

And that was the precise moment when the last piece of the puzzle slotted into place, and I knew the truth. "Your Mum killed Joe, didn't she?"

Jenny gasped.

"I can see by your face that I'm right." I paused. "Why did she kill him?"

Jenny stared at me but stayed silent.

"Who else knows?" I asked.

Her face hardened. "No-one... except you now."

A chill ran up my spine.

"If you'd just let your friend drown up here, everything would have been fine," she said, her voice harsh again. "But you had to come and save her. Be the big heroine." She shook her head. "You only have yourself to blame." Suddenly, without any more warning, she raised the metal poker with both hands and whacked me hard over the head.

I fell back in a daze. Terrible pain seared through me as I lay on the ground. I struggled to get back up, but my body wouldn't move. Then I felt my arms being yanked over my head. I was being dragged along the ground on my back. I tried to struggle, but I was paralysed.

I felt an icy shock again as Jenny hauled me back into the river. I tried to keep my head up, but her hand covered my face and pushed me under. Water poured into my mouth and lungs. I heard rushing water in my ears. I tried to hold my breath and struggle, but I was too badly injured to have the strength to fight. I was going to die.

Suddenly, someone came hurtling into the water, screaming my name over and over. I recognised that voice...Sam!

A tremendous struggle ensued between them, with arms and legs flailing and splashing around.

The girl had to let go of me to fend off Sam. I tried to save myself, but my arms and legs wouldn't move. I felt the force of the water start pulling me away and I put out my hand as a last gesture for help.

A hand grabbed mine and clung on hard. I was conscious of being pulled out of the water, of being hauled onto the bank, of retching as my stomach and lungs tried to clear the water I'd swallowed.

"My poor Grace."

"P-Patrick?" I gasped.

"Yes."

"Help Sam," I spluttered. "That girl…Jenny…is mad."

A commotion rang out behind us. I heard the roar of an engine, then bright lights flooded the riverbank.

"*Grace?*" I heard Blake's frantic voice shouting. "*Patrick?*"

"Over here," Patrick called out while still holding me tight. "Quick," he shouted at Blake. "Help Sam. She's in the water struggling with Jenny."

Blake plunged into the river, and I heard more splashing and shouting. I tried to struggle up.

"It's all right, lass," Patrick soothed, holding me still. "Blake's got Sam. She's all right."

"Evie?" I turned my head towards where she lay. Paramedics were wrapping her up in blankets and putting an oxygen mask over her face.

"Thank God." I slumped back knowing I could do no more for Evie or Sam. I felt myself relax and start slipping out of consciousness.

"No." Patrick shook me, gently. "You mustn't go to sleep, Grace. Stay with me. I've only just found you. Please, stay with me."

"You s-saved me," I choked.

He put his fingers over my lips. "It's only what any father would do for his daughter."

Thirty-one

A watery sun filtering through slatted blinds and making patterns on the stark wall were the first images I saw when I awoke. My mouth was so dry I could hardly swallow, and a familiar smell filled my nostrils. Disinfectant. My limbs were heavy too, and a dull, throbbing pain made me reach up and touch my head. It was covered in bandages.

Then I saw all the machines and the drip in my arm. I blinked hard and started to see the room more clearly. I was lying propped up against a couple of pillows in bed. In a hospital bed.

I heard rhythmic breathing before I saw Patrick asleep in the chair alongside me. His craggy old face was pale but peaceful in the glowing light of the bed lamp as he dozed. Then it all came flooding back. The attack at Lowna Ford. That crazy girl, Jenny.

Patrick was so close, I reached out and took his hand.

He jumped at my touch, opened his eyes, and gave me a smile that lit up his entire face. "Thank God," he said, as he reached over and brushed a tendril of hair tenderly from my eyes. "You're going to be fine, Grace."

"My head," I moaned.

"You've got a fractured skull. A break in the bone. But there's no need for an operation. You lost a lot of blood in the water. The doctors want to keep you in for a few days' observation."

I groaned again as I recalled the whack of the metal poker over my head. "Where are we?"

"York Hospital."

I struggled to sit up. "What about Evie?" I whispered. "And Sam?"

His face turned grave. "Evie's in intensive care."

"How bad is she?" I asked, then I saw him look away. "Don't sugar-coat it. I'm a doctor. I want the truth."

He gave me a weak smile. "She has a fractured skull like you, but also a bleed on the brain. She's going into the operating theatre any minute now."

I felt my heart squeeze in pain. "What do the doctors say? Will she pull through?"

"She has a fighting chance."

I flopped back on the pillow, wishing to God that I'd never persuaded her to come to Mum's house with me.

"Evie didn't try to drown herself up at Lowna," I said. "She was heading back to the car when Jenny ambushed her. I heard a scream as I approached the footbridge. That must have been Jenny hitting her over the head and dragging her into the river."

He nodded. "That's what the police think, but we'll have to wait for Evie to wake up to confirm that." He sighed. "They've put her into an induced coma to give her body a better chance of recovering."

"And the baby?" I asked, softly.

"Still alive. Evie's fighting for him too."

"Him?"

He nodded. "A boy."

I felt tears spill from my eyes.

"Don't blame yourself, Grace."

Then I remembered Sam diving into the water to rescue me. "And Sam? Is she okay?"

"Yes. She's been here waiting for you to wake up. They've just taken her down to x-ray her leg. It's badly bruised but they don't think it's broken. They want to check though." He shook his head. "She's quite a girl, your friend Sam. She shot into that river like a torpedo to save you from Jenny."

I nodded, remembering how Sam had prized Jenny off me. "How did she get up to Lowna?"

"Blake picked her up on the way through Hutton-Le-Hole. They got stuck behind that fallen tree like us. The guys got out to move it. Sam ran ahead and reached you first."

I smiled. "She always was a great sprinter." I hesitated. "And that girl, Jenny? What about her?"

He sighed, deeply. "I'm afraid she died in the river."

"*Died?*"

He patted my hand. "Blake said he'll drop by later and fill you in. He's spent the day interviewing Stella Gray, so he's the best person to tell you."

"Tell me what *you* know," I insisted.

He was going to protest but thought better of it. "Stella has confessed that she killed Joe."

I nodded. "Why though? It doesn't make sense. Jenny told me that she'd shoved Joe; he'd fallen backwards and hit his head on a stone. She insisted it was an accident, yet the police say Joe drowned and it was murder. What the hell happened up there?"

He squeezed my hand. "Now don't get yourself upset. Blake will explain everything when he gets here. All I know is that Stella and Jenny tried to frame Evie for the murder. But the police are certain Evie wasn't involved in any way and won't be charging her with anything."

"I should think not," I said, crossly. "They've treated her badly."

"Now come on, Grace," Patrick said. "You have to relax to allow your body to heal." He took my hand. "Please. Just rest now."

I looked into his worried eyes. I had this man to thank for saving me too. But I also recalled what he'd said before I'd blanked out on the riverbank. *It's only what any father would do for his daughter.* I could see he was wondering if I'd heard that remark.

"So, you're my biological father," I said, softly.

He jolted. "You heard?"

I nodded. "Mum was pregnant before you left for America?"

"She was, although she never told me." He shook his head. "You know your mother, Grace. Such a proud woman. She thought she'd be a burden and didn't want to hold me back. Didn't want me to feel obligated to her." His eyes glistened. "The truth is there's nothing I'd have loved more than to have had you both in my life and be a proper family."

I looked at him. "Why didn't you tell me the whole truth in the church in Lastingham?"

"I tried, Grace," he said, with an earnest expression on his face. "But Blake came in and the moment was lost."

"Tell me now," I said.

He took a deep breath. "Violet told me she met Max a couple of weeks after I'd left for America. He was older than her and they were just friends at first. When it became apparent that she was pregnant, she confided in him. As it happened, Max wasn't in a relationship and had always wanted children. So, they came to an agreement."

"Another one," I said, sourly.

He nodded. "They would marry. He would put his name on the birth certificate as your father and take care of you both." Patrick must have seen the scorn on my face because he added: "Don't judge your mother too harshly, Grace. They were different times. Violet would have struggled to continue her writing career without a partner to help her, especially with a baby." He paused. "I'm sure she loved Max too."

I said nothing because I wasn't sure that she had.

"She never told Max who your biological father was though," Patrick went on. "He found that out for himself when she started seeing me again. She didn't tell him about her house in Hutton-le-Hole either until he stumbled upon the deeds one day. He was furious and said he'd destroy her if she told you I was your real father." He paused. "Max loved you very much."

I nodded. "Do I know everything now?" I asked.

"Yes," he said. "There are no more secrets. I promise."

I studied him, trying to see myself in him and if there were any similar features. The truth was I didn't know this man very well. But I knew he was kind, and wise, and that he'd saved my life and Evie's without a thought for his own.

I could see he was conscious of me studying him and seemed to be almost holding his breath to see how I was going to react. Whether I would reject him or not.

It was my turn to take a deep breath. I thought of Max and everything he'd done for me. I couldn't have wished for a better father. "Max will always be my dad," I said to Patrick. "He brought me up and cared for me. Tended to my every need. I wouldn't be a doctor if it hadn't been for him."

Patrick nodded and looked down to hide the sadness in his eyes.

"But I'd love to have another parent in my life now," I said. "That's if you want the job, Patrick."

He looked up, his eyes sparkling. "That would be wonderful, Grace. Absolutely. There's nothing I'd love more."

Thirty-two

It was much later that day when Blake popped his head around the door of my hospital room. I was just staring into space when he arrived, woozy from all the painkillers.

"Is it okay to come in?" he asked.

"Of course."

He walked in, shoulders hunched, and hovered nervously over my bed, or rather hopped from foot to foot in a wired state.

"Please sit down," I said, "you're making my head worse."

"Sorry." He sat down in my bedside chair. "Where's Patrick?" he asked.

"Gone for a meal in the restaurant with Sam." I grimaced at the thought of hospital food. "You should join them. I don't suppose you've eaten today."

He gave me a small smile, but I thought he looked terrible. His eyes were dark and sunken, and his skin almost yellow with fatigue. He looked into my eyes. "How are you?" he asked.

"Apart from a cracking headache, I'm okay, considering…"

"I'm so sorry, Grace," he said.

"It's not your fault."

"Yes, it is," he said, firmly. "I should have worked it out sooner."

I struggled up into a sitting position. "Patrick said you'd tell me everything when you got here. My mind keeps replaying things over and over. I want to know what happened that night at Lowna when Joe died. The truth, please."

"What's Patrick told you so far?"

"Only that Stella Gray said she killed Joe... and that Jenny died in the river."

Blake nodded. "Jenny hit her head on the bridge during the struggle with Sam and was carried off downstream by the current. She was dead by the time paramedics found her." He gave a deep sigh. "Stella's in pieces... a broken woman. Her kids were everything to her. She has confessed though. That's where I've been all day, interviewing her. She's going to be charged with murder."

"But what happened?" I asked, exasperated.

Blake shuddered and I felt for him having to charge his own Sergeant. Then he gave a deep sigh. "I suppose I should start at the beginning for it to make sense."

"Please do."

"Well, it seems that Jenny and Joe were having a secret sexual relationship. They had burner phones so no-one could trace their sexting. It was all a bit of a lark. Exciting too, I suppose."

I nodded. "Jenny told me about that at Lowna."

"Except their relationship wasn't a secret. One of our police constables had found out. He was called to a hotel in York to arrest a prostitute soliciting in the bar. The woman wasn't a prostitute though, it was Jenny."

"Oh my God."

He nodded. "Jenny had texted Joe and told him to meet her in the bar and pretend not to know her. She would then chat him up." Blake shook his head. "Apparently she was dressed to kill so it wasn't surprising hotel staff thought she was a prostitute and called the police."

"Did your colleague report the incident?"

"No. He let the pair of them go, but not before taking their names and addresses. Of course, he recognised Jenny Gray as Stella's daughter. He didn't record the incident, but he did tip Stella off."

I raised my eyebrows.

He nodded. "After that, Stella wouldn't allow Jenny out of the house except to go to work. She also secretly started tracking Jenny's mobile to keep an eye on what she was up to."

"Ah, I see."

He nodded. "That fateful night Jenny texted Joe to meet her at midnight at Lowna. She snuck out of the house when she thought Stella and her brother were asleep. Except Stella heard Jenny's motorbike rev up and went after her." He paused. "She tracked her through her mobile up to Lowna and arrived in time to see Jenny, dressed up like our ghostly serial Kitty Garthwaite, bending over Joe who was lying unmoving half in and half out of the water. Jenny was hysterical and screaming that she'd killed him."

I frowned. "But Jenny insisted that she *hadn't* killed him."

"That's right," he said. "At that point, Joe was still alive. Of course, Stella realised that and tried her best to revive him. But as Joe came round, he must have been confused from the blow to his head and thought Stella was attacking him. Don't forget he'd never met her before. He grabbed her and pulled her into the river. There was a ferocious struggle. In the end, it was Stella who held Joe's face under the water to stop him doing the same to her. He drowned. So, it was Stella who killed him and not Jenny."

I lay back, letting everything sink in. What a stupid, tragic turn of events. "It wasn't premeditated murder then. No-one set out to kill him."

"True," he said. "But to cover it up and try to frame Evie for murder was a foolish thing to do, especially for a police officer."

"Poor Joe…Poor Jenny. Talk about star-crossed lovers." It was my turn to sigh now. I felt some sadness for the youngsters. "Jenny would have loved the drama of it all on stage though," I said. "She was quite fanatical about becoming a successful actress."

Blake nodded.

"You know…" I glanced up at Blake, remembering Jenny's frantic eyes as she smashed me over the head with that poker. "I found her a strange girl. There was something wild about her… crazy even."

"Mm. Stella says there was always something not quite right about Jenny. That's why she kept such a watchful eye on her. She'd taken her to several doctors over the years, but they just alluded to a personality disorder."

I nodded. "So, how did Evie get mixed up in all this, Blake?"

He pursed his lips. "She was just in the wrong place, at the wrong time."

I could see he was finding this difficult, so I waited a few moments for him to gather his thoughts, then asked: "When did Evie appear on the scene, then?"

"She didn't…Stella was up there for a long time with Jenny trying to make Joe's death look accidental. Trying to make it look like he'd drowned after falling and hitting his head. But Stella knew any pathologist would see through that, especially with the bruises she'd inflicted on him during the struggle and holding his head under."

I inadvertently touched my own head injury.

Blake looked anxious. "Are you in pain?"

I shook my head. "I'm full of painkillers, but my mouth feels dry."

He poured me a glass a water from the jug on my bedside cabinet and held it to my lips.

I took a long gulp and swallowed. "Thanks. Please go on."

He took a deep breath. "Stella did what she could up at Lowna to cover things up. She was driving back home, with Jenny following on her motorbike. They came across Evie walking by the side of the road, just outside Hutton-le-Hole."

"Just outside Hutton-le-Hole?"

He nodded.

"I knew it," I said, firmly. "Evie couldn't have gone far in her state."

"Yes, well, it seems she was sleepwalking. Stella realised something was wrong and stopped the car. She recognised Evie as Violet's friend from last summer. Your mother had introduced them when they all attended the play in the museum. Evie even went back to the museum a few times after that to research their archives for more information on Kitty Garthwaite."

I nodded.

"So, having steered Evie into her car with the intention of taking her home, a darker thought took hold in Stella's mind when Evie fell asleep on the back seat. Here was her chance to divert attention away from her daughter and try to frame someone else for Joe's murder." He shook his head in a disbelieving way. "Stella drove Evie back to the crime scene to incriminate her in any way she could. It was getting light by then. Evie woke up and couldn't remember how she'd got there. Stella told her that she'd found her wandering on the Moors and was driving her home. She never mentioned Joe's death until we were all in your house." He ran his fingers through his short hair, distractedly. "So, when I was notified of the body and arrived at Lowna, Stella and the forensics team were already there. Stella told me that she'd found Evie at the scene. And I had no reason not to believe her."

"But where was Jenny when you got there?"

"Hiding on the Moors until Stella had a chance to go back and pick her up." He sighed. "You see, after they found Evie outside Hutton-le-Hole, Jenny left her motorbike in the back lane, got Violet's car from your house, and drove it to Lowna to make it look like Evie had driven it there."

I frowned. "But how did Jenny get the keys to Mum's car?"

"Off a hook in the barn, apparently."

"Oh God." I sighed. "Patrick again?"

Blake nodded. "He left Violet's house *and* car keys in the barn in case he forgot his own. He's been running the car around to keep it ticking over."

"I see."

"Jenny worked as a volunteer in the museum at weekends and when she could get leave from her job in the department store," Blake continued. "She was always looking for somewhere to meet Joe in secret and knew Violet's house was empty. The pair of them met up in the barn and in your mother's house a few times."

"Oh, for God's sake." I was cross now. "And what a hair-brained scheme thinking they could frame Evie like that."

He shrugged. "Stella insists there was no other choice. And, with her job in the police, she reckoned she had a good chance of pulling it off." It was his turn to get annoyed now, but with himself. "I was a bloody fool. I should have known from the start."

"Hardly," I said. "The whole story sounds ridiculous in the cold light of day."

"Does it?" He lowered his voice. "I trusted Stella, completely. When I got to Lowna and she said she'd found

Evie there, I believed her. Why wouldn't I? And it was Stella who interviewed Evie when you all came to the police station in Scarborough. She changed Evie's statement to make it look like Evie had known exactly what she was doing." He turned to me, exasperated. "Again, I totally believed Stella, but I should have known."

I frowned. "But wasn't Stella soaked to the skin after she'd been in the water fighting with Joe?"

He shook his head. "You may have noticed that Stella is fastidious about her clothes and looks. She always had spare clothes in the boot of her car to change into." He shook his head, looking the picture of misery. "You can easily get messy in this job."

I nodded because it all made sense. I didn't say anything else though. Blake would always blame himself for not seeing through Stella's lies. But there was something else burning away in my mind.

"There's another thing I can't quite make sense of Blake."

He turned to me, eyes questioning.

"Why did Jenny want to kill Evie? She'd plotted with her mother to frame Evie for Joe's murder. Why not leave things like that? Why risk everything and commit another murder?"

He looked straight at me. "Because of you."

"*Me?*"

"Stella feared you'd drive a coach and horses through their story. She kept telling Jenny over and over that you were the problem in their plan. If anyone was going to demolish their story, it would be you. You were a well-respected doctor. You were digging around and fiercely defending Evie. You were also becoming friendly with me. They thought you would turn me around to your way of thinking."

"And would I have?"

He shuffled uncomfortably in the chair. "You must admit that Evie had become more and more disturbed. She told everybody that she'd seen Kitty's ghost in your house and garden. She even told me that Kitty was standing behind me in the kitchen the other night. You can't deny that?"

I stared at him. "Are you saying that Stella and Jenny could have got away with it?"

He looked down. "Maybe. In the absence of any other evidence and explanation."

"Bloody hell, Blake." I could hardly believe it. "I know Jenny and Joe kept their relationship a secret, but what about the police constable who went to the York hotel to investigate the soliciting accusation? *He* knew they were an item. He knew there was a connection."

"I'm not saying there aren't loose ends." Blake looked defensive now. "But that constable didn't *record* the incident. It would have been his word against Stella's, and she knew that." He shrugged again. "There's no such thing as the perfect murder, Grace, especially with no real evidence. Sometimes it's just the balance of probability."

"Tell me this then," I said. "How the hell did Jenny know Evie was going up to Lowna to drown herself? *That* doesn't make *any* sense."

"I'm afraid it does. You see, Evie and Jenny have been in constant touch since they met last summer. Did you know that Evie was trying to complete Violet's novel 'It Began with a Ghost Story'?"

I slumped back on the pillow. "No. I didn't."

He nodded. "She wanted to finish it as a tribute to Violet. And Jenny became her adviser on the project. They often spoke on the phone. Evie confided in Jenny that she'd seen Kitty's ghost in your mother's house and garden when she visited last summer. Jenny thought it was a hoot and played along with her, saying that she'd seen Kitty a lot too since playing her at the museum. Jenny preyed on Evie's mind constantly, talking to her about hating men and wondering what it would be like to join Kitty on the other side."

I gave him a sceptical look. "We'll have to wait for Evie to wake up to find out if that's true or not."

"Of course. But Stella said that Jenny started dressing up as Kitty's ghost and parading around Violet's house to drive Evie over the edge. It was all part of their plan to frame Evie for the murder. Drive her crazy and make her sound even more obsessed with Kitty's ghost. She was an easy target." He paused. "We think Jenny phoned Evie yesterday and talked her into drowning herself at the Ford like Kitty. Stella is adamant that she knew nothing about that." He shook his head. "I guess Jenny thought if Evie was out of the way, there would be no-one to contradict their story about what happened to Joe. If Evie committed suicide, they'd be certain to get away with it."

I stared at him. "Again, Evie's the only one who can say whether that's true or not."

He nodded.

"So, you think Jenny went up there to make sure Evie killed herself?"

"Yes."

"Do you think Jenny always planned to kill Evie if she didn't drown herself?"

"I reckon so. Why would Jenny go up there otherwise?"

I thought so too. It was the manic look in Jenny's eyes that convinced me. "And do you believe Stella when she says she knew nothing about Jenny going to commit a second murder?"

He paused for a moment, then nodded. "I don't think Stella would have let Jenny go alone. She'd have wanted to make sure the job was done properly."

That sounded about right. Stella would have wanted to make sure her daughter didn't screw up. But that's exactly what she did do, losing her own life in the process.

Blake gave another sigh. "Still, they were right about one thing." He glanced at me. "They feared you'd scupper their plan. And you did, almost getting yourself killed in the process."

I was silent for a while as I turned all this over in my mind, then I said: "The trouble was Jenny overplayed her role. She cast herself as the central character in this evil drama and went too far. She came on stage too often dressed up as Kitty, which meant both Sam and I also saw her around the house and in the back lane. She styled her hair and dressed in the same clothes as the girl in the painting of Kitty in the Iron Age roundhouse in the museum. I suppose it was her costume from the play. You should have seen her scary performance on stage when I went over there. Unbelievable."

He nodded. "She was just a kid."

We sat together letting everything sink in until Blake said: "There is one loose end that doesn't make any sense, Grace."

"What's that?" I asked.

"Who set fire to your barn?" He looked puzzled. "Stella swears blind it wasn't Jenny or her. She insists neither of them went anywhere near your house that night. But someone threw petrol on the barn and set it alight." He shrugged. "And whoever it was, left not one shred of evidence. I've had forensics and fire experts crawling all over the place today." He looked at me. "If it was those lads from the pub, I'll get them," he said. "Mark my words I will."

That fire had been playing on my mind too. I shivered, remembering that ghostly woman holding Rufus as if she were about to throw him into the fire. She hadn't though, had she? Maybe she'd started the fire deliberately to make Rufus shriek and wake me up. Had she wanted me to discover that Evie had gone out to kill herself?

"Grace..." Blake said, bringing me back to the present.

I looked into his exhausted eyes but said nothing. Sam was the only person I'd spoken to about seeing that woman holding Rufus at the fire that night. What purpose would be served by telling Blake now? It would sound crazy and add more confusion to the mix. No, the barn being set on fire was a mystery that didn't make any sense. A loose end as Blake called it. I would leave it like that.

Thirty-three

One year later, Hutton-le-Hole

I straightened up with a sigh and leant the rake against the trunk of the old ash. It was the last tree in the garden to leaf in spring, and the last to shed in autumn. The fall was abundant though and raking up the leaves hard work. Hot work too. I pulled my jumper off and draped it over the handle of the wheelbarrow to stop it falling onto the ground. Not that the grass was wet. It had been a dry and warm autumn and nothing like the deluge of last year. There was still warmth in the October sun, and I held my face up to the sky to feel it on my skin.

Over the year, I'd grown to love this house and garden. Something I'd never thought possible after the terror of that night at Lowna Ford. That girl, Jenny, still haunted my dreams. It was her crazy eyes as she hit me over the head with the poker that I couldn't forget, along with her terrifying performance as Kitty on the stage of the old roundhouse in the museum.

After the attack, Evie had spent weeks in hospital recovering. It had been a nerve-racking time for everyone. I thought she would surely lose the baby given the time she'd been in the water and so near death. But, by some miracle, Jamie survived. I put that down to her determination that he should.

The reason I'd recovered so well physically and emotionally was all down to Patrick. He'd moved into Mum's house to look after me and help me come to terms with everything. Every day he would drive me to York Hospital to see Evie, and we'd spend hours talking and catching up on our lives. Over time, I started to relax and accept the past. A piece of my life that had been missing now seemed to make sense and I understood why my mother had fallen in love with this wise and generous man. He was good with little Jamie too.

As if on cue, a gurgling sound came from the nearby path. I smiled and walked over to the pram. "Hello, little man. Are you awake already?"

I was rewarded with a toothless grin, and gobbledegook chatter. He was a remarkably happy baby given his first traumatic months in the womb. He raised his index finger and pointed to the sky.

I looked up to see two wood pigeons sitting in the ash tree.

"Pigeon," I said out loud. "Fat pigeon."

He chuckled and wriggled in his pram.

"*Hey!*" a voice called out. "No slacking or we'll never get this tidied up."

I turned and smiled at Blake whose wheelbarrow was already full to the brim with dead leaves.

He left it where it was and came over to say hello to Jamie. "Cheerful little soul, isn't he?"

"Yes, he's bright and full of personality. He's just started crawling, you know."

"Already?"

"He's seven months now."

He shook his head in wonder. "I couldn't believe the transformation in Evie when I saw her," he said. "She's like a different person."

Instinctively, I turned towards the house and saw Evie wave through the kitchen window. She'd gone in to get some tea and scones for the garden work party. I gave her the thumbs-up to indicate Jamie was okay and turned back to Blake.

"It was touch and go for a while with Evie." I shivered at the memory.

"You're both lucky to be alive," he said through gritted teeth.

Blake was never going to forgive me for not phoning him straightaway that night.

"It was a good job Patrick was here," he said, grumpily. "You wouldn't have made it otherwise."

I knew that only too well.

Then he shook his head as if to get rid of some awful image and changed the subject. "You all seem to be getting on well living together," he said.

"We are. I was happy to sell my London flat and move into Mum's house in Hampstead. It has enough bedrooms and space for all of us. It's a good place to bring up Jamie." I couldn't believe myself how well things had turned out. "I'm back working at my medical practice three days a week, which gives me spare time to look after Evie and Jamie." I smiled at the baby and turned back to Blake. "Not that Evie needs my help now. As you say, she's like a different person and much stronger physically and mentally. She's happier than I've ever seen her."

I heard a shout and looked up to see Patrick waving from the paddock and pointing to the plumes of smoke billowing into the sky. He'd been trying for ages to get a bonfire of all the dead leaves going. Now, he was beaming from ear to ear with success.

Blake smiled. "You've given him a new lease of life too. I've never seen him happier either." He paused. "It says a lot about you that you were able to accept him into your life in the way that you have, Grace."

I smiled back. "He's part of our little family now. He's got his own room in our house and comes and goes as he pleases."

"He's in London with you more than he's here."

I laughed. "To be honest, I don't know how we'd manage without him. He's so good with Jamie." I paused. "Anyway, we get on well. It feels like he's always been in my life."

I glanced at Blake, wondering whether to ask my next question. I didn't want to upset him, but then he'd been asking me all sorts of things. "You scared me when you told me about your fiancée, about her murder I mean."

A shadow flitted across his face. "I'm sorry. I shouldn't have burdened you with all that." His shoulders slumped. "I blamed myself for not being there for Gina, for not taking the threat seriously. I wanted to make sure you understood the danger, that's all."

I nodded. "That night up at Lowna, I could have found myself in the same situation as you. I'd have done anything to stop Jenny killing Evie." I paused. "The sadness of it is that Jenny was a damaged kid. She needed help."

"Mm." He turned and looked me in the eye. "There is still that one loose end," he said.

"What's that?"

"Who set fire to your barn that night? And why?"

I looked over to the spot in the garden where the old barn had once stood. It was completely clear of any blackened or burnt-out materials. Patrick had seen to that. He'd also drawn up plans to put up a new barn.

"Grace..." Blake interrupted my thoughts. "Who did you see in the garden that night?"

I hesitated, then shrugged, although I knew full well who I'd seen. That ghostly woman in the long dress. It was her who had made Rufus shriek. I knew that for sure because of his reaction then and after. In the days and weeks that followed, Rufus was too scared to leave the house. Even now, he avoided the spot where the old barn used to be.

"Grace…" Blake said, again. "Was it Jenny?"

I'd thought long and hard about this over the year. Why would Jenny have set fire to the barn? She wouldn't have wanted to wake me up and have me follow Evie up to Lowna. Quite the reverse. I was convinced the fire had been started deliberately so that I *could* stop Evie killing herself. I was certain too that I hadn't seen Jenny, or her mother Stella, in the garden that night.

"Grace…" he repeated.

There was something else I hadn't told anyone about that night. I knew for sure it hadn't been Jenny dressed up as Kitty who'd met me on the track to Lowna Ford. It hadn't been Jenny who'd shown me the way from the carpark to the bridge where Evie was in trouble. I knew this because in my mind I often picture those dainty feet in the old-fashioned boots that didn't leave one single footstep in the mud, and the hem of the woman's dress brushing along the ground in my torch beam as I followed her. She certainly wasn't dressed in bikers' leathers and big, modern boots like Jenny.

I took a deep breath, wondering whether to confide in Blake. But it would sound so ridiculous if I was called to give evidence at Stella's trial which was to start later this month. Did I really want that kind of attention? Or people hanging around the house and village to ghost hunt?

I shook my head. "I don't know, Blake. The weather was horrendous that night. It was too dark to see anything in the garden but flames spiralling into the sky. That's all I could focus on. The fire."

He gave me a sceptical look. "One day," he said, "you might trust me enough to confide in me."

The crunch of footsteps on dead leaves behind made us both turn round.

"You'll have to earn Grace's trust," Evie said, with a mischievous gleam in her eye. "That's the way she is. But once you have it, you'll be friends for life… maybe more."

Blake turned bright pink but looked pleased too. "I have to come down to London next month on a work trip." He looked at me, hesitantly. "I thought, well, I thought maybe you might show me the sights one day, Grace, if you have time."

He stood there tall and bashful like a schoolboy. Gone was the terse and irritable Detective Chief Inspector I'd first met in this house a year ago. Here was a man I'd come to respect and admire.

I smiled at him. "Of course, just let me know when you're coming."

Blake didn't smile very often but when he did, his whole face lit up.

"Good." Evie's lovely green eyes shone with approval, and she nudged him playfully in the ribs. "That's settled then."

But I could see there was something more on Blake's mind.

Evie sensed it too. "I expect you're wondering what's happened to our friend, Samantha," she said.

He looked at us both in turn. "Neither of you have mentioned her," he said.

"She's in San Francisco," Evie said. "The advertising agency she works for has an office over there. She's gone for a year to help them set up a new project."

He looked at me, hesitantly.

"It's okay," I said. "We're all friends again. We're going over to stay with her for Christmas."

An uncertain look passed across Blake's face, although he said nothing.

But Evie caught that look too. "I expect you're wondering if she's seeing Peter – Grace's ex?"

He blushed.

"It's all right," I said. "It's well and truly over between Peter and me. The pair of them can do whatever they like."

Evie smiled. "They won't be seeing each other," she said. "Peter's not in San Francisco anymore. He moved to New Zealand."

That was news to me, and I stared at her.

She shook her head at me. "No, I haven't spoken to Peter if that's what you're thinking. He rang the school where I used to work to get my new contact details. They wouldn't oblige, so he left his address and phone number for me to get in touch with him." She gave me a kind smile. "I didn't follow it up though. That's all in the past. We've all moved on with our lives."

I wasn't sure what prompted him at that moment, but Jamie started giggling as if someone had told him a joke. His laughter was so infectious that we couldn't help but all join in.

"Right, my little one," Evie said, lifting him out of his pram. "It's time for us to have some tea."

Thirty-four

Late afternoon the following day, I sat on the wrought iron bench on the back lawn looking up to where the old barn used to be, and beyond that to the paddock. It was my favourite spot at that time of day. I enjoyed seeing the rabbits chasing each other around the field in a burst of energy before returning to their burrows for the night, and watching the sun sink slowly behind the trees on the horizon. It was a brilliant ball of orange today, and its rays glowed on the old stone house.

Rufus lay stretched out asleep in the sun on one side of me, and Jamie in his pram on the other. Evie was upstairs. It was her time of day to work on Mum's book. She was determined to finish 'It Began with a Ghost Story' as a tribute to Violet and I could think of no-one more authoritative on the subject than her. Patrick had begun the book's illustrations too and the pair of them spent hours with their heads together working on the project.

Jamie looked so peaceful as he slept. The rise and fall of his chest promoted a feeling of calm and wellbeing, which was a far cry from the craziness of the year before when I first came here. I could hardly believe the change in me. I'd hated this house and everything in it back then. Of course, I was upset about Mum dying and deeply hurt by her secret life. Now though I understood why she'd loved this place. Everything in the garden, from the fragrant white climbing roses to Scotch thistles to the clump of marguerites and the abundant apples, pears, and plums from the fruit trees, appeared in her books somewhere, along with the mice, rabbits and pheasants that strolled around the paddock and back lane. It was a country paradise.

A sudden squawking in the tall beech tree caught my attention. A gang of jackdaws flew out and up into the sky. The young ones born that year in the village were nimble in the air now as they wheeled and squabbled with each other. Soon they would be moving to the woodland treetops to sit out the winter before coming back to the same chimney pots to breed next spring.

Even the spot where the old barn burnt down held no fear for me now. I knew I had nothing, or rather no-one, to be afraid of. The legend of Kitty Garthwaite held no terror for me either. I could imagine how badly 'fallen' women were treated back in those days and what a terrible time Kitty would have had. I didn't believe the folklore about her ghost sitting naked on the riverbank and luring men to their deaths either. That was rubbish. Perhaps one or two men might have fallen from their horses over the years while crossing the ford and hit their heads on the bank or stones. But to turn the poor girl into a ghostly murderer was ridiculous.

I heard a gurgling noise and turned back to see Jamie was already awake. His bright, green eyes, just like his mother's, were open and eagerly watching the birds in the sky.

"What a noisy lot they are," I said to him.

He smiled and raised his arms to be lifted out of his pram.

"All right." I got him out and sat him on my knee.

Immediately, his head turned this way and that as he looked about to see what was going on. Then he pointed again to the sky.

"Jack…daws," I said to him. "Jack…daws."

That word always made him laugh and soon he was bouncing around on my lap. I knew that meant he was eager to get moving. I stood up and held him in my arms. "Shall we go for a walk?"

He babbled something in reply which I took to mean 'yes'.

Rufus stirred from his sleep too and stretched out his back legs. I'd seen him do that more lately and made a mental note to take him to the vet. He was getting on and I reckoned his joints were stiffening. I didn't know whether it was old age, or the scare he'd got from the fire that night, but he never went off roaming the Moors anymore when we were here. In fact, he never left the house or garden. And I might have been imagining it, but he seemed to keep a close eye on Jamie when he was alone outside in his pram, behaving like a kind of sentinel.

"That's it, Rufus," I said. "You come too."

He walked alongside me on the path. It amazed me what friends we'd become. He wouldn't sit on my lap in the way he had Mum's but, sometimes, when I was on the sofa watching TV, he'd spring up next to me, make himself comfortable and go to sleep. That was his way of showing companionship.

Now, as I walked along the path to the top of the garden, I chatted to Jamie all the while, pointing out flowers or birds by name. Of course, he didn't understand, but he was curious and eager to explore. And what a joyous place it was for us all to come to. There was no way I'd sell it now.

Suddenly, as we approached the gravelled area next to where the old barn used to be, I caught sight of someone in the back lane. I put my free hand up to shield my eyes from the dazzling sun to see who it was. I'd got to know most of the neighbours who'd turned out to be a friendly lot after all. They liked nothing more than to stop and have a chat over the wall.

I stopped dead and felt goosebumps shiver up my spine as I stared in astonishment and incredulity.

A young woman stood in the back lane, just outside the gate. She was small and slim; and wore a simple grey dress that touched the ground. In the shock of that moment, the one feature I remember distinctly was her long dark hair shining in the sunshine.

The woman stood perfectly still and didn't speak. She looked straight at me, her eyes locking onto mine in a curious stare. I felt a kind of power emanating from her, and I couldn't look away, until Jamie suddenly bounced up and down in my arms and reached out in excitement.

Distracted, I grabbed him with both hands to stop him falling. But, when I looked back to the gate again, there was no-one there.

I stood stupefied, staring all around. Then I went up to the gate and checked both ways along the lane. No-one. Had I imagined that? Had my head been so full of Kitty and her ghostly story that I'd fooled myself into thinking I'd seen her?

Maybe. But when I turned back, I saw Rufus scamper across the lawn, then dive through the cat flap into the house as fast as his old legs could carry him.

Follow the author, Jean Harrod,

and sign up to her newsletter on

www.jeanharrod.com